28x (6/11) ✓ 2/12

Fortune's Fool

Praise for Mercedes Lackey's
A TALE OF THE FIVE HUNDRED KINGDOMS series

One Good Knight

"*One Good Knight* delivers the literary goods in a big way: nonstop action and intrigue, ill-fated romance, jaw-dropping plot twists and, of course, the proverbial 'and they lived happily ever after'—except this happy ending has some huge and completely unexpected twists. Enjoy!"
—*Explorations*

"A lot of fairy tale conventions get turned on their heads…for an entertaining light fantasy with just a touch of romance in the end."
—*LOCUS*

The Fairy Godmother

"Lackey's satisfying fairy tale will captivate fantasy readers, with its well-imagined world, and romance fans, who will relish the growing relationship and sexy scenes."
—*Booklist*

"Lackey starts off Harlequin's new LUNA imprint with a bang, proving why she's an acknowledged master of her craft with this awesome take on the world of fairy tales. If this is what we can consistently expect from LUNA, fans of fantasy and the paranormal are in for a real treat."
—*Romantic Times BOOKreviews*

MERCEDES LACKEY

Fortune's Fool

LUNA™
www.LUNA-Books.com

LUNA™

FORTUNE'S FOOL

ISBN-13: 978-0-373-80266-1
ISBN-10:   0-373-80266-8

Copyright © 2007 by Mercedes Lackey

First trade printing: March 2007

Author photo by: Patti Perret

This edition published by arrangement with Harlequin Books S.A.

® and TM are trademarks of Harlequin Books S.A., used under license.
Trademarks indicated with ® are registered in the United States Patent
and Trademark Office, the Canadian Trade Marks Office and in other
countries.

www.LUNA-Books.com

Printed in U.S.A.

To Larry: Because he makes me laugh.

Chapter 1

Shafts of golden light pierced the green twilight, penetrating the waving fronds of the forest to leave pools of light on the ground. The path to the Great Palace, paved with pearl shell, unraveled along the sand; a broad ribbon of iridescence, suddenly burning into a patch of blinding white when one of those shafts touched it. On either side of the path, at charmingly irregular intervals, stands of long, waving kelp, beds of colorful anemones, and coral "bushes" were being carefully tended by a small horde of tiny sea creatures.

No one ever actually set foot on the path, or truly even needed to use it. This was, after all, the bottom of the sea. People swam. Even the few two-legged people, like the Sea King's children, swam.

Nevertheless there was a path, winding through a "forest," though the forest was kelp, the "birds" were fish, and even the "hawks" had an analogue in the form of sharks and other predators.

There were all these things because the path went to a palace. The Tradition said that all palaces should have winding paths traveling through mysterious forests filled with enchanting wildlife.

So this Palace, although underwater, had such a path.

In many ways, it was a good thing that no one ever actually walked on the path. Pearl shell, while pretty, had very sharp edges, and no one down here wore shoes.

And that, Ekaterina, the youngest daughter of the Sea King, reflected, as she swam in a deceptively languid manner toward the palace, was a pity.

Katya loved shoes. Dainty, embroidered silk slippers. Thigh-high leather boots. Strange wooden things that were like walking with tiny tables strapped to one's feet. Dancing shoes, red-heeled shoes, shoes that were hardly more than thin little straps, shoes that were substantial enough to pound a nail with. She loved them all.

In fact, she loved clothing. She adored clothing. It didn't matter what the style, the fashion was, she loved clothing the way she loved shoes.

Sad, really, since no one wore clothing, or at least much that was like clothing, down here.

As a warrior in her father's Personal Guard, she wore her fish-scale armor of course. In fact, she was wearing it now, since she had been summoned for official business. It was as pretty as she could engineer, despite being first, and foremost, very functional. The fish scales glittered in the errant beams of sunlight filtering down through the kelp branches. It was the same pearly white as the shells beneath her, and gleamed with the same iridescence. The scales of the formfitting tunic were about the size of her thumbnail, while those on the sleeves of the tunic and the equally formfitting leggings were much, much smaller, about the size of the nail of a baby's littlest finger.

Her sharkskin boots were a dead white, matching the shark-skin belt and gloves. The belt held nothing at the moment. No sword, no knives. But Ekaterina didn't need a weapon. Ekaterina *was* a weapon.

Her hair had been bound up into a severe knot…another pity. She had lovely hair, as pearl-white as the shell also, and the fact that living under the sea allowed only two basic hair-styles—severe knot, or floating free—was another source of private regret for her.

Small wonder she welcomed her father's regular summons.

Hopefully this would be another trip to Dry Land! Even better if it was to a new bit of Dry Land, a place she had never been before! That would be glorious!

The nearer she came to the Palace of the Sea King, the more people she encountered, though most of them were dolphins and the smaller whales, who served as her father's Palace Guard. You could always tell a Guard creature from the fluke studs denoting rank; small gold or silver rounds much like earrings, and put in the same way. She always winced at a fluke-piercing, though the cetaceans were quite proud of enduring the pain. She supposed it must be like islanders' tattoos. They, too, made a point of experiencing the pain of their decorations.

There were a few mer-folk as well; a couple of the mermaids of her mother's Court, sitting, gossiping, and combing their hair. Mermaids did that a great deal. Part of it was because when your hair was long and floating free in the water and you didn't have two dozen little cleaner-shrimp to keep it disentangled and sorted the way the Queen did, it got knots very easily.

But part of it was The Tradition, which said very clearly that mermaids spent a lot of time combing their hair, sitting on rocks and singing, or both. Her father had managed to put an end to the part of The Tradition that had once made them sit on rocks and sing sailors to their doom—now they only enchanted the poor lads so that they forgot their One True Loves, at least until the One True Loves managed to break the spell. Her father was clever that way. He hadn't wanted sailors with their ears stopped up with wax or clay slaughtering his subjects, so back when he'd been the Sea Prince, he'd gotten hold of half a dozen very good bards and paid them generously to write songs on the new theme. It had taken several years of concentrated effort, spreading the songs, singing them in contests, even introducing very elegant versions into several nearby Royal Courts, but the effort had paid off handsomely. Now the only sea creatures that lured sailors to their doom were the Sirens, and they didn't acknowledge her father's authority, claiming to be descended from gods. So the Sirens could handle the odd clever hero with murderous intent on their own.

Katya reflected that her father really was one of the cleverest Sea Kings of his line. He wasn't the only King of the Sea, of course; for one thing, the sea was twice as big as the Dry Land, and it would be absurd to think that one person could govern all of it. But he was certainly one of the cleverest of those currently ruling. As a young Prince he had quickly come to understand how The Tradition shaped the lives of everything, and had determined that it would no longer be The Tradition that controlled the lives of his family and his people, but the other way around. To that end he had studied as much about it as he could, certainly as much as many Godmothers, and had educated his subjects in how it worked as well. But when you were a magical creature, as the peoples of the sea generally were, The Tradition had a tendency to shove you about more ruthlessly than any mortal.

Unless you knew how to do a little preemptive shoving of your own.

As Katya swam past the coral garden, she caught sight of her sister Tasha with her nose buried in a book, her back cradled by an enormous sea fan. There were no Godmothers for the sea creatures; evidently only mortals got the services of such cleverly manipulative creatures—but the Sea King was doing the next best thing to getting one.

He was training his very own Sorceress.

Now, all of the Sea King's children—and he had quite a few— had positions of real authority or meaningful jobs. He had told Ekaterina once that this was the way to make sure none of his offspring "went to the bad." "Everyone needs to have responsibility," he had told her. "The cleverer you are, the more responsibility you need. Nothing breeds discontent like idleness."

Tasha was one of the cleverest of his daughters, and she had a real aptitude for magic. Not that Katya envied her the special tutors, the tower of her own, and all the special considerations. Not once it had become obvious that Tasha was never going to leave the Palace grounds again.

Not that Tasha cared. That was the genius of the Sea King; his children were all considered and studied as carefully as any sculptor would study a block of stone, and then positions were created for them that suited not only their talents, but their aptitudes, and not only their aptitudes, but their desires.

Katya had enough wanderlust for twenty sailors. She was never happier than when she was sleeping in strange beds, eating strange foods, and wearing strange clothing.

Oh yes. Especially wearing strange clothing.

Tasha did not even notice as her sister swam past. But then, it would take the eruption of a volcano beneath her feet to get Tasha out of a book of magical theory once she was deeply engrossed. Such ability to concentrate was invaluable to a Sorceress, whose life might well depend on being able to carry out every step of a complicated ritual while an Evil Mage was throwing everything he had in the way of an attack at her head.

Now, Mischa, the Crown Prince, would not dare to allow his mind to be so focused. A King—or a Prince in line for the throne—needed to be able to divide his attention among a dozen or more things at once, and change from task to task on an instant, exactly like a juggler keeping a complicated number of balls in the air at once.

Mischa was superbly suited for such a thing, to the extent that the people were already calling him "Prince Mikael the Clever."

That was a talent he shared with Ekaterina, though the throne was absolutely the last thing she wanted. Ever. Not all the lovely dresses in the world and the ability to wear them underwater could have bribed her to take the throne.

The kelp forest abruptly gave way to open sand, and the Palace rose up before her in all its splendor. A dazzling ray of sun pierced through the surface of the ocean far above, and bathed the intricate spires and delicate towers in green-tinted glory. It looked for all the world as if nature had conspired to put that shaft of sunlight right there—

And of course, Katya knew very well that it *had*.

Here again was the hand of The Tradition at work. The Tradition decreed that the first sight of the Sea King's Palace should be of it bathed in a shaft of sunlight piercing the depths.

So, of course, it was. All the time—well, all the daylight time at any rate. By night, as long as there was a moon of any strength, it was bathed in moonlight. As a child, Ekaterina had taken particular and mildly mischievous delight in dragging visitors through the kelp forest on wretched and stormy days just to see that shaft of sunlight break through the clouds in time to perform its magic.

The walls were made of pink coral, carved and polished to a soft glow. Beautiful patterns had been inlaid around each window in mother-of-pearl, black and red coral.

Unlike the fortress-palaces of Rus, this place could not possibly withstand a siege, or even the attack of a child with a sling and a stone. There looked to be two dozen spiral spires, like the long and delicately pointed seashells or a narwhal's horn, and half again as many filigree towers. In fact there were twenty-one spires and nine towers, each of them the private domain of someone in the Royal Family. Not just the King and Queen and their brood, but the Dowager Queen, and several assorted Aunts and Uncles. Whenever another family member turned up, if there were no vacant places available for them, another was created.

This wasn't just whim or fancy. This was, after all, the sea, and such an arrangement made it possible for the Royals to come and go as they liked without having to pass through the rest of the Palace. When you lived at the bottom of the sea, an exit was as easy as swimming out your window, and the towers gave discreet points from which to do so. No doubt many Royals in the past had taken such exits to have adventures— or even to meet with a paramour they had rather their spouses didn't know about.

To Katya's immediate right, the parade grounds, which just now were empty, but often as not held her brother Mischa as he drilled his troops. For the most part, the Sea King's troops were ranged in "battles" that had very little to do with war. There were monsters in the sea, enormous behemoths that came with ravening appetites for which a whale was nothing more than a morsel to whet the appetite. When they appeared, they had to either be killed or driven away, and it took strong creatures armed to the teeth to do so. Mischa thrived on combat, hence his position as the Commander of all of the Sea King's forces.

And though the army was a small one, it was formidable, for Mischa employed magicians alongside the armsmen, training the two to work together as a seamless whole. To Ekaterina's certain—and it was very certain—knowledge, no one else in the sea kingdoms did such a thing. As a consequence, it was vanishingly unlikely that any attempt to take this kingdom by force would succeed.

Today Mischa was out there alone, drilling. The resistance of the water to fast movement made sword-work impractical, so the most common weapons beneath the sea were extremely powerful bows and arrows, trident, spear, and knife. Today he was working with knives, battling a seaweed-stuffed dummy that already was losing its stuffing.

She swam a bit faster; this close to the Palace there was always the chance of being ambushed by a would-be suitor, some acquaintance trying to find a way to the King more direct than waiting his turn for an audience, or one of the young women at the court hoping for one of Katya's brothers to happen along.

Katya was of the mind that her brothers were perfectly capable of deciding for themselves who they would and would not court, she was not about to play the stooge for yet another sycophant, and as for would-be suitors for herself...

Those, she could do well enough without. So far there had not been a single young man she had ever met that could keep up with her. To be brutally frank...they bored her silly.

All they ever thought about was the Court. Who was advancing, who was declining, who was allied with whom, and what that meant for the tiny, tiny circle of "those in the know." They never looked past the boundaries of the magical barrier around the Palace grounds to the greater and far more dangerous world of the open sea, much less to the Dry Land. Most of them didn't even know the names of the countries that bordered this Kingdom, if they weren't also Sea Kingdoms.

They didn't think twice about the very powerful and, at the same time, very delicate magic that kept the water warm, those without gills breathing, and predators peaceful. This was the only place in the Kingdom where a seal could swim with an orca and the orca wouldn't even think of harming it.

Sea Kings many generations ago had bargained for that spell. Up above the surface, storms might rage and winter snow might pepper the waves; here it was pleasant enough that tropical fish and other creatures of warmer climes played among corals.

And it was the day that Katya caught one of her would-be suitors trying to use some unauthorized magic here—magic that might well upset that finely tuned balance—that she realized that the young men of her father's Court were either empty-headed idiots *or* one of Mischa's warriors. There just was no middle ground.

Perhaps that was because any young man even remotely useful to his parents was either sent to the Royal Guard or kept at home to manage the business or estates. But when you had an ornamental dunce sitting around doing nothing but making idle trouble, your only real solution for what to do with him was to send him to court and hope he could make a good marriage alliance. If he could snare a Princess, all the better.

If there was one thing the various peoples of the Sea were, it was prolific. The Royal family was by no means the only one with an entire shoal of offspring. The Sea was dangerous; outside the protections of the Palace there were killing storms, giant octopi and squid, and an entire bestiary of monsters. There were undersea quakes, volcanoes, whirlpools, and land-slides. And then there were the wars between Kingdoms, and the inevitable appearances of SeaHags and other evil magicians whenever things threatened to remain peaceful for a while. The Tradition might not rule beneath the waves with quite so firm a hand as it did on Dry Land, but it was powerful enough to stir up trouble, and plenty of it.

Now, the North Sea Kingdom had been peaceful since Katya's father—who, according to her sources, people were starting to call "Vladislav the Merry"—had fought his way to the throne over the bodies of several would-be rulers who'd tried to keep him from taking it. Vladislav wanted to keep things that way. Although he was an awe-inspiring fighter, he hated conflict—but he was very, very good at handling people, at politics, and at history.

The result was that his reign so far had been *so* peaceful that the various Noble families had seen a great many sons survive, who would in previous reigns have made fatal errors of judgment.

That was what, in this generation, had been sent off to Court.

When Katya had reasoned all that out, she had vowed that she was not going to even *think* about courtship unless the young man in question was at least as skilled and clever as she. He didn't have to be skilled in the same ways—she'd be perfectly happy with a highly intelligent scholar, for instance—but he had to be a match for her.

So far, the crop of young fellows swarming her had failed miserably in producing someone of that order.

She had the sense that her sisters, and perhaps her brothers, too, felt the same way. Certainly Tasha was not showing any signs of welcome to the few who dared approach her. In a lot of ways, Katya envied her. She might not look intimidating, but the fact that she was a sorceress-in-training scared the scales off most of those poor fish.

Whereas the essence of what made Katya just as dangerous was by necessity cloaked in secrecy. She couldn't be her father's hidden weapon if everyone in Court knew what she was and where she went.

She wound her way through the halls of mother-of-pearl and coral, of abalone and amber, checking the usual places where Vladislav might be. And finally she found him.

The King was in his counting house, but he was not the one doing the counting of the money. Four earnest, clerkly Tritons were tallying up the contents of what must have been a treasure ship. Gold and silver bars already lay neatly stacked, awaiting transfer to the vaults. At the moment, it was the contents of several chests that occupied their attention.

Katya's eyes gleamed a little as she surveyed the wealth. From the fact that the styles and gems of several different lands were jumbled together in the one she was nearest to, she suspected that the vessel that had sunk must have been a pirate raider. If so, good riddance. The Sea People were always being blamed for the depredations of pirates, and many a war had been started between Dry Land and Sea because the Drylanders were certain that the Sea People had been plundering their ships.

"Ah, now, save this out," the King said, pulling out a delicate tunic woven of tiny gold and silver links. "This should be in Galya's wardrobe."

In her arsenal, you mean, Father, Katya thought with amusement. Galya was the most beautiful of his daughters, the one that displayed the Siren blood they all had from their maternal grandmother most clearly, and she was, next to Katya, the most subtle weapon he had to deploy.

Not subtle in and of herself; her seductive lure was more like a bludgeon to the head. But subtle in how Vladislav used her.

Any time he wanted to read a man, or deflect his questioning, or confuse him, or make him forget all about caution, all he had to do was bring Galya in for some pretext or other. Katya hadn't seen a man yet who didn't end up with his eyes riveted on Galya's magnificent bosoms—or, rarely, some other part of her—within the first few heartbeats. And it was certain that as he stared, he was not thinking of how best to negotiate with Vladislav.

This delicate tunic would allow Galya's body to shine through while giving the illusion of modesty. It was exactly the sort of thing that delighted her.

It would also be cursed heavy. For all that the garment was a work of art, Katya did not envy her the wearing of it.

"And what of you, *belochka?*" he asked. "Do you see anything here your heart craves?"

His eyes flickered from her to the chest and back again and she read the wordless message clearly. There must be rumors about her again. Possibly only that she was too serious, too unfeminine, but those were rumors easily quashed with a moment of girlish vanity.

Fortunately there were some things in that chest that she would like. With a squeal of glee, she pulled out six elaborate hair sticks of the sort the people of Qin wore. One pair was done in the likeness of cascading fuchsia blossoms, the blossoms and leaves being formed of delicately carved, whisper-thin semiprecious stone. One pair featured the Phoenyx-bird and the Dragon, wrought in gold and silver, every feather and scale perfectly represented. And from the final pair, chains of tiny golden bells descended, so that the wearer would be surrounded by gentle chiming as she moved.

Of course, the fact that these "hair sticks" were absolutely lethal weapons was something best kept between the two of them. How these ornaments had come into the hands of pirates she had no clue, but they were one of the many weapons used by a certain class of courtesan-assassins, who would insert themselves into a Qin-lord's concubines and wait, sometimes for years, before striking.

It was a good tactic. One Katya did not have the patience for, but a good tactic nonetheless.

"Come, my daughter. My business here is finished, and these young men can complete the tally without me. Tell me of your day." Vladislav smiled at his daughter. He was possibly one of the most gorgeous Kings of his line to date, and that was not just her admittedly biased opinion. The Siren blood that made Galya so stunningly beautiful was expressed in him as powerful masculine charisma. He truly was a "golden king;" blond, clean-shaven, he had all the physical perfection of a statue of a god. Square-jawed, with startling blue eyes, a musical voice, and a ready wit, it was small wonder that he was also known as "Vladislav the Handsome."

But this was his cue to her. It was time for them to find a place in private to talk.

Her heart leaped with excitement. This could only mean he had a task for her that she must carry out in secret.

And that almost certainly meant a spying trip to Dry Land.

Chapter
2

"Sasha Feliks Pavel Pieterovich, Prince of Led Belarus, you are a fool." King Pieter Ivan Alexandrovitch glared at his youngest son, who looked back at him with a winsome smile.

"Thank you, Father," he replied. "It is nice to know I am doing my job."

Both men burst into laughter, quickly joined by the other four of King Pieter's sons. The six of them were gathered beside the biggest fireplace in the private quarters of the King's family. This was a smaller stone fortification inside a stone fortification, an actual building separate from the rest of the granite crag that was the Palace of Led Belarus.

Nevertheless, despite that this place looked like a prison from the outside—since it had began as a fortress, there was no gentle, winding path to it—on the inside it was warm and welcoming. This was thanks in no small part to the fact that some long-ago King had decided he was fed up with living in a cave, and had created entirely new inside walls, floors, and ceilings of warm, light-colored wood. The floor was polished and shining, the walls looked surprisingly festive with their ancient weapons and hunting trophies; bright embroidered cloths covered every flat surface, and benches with cushions beckoned an invitation to come and sit. Even the ceilings were cheerful, with every inch of every beam carved and fancifully painted.

Sasha grinned. King Pieter looked like a bear, sounded like a bear, and people tended to dismiss him as one of those fellows who had become King only because his father had been King.

But Pieter was as shrewd as they came, as his father and grandfather before him had been. And being the Fool was, indeed, Sasha's "job."

Sasha plopped himself down on the hearthstone, put on a simpleton's expression, and grinned up at his father and brothers.

Led Belarus was a Kingdom that had no Godmother, nor a Wizard or Sorcerer, but King Pieter's grandfather, the then-Prince Rurik, had surveyed this situation, pondered it when his own father had still been alive, and had decided to do something about it.

He'd lured a Godmother into teaching him.

It hadn't been easy. First he'd had to get some dragon blood so he could understand the speech of the beasts and birds. Fortunately, he had been able to make a bargain with a Great Wyrm laired up in the nearby Cassian Mountains. That bargain still held, in fact. There was a herd of very fine cattle that, in effect, belonged to the Wyrm Lukasha now, but was tended by the Royal Herdsmen. Every other day, Lukasha helped himself to one; when the herd grew too thin, another lot was driven up to replace it. In return, Lukasha came to a secret meeting place three times a year to be bled. Dragon's Blood was potent stuff, with many magical uses, and the Kings of Led Belarus were able to barter many favors from those magicians they trusted for a small vial of it. This more than made up for the cost of a few hundred head of cattle a year.

But of course, having a ready supply on hand meant that from then on, the entire Royal Family of Led Belarus could speak and understand the beasts of the field and the birds of the air.

Now to be honest, the gift was something of a nuisance, so far as Sasha was concerned. For the most part, the beasts of the field and the birds of the air didn't have a great deal to say. You had to learn how to ignore them, like the background chatter of old gossips; when he'd first drunk the Dragon's Blood, he'd spend the whole day listening to dogs barking, "Hey! Hey! Hey hey hey hey hey!" Only when the beast was, itself, intelligent—either because of a spell cast on it, or because The Tradition deemed it appropriate—did the Gift really come into play.

Although…his elder brother Kostenka did claim it was useful to listen to what the crows, ravens, and jackdaws were saying when he was hunting.

Well, once Prince Rurik had made his bargain and gotten the Gift, his next task had been to catch the Mare of the Night Wind, and get from her the boon of the services of three sons in return for her freedom. But the horses followed the Tradition. There was beauty, intelligence, and magical ability and most creatures only got two out of the three. The first two stallions were stunning, fleet, and utterly worthless to him except as the bride-price for the Princess he eventually determined to wed. And that was only later. The third, however, was the Little Humpback Horse…wise, clever, ugly, and very, very magical.

But he had not wanted the services of the Humpback Horse for himself. The little fellow could fly, travel as fast as his mother, and offer the best of advice. And after a careful negotiation with the beast, he had found a Godmother willing to teach him as a trade for the Humpback Horse's aid.

And so Prince Rurik had learned all about The Tradition, that insensate force that guided all life in the Five Hundred Kingdoms. He'd learned how it worked, what drove it, and how it could be manipulated to work in your favor. And he, in his turn, had taught all this to his children and his grandchildren.

He had made it very clear to them that there must always be a Scholar of The Tradition among the King's offspring. Magic was not a gift in the lineage, so none of them could ever aspire to become a Wizard or Godmother—which was rather too bad. But at least the Kings of Led Belarus would always be able to have someone who could predict what The Tradition might force on them and the Kingdom, and act accordingly.

Right now, that Adviser was Sasha's Uncle Zhenechka; always scholarly by nature, he found following the twists and turns that The Tradition made fascinating to puzzle out. Zhenechka's successor would be Sasha's brother Yasha, dedicated with all his earnest heart to keeping the people of Led Belarus safe from all the possible evils that might befall them.

And here was how very, very clever Rurik and the current Advisers were with regards to the Royal Family.

The Tradition in Led Belarus had a great deal to say about how the young Princes would turn out, based on how many of them there were. The Traditional role for the eldest and heir was that of the Arrogant Bully, who nevertheless could be redeemed by insulting some magician or spirit and performing its tasks until he learned humility. Prince Adrik had walked through that particular lesson before he was thirteen.

The Tradition for the second born was as his brother the King's right-hand man, the leader of his troops. It had been no problem for Prince Anatolii to fit into that role.

The third, fourth, fifth, and sixth born were the luckiest in a way. They were able to choose their lot in life. Yasha had happily apprenticed himself to Zhenechka as Adviser-in-waiting, and the rest had found themselves niches here and there as Zhenechka advised them.

But Sasha, the seventh born...

He had come late in his mother's life, and been entirely unexpected. And The Tradition had a lot to say about the seventh born. Though not usually magical by nature, although there were exceptions, nevertheless, Traditional Magic was destined to circle strongly about him. And his role would be—the Wise or Fortunate Fool.

Now, the Wise Fool was a feature in so many tales and legends that Sasha had long since lost count of them. That made it a pattern that The Tradition was going to be working very hard to force him into. But the Wise Fool was not really a fool as such....

No, he was a dreamer, a planner. Not a warrior. Very often a poet. And there was one thing that he did for his country that could not be Traditionally duplicated in any other fashion.

He brought them all Luck.

Traditionally, there was no particular way in which the Wise Fool needed to bring the Luck, as long as he did something that could be linked into the magic of The Tradition itself.

Now as it happened, there could not possibly have been a better match, temperamentally, for the role of the Wise Fool than Sasha.

He *was* musical, and music was a potent link for The Tradition. He was not much like his older brothers, being smaller and lighter than they. Not that he was bad at combat, but not the sort that they were *good* at. If it ever came to a war, and he had to fight, he would be darting in and out with light armor and long knives while they laid waste to their foes with ax, mace, and heavy broadsword. Prince Adrik called him "Ferret"—mockingly in public, jestingly in private.

He *was* a thinker, a scholar, and studied The Tradition and anything else he could get his hands on alongside his brother Prince Yasha. In private, Yasha called him "Little Owl." In public, Yasha berated him and called him "Little Fool."

For that, too, was an aspect of the Wise Fool. So far as the rest of the world was concerned, Sasha's family despised him. That was how The Tradition wanted it.

But from the very beginning, the tiny boy with the too-wise eyes had gotten it all very carefully explained to him. *We must shout at you before other people, but it is all a game. We love you. You are our treasure, our blood, our Fortune.* And he had been precocious enough to at least understand the difference between what was said and done in public, and what was said and done in private. Before too very long, he was clearly enjoying the "game" aspect, the way his entire family fooled the rest of the Court and indeed the whole kingdom. His greatest joy had been when he had acted particularly stupid, been threatened with a thrashing, chased into the family's private quarters, then picked up, swung around and praised for his inventiveness.

Not that, as a child, he hadn't gotten into some trouble for taking advantage of his position. He'd been soundly thrashed, and more than once, for exceeding the bounds of what was permitted in his mischief and foolery. He was not as a child, and was not now, any kind of an angel.

"You skirted very near the pale today, my son," his father growled, an expression of mixed pride and irritation on his bearlike, bearded face. "That business with the boyars—one more prank and I would have been forced to thrash you in public."

"That business with the boyars" had involved Sasha getting tangled up with their huge fur cloaks, tumbling among them, tripping them up and destroying their dignity and tempers, all the while easily dodging the blows they'd aimed at him.

"Yes, but you got to soothe their tempers with vodka, and got them to sympathize with you. You had them eating out of your hand, Father." Sasha had known what he was doing—they had entered the doors of the Palace hating one another and determined to do nothing to cooperate. He had forced them together, and given them something else to vent their ire on.

Well, all right, the truth was that they were a lot of pompous windbags and he had wanted to see them deflated. He'd counted on vodka and his father to smooth things over again.

King Pieter aimed a mock blow at his head. He ducked. "Now I am going to have to chase you out to give credence to the tale that I am angry with you," his father said. "Don't do that again, or it will be more than pretense. These men are touchy, and I'm negotiating for a bride for your brother. I don't want that to fail because of your mischief."

Instantly, Sasha was abashed. "I didn't know, Father," he said apologetically. "I wouldn't have been so irritating if I had."

"Hmph," his father grunted. "Keep in mind that I don't tell you everything. Nor should I. Now—wait, let me find something I can throw at you without harm." His eye lit on an old boot one of the Wolfhounds had dragged to the fire to chew on, and picked it up. "All right, out you go."

Sasha kicked the door open and tumbled out it, looking from outside as if he had been thrown at the door and it had sprung open under the blow. He rolled to his feet and ran off, arms and legs flailing, while his father flung the boot at him.

"Sleep in the pigsty!" the King shouted. "It's all you're fit for!"

He had landed out in the main courtyard, beside the stables, and all the boyars were there, mounting their horses to go to the guesthouse outside the Palace walls. There were no guest quarters in the Palace itself; there was only the inner building for the family, and the barracks built into the fortifying walls that surrounded it. In less gracious times, guests would have been housed in the Great Hall, sleeping on the benches and under the tables there. But for at least four generations now, life had been a good deal more gracious than that. There were guesthouses enough to hold up to a hundred important folk, with their servants and guards, and nothing could possibly be wanted from the accommodations. There was even a steam bath attached to each, and from the stink that had come off some of those rancid old men, they could well use it.

The boyars hooted and tossed insults after him. He was laughing as he ran; he used Beast-Speech to call the Wolf-hounds to him, so that it looked as if he were being pursued by the pack, when in fact, they were running with him.

He hoped that his father would get the bride that he wanted. But if he didn't—it would not be because of Sasha; it would be because The Tradition didn't want that girl married into this family at this time.

In order to keep up the pretense, he had to flail his way past the guesthouses, then through the village, inviting further insults from the peasants. This was why he had called the pack; they would protect him from anything like an actual attack. "Prince Borzoi," the peasants called him, after the hounds he so often ran with. He'd even been known to sleep with them as a child, in summer, all of them tumbled together in a heap in the kennel. He didn't do that now, of course....

Though in a way, he missed it. The hounds were just about the only creatures on the Palace grounds that he didn't have to keep up some form of pretense with.

Once out of sight of the village, he dismissed most of the pack and sent them home. He kept his favorite, his particular pet, a stunted fellow he called Ivan. This was no Wise Beast out of The Tradition, but he was a faithful old fellow, and good company, and quick to warn him if someone was approaching so he could put on his Fool face.

The two of them ambled down a path they both knew well,

to a spot deep in the forest that long ago had earned itself the designation of the "Heart of Led Belarus." As Sasha understood these things, it was not so much the physical center of the Kingdom, and it certainly wasn't the cartographic center, but something about the place ensured that anything done there would have resonance with the whole of the country.

And now that he had been insulted, derided, and thrown out of the Palace, Sasha took his brimming Luck into the Heart of his land to be spilled out over it all.

The path wandered, twisted, and turned like a snake trying to tie itself into five different kinds of knots. The trees here were old, old, old, very tall, broad of trunk and spreading of branch. Sunlight penetrated only here and there, piercing the gloom with shafts of slanting light; his feet made no sound on a path layered years-deep in evergreen needles. In fact, the only sounds were the trickling of water from one of the many little streams that cut through here, and the calls of birds high up in the trees,

He understood those calls perfectly, of course. Nesting season was over, babies fledged, so mostly the calls were all "I'm here! I'm here!" Not even "Get out of my space! Interlopers beware!" nor "Where are you, gorgeous creature, whoever you are?"

But there was one, far off in the distance, a heartfelt outpouring of "I'm happy!"

Oh, how he envied that bird.

Occasionally the dog would dart off after something scuttling in the underbrush, but he always returned without having caught anything. This was not a good place for a dog of his sort to hunt. Wolfhounds needed space and plenty of it; they were coursing dogs, and needed room to run. There was nothing like that here.

Still, it didn't keep Ivan from trying.

This was, in its way, a very sacred place. The air was thick with the scent of cedar and age, the woods weighed down with years.

Then, in the distance, a shaft of golden light as broad as a courtyard and bright enough, in the gloom beneath the branches, to dazzle the eye lanced down through the trees, il-luminating a very special place indeed.

He hurried his steps, beginning to feel the press of magic around him. He couldn't see, taste, or smell it, as a real magician might, but he got the sense of it closing in on him. He needed to discharge it before it found some other outlet. The last thing he needed right now was for The Tradition to decide to "reward" his persecution in its own way. He could just imagine what sort of "way" that would be. With his luck, his brother's intended bride would come wandering in here to pick berries, discover him, and fall in love.

And if that happened, he thought with ironic amusement, *Father would have every reason to be quite angry. And rightfully so.* After all, it was also his job to know The Tradition well enough to keep things like that from happening.

He stepped out of darkness and into the light. The sun poured down on him like warm honey as he stood beside the spring-fed pool of clear water that was the Heart of Led Belarus.

This pool of water never froze over, not even in the depth of winter. It was as pure and sweet as water could be, which was hardly a surprise since unicorns drank at it twice a day. And in general—

"Oh! It is the prince!" The voice was not familiar, but it didn't need to be. He knew what it was, if not who.

The words carried an overtone of whinnying, and Sasha braced himself. In a moment, he was overwhelmed by five doe-eyed, adoring female unicorns.

"Prince Sasha, would you comb my mane?"

"Prince Sasha, I have this dreadful itch behind my ears."

"Oh, Prince, could you please—"

They pressed in around him, nostrils quivering, horns glowing with magic, all trying to touch him at once.

Predictably, getting in the way of what he actually needed to do.

"Ladies, please!" he said, after a moment of being softly jostled and inundated with pleading. "I need to let some magic free! If I don't, something might happen that you wouldn't like!"

They giggled, but backed up. Trotting around to the opposite side of the pool, they lined up, watching him expectantly. He didn't know what male unicorns were like, but the female ones seemed to have the same intelligence and good sense as any empty-headed young human in the presence of his or her first love. Which was to say, none at all. In fact, he'd seen toddlers with more sense than the unicorns.

And it made him wonder, how on earth did they reproduce if they were besotted with humans and not their own kind?

Maybe they didn't. Maybe new unicorns were spontaneously generated out of something. Nectar and dandelion floss. Honey and milkweed seeds. Spiderwebs and leftover magic. Or maybe the forest spirits created them; some of them were quite mischievous enough to do so.

Now that he was free of attention, he pulled his flute out of the front of his tunic, made sure that it hadn't been damaged in his falls, and put it to his lips. Music was how he called on the magic that The Tradition packed around him, And while he couldn't say that he controlled it, he certainly guided it.

He sensed the magic flowing from the first note. Using him as a conduit, and the music as direction, it poured out over this place that was somehow integral to all of his Kingdom.

Bring us Luck, he urged the magic. *Give us the reddest cherries, the juiciest apples, the sweetest berries. Make all the nuts sound and savory. Let the cattle and sheep, the goats and the horses, the donkeys and swine and fowl of all sorts bring forth their young in ease and health and abundance. Let the land flow with milk and honey. Let all things flourish…yes, even unicorns….*

He almost heard the magic reply in agreement. It was as if there were something just on the edge of hearing that said, But of course! The Fool is the Luck of the Land!

And the magic stopped looming over him like a wave about to break, and flowed off to make all things in Led Belarus as bucolic as an illumination in a manuscript.

Meanwhile the unicorns sighed and gazed at him with undisguised longing, their eyes growing moist and soulful as he played. He suppressed a chuckle; it didn't do to laugh when you were playing a flute. It would have been nice if he could have turned their passions toward a more appropriate species, but he knew better than to charge the magic with *that* task. He was no mage, and anything subtle would almost certainly backfire on him.

Now there was one more thing he had to do. With the last of the magic waiting to be released, the tone of his song grew dark. The unicorns shivered, and even the golden sunlight dimmed a little.

In his way, he was not only the Luck of the Land, he was its protector.

Demons, and monsters, and night-walking vampires, all things that would harm my land and my people, hear now my music and flee from this Kingdom—

Again, the simplest of commands, and one with no ambiguity. Whatever was evil was ordered to run to the other side of the borders. When he was not riding about the Kingdom to apply the Luck and the magic to specific problems, he did this as often as twice a week, never going more than a month before having to come to this pool to discharge built-up magic. He'd been doing this roughly since he was twelve. No one had taught him, it had just all felt right. He really wished with all his heart he could have had some more guidance on this but the truth was, magicians never came here since he'd begun discharging the built-up power on his own.

Sometimes he wondered if maybe he was driving all magicians away, not just the ones with bad intentions.

Ah well, that was unlikely, since this actually didn't drive *all* evil things away, just the weakest, the easiest to influence. For others…well, others needed to be dealt with directly.

He sensed the last of the power go; it was like being clutched in a fist and suddenly sensing the fist relax.

He ended the tune, and the unicorns sighed in unison.

Then surged back around him. "Prince Sasha, Prince Sasha, would you—" Nudging and cajoling, they begged for his attention. And soft-hearted as he was, he just couldn't tell them no.

Well, he wouldn't be leaving here any time soon. With a rueful sigh, he pushed one of them aside and made his way to a tiny hut built just outside that circle of golden light, a hut so artfully hidden that even he, who had built it, had a hard time spotting it.

He went inside and came out with a pair of currying brushes and a comb, and as soon as they saw these implements, the unicorns gasped with happiness. Whether they were familiar to this spot or strangers, they all seemed to understand, by some kind of arcane migration of thought, what lengths he would go to in order to make them happy.

He spent the rest of the afternoon brushing and combing them, carefully saving out the mane and tail hairs. Unicorn hair wasn't quite as valuable as dragon's blood, but it was potent, and there was a demand for it.

The unicorns themselves were in ecstasy.

"Stay with us!" they pleaded, when he was done. "We scarcely see you anymore," added the one that seemed to be the leader this time. "You used to be here much more often than you are now."

He didn't bother telling her that he was here in their glade far more in the past several months than they thought. Unicorns weren't good at counting. Or at telling time, either. And their memories weren't very reliable, sadly enough. Now that he came to think of it, they were rather like dogs—good-natured, overly affectionate, not very bright dogs. The ones whose conversation mostly consisted of "Hey! Hey! Hey!"

"I'll stay, but only if one of you go fetch my provisions," he said. Why not? He didn't have anywhere he needed to be this evening. Whenever he was thrown out of the house, a basket of food and other needed things would have been left at the head of the path by one of this brothers. This was good, sound sense. If someone were to see him, they would never think to question what one of the Princes were doing with extra food. A Prince could do what he pleased, when he pleased, and had to answer to no one. A servant, on the other hand, might well be stopped and questioned.

"I'll go," said the smallest of the five, and, rearing slightly and pivoting on her hind feet, she shot off like a silver arrow through the shadows under the trees.

She was back in short order with the basket dangling from her horn.

He took it from her with thanks, and lifted the napkin to see what his brothers thought was appropriate to keep him from starving.

Bread, soft cheese to spread on it, dill and onions, and smoked sturgeon. A bone for the dog and honey cake for the unicorns. No, his brothers hadn't packed this. This could only have come from his mother.

He smiled, and felt warmth spreading over him. He gave the dog the bone, and set the rest inside the hut.

"All right, ladies," he said, getting out his flute again. "You have me for the night. What would you like to hear?"

Chapter

3

"Well, my Cunning Little Vixen," said the Sea King, as an errant current sent a little clown fish to thread through his hair, thinking it was an anemone. It realized its mistake a moment later, and darted off to swim down to the garden again. "I have a real challenge for you. I know that something is amiss, but I do not know what it is."

Katya ran her hand along the polished edge of the pink coral parapet on which she sat. This was just about the only thing that she missed badly when she went onto the Drylands. Here in the Sea Kingdoms, she was essentially "flighted," since everyone swam in three dimensions. Once on dry land, she was restricted to her own two feet. She was not alone in this. The King hated that so much that he could scarcely bring himself to poke his head above the surface.

The two of them rested atop one of the many towers of the Palace, which, besides having a view as far as the obscuring nature of the water would allow, meant that no one could possibly eavesdrop on them. This was a wise precaution considering what it was that Katya actually did for her father.

It was not always easy being the youngest of fourteen children, but there were great advantages to the position if you were of an observant nature, and Katya was. You watched how people with bonds of affection acted toward one another. You saw how other people would try to use or intrude on those bonds. When your family was important, you saw every possible manner of exploiter turn up and attempt to use them.

You watched your siblings fall for some gambits, make mistakes, have to repair them. You saw your parents forced to fix the ones that your siblings themselves could not save.

You were a child, considered insignificant, safe to ignore by those outside the family. And by the time you were old enough to be significant, to be used yourself, you knew all of the tricks.

The Sea King's brood was enormous, even by Drylander standards. Seven sons and seven daughters, one for every year, until both the King and Queen had decided that any more would stress the capacity of the Palace itself, not to mention the ingenuity of their father in finding places for them. Eventually, for the major positions, he had decided to mirror his offspring; similar duties, different titles. And being a creature of the Fey, of the Sea, and not nearly as bound in these things by The Tradition as mortals, he elected to mirror the boys against the girls. Each of the daughters was being trained, groomed, and nurtured toward the same sorts of lives as the sons. Take Raisa, the eldest. Like Mischa, she was a warrior. Unlike Mischa, she was not apt at tactical thinking, but her combat skills were exquisite. Fighting in the Sea was not nearly so driven by power and bulk as it was by finesse and quickness. So she was training as the King's Champion, a Traditional role with a lot of the same Traditional magic behind it as a Godmother's Champion, and she in turn handled the combat training of exceptional individual fighters.

Tasha was training as a Sorceress, Tanya as her father's Seneschal, and Galya as his…distraction. Among the brothers, middle son Yerik was the male counterpart to Tasha; Vitenka hard at work already as the Steward—at the moment, sisters Svetlana and Inna were not sure what they wanted to do, but given their bent for diplomacy, Katya foresaw both of them happily making alliance marriages, so that they could go exert their influence in another of the Sea Kingdoms. Which was also what Leonide might do. The highly amusing analog to Galya was the other sort of distraction, the irritating kind—seventh son Fabi had virtually leaped into his Traditional role of the Wise Fool. Fortunately for Fabi, the Tradition of the Wise Fool was not so strong nor demanding in the tales beneath the waves as it was on Dry Land. It allowed him the luxury of being the artistic sort of Fool, the dreamy kind, whose wit was admired as well as just barbed enough to serve as a correction. Fabi was a poet, and a good one. He was, Katya thought, entirely in love with words. In a way, she pitied the girls who yearned after him; they could never, ever compete with poetry to claim his heart.

There was no analogous position to Wise Fool for a seventh daughter, for which Katya was very grateful. Like the rest of her siblings who were not "destined" for a particular life, she had been able to choose, with her father's guidance, what it was that she wanted to do.

It had not been the most obvious choice and, in fact, had she not been blessed with a very particular sort of magical ability, it probably would not have been possible.

"Your magic is still as strong as ever?" the King asked his daughter. "You still have no difficulty?"

"Stronger and easier to wield, Father," she said with confidence. There were, of course, always doubts when one first came into a magic. It could leave, or change, or fade instead of strengthening. But once one passed the magically significant milestone of the twenty-first birthday, as Katya finally had, it was generally stabilized for good and all.

This was important, since Katya's form of water-magic, though not nearly as powerful as her Sorceress-sister's and virtually identical to it in such things as "calling water" or forcing water creatures to obey her at need, did one thing that none of the rest could do.

She could walk on the Drylands without precautions or a second thought. That was the gift that touch of Siren's blood gave to her. Beneath the waves, she breathed the water, while above it, she breathed the air. Transitions were effortless and instantaneous.

That, combined with her appearance—tiny, white-blond, like an exquisite and fragile doll—made her the ideal secret agent for the Sea King in the Drylands as well as within his own Court.

He had been the first to suggest such a thing, when she'd brought some of her uncannily accurate observations to him when she was only nine, though he had not proposed anything of the sort at the time. *"Keep watching, my cunning little vixen,"* he had said. *"Keep watching and come to me and we will talk about what you have seen."* She had nodded, pleased that she had pleased him. On her thirteenth birthday, he had told her what she was actually doing. On her sixteenth, he asked if she wanted to continue. On her seventeenth, he'd had sent her to the Drylands for the first time. No one else had known what she was doing. Not even her mother. She had returned with the information that wreckers were taking ships and blaming the Sea King. With that, her father had stopped a war before it started.

Now she had passed the last hurdle. Now that they both knew that she could go anywhere, any time, the King would be free to send her anywhere he needed her.

"Well this should be interesting for you," the Sea King said, nodding with satisfaction. "The seabirds tell me that something dreadful is arising on the island Kingdom of Nippon."

Katya felt her eyebrows rising, as she looked into her father's handsome face. "I have never been to Nippon." This was definitely promising! She tried to recall what she knew about that Kingdom. Nothing really. It was a chain of many small islands and one very large one; she could not really think of anything else. This island Kingdom was as far from the Palace as it was possible to be and still be touching their borders.

"Nor I, actually. I know only what is in the library. But if the seabirds are noticing something bad, it is likely to be very bad indeed." He grimaced. "Since normally all one ever hears out of a seabird is *'Mine! Mine! Mine! Mine!'* this does not bode well. I tend to leave Nippon alone, as they are very touchy, but—"

"They are an island and touch the Sea on all sides, and anything arising there will have to cross the Sea to go elsewhere." Katya nodded. "Lord King my father, I will visit the library to acquaint myself with all that we have, and then I will be on my way."

His look of pride filled her with confidence, even though this was the first time he had set her a task in a place where neither of them had any real previous experience. If he believed in her, and believed she was ready—then she was ready! "I depend upon your eyes and ears and cleverness, my daughter. I know you will not fail me, nor your Kingdom."

He returned to his counting-house, and she swam down to the repository of knowledge they all referred to as a "library" although it hadn't a single book in it. It couldn't have real books, of course; paper would rapidly disintegrate here. All the magical books that Tasha read were especially created just for her, the letters incised into paper-thin metal pages, the bindings all of metal-covered wood. But to preserve a library full of real books would mean the casting of many spells to protect them, more to allow them to be handled and read. Again, the question of the delicate balance of magics inside the protective shield around the Palace arose, and the answer was the same as always. It was not worth the risk.

But the "library" had been here forever. It had been here since there had been a Sea King in this Kingdom. The magic around the Palace had been put there when it had already been in place for centuries. It was very likely, in fact, that the Palace had been erected here in the first place primarily because the library was already here.

She swam through a coral garden, the most popular garden surrounding the Palace, full of secluded, blue-lit grottos, great staghorn branches of black and red corals surrounding soft pockets of sand, sea fans providing endless places for children or adults to play hide-and-seek. But in the center of the coral garden was her goal, hidden within a sea cave, and illuminated by the glow of a set of strange, luminescent corals she had never seen anywhere else.

She swam inside, waited for her eyes to adjust to the dimmer light, then approached the library.

In the center of the cave was a slab of stone; something translucent and white. She thought it might be quartz, but no one knew for sure, because no one wanted to upset the magic here, and it would probably take magic to find out. It was precisely cut into the shape of a triangle. By whom? No one knew.

On the top of the stone lay a shell.

Not an ordinary shell, mind. In the shape of a conch shell, this one was made of the same translucent white stuff as the table. It must have been carved, although every detail was precisely identical to a real conch, including a few little irregularities and places where it looked as if barnacles had tried to attach.

This, in fact, was the library.

And unlike a real library, it was not portable. You could not move the stone slab; it was somehow rooted to the rock beneath it. You could not take the shell, either. The moment you left the grotto, it would vanish from your hand and reappear back on top of the slab. Whatever magic had created it also appeared to protect it. You could smash both shell and slab with hammers, and both would heal themselves within moments.

She picked the shell up. "I need to know as much as possible about the Kingdom of Nippon," she said carefully. Then she drifted up onto the white stone triangle and settled down on it. When she was comfortable, she put the shell to her ear and closed her eyes.

At first, she heard only what you would hear up on the Drylands if you put a shell to your ear; something like the sound of the sea. It was *like* the sound of the sea, although it was not the actual sound of the sea of course; you could not fool someone from the Sea Kingdoms into thinking it was. But under that sound came a soft murmuring, and she listened deeply to that murmur, allowing it to lull her, as the voice became clearer and clearer. She never exactly went to sleep; this was more like a state of trance, though that was something she never achieved except when listening to the library. For a very, very long time she remained this way. Somehow her arm never became fatigued, nor her legs cramped from sitting in one position for so very long without moving.

She literally could not tell how long it was that she sat there. The grotto was a timeless place, and there was no light leaking in from the outside.

It was dark when she emerged from the sea cave, with everything the collective scholars of this Sea Kingdom knew about Nippon stowed away in her mind. Alas that it was not a great deal. She knew nothing, for example, of what the people wore, though she did know what they looked like. They were small, but not blond; though another aspect of the magic she got from the Sirens—the ability to look like anyone she cared to—would come into play here, she would not know how to dress. She would have to rely on The Tradition to help her. Tricky, that. It would do so only if the story needed her intervention, or if *her* story needed its intervention. Still. It had helped her before, and it would likely do so again, and it was always worth trying.

Her eyes were drawn inexorably to her home. Now that it was night, the Palace glowed against the dark water like a giant lantern, all pale pink, and if possible, looking even more like a creation out of a dream. The lights from within glowed through the coral walls; except when the Palace settled down to sleep, no room was ever left unlit, so the effect was never spoiled by dark patches. Even then, there were always small lights left burning, so that there was always a faint glow to the place. Down in the gardens, the night fish had come out; luminescent, they sported patterns or lures of glowing green or pale blue along their flanks. Some of the little squid and octopods that lived in the garden also glowed. Some of the patterns moved, or flashed on and off. Some of the anemones glowed as well. The glowing Palace was surrounded by a garden full of tiny, moving lights. And on the surface above and just a little below it, the glow-drift gleamed, thin scarves of pale light that were really made up of millions and millions of tiny sea creatures almost too small to be seen. This served as stars for the Sea Kingdoms, though no one who had ever seen the actual stars ever found the glow-drift as satisfying.

Armed with her information, and already wearing her fish-scale armor, Katya was ready to go.

Now, it was a curious thing with her father; he hated goodbyes. He liked the illusion that if he turned a corner, he just might come across the person that he knew very well was somewhere far, far away. Maybe it had something to do with the fact that as a young child, most of the people he had actually said goodbye to had never returned. That had been a turbulent time, when war raged between this Kingdom and the Dryland-ers of the south, and she could hardly fault her father for having such a reaction.

And although the rest of the family was well aware of how she served King and Kingdom, as were his advisers and other special agents, he had made it very clear that the family was not to know when and where she had gone when she took on a task for him. It could be dangerous for her, for even as cautious as they were, it was possible for something to fall in conversation where it could be overheard. As for the Court—well, since more than a few of those tasks she'd been set when she was younger had been about uncovering the true motives of one Court member or another…it was not wise to inform them, either.

As a matter of principle, she allowed herself to trust no one in the Court. Not even when her father trusted them.

So she never said goodbye to anyone. Ever. She just went.

That was what she did now; she swam to the stables to find herself a ride.

Stables was a misnomer, really. It was really an enclosure, with walls of net strung between pylons formed of old ship masts, where various small whales and dolphins who were visiting the Palace could stay. The net kept them from drifting off when they dozed, and mullet was served to the visitors several times a day. That made it a good spot for them to relax and hang about; some to gossip with each other, some to get fed without effort, some just because they were willing to lend a fluke now and again to some task like Katya's. Normally Katya would select a dolphin, porpoise, or a pilot whale to carry her where she needed to go, but this time, the journey would be a long one, and she needed strength, speed, and stamina. With the smaller cetaceans, you could have any combination of two, but not all three.

So she was going to have to choose something very different from her old friends, and no little bit dangerous.

She needed an orca.

When she entered the enclosure, there were three orcas there, all habitués of the Palace. Two of them were old, seasoned veterans, one with his flank scarred by the marks of squid suckers, the second with a lopped-off dorsal fin where a shark had bitten it off. The youngest was the one she was most interested in; he was known to be a fast swimmer, not because he had ever taken a rider before, but because he had won several inter-pod races. He was handsome, but not unscarred; there were the marks of combat on his flukes, a clear impression of teeth.

He was awake, too, which was good, as the other two were already dozing. Orcas tended to be testy if you woke them.

Like all the Royal Family, Katya had tasted Dragon's Blood, that of an ancient Sea Drake that lived in a sea cave beneath the Palace itself, and woke only once every hundred years or so. She had never seen it awake, though her father had. She envied him.

She and the last four of her siblings had all tasted the blood at once. The Drake was impossibly beautiful, like an enormous cross between a Sea Serpent and a Lionfish. In sleep, it lay coiled around a stone in the center of its cave that had been worn smooth by its movements as it slept. It had an enormous frill of black-and-white striped spines, and a ridge of similar spines down its back. Both were folded flat, but moved a little as the King took a knife, nicked the membrane between two toes and collected a thick drop of blood. She had moved forward very carefully and with the others, tasted it from the point of the knife before it could wash away.

And then…then she had understood the language of the Beasts. Interestingly enough, it had also given her the Gift for understanding the various spoken and written languages of every race she had ever encountered, though it had not done so for her siblings. She had spoken first to a dolphin, and her life had seemed changed forever.

The Dragon's Blood had unlocked the speech of every cetacean, of course. So it was no difficulty at all for her to bow to the orca and say to it, "Eagle of the Sea, I wonder if I might trouble you for a moment," and be perfectly understood.

The orca regarded her with its right eye, round and shrewd. "The Sea King's youngest daughter comes to have words with me, although we have never met. Presumably, you want something."

Orcas were odd beasts. They absolutely required formality and deference from those who initially approached them, then tested them with rudeness, or sometimes even threats. It was probably because that was the way they treated each other. Big predators were always testing each other.

So she laughed. "But of course! Doesn't everyone? This offers challenge though. An epic swim, if you will, and perhaps at the end of it, something interesting to see. Have you ever been to the place the Drylanders call Nippon?"

He rolled so that he looked at her with his other eye. "Hmm. I have not. It would be a new place to see. An epic swim, you say?" He blasted her with a jolt of sound that jarred her insides for a moment. She didn't even flinch; definitely another test. "Such a thing would make me attractive to the females. I am looking to start a pod soon. A strong swimmer, a good hunter. Hmm." He rolled back to the other side. "And you…you are a warrior."

"Of sorts," she agreed.

"You do not show fear, only proper deference." He blew a blast of bubbles. "You would be a good companion. We will go."

"My thanks. May I know your name?" she asked, going over to the side of the enclosure, which really served only to keep the visitors from drifting off on the currents as they slept, and as a place to hang the various sizes of traveling harness and the weapons one needed when traveling.

"Sharptooth. You would be the one called Tsunami."

That pulled her up sharply. She had never heard her Orcan name before. "Tsunami? Why am I called that?" she asked, as she fitted the harness over his nose.

He blew a string of laugh bubbles. "Because nothing at all of you shows on the surface, and only at the last moment do you reveal yourself. And those who see you are swept away."

She had to admit, that was a fairly good encapsulation of her style. "I trust you approve and agree with such a name," she said dryly, slowly working the traveling harness over his tall dorsal fin.

He blew another string of laugh bubbles. "I am of the People. You need to ask?"

* * *

Orcas were the fastest swimmers in the sea. Sharptooth was probably one of the fastest orcas in the Kingdom. Katya held to his harness, flattened herself down along his back to reduce resistance, and let him go. As for giving him directions—this was an orca. He had access to the best guides in the world. Other orcas, and the only great whales that could rival an orca for fierce nature, the sperm whales. He simply set out in the right general direction and began calling out his destination. Soon, someone replied. "This way." He oriented himself on the call without slackening his pace.

Once out of the shelter of the magic around the Palace, the water had turned cold and the magic that allowed anyone to breathe water vanished as they crossed the invisible barrier, and her body had reacted by changing, just as the Sirens' bodies did. There was one moment of icy cold, and a moment when it felt as if she was choking.

Then she was warm again, and she could breathe.

They paused to chase down, catch, and eat some salmon. She spread a purse net vertically in the water; he chased the school toward it. The school hit the net and she pulled the cord that turned it into a bag, catching enough for him with one left over for her meal.

As she sliced raw bits off and ate them, he eyed her. "There were seals," he offered. "I did not chase them."

She eyed him back. "If it is a choice between seal and starving…"

He blew bubbles. "Good, you are practical. I doubt you would let me take porpoise under any circumstances though…."

"I'd rather you didn't eat my allies." She suspected, from the tone of his voice, that he was teasing her. "It makes for bad feelings all around if you eat allies."

"True. And we should be gone."

"So we should." She sliced off the fillets and stowed them in a fish-skin pouch on the harness. She was set for food now; all they had to worry about was keeping him fed. She secured herself to his harness, tucked herself down again, and they were off.

A journey like this had a curious timelessness about it. They stopped to rest when they were tired, hanging together in the featureless, empty blue that was the mid-ocean far from any shore. When he was hungry, he would query the surrounding water until he got an answer about where the food was, and they would make a slight detour. The sun rose and set above the water; once they waited as it touched the horizon to see if they could catch the "green flash" that supposedly came as it passed beneath the waves, but neither of them saw anything. So they moved on.

Finally, there were gulls in the sky, bits of greenery on the waves, and they knew they were nearing some kind of land.

Then they saw it.

Journey's end, but the mere beginning for Katya; though Sharptooth would be a part of this for a bit longer. First, Katya had to find the right part of what was really a very large island.

For that, they needed to listen to the seabirds.

At their first landfall, the birds were acting perfectly normally. Nothing much to complain of, it seemed, other than that someone was always stealing food. And there was the usual gull chorus: "Mine! Mine! Mine! Mine!" They turned their faces southward along the coastline and plunged on, pausing long enough to give the hungry orca a meal of good mullet.

The second time, half a day later, was equally fruitless. It was a full moon, though, so they elected to cover more leagues in the search.

But the third time—as sunrise flooded the sky with light, and the seabirds rose to meet it.

"Death! Death! Death!" cried one.

"Despair! Despair!" cried a second.

Katya turned to look at the round, bright eye of her companion. "I think we have found the right place,"

Chapter

4

Sharptooth had left, after giving the unusual pledge that if she needed *him*, she must summon him through the Sperm Whales or the Orca pods. She stepped out of the water and shook herself off, waiting while her body shivered in the shock of change, her lungs took in the first gasping breath of air, and she felt things subtly shift inside her.

Then, she spread her arms wide, spun out a thread of magic, and sent it questing after The Tradition. Not that The Tradition was anything like an entity, except…

Except that sometimes it acted as if it was.

Well, no matter. She knew when her magic touched it, and she promptly insinuated her will into it, cajoling. *I need to fit in here,* she told it; if there was one thing that The Tradition "liked," it was for everything and everyone to follow down its favored and predetermined paths. This was a land full of small black-haired people who looked a certain way. She didn't look that way, and wanted to. She sensed its interest, then its power. Quickly, before it could elect to do something annoying, and seized on that image of *fitting in*, and decided to make her fit in as a beggar, she needed to take control when the power was there.

I need to fit in here, she told it.

And the moment when it decided that it needed to help her do that, she invoked exactly how she wanted to fit in. As a high-ranking noblewoman—with whatever was the most beautiful clothing that was available!

Because, after all, it was no fun being a peasant.

She had her eyes closed in order to concentrate; the magic was thick, very thick around here. No wonder the seabirds were crying doom; whatever was happening was powerful and The Tradition had taken note quite strongly.

But she was a bit taken aback when it suddenly felt as if someone had draped her in a hundred bolts of fabric all at once.

Legs muffled, arms enveloped, head bowed forward—her eyes flew open and she looked down at herself in shock.

It not only felt as if someone had draped her in a hundred bolts of fabric—it looked that way, too.

She must have been wearing six layers of clothing.

In form, the main article she was enveloped in was a heavily embroidered blue silk robe, but the rectangular, lined sleeves swept down to and along the sand, the robe itself trailed along behind her by the length of her arm, and it was bound around her by a broad, stiff, embroidered silk sash with an elaborate bow or knot that she could feel at the small of her back. Beneath this robe was another; beneath that still another—

there must have been six or seven of these robes, each carefully layered so as to show a sliver of colored silk at the neckline. Her hair had been bound up and hidden beneath a wig made in a stiff mounded style with hair sticks thrust through it, and on her feet were wooden sandals so tall she was afraid to take a step in them. Not that she could have even if she had wanted to. She couldn't move.

The clothing was beautiful but—

This was utterly ridiculous.

Would The Tradition give her another chance? She closed her eyes and tested the potential magic about her.

There was nothing there. She'd had her chance. Now she had to find some other way of getting the job done.

Drat.

With a sigh, she began divesting herself of all of the many garments. She would just have to do this the hard way.

By dusk, she was quietly moving through the underbrush at the side of a road, following her instincts into the north. She had found a peasant farmer's house with commoner's clothing drying on bushes outside it. Figuring that one of those silk robes was probably worth more than a hundred outfits, she left all seven of the robes neatly folded beneath the bush, with the wig on top. She kept the jeweled hair sticks, the jade ornaments attached to the sash, and the handful of trinkets she found tucked inside sleeves, in the sash. She might not need them, but you never knew.

How do women manage to do anything in this place? she thought crossly, slipping from shadow to shadow. This did not bode well for accomplishing her father's task quickly. If women were so confined by their clothing, what other fetters did this land put on them?

What a confounded nuisance.

The Temple was in shambles.

Katya knew it had to be a Temple; religious structures in nearly every land she had ever been in were generally very similar, though this was very small and rather humble. Perhaps it was a Shrine rather than a Temple? This place had a very large front gate, all of wood, which stood open, and a broad avenue lined with stone lanterns leading directly to the front doors, also standing open. There was a large bell and hammer to one side of the door, although one side of the bell frame was splintered and broken. The once- manicured grounds were overgrown with weeds, and the gravel paths had bits of grass sprouting in them. Katya climbed the steps leading to a porch around the entire structure, then stepped quietly through the open doors and peered around in the gloom. The exterior walls were all of wood, and the place appeared to be just one big room with a wooden floor. There was an altar with the statue of a man seated in a cross-legged pose on it. The serenity of the man's expression was marred by the hole gouged in the statue's forehead.

Violation of a sacred space. This is not good.

The destruction was not new; in fact, it looked very much as if it had happened many months ago, and yet there had been no attempt to repair it. The Temple looked abandoned.

She prowled around the edges of the room. It was curiously barren, but the walls behind the altar seemed to be composed of nothing but paper stretched in frames. Odd. Very odd. There were no doors, and yet there seemed to be further space beyond the paper walls.

She examined the walls further, and her curiosity increased. It appeared that the center section of each wall moved. She gave the one nearest her an experimental push.

It moved sideways with a faint sound, and she stared at the room beyond…

…and the old man sitting disconsolately in the corner. He looked up at her.

He looked like a more ancient version of the Qin sailors that she had seen, very rarely, among the crews of sailors from other lands on trading ships. He was quite small, no taller than she, and his skin was like parchment, his eyes narrow and slanted. He looked—broken. "It's no use," he said dully. "If you have come on *her* behalf, you might as well know that she has already taken the only valuable thing we had. If you have come for solace, there is none to be had here. I have tried my best, but I am old and hurt, and the others are all dead."

"What others, Grandfather?" she asked, coming over to help him up as he tried to stand. "I am a stranger here—"

"I can offer you shelter for the night, but little else," the old man said, as if he had not heard her. "My brother monks are dead, and no one comes from the village anymore. I think they may be dead, too. I have not had the strength to look."

She helped him to his feet and at his direction, into a little building behind the shrine, which proved to be an open room with a kitchen at one end. There was a small fire burning in a brazier, with a kettle of water over it. "I have tea—" he began.

"Grandfather, you will sit, and you will let me tend to

things," she said firmly. Princess she might be, but she was also not a stranger to every sort of work. That, too, had been part of her training, so that she could counterfeit virtually anyone of any station. Before long, she had the old man comfortable beside a much larger fire, cradling a cup of hot tea. At his direction, she had started a pot of some sort of grain cooking, then went out to survey the rest of the Temple and its grounds.

It had been pretty much ransacked, and the more she saw, the angrier she became. A great deal of the destruction was purely wanton damage. There was no reason to it, if, as the old man had said, there was only one object of value here. It appeared that five or six others had lived here with the old man in lives of quiet simplicity, which had in one day been shattered by an outside force. She did manage to find some bedding that was not too torn up, and the pallet the old man himself must have been using, and some of the same short robes and loose trews of plain dark cloth that both of them were wearing, which had been stored in a closet. That would give both of them a change of clothing.

She returned to the old man laden with her gleanings to find he had gotten enough energy to tend to the food. He looked up at her entrance, his face much more alert this time. "Little daughter, you are too kind."

"Grandfather, it is my duty," she replied. "Can you tell me what happened here?"

He bowed his head. "It was a witch," he said sadly, "and we were not prepared to combat her. But we did not know. How were we to know?"

Slowly, as the grain cooked, as she made up beds for both of them near the warmth of the fire, as they ate, she pieced together the story. This was not an important shrine, but it was regularly visited by the folk of a nearby village, and the old man and his five fellow priests tended the shrine and the grounds, and the spiritual needs of the village, faithfully. The statue— she could not make out from his sometimes rambling speech whether it was of a god, or of a great priest of that god—had been unearthed accidentally several decades ago by a farmer plowing his fields, and the shrine built to house it, priests found to tend the shrine once it was completed. No one had thought that the statue was of any particular importance; the dark stone embedded in its forehead had seemed nothing more than a simple bit of ornamentation.

This old man had been one of the first group of six priests to be sent here; as old age had thinned their ranks, others had been sent to replace them. Katya gathered, as she ate the boiled grains and listened closely, that although there were branches of priests that were martial in nature and trained in combative techniques, these were not of that order, being strictly contemplative. "This was just a forest shrine," he repeated, over and over, his bewilderment evoking her pity. "What did we have that anyone would want?"

Then, two months ago, *She* had turned up at the door.

She hadn't been subtle, either. The way the old man described it, she hadn't even issued a challenge. The first they had known of her arrival was when the doors had blown open, and a white-clad, white-haired woman surrounded by a whirlwind of grimacing demons strode into the sanctuary.

"A witch," the old man called her. Katya would have called her a sorceress, but whatever you called her, it was pretty clear that she was very powerful. It was also quite clear that she was both ruthless and evil.

The old man himself had been the first to bar her way, with amulets binding both wrists and a blessed staff to protect him, he had interposed himself between the witch and the others.

Amulets and blessed staff had been utterly useless. With a simple gesture, she had flung him through the air at the bell frame just outside. And that was literally the last thing he knew until he'd woken up again, in terrible pain, lying at the foot of the bell shrine with a broken arm and cracked ribs.

He had staggered into the sanctuary to find his fellow priests dead, lying where they too had been thrown, and the stone wrenched out of the statue.

"It must have been important, some sort of amulet or talisman," the old man said brokenly. "But we were simple priests. We never had any magic of our own, only magic in things we were given and the power of our faith. How were we to know?"

"You couldn't," she soothed him, as she helped him into bed. "You could not have known."

It was clear that the attack had broken his spirit as well as his body.

The old man had cremated his fellow priests by the simple expedient of dragging their poor bodies to an unused shed, drenching them with oil, and setting fire to the place. He had then waited for someone from the village to come to send word of what had happened to his superiors.

But no one ever came, and he was too weak to make the walk himself. And by now, he had lost faith that they still lived.

"Be easy, Grandfather," she said into the darkness. "Tomorrow this will be dealt with. I am young and strong. If there is help to be found for you nearby, I will find it. If there is none, I will take you to where help is."

As soon as he was asleep, she got up again, and stole out.

She needed very little sleep, and right now she needed information far more than sleep. Thanks to the old man, she knew where the village should be, and the first piece of information she needed was whether or not there was anyone still alive there.

Under the cover of darkness, she sprinted down the road and before the moon was very high, she had come to the village. She had feared that what she uncovered would be "what was left" of the village, and to her intense relief found it still standing.

Easy enough to see from a distance, it was like a collection of toy houses all lit up. She caught a hint of the steep thatched roofs in the moonlight, but most of the light came from lanterns outside the doors and being carried by people milling about. The houses all seemed to be like the shrine; substantial in size, raised off the ground, and sometimes going to two or three stories.

Evidently, there was a meeting of some sort going on in what looked like a village square. Katya slowed to a walk, and then, after pausing for a moment in the shadows, worked her way toward the ones that seemed to be doing the most talking.

She listened silently, on the outskirts of the crowd, keeping herself in shadows. She had the notion that if she stayed very quiet, since she was a female, the men might not notice her. And she was right. There were other women and children hovering half in the shadows, listening, but none of them said a word.

She examined these villagers as well as listening to them; for the most part, they wore the same kind of loose trews and wrapped tunic that she had purloined. The men were quite muscular. The women looked quite strong, too, leading Katya to think that, as in the Sea Kingdom the women of this land were not inclined to hide behind their menfolk, even if they did defer to them.

The "meeting" consisted of a great deal of quarreling, not to the point of shouting, but very near. A minority of the men, mostly young, wanted to find out what had happened at the shrine. The majority were still too frightened to go, and kept reminding the others that "she" had said it was none of their business, and to stay away.

Well, after the priest's story, Katya had a good idea who "she" was. The witch had given some sort of demonstration of her powers and managed to thoroughly cow the leaders.

Katya heard the fear there, fear and even some panic that made the voices of most of those speaking a bit shrill. The faces in the lantern light were strained, and several of the speakers kept looking back over their shoulders as if they were afraid they were going to be overheard.

But to Katya, the interesting thing was that this witch had threatened the villagers rather than actually doing anything to them.

She must have made some display of power, or they wouldn't be so frightened, but it didn't look as if the *display* of power included much actual harm. Not like what had happened to the monks. Katya doubted that this was out of the kindness of her heart, or a disinclination to slaughter an entire village full of people. Oh my, no.

It had to have been because she *couldn't* do anything to them.

As she listened to the arguments go back and forth, she wondered what the difference was between the villagers and the monks. Because the witch hadn't hesitated a moment before going all out against the shrine.

What was in the shrine, besides the talisman?

Perhaps the answer lay, not in *what* but in *who*.

Six unarmed priests, none of whom were trained in fighting, most of whom were probably old or elderly? *I suspect that may be the answer. They were not a challenge.* But a village full of working men and women, with weapons or weapon-like objects…

Whatever it is that the talisman does…might have very little to do with combat.

She might have demons, but evidently not enough of them. Not enough that she could take on a village. Or else…her demons couldn't cope with something that the villagers could use against them.

She began casting glances around at the homes and work-shops. There were carvings and written symbols everywhere; they could be nothing, or they could be guardians and runes of protection. But the shrine presumably would have had the same sort of protections. That couldn't be it.

Something common, so common as to be easily overlooked.

The iron of their farming implements? The bird- frighteners in the fields? The presence of ancestral spirits about the village?

The presence of children in the village? Without having the sort of concentrated and focused magic that a real magician or sorceress had, rather than the bits and bobs that she had as the daughter of the Sea King, there was just no way for her to work it out.

Katya circled the group, looking for clues, hoping for ideas. At least at the moment, it appeared that the witch was not all that powerful—certainly not so powerful that she could not be overcome by someone who actually had strong magic. But Katya knew better than to trust appearances. She wanted to see this creature with her own eyes, to judge for herself just how dangerous she was.

And then there were the seabirds. They would never be crying doom if the danger wasn't real. So just because this witch wasn't strong enough to take on a group of simple villagers at the time of the confrontation—

She might be very strong now. She had her stone, and as far as she knew, all the priests were dead. The threats had served their purpose; the villagers had stayed away from the shrine long enough for her trail to have gone cold. That may have been exactly what the witch wanted.

Well, this would not be the only cold trail that Katya had pursued. Meanwhile, she also needed to get help for the old priest. It was a very good thing that she knew exactly how to get that help.

On the outskirts of the crowd were the adolescents, huddled in a knot, listening intently and doing no small amount of grumbling. Katya went to eavesdrop.

"Who is this foreign witch to tell us we are not to visit our own shrine?" hissed one of the boys, keeping his voice down. Katya smiled.

"That's right!" One of Katya's little magics was the ability to make her words seem to come from anyone other than herself. Right now it seemed to be coming from a group of four, each of whom would swear one of the others had spoken just now. "Besides, those priests aren't fighters! What if something happened to them?"

"I'm sure something *did*," replied the first boy, grimly. "Someone should have been sent as soon as that witch was out of sight."

"I never thought I would ever feel ashamed of my father." That was another of Katya's little prods. It struck home with more than one of the youngsters.

"If the old men won't act, we should," growled the first boy, and within moments, with a little more prodding on Katya's part, the young men had withdrawn to where they wouldn't be overheard by their elders. Katya followed them just long enough to be sure that they were of one mind on going to the shrine in defiance of the witch's orders. But once she was sure—once she had actually seen them marching out on their way—

She felt a little badly about it; she'd manipulated them shamelessly and now they thought of their own parents and grandparents as cowards. On the other hand…

There was an old man, sick and hurt, who had been trying to take care of himself for far too long now. It was more than time that someone helped him.

As she left the village, slipping silently through the shadows with the cool, damp scent of water strong in her nose, they were on the road back to the shrine. And their elders were still arguing whether or not anyone ought to see if the old priests were all right.

Once she got out of earshot, and down to the banks of the stream she had smelled, she put it all out of her mind. She had far more pressing things to think about.

Now if I were a witch, and I wasn't planning on fighting my way to power, where would I go?

Chapter 5

At some time near midnight she stopped.

Before her, silver with the moon etching a path across the mirror-smooth waters, stretched a truly beautiful lake.

There was not even a breath of breeze to ripple the glassy surface, and Katya stared at the pure, clean water longingly. It would be cold, of course, but for the Sea King's children—

Well, they swam through, and fought in the waters of the Arctic. This lake was not that cold. And there would be so very many advantages to being in her proper form, not the least of which was that she would be able to interrogate every water spirit there was hereabouts.

She stared at the moon path for a long time, then sighed. She felt sticky and dirty. It was one thing to be able to disguise one's self as a person of rank, comfort, and privilege. It was quite another to experience life as a Drylander as a peasant. Not that she hadn't done that before but…it made the task less of a pleasure and far more like work.

It didn't take a great deal of thought to convince herself; after a thorough check to make sure she was not being observed, she reverted and slipped under the water.

Quickly, she swam down to conceal herself in a kelp forest and sent out the silent call. As her father's daughter and a princess of the Royal Blood, she could summon and direct any creature of the water, whether it be natural or magical in nature. Some, she could even coerce, though she rarely did so. Although they were by no means as mobile as air spirits, the little creatures of the water did go many places unseen and unheard, and if the witch was anywhere about, they would probably know something about the creature. Her movements at least, if not her motives.

She expected some information. She did not expect to be virtually mobbed by the little water creatures of this Kingdom.

The moonbeams piercing through the surface of the lake illuminated a horde of creatures large and small, in a bewildering variety of forms, which homed in on her as if she were a loadstone and they were bits of iron. Some were actual fish, frogs, and turtles. Others were pure spirits of the water, tiny water-fairies in the form of impossible fish-like creatures, wildly colored and with a vast variety of fins, spines, and crests. Others were strangely transparent snakes, or miniature dragons.

Some were ghosts—which rather startled her, as in the lands where she was accustomed to walk, ghosts were a rarity. Some of the ghosts were true haunts, spirits that, for whatever reason, were unable or unwilling to pass on—those were generally the spirits of people who had met with an untimely and water-related end. Some were guardians to their families of fisher folk. Some…their motives were unclear to her, and she wasn't at all sure she wanted to probe any further to find out.

All of them were desperate to tell her about the witch. And very, very quickly indeed, she got the sense that the seabirds had not been crying doom frivolously.

Gradually, as she listened to them, she got a sense of what the witch was up to. It was a diabolically clever scheme, for it was always more difficult to remove someone who was the power *behind* the throne rather than the power on it.

Despite her acquisition of the stone, she still wasn't all that powerful, not by the standards of a great Wizard or Sorceress. But she was certainly powerful enough to cause a ripple across the land. And it was entirely possible that this talisman, this artifact, was not one that granted overt power, but rather one that granted something more subtle.

That was going to make Katya's job infinitely more difficult.

As for what the witch was doing…

"She appeared at the lord's gate in her litter," fretted a child-like ghost with hair that pooled on the ground at her feet. *"The litter-bearers were all demons, of course. She said she had been sent, as a gift, and one look at her and the lord was under her spell."*

That seemed to be her pattern. She appeared on the very doorstep of powerful lords. She said she had been sent as a gift; Katya could only assume she was posing as a courtesan of some note. The moment that the lord saw her, he was under her spell, dismissing other concubines, sending his wife away, and generally acting besotted. She would consolidate her hold over him, then move on to the next conquest.

And then…nothing. One would think she would then urge her conquest to some conflict with his neighbors but…not.

In fact, it seemed she actively discouraged any such thing. She merely consolidated her position, then moved on to the next lord.

Katya pondered all of this and frowned, as agitated water spirits circled her. Others might view this differently, but she saw a pattern.

Once she had all the warlords in this place following her will, she could choose one to become the figurehead, and take the Kingdom. Since this Kingdom had no Godmother, it might be a very long time before she found herself challenged. And if this Kingdom possessed some powerful magical artifacts besides the one she already had—she could challenge the Sea King.

That…would be bad.

As it happened, since this lake was very large indeed, the witch was not far by a straight swim. Katya pushed off from the kelp bed, invoked the webbing between her fingers and toes, and set off at a pace that left most of the water dwellers behind.

And before she was halfway to her goal, it became obvious that this time, the witch was not going to have it all her own way—for flashes of magical power were lighting up the night sky.

Katya put on an extra burst of speed.

She leaped out of the water, but did not bother to change to a more human form. Looming above the water was a Palace—for that was all that such a huge and ornate building could be—and it was from within this structure that the signs of a magic struggle in progress were coming.

As Katya sprinted up the path to the Palace itself, it became very obvious that the witch was taking no chances on unexpected friends or allies showing up and weighing in on the side opposing her. The path was strewn with the apparently lifeless bodies of the Palace guards....

Katya stopped dead in her tracks beside the first one and frantically felt for a pulse. To her intense relief, the man was still alive. So it was the usual trick of shutting the inhabitants of an entire area in sleep.

She wouldn't be able to wake them until the witch was defeated, but at least they were still alive.

And there was this much. At least they wouldn't be either at the command of the witch, or able to spring to their mistress's defense.

Katya hoped not, anyway.

Up a flight of stairs to a stunningly beautiful wooden porch, she ran. The porch was strewn with flat, square pillows, and she guessed that it was a favorite place for the warlord and his family to spend time. Nothing in sight that she could use as a weapon, though, not even a chair or a stool.

The doors were wide open, and she charged inside.

Katya got only the vaguest of impressions of the place—that it was huge, that it was as barren of furniture as the porch—when her attention was riveted by the two combatants and their hostage.

He had to be a hostage. The combatants wouldn't have left him standing there unattended otherwise.

His eyes were glazed over and he swayed a bit where he stood, which was off to the side of the room. He was in no danger *yet*, but it was possible that once the witch saw a new element enter the affray, she would cut her losses, kill the warlord, and vanish.

So as her first act, Katya leaped across the room as she drew her sword out of the ether, and interposed herself between the warlord and danger. At the moment, she couldn't tell who was who, except that the warlord was the only "innocent" here.

Only then did she stop to really look at the two mages.

Both were female. Both were stunningly beautiful. Both were clothed in more practical versions of the robes Katya had conjured when she'd first arrived; the brocades and embroideries were just as elaborate but sleeves, sash, and hemlines were nowhere near as exaggerated. One was all in blue; one was all in red. The one in blue had white hair, the one in red had red hair, and by now Katya knew enough to know that on a young woman, white hair was not an auspicious color, and for the uniformly black-haired people of Nippon, red hair on anyone was the sign of a something not of this world.

It was entirely possible that not one, but *two* inhuman women had their sights on this particular warlord. That would make things…interesting.

But it was also possible that the motives of one of these two were, if not pure, at least benign.

When you don't know, you wait.

There were no other entities visible right now, and the witch, at least, had been reported as being served by demons. That could mean that the witch was withholding her demons for a later strike, or that they had all been defeated. It was possible that the witch had already lost that part of this battle. But in case they were in hiding somewhere, Katya needed to be alert for a possible attack.

Meanwhile, although this might not have been one of the most spectacular mage battles that Katya had ever seen, some of which had involved the wholesale destruction of entire fortresses and villages, it was definitely one of the more colorful. The woman in red was using a fan to direct her powers. As Katya stood guard over the rigid and unresponsive warlord, the woman in red made an attack. A backhanded flip of her unfurled fan sent a wave of daggers of white light singing toward her opponent. The woman in blue hastily scrawled a glowing glyph in the air with both index fingers that deflected the daggers to either side, where they struck the wooden walls and vanished. The woman in blue cast something invisible at the one in red, and a moment later, a gigantic, transparent serpent formed out of the air itself, materializing in a loose coil around the feet of the woman in red. It reared up until its head was higher than hers, and stared down at her out of cool, translucent eyes. Then it wrapped itself around the one in red and began to squeeze. With a contemptuous sniff, the one in red bent her head down and blew on the coils, a long, foggy breath that sparkled with frost crystals. The serpent stiffened, and a thin rime of ice and frost spread across its body with unbelievable swiftness. The serpent stiffened further, then stopped moving altogether. The woman in red stamped her foot, and with the sound of breaking glass, the serpent shattered, the pieces of it raining down around the woman in red, then vanishing. The woman in red was already making the next move. A forward flip of the fan created a wash of fire that raced toward the woman in blue and engulfed her. She was hidden from view by the flames for a moment, then with a thunderous crash that shook the floor, the flames were extinguished by a blast of wind. She retaliated with an overhand throwing motion; halfway between herself and the woman in red, a hundred spears manifested. The woman in red spun, literally like a top, and the spears splintered as they touched her. She spun to a halt, then fluttered the fan to and fro faster than a bird's wings in flight, as if she was trying hard to cool her opponent off. But that action created a whirlwind that, even as Katya watched, blew her opponent nearly off her feet. The blue woman braced herself against it, a frown on her face, then her eyes flickered toward the warlord.

She opened her mouth. The sound that came out of it was like nothing Katya had ever heard before. The word *scream* did not even begin to describe the mind-breaking, ear- shattering howl that emerged from this lovely white-haired woman's throat.

The sound was enough to send Katya to her knees with her hands clamped over her ears, her sword dropping to the floor. But its fall somehow shattered the howl.

The woman's mouth snapped shut, leaving an echoing silence as Katya and the woman in red both shook their heads, trying to clear their minds. Then, in the next moment, the woman in blue made that same "throwing" gesture, and a thousand spears flew toward Katya and her charge.

With a cry of horror, the woman in red flung herself between both of them and the spears, spreading her arms wide and making a shield of her own body.

"*Nyet!*" Katya cried, and slashed her hand down. Water burst up out of the floor just in front of the woman in red, in a geyser that deflected most of the spears up and to either side. Only one got through, pinning one of the woman's long sleeves to a pillar.

Well, now she knew which of the two women the witch was. The witch would not have interposed herself, but would have taken the attack on the warlord as an unexpected opening for an attack of her own.

As the woman in red yanked the spear from her sleeve and cast it aside with a snarl, Katya made a fist and jerked down, and water poured straight down on the witch from the ceiling, exactly as if she were standing under a powerful waterfall.

It knocked the witch off her feet, giving the woman in red time to make a slashing movement with her fan. A line of force split the air between them, sending the witch tumbling. Katya closed off the torrent as her ally made a second slashing motion, this time upward, which sent the witch against the wall.

But the witch recovered faster than Katya would have thought possible. She whirled, her face contorted with rage, and made a clawing gesture with one hand. It looked as if she was seizing something with that hand, and with the other, she snatched open the neck of her robes. A strange, blue-black gem, oblong, and strung roughly on a cord, gleamed for a moment at her neck before she clutched it and hid it. And *now* she summoned her demons, with a single screeched word.

They were like no demons Katya had ever seen before.

They were nothing but heads. Horrible heads that flew through the air, laughing and howling and spitting curses.

They had horns, as many as three, curling horns like a ram, nubbins like a young goat, long spikes, ridged, ringed, and spiraling. Some of them had worms for tongues, or snakes, or no tongue at all. Their eyes bulged, red eyes or yellow. Some were fanged, others had the teeth of wolves or sharks. The heads dove at them, and Katya was the first to react.

She swung at the first head to dive at them, with the flat of her sword, for she was not at all certain she could cut them, but she knew she could certainly hit them. She connected with a solid *thud*, and with a wail, the head careened into the wall, where it smashed, and vanished.

And now the woman in red unwrapped her sash. Her robes slid from her shoulders and dropped to the ground, leaving her wearing the same sort of thin, white silk trews and wrapped shirt that Katya had found underneath all the robes she'd been in. She kept the sash though, and passed it around behind her back, wrapping each trailing end around her arm three times, leaving a puddle of scarlet, rust, cream, and burgundy silk on the floor below both wrists. And then…

Then she began to dance.

But *what* a dance!

She moved like nothing Katya had ever seen before, except, perhaps, her brother and sister in full battle fever. She spun, she kicked, she flipped. She tumbled in midair and on the ground. She ran up the wall and cartwheeled off it. She did moves that Katya had never seen anyone do before, and every time she moved, one end of the sash lashed out. When it did, it generally connected with a head. Where the sash struck, it left a bleeding gash. Or took out an eye. Or sliced off a horn, or smashed in teeth.

Soon there was not a single one of the demons that were unmarked. They wailed in protest, voices shrill and unearthly, and a glance at the witch proved that she was having difficulty controlling them. Her hands moved in the air in stiff, frantic gestures, and her brow was beaded with sweat. Her hair lifted, as if being pulled by invisible hands, and when Katya squinted her eyes—in between devastatingly effective swats with the flat of her sword at the demon heads—she thought she could make out more of the heads, so transparent as to be just this side of invisible, with strands of her hair in their mouths. They were lifting it, tugging at it. Katya wondered why.

The sash lashed out again, and for one moment, Katya thought it was one of the red-haired woman's rare misses.

But…no…

The end of the sash licked across the witch's forehead.

The witch shrieked at the top of her lungs, a blood- curdling sound that made Katya's hair stand on end. The witch's hands were a blur of motion, the demon heads were clearly fighting her control, none of them were coming anywhere near Katya now, and the strange stone burned a terrible blue at the witch's throat.

And *now* Katya saw what the demon heads were doing. They were holding her, keeping her from running. Did they know that if she got the chance, now that she was losing, she would run and leave them to face the red-haired woman alone?

But this was providing something else. Something that Katya had been hoping for since this fight had begun.

She turned her concentration to the red-haired woman's dance, tracking the rhythm, the moves. *She* was still being swarmed by demon heads, and some of them were getting through to her. The white silk of her garments was spotted with red, and not all of it was from the demons.

But that shot to the forehead was not the only mark that the red-haired woman had put on the witch. So if Katya could time this just right…

The opening she was hoping for came. The creatures tangling themselves in the witch's hair gave a pull back. The red-haired woman scored a cut to the witch's cheek. The witch screamed again and winced back, her eyes closing involuntarily.

And Katya dropped her sword and pulled her short dagger—

She dashed in, seized the stone in her left hand, and lifted her dagger in the right—

And with a single, swift slash, Katya cut the stone from the witch's neck.

A scream literally split the air, joined a moment later by a disharmony of howls from every part of the room. The witch made a snatch at her, hands outstretched, turning into claws, into talons, elongating in a way that made Katya gag even as she spun away.

She fell back rather than trying to run, tumbling over and turning the fall into a roll, with the stone tightly clutched against her chest. She had been afraid that it was some kind of talisman of evil and would hurt her when she touched it, but it wasn't, and hadn't. In fact, it felt warm and smooth in her hand, as if it welcomed her "rescue," as she used the momentum of her roll to spring to her feet and whirl to face the witch again.

What she saw, though, was nothing like the elegant, beautiful courtesan who had stood there. The face, skull-like and a cadaverous white, had baleful yellow eyes that glared at her with hate that had a life of its own. In place of the elegant robes, she was swathed in garments the color of dried blood, and the body inside those garments promised not pleasure, but the grave.

The only part of her that was the same was the long, long white hair, hair that, unbound as it was now, was easily twice as long as she was tall. Like a spider stuck in the middle of its own web, she was trapped in her hair, trapped by the now-visible demon heads that held the hair tight, while she screamed out unintelligible syllables and her claws—not hands anymore, but nasty, scabrous things of bone and talon—moved to form shapes that made Katya's stomach churn. Even though she had no idea what the witch was invoking, no knowledge of her magic, those sketched shapes somehow twisted the space around the witch into something utterly *wrong*.

The demon heads continued to howl, and swarmed the red-haired woman. Katya moved in, swatting furiously with her sword in one hand, the stone in the other. With a look of intense concentration on her face, the red-haired woman suddenly unwound the sash from her arms, whipped one end of it over her head in a circle, and let fly.

The sash flew across the distance between her and the witch as surely as any arrow from the bow of Katya's sister.

The instant it touched the witch, it twisted in midair as if obeying a command, and as if being manipulated by unseen hands. One end whipped around and around the witch's hands, binding them, mummifying them. The other slung around her neck, then continued to wrap around and around her head, sealing her mouth, until all that could be seen of that wreck of a face were the glaring, hate-filled eyes.

And the moment the woman in blue had been rendered immobile—the demon heads turned on her.

They swarmed her.

Like sharks converging on one of their number, wounded and bleeding, they moved in on her, teeth clattering angrily. Like sharks, they began tearing at her—the witch struggled and staggered backward, struggling with her bonds, flailing at the heads with her bound hands. Blood spattered the wooden floor as the demonic teeth found their marks.

The red-haired woman shouted a single word, and clapped her hands, and a whirling hole opened in the air above the witch, like a whirlpool in reverse, except that in the heart of this creation was a glow of ominous green. The red-haired woman bent to the pile of her garments and snatched up her fan, holding it closed, and pointing it at the witch. For the last time she flicked it open and made a complicated twisting motion with it, the hole became a whirlwind that surrounded the witch and all her hideous little helpers, and in the time it took to gasp, sucked them into itself—

Then it spun itself closed.

And winked out of existence, taking the witch and all with it.

Katya sat down abruptly, the stone still glowing softly in her hand.

Silence filled the wide wooden room, as the splotches of blood faded from the floor, leaving no sign that a struggle had taken place except for the condition of the two that remained. The red-haired woman dropped the fan on her clothing again, and pushed her hair back from her face with both hands.

Only then did Katya notice the furry, pointed ears poking up from her ally's hair….and the bushy, red-furred, white-tipped tail that had been half-concealed by the long fall of the red hair down her back.

Before she could wonder if she had merely exchanged one demon for another, the fox-woman knelt on the floor, rummaged through her clothing, and came up with an elaborately carved box. With shaking hands, she pried it open and shook something small out. Stumbling to the side of the warlord, who still stood like a statue, she pressed the object—a small, glowing stone, much like the larger one that Katya still held—to his forehead. Katya bit back an exclamation as the stone in her hand suddenly came to life, flaring with light and power that turned it from blue-black to white in an instant. There was a brief flash, and then the warlord blinked.

With a sob of relief, the fox-woman flung herself into his arms. "She almost had you!" she sobbed. "She almost took your spirit! It was in the stone!"

"Shh, my brave one, my dancing warrior," he soothed, stroking her hair, then her ears. "It is over. You saved me. You and—"

Then he looked over the fox-woman's head and seemed to see Katya for the first time.

"Tamiko-san," he said carefully. "Who is this foreign devil sitting on the floor of my house?"

Katya cleared her throat. "You might not believe this, most honorable Prince," she said carefully. "But I am the seventh daughter of the King of the Sea…."

Tamiko resumed her garments, the garb of the courtesan of a prince, and with them the illusion that made her seem like any other mortal. Her hair changed from red to black as well; the warlord watched all this with a calm that told Katya he had seen this particular transformation not once, but many times before. Katya found this reassuring, since it seemed to her that this meant there were no secrets between the warlord and his nonhuman companion. For her part, Katya resumed her own illusion, then Tamiko fetched robes to clothe her. Only then were servants summoned, food and tea brought, and full explanations on Katya's part made. She was content to wait to hear just what it was that Tamiko was, how she had come to be with the shogun, and why she had defended him.

Through it all, the warlord listened, silently, courteously, only asking an occasional question. Finally, when Katya was done, he nodded.

"I believe you, Princess," he said gravely. "I would have believed you anyway, even had you not aided Tamiko in saving my life." He chuckled. "My family is prone to attracting the attention of the Spirit Realms. My great-grandfather was rewarded with this very palace and our lands and titles as a reward for his demon-slaying. My father was notable for laying ghosts to rest. All but one, that is. That one he returned to her slumbering body, broke the spell that held her, and wedded her. And me—" He smiled at Tamiko. "I seem to have won the heart of a kitsune."

Tamiko blushed, and politely hid her smile behind her hand. It was hard to believe that this shy and delicate creature had been the dancing warrior not so long ago. "I came to make mischief in the house of the son of a ghost," she murmured. "I stayed because instead of mischief, I found my love."

"So I believe you, Sea Princess," the shogun continued. "Tamiko has said that without your aid, she would not have been able to overcome the witch. For that…there are no words adequate to express my thanks."

"What was she doing, this witch?" Katya asked. "All that I know is she was leaving a string of men who were her puppets behind her."

Tamiko sighed. "She was stealing their spirits, putting one of her tame demons in its place, and putting the souls in that stone." She pointed to the glowing stone on the floor mat between them. "From those souls, she gained magic power. From the demons doing her bidding in place of men, she gained temporal power. There is no telling, now that she is gone, but I believe that she intended to make herself Empress here eventually. Perhaps even set herself up as the rival to the Good Goddess." Tamiko shrugged. "If your words are true, and the seabirds were crying 'doom,' I can well believe that. If the Good Goddess abandoned us…"

She and her warlord exchanged a somber look.

"But it didn't happen," Katya pointed out. "My father takes a dim view of that sort of thing going on at the border of his ocean. If I had failed, he would have come himself, with allies." She raised an eyebrow. "With Godmothers, and more than one if he could. Even a would-be goddess should beware of Godmothers."

That made them both laugh. "Then perhaps," suggested Tamiko, "I might speak to the Twelve-tailed Kitsune, the head of our clan, and she might find a way to keep your father better informed on the matters within Nippon than relying on the gossip of seabirds."

"That," Katya said with satisfaction, "would be excellent. My father is always glad of allies, and it is one of the reasons he sends me out to be his eyes and ears, and sometimes his hands. But what about the spirits that are still in this stone?"

"Ah," the shogun said with a raised brow. "I think this is where I come in. I have arranged for all of us to take a journey on the morrow."

And so it was. The next day, three litters and an entourage embarked from the shogun's palace. Runners went out beforehand, looking for men of rank and influence who had suddenly collapsed in the night. This had happened, of course, as the demons controlling them had been ripped from their bodies at the defeat of the witch. Each time one was found, the shogun offered to resolve the tragedy. As the son of the famous Ghosthunter Prince, he was welcomed warmly by desperate and frightened families.

Once in the presence of those families, the shogun soothed their fears while the kitsune went to work, taking the stone from Katya—for it seemed to be most "comfortable" in her presence—and releasing the spirit held within it back into its proper vessel.

After a night of hospitality, they would move on. With every soul released, the stone grew dimmer, quieter.

Finally there was only one left. And this was where they made a slight detour. The shogun diverted them all down a path through the forest, a path so overgrown that Katya wondered how he could find it. And yet, when they came to the end of the path, there, in the midst of forest that seemed to have never felt that presence of man—

There was a Temple. And not merely a Temple, but an entire complex that included living spaces, smaller shrines, teaching rooms, halls for meditation, and several spaces for the training of martial arts. This was a place full almost to bursting with priests and monks.

But before they could step onto the grounds of the Temple, a priest appeared before them, holding up his hand.

"It devastates me to demand this of you, honorable visitors," he said, "but only you, Prince, may go forward. I beg your companions to remain here."

The kitsune looked startled, the Prince frowned, and Katya felt as if she had been slapped.

"Why?" Katya asked, making no effort to hide the fact that she felt insulted by this. The trek through the forest had been long and tiring and she had been a long time from open water....

"It is not because you are female, valiant foreign devil," the Priest said, with a smile that softened the unflattering term. "Nor is it because you are a foreign devil. It is because you are both creatures of magic, and your presence will disturb some delicate magical workings, I fear. That stone you bear, weakened though it is, certainly *will* affect those workings, and I doubt that you would care to leave it in another's custody."

Katya blinked. "Oh," she said, as Tamiko, who had been looking a bit irritated herself, relaxed. "I understand that completely. In that case—"

"And in that case, perhaps you will honor us by accepting our hospitality here," the Priest replied. And before they could blink, a swarm of young monks had assembled a pavilion, brought tea, and a delightful old scholar had come to ask them about their adventure.

When they left, they did not go empty-handed. With them came six monks of a martial and magical order, and a magical craftsman.

And within three more days, it was all over. The last spirit was restored to his body, the craftsman had replaced the stone in the statue where it belonged, and the six monks were installed in the shrine to guard it from any more thieves. The old man was retrieved from the village, and set up as the chief of the new order here.

The shogun remained at the shrine while Tamiko escorted Katya to the sea coast, for the two women had become quite fond of each other over the past several days. They both had a passion for lovely things to wear that had left the poor Prince looking at them with bewilderment from time to time. And Katya was determined to learn as much about Nippon as possible. The next time she came here, she would be better prepared.

"Now you must go, I suppose," Tamiko sighed, as they both stood on the rocks above the water. Katya had already removed the lovely robes she had just about gotten used to wearing, and given them over to Tamiko's servants. "You have done more than you expected, I think. My lord has the gratitude and loyalty of all of those you rescued. He had not before given any thought to power within the Emperor's Court, but now…"

She shrugged.

"Oh, dear," Katya said, feeling a little guilty now. "I didn't mean to—" She flushed. "I know that you would rather live quietly with him."

"It is no matter," Tamiko said dismissively. "It may be that he was fated to become more of a power, and this was merely one of many ways it might have come to be. Whatever happens, he and I will do what we must for the good of our people. But I have something for you." The kitsune reached into her sash and brought out a little red paper bird.

Now, since being in the company of Tamiko and the shogun, Katya had seen the kitsune fold squares of paper into dozens, if not hundreds, of shapes. It seemed to be a common pastime for the people of this place. Katya had even learned to fold a few herself.

But she sensed that this little bird was something very different.

"This," said Tamiko, "is no ordinary origami bird. I have had it enchanted with a spell that will last as long as the bird itself does. You have told me that your father sends you to perilous places alone. This bird will serve as your messenger when no help is near. Unfold it and write your message, then fold it up and send it on its way by saying 'Do my bidding, bear my word, then come you back my paper bird.' It will fly to the one you want, unfold itself, then when the message is read, fold itself up again and fly back to you. It will also wait for an answer to be written on it before flying back."

Katya's eyes went wide. This was no trivial magic!

The kitsune smiled. "There is a bit more," she said. "You need not send it to a specific person, for that person may take too long to arrive. You can imagine what *kind* of person or being you need—the nearest good magician, for instance, or the nearest of the Godmothers—the nearest bear-man or fox-woman. So long as you keep firmly in your heart the sort of help you need, the bird will find it. But you should keep it very safe and away from water. It is only paper, after all."

"Of course," Katya agreed, then impulsively hugged her new friend. "This is a gift beyond price," she whispered, as the kitsune returned her embrace. "I can never thank you enough."

"Nor I, you," Tamiko countered. "After all, you saved my beloved. And do not try to tell me I could have done so myself! Did not the seabirds cry 'doom'? Without you—" She shook her head, and pulled away. "I brought this as well," she said, offering a little jar into which the bird could be slipped, and a stopper and wax to seal it with. "Until you find a better container, this will do."

"Clever as well as brave and beautiful!" Katya exclaimed, with a wink that made Tamiko blush and giggle. The two of them sealed up the bird, "And now—"

"Now it is time for us both to go." Tamiko held her hands for a moment. "*Sayonara*. For we will meet again. I am sure of it."

"*Dosvedanya*," Katya agreed. Then, securing the jar to her belt, she turned and plunged into the sea. She could hardly wait to be home again, and see what new problem her father had for her.

Chapter 6

"Time for the songbird to awaken, little brother!" As Sasha blinked in the cozy darkness of his bed-cupboard, Prince Yasha grabbed Sasha's foot and shook it. "The kingdom will descend into darkness if you don't sing it into happiness!"

Sasha stretched and yawned. "Good thing I like mornings, brother, or there would be a mischief played on you today."

He threw back his blanket and swung his legs over the side of the bed-cupboard, letting them dangle while he scratched his head. The shutters that kept out the light—and in the winter, kept in the heat—were folded back. Morning light never bothered him, and in this weather, it was folly to close yourself in when you could wake to a fresh breeze and birdsong.

He wriggled his toes at Yasha, who laughed. "If anyone was ever to doubt your parentage, or mine for that matter, they would only need to see us awake and cheerful as the sun starts to rise. Father has been up for ages."

"Bah! He beat me awake? What kind of a slug am I this morning? A good thing you came to get me." Sasha jumped out of the bed-cupboard and snatched up the clothing that the servants had laid out for him. "You go do whatever it is you do, brother mine, and leave me to my foolery."

Yasha laughed again, and gave Sasha a mocking bow before leaving.

Sasha had the smallest bedroom of any of the Princes. Even so, by the standards of the boyars, who slept two and four to a bed when they came on state visits, this was luxury. Because the room was so small, the bed-cupboard was a necessity or he'd not have had room to move.

But all his life, Sasha had loved his bed-cupboard. It had been a retreat, a sanctuary in the times when he had misjudged the acceptable level of foolery and been punished for it. It was a nest when winter winds howled around the Palace and there was scarcely any daylight. He'd had some changes made to it over the years, and now it was a kind of miniature room within a room, with a hanging lamp for reading and a set of shelves for the books and anything else he wanted to tuck in there.

Such as his instruments.

He went over them in his mind as he pulled on a fresh tunic and set of trousers. It was about time to sing prosperity again, and check for things that didn't heed his warning to stay away. Especially with negotiations going forward for a bride for the Crown Prince. Time to burnish up an already shiny little Kingdom to speed things along.

He took the balalaika out of its storage shelf and unwrapped it from the layers of silk surrounding it. Slinging it over his back, he went hunting in the kitchens for some breakfast and a wash-up.

Then fed, clean, and ready to go to work, he strode out to face the day.

The sun was barely a sliver above the horizon when he made his first stop. Magic and The Tradition being what they were, it was often just as effective to use a symbol for something as the thing itself. And in this case, the Royal cattle herd stood for all the cattle in the kingdom.

It was, and had always been, possible to steer The Tradition through songs and stories. It was only that it was a bit tricky and took a lot of planning to successfully pull it off.

And you had to start with good material; in the case of a song, it had to be—well—singable. Memorable. Something that people liked to sing themselves of a winter night in a tavern.

Sasha had a talent for creating just that sort of song out of the most unlikely of subject matter, such as the health of cattle.

He stationed himself right inside the fence surrounding their pasture, made sure his instrument was in tune, and began the song he called "My Little Brown Cow."

It was an absurd little piece, really. It was sung in the persona of a herdsman, boasting about his prize milch-cow, and claiming more and wilder abilities for her with each verse, then turning it all around in a chorus that admitted that the claims might be stretching the truth a bit but that there was no doubt that this cow, and every cow in the Kingdom of Led Belarus for that matter, was the healthiest, happiest, most perfect specimen of its kind in all of the Five Hundred Kingdoms.

The cattle listened with bovine interest; the herdsmen sang

along on the chorus. And once again, The Tradition was thwarted. Or at least, it was convinced to ensure that the cattle of Led Belarus were plump, fertile, and tractable.

From the cattle pasture to the sheep enclosure he went, with a variant on the cattle song. On the way there, he sang what he thought of as the "Perfect Day" ditty, in which he extolled the weather in Led Belarus, with the chorus suggesting that every day was a perfect day here with enough sun, enough rain, fall not coming too early, spring not arriving too late.

He had a song for every sort of livestock, actually, and he sang them as often as he could. He had found that each sort of herdsman was, in general, very proprietary about the animals he or she cared for, and they *liked* having songs about their charges. From the goose-girl to the breeder of fine horses, he had created a song for each of them and it was a fair bet that over the course of a day, a person who was paying attention would hear several, if not all of them.

And all of them created Traditional paths that ensured that Led Belarus was living up to the songs.

He'd taken the precaution of filling a wallet with food, but as it happened, he didn't need to eat what he'd brought, for around about noon, he ran into a wedding.

Now this was the best possible encounter for his purpose. Everyone knew Sasha the Fool, and when people knew they would not be the butt of his foolery, they welcomed him. When he was walking about with instrument in hand, he could go just about anywhere and be welcomed.

Especially at a wedding.

His wanderings had taken him down to the little village of

Chersk down below the Palace, and he encountered the wedding party coming out of the church. They swept him up in their wake and the next thing he knew, he was being plied alternately with food and drink and requests to sing.

He embarrassed the bride, of course—it was expected that he sing at least one song about all the fat, happy babies she was going to produce, with some sly innuendos that no one was going to be very strict in counting the number of months between the wedding and the first of them. People would have been disappointed if he hadn't made the bride blush. He also managed to work in some songs about weddings in general that he hoped would shove The Tradition in the direction of a *nice* bride for his brother. Someone pretty, and pleasant, who was prepared to make friends with her husband. Just because this was going to be a marriage of state, it didn't follow that husband and wife needed to make each other miserable.

The wedding feast was "peasant fare," but Sasha had learned long ago never to ask what was in his sausage. He ate and drank and sang with a will, and heard no complaints from anyone. He played a few harmless pranks, things guaranteed to make sober and nervous people comfortable.

Then, as the afternoon passed into evening, he returned to the Palace long enough to pack a saddlebag and get his horse. It was time to make his rounds of the Kingdom and for that he would need several days. He told Yasha where he was going; that was enough warning. It wasn't as if anyone at the Palace needed him specifically.

Whenever he decided to make a round of the Kingdom, it was always like this—on impulse.

By the time he finished packing and carried his bags out to the stable, his horse was waiting, saddled and bridled. This was a solid, calm beast of the North Wind get; the gelding had none of the North Wind horses' good looks, but a great deal of sense and an unflappable nature. Sasha needed that…just in case.

Because he wasn't just singing prosperity into the land. As soon as the sun went down, Sasha went hunting when he made his rounds.

The signs that evil was trying to make its way into Led Belarus were obvious. And they should be, as Sasha had specified in his songs exactly what evil-doers said and did the moment they entered his Kingdom and started on their own nefarious plans. They might think they were acting on their own, but The Tradition, directed by Sasha, was making them give telltale signs. All Sasha had to do was look for them….

And on his third day out, he found them, too.

There it was. A stretch along the border where the woods suddenly turned…dark. Haunted. Where the trees looked as if they might actually snatch you up and use you as fertilizer, and where every path seemed to close in on you the moment you set foot on it.

Sasha smiled to see it. This was precisely as he wanted it.

He turned back on the road to the village he had just passed through. And he knew without even asking that the villagers would tell him not to go there. So he didn't trouble them with what he was going to do. After all, he knew what he was doing; he'd written the song.

Sasha left his horse at the inn and walked about the village, making a few inquiries about that place in the forest that the locals were starting to avoid. The answers he got gave him some relief. It wasn't bad yet. No children had gone missing. No travelers had vanished, or at least, none that anyone was aware of. But horses didn't want to go in there, mules flatly refused to, the birds avoided it except for ravens—

All those things were the signs that something nasty was trying to get established in Led Belarus by stealth.

Ha. You do not know who you are dealing with, whatever you are.

He would neither say nor think, "You're welcome to try," because whatever it was, it most assuredly was *not* welcome in his Kingdom, but when a thing was attempting to get in, thus far, he had been able to seize it by the metaphorical ear and throw it out again.

He went on foot to the "troubled place" as the locals were calling it, waiting until they were all at their dinners so that no one would notice where he was going. Very often locals took a dim view of someone meddling with such places, and wisely, too. Meddling could stir up things best left alone, when said meddling was done by someone who had no idea what he was doing.

But Sasha had written the song.

With his balalaika slung on his back, he made his way afoot. The road moved into the forest itself, trees arching over it, making a green tunnel that was very pleasant to walk inside. This was the part of the job he relished, the parts where everything was lovely and normal, but where he knew he was about to face an unknown foe of unknown strength, which made all the peace that much sweeter.

Sometimes the transition from "normal forest" to "possessed forest" was subtle. This time, it was not.

On one side of the path, the last light of early evening lingered pleasantly on the land, sending mellow beams of light slanting down through the leaves. The forest floor was cushioned by leaf litter aged to a warm gold. Birds were coming in to roost, twittering softly to each other as they settled in for the night. In the far distance, he caught a glimpse of a stag slipping warily between the trees.

On the other side of the path—

The last light of early evening was swallowed by shadows that were just a little too dark, just a trifle too cold. The air was damp and chill, and felt like the air of the last days of dying autumn. The forest floor was covered in the blackened skeletons of leaves, scabrous grey and charcoal, that shattered like ancient bones when walked on. There were no birds, no animals in sight, and the air smelled of rot and mildew.

So the battle lines were drawn.

Sasha pulled his balalaika around to the front and began to strum it.

The first song he sang was for his own benefit; it was a riddle-song that was designed to tell him exactly what sort of creature it was that he faced. Was it some evil thing out of legend, was it a demon, or was it a very powerful ghost? He sang the riddles and read the answer in the rattle of the dry branches, the sighing of the wind, and a glimpse here and there through the trees of something moving.

Rusalka came the answer, and he sighed. This would be both easy and hard. Easy, because the Rusalkas were quite single-minded and at the same time, not very tenacious. Hard, because the Rusalkas, whether they were ghosts or water-spirits, by and large were born of the anger and despair of young women who had drowned themselves, usually over a young man. And he, of course, was a young man. The Rusalka would try to seduce him in order to do him the same favor, and when she could not…

Well, now, this was where he had to be clever, persuasive, and if need be, ruthless.

But first he had to find her pond. Because a Rusalka always lived in a body of still water.

To do that, however, he would first have to get through the forest. The forest knew what he was, even if the Rusalka was not aware that he was here.

This could be very tricky.

Sasha stood on the bank of the Rusalka's pond, picking twigs out of his hair. The forest had not wanted him to get through. It hadn't been strong enough to actually prevent his passage, but it had made it as difficult as possible, trying to protect its progenitor.

But of course, it wasn't all that intelligent, and couldn't know that it was actually telling him the way. When it yielded, Sasha knew he was going in the wrong direction. When it blocked him, he knew he was on the right path. The more it tried to prevent his passage, the closer he knew he was.

There was no doubt that this was his goal. The pond and its surroundings were a curious mixture of ethereal beauty and shadowy menace. The pond itself was bathed in moonlight. Or at least, what *appeared* to be moonlight. The only trouble with that was that the moon wasn't up. The water was crystalline clear, so clear that it was easy to see the gracefully waving streamers of water plants and the tiny silver fish that darted among them. Of course, the moment anyone entered the water, those harmless-looking plants would wrap themselves around the victim and pull him under, and the little silver fish would strip him down to the bone.

Everything here told him that she was here, and thought she was here to stay.

Now what Sasha did to her was going to depend entirely on what she was. If she was a ghost, and there was any vestige of humanity left in her, he would try and touch it, to awaken her conscience and maybe, just maybe, persuade her to leave on her own.

If, however, she was nothing *but* hate…

Well, in a lot of ways, that would be easier. Harder, in terms of a fight, but easier in terms of reducing the problem to a situation of pure black and white. She would be evil, he would be good, and he would have no compunction about singing her into oblivion if he had to.

"Who are you, who lingers at the water's edge?" came a voice from behind him. It was a sweet voice, yet cold, as if the sweetness was a mask over something much darker. There was an echoing quality to it, and the sense that the speaker was somehow not altogether in this world.

He turned.

Like the pond, the young woman before him was a mixture of ethereal beauty and menace, although he doubted that most men would notice the "menacing" aspect. She was dressed in a simple gown of white with silver and pale blue embroidery at the throat, the wrists, and the hem. Her long, silvery-blond hair flowed down her back like a waterfall. She was slender, delicate, and very pale. There was a transparency about her that told him that this was, indeed, a ghost. He wondered how she had died. How it had happened would have a lot of bearing on what was going on in her mind.

And her eyes were utterly empty. Though he doubted most men would recognize that either.

But her expression changed the moment she got a good look at him, from sweetly cold to shocked.

He had anticipated any number of reactions on her part, but shock wasn't one of them.

"You!" she exclaimed.

He lifted his eyebrows. "I don't believe we've met?" he replied, carefully. "I certainly do not recall ever seeing you before this moment, and believe me, I have a very good memory for names and faces."

But she was already backing away from him, drifting just an inch above the grass, her hands upraised. "If I had known that this was *your* Kingdom… Do not touch that instrument! I have no wish to be sung into oblivion!" Her expression turned angry and sour. "Just let me withdraw in peace. I will find somewhere else. You have won, I have lost and—"

He felt suddenly guilty, even though he had not done anything, and went on the defensive. "Of course I won't let you settle in to my Kingdom! You Rusalkas lure men to their deaths! Any young man, any man at all that crosses your path! You don't even trouble to discover if they deserve *any* punishment, much less that!" He glared at her. "Of course I sing Rusalkas into oblivion, or at least, out of my kingdom! What do you expect?"

She bristled; her shoulders squared, and her eyes flashed. "I haven't lured *any* young men to their—"

And then she stopped, and a faint flush came over her cheeks. She looked first embarrassed, then mortified.

He blinked. "You haven't? But I thought—that's what all Rusalkas did."

"Well of course we want you to think that's what we all do!" she exclaimed, now bright red. "This is what a Rusalka is! Only…it…isn't. Not always. Not…even…mostly."

"Since the only other Rusalkas I have encountered were certainly luring men, young and old, to drown, you can scarcely blame me for assuming that common knowledge was accurate," he pointed out dryly. He wondered if he could believe her. He wanted to believe her. Then he looked about, spotted a rock, and sat down on it. "All right, then, tell me—"

He was interrupted at that moment by a whinnying scream and the flash of three glowing white bodies charging out of the forest, heading straight for the Rusalka. With a scream of her own, the Rusalka dove into the water, and the unicorns skidded to a halt at the edge, snorting and dancing with fury.

"We have come to save you, Prince!" one of them shouted, shaking her horn menacingly at the Rusalka, who had poked her head cautiously above the water. It was a sign of her other-worldly nature that her hair wasn't the least wet, though it floated around her on the surface of the water.

"We will not let this creature of evil harm you!" said another, her hooves thudding on the ground as she reared and curveted.

Safe in the water, since the unicorns were hardly going to go in after her, the Rusalka looked from Sasha to the unicorns and back again, with puzzlement at first, and then the dawning recognition of why they were there. She put her hand up to her mouth, and burst out laughing.

Sasha gritted his teeth. "Don't say what you are thinking," he warned. "My patience is not endless."

"I would not venture a word," the Rusalka said, then laughed again.

The unicorns stopped dancing angrily, and looked from Sasha to the Rusalka and back again. And back to Sasha. And back to the Rusalka.

"Um," said one, hesitantly. "A problem…"

"No problem," said the first immediately, tossing her head. "This is a creature of darkness!"

"But…" the hesitant one said, as she dropped her head to sniff at the water. "A virgin creature of darkness…"

It was the Rusalka's turn to flush as bright a red as a ghost could manage.

"No problem," insisted the first, who was evidently the leader of this group. "That is a female. So are we, and we do not protect females. And she is a creature of darkness. We destroy creatures of darkness. Virginity doesn't enter into it."

"But…"

"I'm sure there are virgin creatures of darkness *all the time*," the leader retorted, stamping her forehoof. "The fact that they are virgins does not make them good or worthy of protection. I would guess that most creatures of darkness are virgins, unless part of their darkness is that they seduce men. After all, who would want to take one to bed if he were not being deceived in the first place?"

The Rusalka flung her head up, angrily, and glared at the unicorns with a dangerous expression. "Now *look*—" she began hotly.

The leader of the unicorns continued on, ignoring the Rusalka altogether. "It is a creature of darkness. It is a female. We are female, and we do not protect females. It is menacing our Prince—"

"I wasn't menacing anyone!" the Rusalka said indignantly.

"—therefore, no prob—"

An equine scream rang through the forest again, interrupting the unicorn. A fourth gloriously white body slammed through the underbrush and skidded to a halt beside the pond. The very male unicorn reared, pawing the air with his silver hooves and brandishing his pearlescent horn. "Begone, wretched, bestial man!" he shouted. "Unhand that virgin! Maiden, I have co—"

"*Ilya!*" snapped the leader of the female unicorns, "You *idiot!* Shut up!"

Ilya dropped to the ground, abruptly, sapphire eyes going wide, suddenly deflated. "Um…Zhenya? Nelli? Galya? What are you doing here?"

"Protecting our Prince from that creature of darkness!" retorted Zhenya, the leader, with an emphatic stamp of one hoof.

"But that—" Ilya fumbled "—and she—and—"

His head whipped back and forth as he stared at Sasha and the Rusalka in turn. His nostrils flared as he sampled the air. "—and he—he's a virgin!" the unicorn all but shouted. Sasha groaned.

"Tell the rest of the kingdom, why don't you?" he muttered crossly. "I'm sure there are a few people at the border who didn't hear you."

But the unicorns were ignoring him as they looked from one to another of their number. Finally Ilya spoke.

"Um," he said hesitantly, "problem."

The other three just sighed. "There is now," said the leader, with resignation.

The full round of the Kingdom of Led Belarus took several days. Summer was a good time for that, though Sasha had no set times or seasons when he made his rounds. For one thing, although he might be the Fool to the ordinary folk of the Kingdom, the magical folk knew very well who he was and what he did, as evidenced by the fact that the Rusalka had recognized him. That meant magical folk both kindly and unkindly. If word spread that, say, on the day after Midsummer's Eve, the Fortunate Fool made his rounds, the unkindly could go into hiding until he returned to the Palace.

Or something much more powerful than anything he'd ever had to face could ambush him and do away with his possible interference.

There were some very nasty pieces of work out there, Traditionally speaking. He just considered them all fortunate that they seemed to concentrate on larger Kingdoms than Led Belarus. Perhaps it was the name, which meant "Lovely Land of Ice," although the winters were no worse here than in other Northern Kingdoms. The Kingdom of the Sammi was far, far colder. But the name might well be one of the reasons why they were left alone. Who wanted to rule over a kingdom of ice?

Perhaps it was that it was so small, small enough to ride around in a fortnight. Perhaps it was that, although it was a happy and prosperous place to live, Sasha took care that it was not *too* prosperous. He made sure never to sing of gem mines, for instance, nor silver, nor, heaven forefend, gold. In fact, he didn't think there was more than a bucket-load of gold in the entire Kingdom, and that was just fine with the entire Royal family.

The most complicated problem that Sasha had ever been forced to deal with was that of the Rusalka, and that was mostly because the unicorns had come charging into the middle of it.

He felt himself blushing, and was glad that there was no one on this coast road to see him.

Once he had been assured that the Rusalka was going to keep her word and not go egregiously about drowning people, he'd negotiated with her for her right to remain. She would be permitted that patch of forest and he would leave her alone. In return, she had to pledge never to harm anyone—

But she did have the right to frighten them, because that was not entirely a bad thing. Sasha had always made it a policy not to chase every dark thing out of the Kingdom, so long as they kept themselves and their powers under control. A story that was all sunshine and roses quickly became boring; a Kingdom without some frightening places grew people that were complacent about the darkness. And when people grew complacent, and were sure that terrible things could never come to their homeland, they became easy targets for those terrible things.

This was the sort of opening that The Tradition would seize on and exploit to dreadful results.

So Led Belarus was never perfect, and the Rusalka fit very well into that scheme of things. "After all," he'd told her, "which would you rather? Go about avenging your wrongs on fellows who have never even heard of you? Or prevent little boys from growing up into the kinds of lying blackguards who use and discard women without a second thought?"

When that caught her interest—which it did immediately, her being a ghost and all—he had outlined his plan. It was simple, really. All she had to do was frighten the boys and girls who ventured into her part of the forest. The boys, she would terrify, letting them think she was going to drown them for the wrongs she had suffered—and she would go into great detail. The girls, however, she would frighten in an entirely different fashion. She would take them to the rankest, swampiest part of her pond, let them think that this was her home, and then tell them her own story, with emphasis on how you could tell when a young man was the kind of blackguard who would use and discard women. She would make them see that there was nothing romantic about being bound to avenge herself over and over as a Rusalka. That probably wouldn't completely stop the girls from doing foolish things—people who thought they were in love were not known for rational behavior—but at least it would prevent *some* tragedies.

At least, that was what she promised. Whether she could be trusted to keep that promise, only time would tell.

"Maybe I am a fool, a real one," he said out loud. His horse cocked its ears back at him and snorted, then turned its head a little to look back over its shoulder at him. "What do you think?" he asked it.

It shook its head, but there was not enough of North Wind blood in it to make it truly intelligent. Not that he particularly needed or wanted a smart-tongued horse in his life to make fun of him....

Well, what was done was done. He made a note to ask Yasha to keep an especially close watch on that part of the Kingdom. If people started going missing...

He could *still* sing her out of the Kingdom if he had to. It was even easier, since she was a spirit, than it would have been if she was something of flesh and bone.

Or he could get a real magician to banish her....

Oh, he was thinking too hard about this. And one more day and he would be back at the Palace.

But first, he planned to spend a day or two here at the seashore. He almost never got the chance to come here, except when he was making his rounds. There was a nice little inn around the next turn of the road, where they knew him, but only as a traveler. He'd planned to be there by noon at the latest and it wasn't even midmorning now.

Yes. He would spend a day, perhaps two here. And then—

He sighed.

Then it would be back to the foolery. This had been a nice change, but alas, it was time to get back to work.

He wondered though, as he rounded the curve in the road and saw the inn in the distance, if anyone ever realized just how much work it was....

Chapter

7

The inn was full of people, the smells of good food, the murmur of talk. Sasha stared morosely into his mug of honey mead and toyed with the remains of his apple tart. This was not going as he had planned.

It wasn't because the inn wasn't warm and welcoming, because it most certainly was. And it wasn't because he wasn't remembered as a good customer and treated as such. No…no it was none of that.

It was that for some reason—maybe it was the season, maybe it was because the current crop of local youngsters was just old enough to begin thinking of love and lovers—the inn was full to the rafters with courting couples. What they were all doing here, he had no clue. It was the middle of the day, and surely they should all be out working. Fishing, cleaning, baking, mending nets or boats—what have you. Yet here they were, mooning at each other over their midday meal.

Maybe he had been a little too good when he'd sung all those songs at the wedding. Sometimes even he couldn't tell what The Tradition was going to seize on and run away with.

The barmaids each had their swains, who teased them as they worked, under the indulgent eye of the innkeeper's wife. There were couples at every table, inside and out, in every possible stage of courtship. One very young pair, who from their costumes were a couple of apprentices to a potter, was at the shy, tongue-tied stage, hardly looking at each other, yet the tension between them was palpable. Another, who could hardly be separated, and he learned from overhearing bits of conversation, were newly married; he a fisherman, she a net-maker. Two couples were awkward for another reason; dressed in their finest, these were arranged engagements and the young men were awkwardly, and dutifully, trying to win over the young ladies while their match-makers looked on. It didn't look to Sasha as if they were getting bad bargains either; both girls were clean, nice to look at, and seemed to be amiable and cheerful, both young men looked as if they were hardworking and not unkind. As arranged marriages went, these were certainly not going to be the worst. And—well, it looked as if the girls were beginning to think well of the boys.

That wasn't a bad thing at all.

There was an old couple near the fire, quietly sharing a meal, but with obvious affection between them; those two he could understand being here in the middle of the day. Though he wore the garb of a fisherman, it was clear that his fishing days were long past.

And the innkeeper and his wife were clearly bound by both love and a strong partnership.

It was all a lovely atmosphere of contentment, affection, cordiality.

And the result of all of this was to make Sasha feel terribly lonely.

It was one of those moments when he realized how very *apart* he was from the rest of his family. His very nature set him apart from them; he would always be one thing to them in private and something different in public. Out here he wasn't the Fool; he was Sasha the Singer; a bit of a mystery, but he'd made this trip often enough that people took him at face value. When he got home, though, it would be back to being Sasha the Fool, and no one was really kind to Sasha the Fool except behind closed doors.

Certainly he had never seen a young lady regard him with any kind of interest. It wasn't going to get any better, either. By now, the Palace would be full of news, speculation, or both, about the Crown Prince's new bride. Once the Crown Prince was settled, there was a strong likelihood—a certainty in two cases—that the rest of his brothers would bring up the brides of their own choosing for approval, Yes, it was that season. It seemed as if Sasha was the only creature in Led Belarus that wasn't paired up, or about to be paired up.

Nor was he ever likely to be. Not even by an arranged marriage. Who'd marry the Fool? Who'd betroth his daughter to the Fool? The very scorn that made his magic possible also made any kind of a normal life impossible. The only chance to find a woman lay among the magical creatures of the realm…and he wasn't at all sure that he wanted to make that kind of alliance with one of them. That could be very dangerous.

Besides, which of them would care to take up with a mere

human? Mortal, short-lived, it was the kind of relationship that could only end in sorrow. Songs were sung about that very thing—which, Traditionally, made it all the more likely that any love between him and a creature of legend would end badly.

Maybe a witch...

Or maybe not. Witches were settled, and wouldn't want to pack up and move to be near the Palace. And he couldn't leave the Palace except to make his rounds.

He stared glumly down at his reflection in the mead, thinking with resignation that he was, in all probability, doomed to live and die as unicorn bait.

Finally he couldn't bear all the couple-ness around him; no one had asked him for a song, in fact, they were all so engrossed in each other that he doubted they had ever noticed him. He went to his room.

It was a good room in a good inn. He had the narrow bed and the small room to himself; most travelers slept two to four to a bed, whether they knew each other or not. The feather mattress was nicely stuffed and clean, the bedding was clean, the blankets newly aired. Clean, neat—those were the touchstones to this place. And at least he wasn't staring at courting couples. But it was not much better for his loneliness than being down in the common room had been.

After lying on the bed staring up at the wooden ceiling for a while, he finally decided that this was doing him no good either. But the afternoon was still young. He didn't have to stay here. And out there was the reason why he favored this inn and this road over all others, including some inns that were downright up to the standards of a Prince. And he could hear its voice calling him through the little window in his room.

The sea.

He loved the sea. If he hadn't been born into the Royal family, he thought he might have been a sailor. He loved everything about it, the ever-changing color, the scent, the sound. Really the only time he didn't love it was in the winter…and even then, he loved the look of it, just…no one sane wanted to be on or near the sea in a Led Belarus winter, when the Kingdom lived up to its name.

His mind made up now, he swung his legs over the side of the bed, pulled his balalaika out from under it, and headed out the door and back down the narrow wooden stairs. No need to lock up here. These people were as honest as they came, and no one would touch his things while he was gone, which was another reason why he liked this inn. If ever he was able to leave the Palace, and give over being the Fool…this would be where he would want to live.

As if he ever could. As well wish for the moon.

Bah. Tell your troubles to the sea.

The odd thing about the sea was that he had always had the feeling it was listening to him, from the very first moment he'd first walked down onto a beach. Well, stranger things had happened, and he had been a part of some of them. Maybe it did listen to him.

Though if he got a wish-fulfilling flounder one day when he was singing his sorrows…he might well ask it to fulfill three of its own wishes. Wishes were dangerous things, and The Tradition was just waiting for an injudicious one.

The various couples were so engrossed in each other that

they never even noticed him go through the common room, even though normally the sight of the balalaika would have elicited calls for music. He sighed heavily as he opened the bulky front door, made like the rest of the inn from salvaged ship timbers, and let himself out.

The village was situated a prudent distance back from the shore, behind a ridge of sheltering hills and dunes. Despite that most of the folk here made their living as fishermen, it was a lot wiser to have to make a long hike down to the beach than take the chance that your house would wash away in a storm. There was a well-worn path that led down to the shore, over the ridge, around one of the hills, and then wound among the dunes. But he didn't take it. He wanted to go somewhere that he wouldn't be running into yet more courting couples; he'd had quite enough of them already, really.

As the sun began the slow, downward slide into late afternoon, he found a stretch of beach that was just as deserted as he could have wanted. Settling himself into a little nook among the rocks, he closed his eyes and began to play. The sound of the waves near at hand set his rhythm for him; the sand was soft, the rock at his back sun-warmed. Since there was no one to hear him but himself, he gave in and indulged in the most melancholy of songs; though none of them were anything he had ever written. He just wasn't the type to write sad songs, even when this mood was on him.

He had moved on to his third song when, eyes still closed, he had the distinct feeling that someone was watching him. Irritated, because, after all, he had come down here to be alone, he opened his eyes.

His irritation vanished without a trace.

He was being watched and listened to, quite attentively in fact, by someone who had perched atop a nearby rock herself. But she was possibly the most adorable little creature he had ever seen in his life.

She was blond, with silky hair the color of silver-gilded thistledown, done in a single thick braid down her back with a red bow at the end, and a much bigger one at the back of her neck that framed her face like a pair of wings. The top of her head was probably just below his collarbone, and he wasn't a tall man. Her bright green eyes were slightly slanted, and her mouth looked as if it smiled a lot.

One thing was certain though; this was no peasant girl.

Her clothing was a little odd for sitting on the beach; a bright red skirt, a white blouse embroidered heavily in red, and unless he was terribly mistaken, both were silk. She had a bright red leather belt and boots to match, and looked like a little czarina about to go for a ride.

There wasn't a horse to be seen, however. He hadn't heard a horse anywhere near here. There were no boyars at all close to this village, and no one's summer house either. No one in this village was prosperous enough to dress their daughter in silk. There was certainly something odd going on here.

Something magical? Probably. He should be wary, perhaps. On the other hand—

On the other hand, he thought wryly, *if there was any danger, or any danger develops, I suspect my unicorn brigade would come charging down to the beach to save me.* Very embarrassing, but he could probably live with embarrassment if it got him out of a tight spot.

And she was very, very pretty.

Where was the harm? How often did he get pretty girls smiling at him and wanting to spend time with him?

"You play very well," said the girl, with a smile. "But whatever are you doing, sitting in the sand?"

"I'm staying at the inn and at the moment it is rather overfull of courting couples," he replied. "They wouldn't pay any attention to my music anyway—they're too busy looking deeply into each others' eyes, and listening to each others' voices. I'm Sasha."

"My name is Katya—Ekaterina," she replied. "Would you rather be alone? I can go. The last thing I would want to do is to disturb a musician. I expect you get little enough peace."

He noticed that she made no immediate move to get up. In fact, she looked very much at ease on her rock. Definitely magical. Who or what else could find a rock comfortable to sit on?

He grinned at her. "Well, I would be very pleased if you would stay. A musician always likes an audience." True on both counts. His dissatisfaction and loneliness at the inn had everything to do with being the only person there who was not with someone. He felt immensely cheered now.

"I'm not a musician by trade," he added. "I just travel about on business for my father." Also true. It was not wise to tell false-hoods in the presence of a magic creature. They could take those falsehoods and make them true. "I play what I can remember, and some music of my own, but I can't claim to have a large number of songs in my head. Is there anything you would like to hear?" he asked.

She shook her head. "Anything at all. I don't know enough of your music to give you names of songs. I only know that I very much like what I have heard you play so far."

Well the last thing he was going to do was lapse into melancholy again. So what would be cheerful? He thought about all the couples in the inn, and smiled slightly. Well, why not? He sang one of the songs of his own making, about weddings and the contentment of a couple who were happily suited to one another. He preferred that to a love song, because not every contented couple was madly in love. In fact, being madly in love wasn't always a good thing. Being madly in love could lead to jealousy, suspicion, any manner of negative things. The Tradition had a way of twisting what you did to its own purposes, and *his* purpose *was* to keep his land from having too many bad things happen in it.

From there, he moved on to other songs, some with a purpose, some without. It did no harm to sing the songs of peace and prosperity here…and in fact, now that he came to think of it, he modified a couple of them on the fly to include the sorts of things that fisherfolk would need. Fair winds. Good catches. Safely out and safely back again. And—always, always remembering to honor the Sea King. Many a Traditional tragedy had begun by angering the Sea King. Katya nodded her head and tapped her feet in time to the music, and once or twice even got up and danced to one of his dancing tunes.

He played past sunset and into moonrise, and finally it was his tired fingers and not a lack of will to continue that caused him to halt.

"I hope your parents are not going to fly in a rage that you are out of the house at this time of night," he said—fairly sure now, since she had said *nothing* about parents or needing to be home, that she was not going to have that particular difficulty. In fact, he was fairly certain that she was not human...or at least, not an ordinary human. She had told him nothing about herself save her name, and he was quite, quite certain that it wasn't her "true name" either. No, she was something magical. But whatever it was, he was just as sure that she meant no harm.

"Oh, I am my own person and need ask leave of no one for my comings and goings," she replied with a toss of her head and a grin. "But you are right. It is late and I should be going. I will come here tomorrow, though, if you like."

Sasha, you goose, you're half in love with her, aren't you? He couldn't help chiding himself at the same time that he was congratulating himself that she wanted to meet him again. But how could anyone not be in love with her? She was altogether adorable.

"In that case, since I am not particularly needed at home, I'll just prolong my visit to the seashore," he said with an answering grin. "I couldn't possibly leave you here to stroll on the sand alone."

"Then I'll be off until tomorrow!" She jumped to her feet, laughed gaily, and ran around the boulders they had chosen to keep the breeze off.

And when he rounded them himself, she was nowhere to be seen.

Definitely magic.

Sasha, you're such a fool.

That I am, he told the sensible part of himself. *But at this moment, a happy one.*

Katya thought that this might have been one of the happiest days of her life. Not a delirious happiness; a quiet happiness, something not to be shouted, but to savor.

She hadn't thought it was going to be nearly so nice; when her father had first told her she needed to go to Led Belarus.

The Sea King had sent for her as soon as she was rested from the long swim home from Nippon. As always, when her mission was successful, he let her recover before needing to hear the detailed account of what had happened.

They sat together over breakfast…which was, she reflected a little sadly, nothing like a breakfast on the Drylands. Raw fish, kelp, some fruits and vegetables from the Drylands, but nothing that couldn't stand immersion in water and nothing cooked. It was probably very healthy, but…

But the food wasn't why they were meeting together, and she continued on with her story—leaving out the early misadventure with the courtesan's robes. When she was done, it was clear that he was quite happy with how she had conducted herself, so far from home. He was very interested in the overture from the head of the kitsune clan. "I think I had heard once they were notable for mischief," he observed, "but also for loyalty and wisdom. I believe we can strike a good bargain here. But now—" He grimaced. "I hate to send you out again so soon, but…I am presented with a puzzle. It is the Kingdom of Led Belarus."

She tilted her head to the side. Led Belarus was very close, geographically speaking, to the Palace. And never once, in all the time that she had been alive, had there been any problems with that little Kingdom.

But then, her father hadn't exactly said there was a *problem*.

"A puzzle? But they have been quiet for three generations, Father. No great evils, only a modest prosperity and—" and then it struck her "—and they are too quiet, are they not?"

He nodded glumly. One of the little reef fish flitted over to their table to beg scraps, and he absent-mindedly fed it bits of lettuce. "The real peace and prosperity is little more than twenty years long. This troubles me. It may be nothing. But such quiet invites The Tradition to create some dreadful catastrophe, or put it in the mind of some evil mage to move in and take over. People become complacent about bad things happening, and it becomes easy for evil to invade. The Tradition does not like quiet."

"Quiet does not make for stories and songs," she sighed. "You are quite right, Father. This should be looked into. Even the tiniest of Kingdoms can attract great evil." Then she smiled. "At least it is not far. And Led Belarus does not live up to its name in summer." And besides…there would be good breakfasts….

So she went. As soon as she set foot on the beach, she asked The Tradition to give her proper clothing, and got the most delightful red-and-white outfit in lovely silk! A grand full skirt that stopped at about the calf—a wonderful embroidered blouse with a high neck—a red leather waist-cincher and matching boots. She pointed the toe of the boot outward, looking at its decorations. Boots fit for dancing in! She smiled happily. The colors delighted her eye, and there was no doubt it was very practical. And by the sort of sheer happenstance that could only be the hand of The Tradition at work in her favor, no sooner had she gotten clothed, than she heard music from farther up the beach. There was something about the music, too. This was no ordinary musician, she was sure of it, the song carried a burden of melancholy far heavier than mere words and tune could convey. Of course, at that moment, she had no notion of just *how* fortuitous this meeting was to be.

Picking her way carefully through the wrack and flotsam cast up by the last tide, she found the source of the music. The playing was solid and skilled, though not masterful. The singing had a great deal of heart, and the singer's voice was pleasant. But there was some hint of something behind the music that she couldn't quite identify.

She climbed carefully and quietly up to the top of a boulder, taking care not to disturb the singer, and got her first glimpse of him. What she saw made her smile with pleasure.

Oh my. Now there is a handsome fellow!

He was blond, the sort of white-blond like hers, which looked unreal; his shock of hair was a bit untidy, but that was to be expected, given that he was out in the wind. He had a good, broad brow that suggested a lot of intelligence. His eyes were closed, so she couldn't see what color they were—but he had high cheekbones, a good nose, and a strong chin. His mouth looked as though he smiled more than he frowned, but there were some odd worry lines creasing his forehead.

He was not a tall man, but he was very well built, and his hands were those of a musician rather than a warrior.

She couldn't place his clothing; a white, high-necked, em-broidered shirt, a wide sash, soft suede trousers and riding boots. It wasn't peasant gear, but other than that, she couldn't identify what sort of job he did, although it did seem rather too well made and unworn for that of an ordinary minstrel.

As she examined him, he seemed to sense that she was there, finished his song, and opened his eyes.

She had expected blue eyes, but instead, they were a startling and striking shade of intense violet.

His speaking voice was as good as his singing voice.

And there was something about him… She coaxed him into talking, though it didn't take a lot of coaxing, and she listened carefully to what he said.

She heard the truth in what he told her, but also heard, beneath the words that he gave her, that he was not telling her *all* the truth. That was fine. She would learn all of it eventually.

And she could tell he was good, that he had an instinct for goodness. When he offered to sing more, she seized on that as a fine excuse to remain.

She sat cross-legged on the sun-warmed boulder, and listened; from the first note, she knew that she had not been wrong. There was something more there. Something powerful that ex-plained exactly why Led Belarus was so peaceful, so prosperous.

This man was a Songweaver. And a Seventh Son. She could sense both those things, now that she was looking for them. The power of the Songweaver put gentle persuasion behind every word he sang. The signs of the Seventh Son were less obvious, but the violet eyes were what had started her down that path of reasoning. When he mentioned he had six brothers she *knew* he had to be the youngest.

And—for that reason, he must also be a Fortunate Fool.

So he was a triply blessed young man, with the power of a Fortunate Fool, a Seventh Son, and a Songweaver.

These might not be *powerful* magics, but tiny magics, worked wisely...

Now, the Songweavers were not Bards as such; they had a different sort of magic. Rather than forcing The Tradition to aid them, or outright undermining it, the Songweavers coaxed it, placated it, and led it along gently into the path that they wanted it to travel. Songweavers worked in small ways, not large ones, and yet small corrections, made early, rendered the powerful magics unnecessary.

Songweavers worked by modifying Traditional paths that already existed rather than inserting new ones. Wish to make your Kingdom prosperous and peaceful? Sing it that way, then make sure that the songs spread, that they are the sort of thing that ordinary people whistle, hum, and sing while they're working. They don't have to be the great, earth- shattering Songs of the Bards; in fact, you'd really rather that they weren't. Not when what you want is the small, gradual changes.

So *this* was why the Kingdom of Led Belarus was so quiet. They had a little guardian to make it so. And if he was wise, he allowed a little bit of evil to come in, flourish briefly, then fade, or be taken down if need be. Nothing should be too perfect. The Tradition did not care for perfection.

The more she listened to this man, the more she liked him. And it wasn't too terribly difficult to work out who he was, as what she had learned from the Library about Led Belarus meshed with what she was learning now. A "Sasha," who traveled about Led Belarus on behalf of his father? A Seventh Son to boot? This could only be Prince Sasha, Seventh Son and Fortunate Fool.

And, of course, Songweaver, though she hadn't known *that* until she'd met him.

Somehow she'd found herself promising to come back to meet him here on the beach. Somehow, he'd promised to extend his stay here to meet her....

Somehow...or with the impetus of The Tradition.

Well, this was one time when she would willingly go along with The Tradition.

The swim back to the Sea King's Palace seemed to take no time at all, and her father was free and taking a brief bit of leisure in the garden when she sought him out.

"Have you not yet gone, daughter?" he asked, looking surprised. She smiled.

"There and back again, Father," she assured him. "The answer is simple. A chance meeting gave me all the answers. Prince Sasha, the youngest of the seven Princes, is a Songweaver."

Understanding dawned on her father's face immediately. "Ah! And Seventh Son...that would make him a Fortunate Fool as well?"

"Yes," she agreed, "only not so foolish."

She outlined all that Sasha had told her, and all that she surmised. Her father listened carefully and nodded now and again.

"Is it possible," he asked at last, "that the King of Led Belarus is canny enough about The Tradition to make the boy a Fool in public and something else altogether in private?"

"I would say that is a certainty, Father." She gazed off for a moment over his shoulder. "Sasha's songs are carefully worded. Not so powerful that The Tradition would ever feel the pressure of his words. And what was more, they are very singable. He has a gift for that."

"And what sort of a man is he?" asked her father shrewdly. "All this is well and good, but if there is greed or overweening ambition in him—"

She shook her head. "He's kind, Father, and very dedicated to caring for his Kingdom. I think that the moon is going to come down into the sea to ask for one of us in marriage before Sasha uses his power for his own gain."

"And your instincts tell you to trust him." The King looked at his daughter shrewdly. Katya blushed, and he chuckled. "Well, the day has finally come. My daughter has found a young man who interests her. You fancy this minstrel, Katya?"

She blushed even harder, and he laughed. "Then by all means, so long as you remember your primary duty is to me and this Kingdom, pursue the young man. Take him to your bed, if you like. It is not our way to meddle in love affairs. But keep your eyes open and your wits about you. Remember all the advice about young men that you have given others. I wish to have no Rusalka daughters. Do I make myself clear?"

She nodded. And she knew that her father was right. She knew very little about Sasha.

But she wanted to know more. She wanted to know everything....

"As a Songweaver, he could, if he wished, do us a good turn or two," the King mused aloud. "I would be very grateful for such help."

"I will see what can be done, Father, but I have only just met him—" she began.

He laughed. "And you know how to rectify that. Go, my dear. And be glad that you have Siren, and not Mermaid blood in your veins."

She blushed even harder. But she also lost no time in retracing her path back to the shores of Led Belarus.

Chapter 8

Sasha sat on the edge of his bed and stared at the message that had finally caught up with him. He had been sending Yasha short reports from every significant stop he had made, more as a way for his family to keep track of where he was than because they needed any news about what he was doing.

It was a message that came with a gift, which told him immediately that he probably wouldn't like it. Had this message arrived at any time previous to yesterday afternoon, he would have been angry, a little hurt, and a great deal resentful.

Dear Sasha, We are at a delicate position at the moment. The negotiations for your brother's bride are going very well. But any little thing could bring it all crashing down. Therefore, if you would, please remain where you are until we send for you? With the letter had come a substantial pouch of money, enough to keep him well for quite some time, and the messenger waited patiently down below for his answer. Which, because Sasha was a good son, and would do as his father asked, would be to agree to the request and not make trouble.

Now at any other time, he would have been annoyed, and even hurt by this. After all, it wasn't as if he chose to be the Fortunate Fool. Given the option he would much rather—

He weighed the pouch of money in his hand. What *would* he rather be?

If he was to have the choice without needing to factor in starvation…he'd be a minstrel. He could still sing the Kingdom to make it prosper and protect it as a minstrel. In fact, it might be easier.

He entertained the fantasy for a moment—for it was a fantasy—of spending his time riding from inn to inn, enjoying the sun and sky by day, tucked up in a cozy corner with an appreciative audience by night, and after the inn was closed, finding a saucy serving wench waiting for him in his bed….

But the reality for minstrels, as he very well knew, was traveling afoot, or if lucky, catching a ride with a farmer. There were very few minstrels who could afford a horse, and most of those were with a troupe of entertainers, sharing a wagon, which had its own advantages and drawbacks. Since he didn't think he'd fit in well with any such group, he would have to go it alone. The life of a minstrel was filled with lots of rainy days, cold days, days of endless snow, and the occasional blistering-hot day just for variety. It was smoke-filled, filthy inns that, unlike the Jolly Sturgeon, were full of the stench of stale, thin kvass— a thin, bitter beer—burned food, unwashed bodies, and vomit. And most of all, the life of a minstrel was going hungry, sleeping without shelter, most of the time. When there was shelter, it was in someone's barn, in a shed, or on the hard floor of one of those wretched inns.

I am a pampered Prince, he thought wryly. *I wouldn't last out the season.*

Of course, if he could manage to be a Prince incognito, to have money sent to him whenever he needed it, to have a good horse under him and good clothing on his back, that would be very different.

I wonder if it would be possible to simply make the rounds all the time? Or, well, not all the time, but there would be no difficulty finding a nice, cozy inn to spend winter months. Would he still then be the Fortunate Fool for the Kingdom? That would be the real question. Probably only a Godmother could answer it.

If he couldn't then—no. He could not in all conscience do something like that. The Kingdom, and his family, depended on his Luck. He couldn't do anything that would diminish it, not and feel anything but guilty.

But if he could…

Well, this was not the time to daydream. For once, when he'd been told to stay away, he was happy about it. He was at his favorite place, it was the middle of summer, and a pretty girl was interested in him.

Leaving aside the fact that she certainly was some sort of magical creature, and there was a possibility, however remote, that she had come here to kill him…

Coming ashore again, on the deserted beach, Katya busied herself at first in fussing with her costume. Sasha had liked her in red, would he like her in blue? It didn't take much magic to change the colors. But she was stalling for time, feeling nervous, and finally she had to laugh at herself. She had faced all manner of dangers and never been half as nervous as this!

Do I tell him who I am? What I am? It only seemed fair. She resolved that she would, but she would have to pick the right time to do so. It wasn't the sort of thing you wanted to just blurt out.

But at least, being what he was, he would believe her. With anyone else there was the very real possibility that they wouldn't. Humans, she had noticed, didn't much like the idea of magic that intruded on their lives. They much preferred it to be somewhere else. Magic, and those who wielded it, took the power of most everything out of their hands, and no one liked to feel powerless. At least, that was what she thought was the reason.

She had come ashore some distance from their meeting place, and once she was satisfied with how she looked, she began the walk with the gulls and terns crying overhead. Once she had the spot in sight, she ran up the beach to the cluster of boulders where they had first met, steeling herself for disappointment. He might have forgotten. He might have had to leave this village. He might have made the promise idly, without ever really meaning to fulfill it.

But as she neared the rocks, she heard the merry sound of the balalaika and felt her feet grow lighter.

He was waiting for her!

She rounded the large boulder, and there he was! He was standing up this time, leaning against the rock as he played. He grinned when he saw her and ended the dance tune with a flourish.

"Well met, Katya!" he said, laughing. "I have come better provisioned this time! Have you eaten?"

"Only breakfast," she replied, and felt her eyes widen as he pulled a basket out from behind a smaller rock.

"Then I shall be more than happy to share my midday meal with you," he told her, eyes dancing. "Though I warn you, it is only tavern fare. Good, but nothing like lark's tongues and roast peacock."

"I can't imagine anyone heartless enough to silence a lark for the sake of eating its tongue!" she exclaimed, as she settled down on the soft sand next to him while he spread out a cloth and began to unpack the basket onto it. "Nor can I imagine wanting to take a beautiful peacock out of the world just to have a moment of devouring it."

"Well, in that, we are one, Katya. I had much rather have plain good food that doesn't require taking beauty from the world to get it." He finished unpacking the basket. "There we are. My hostess's good honest bread, a very nice goat cheese, lovely onions as sweet as you'd like, and a bit of cold hare that we won't inquire too closely about." He winked, and she grinned, knowing that he must suspect the hare was poached, but wasn't going to say or do anything about it.

"I'm sorry there isn't any fish—" he began, but she shook her head as she reached for a piece of the substantial dark bread he tore off for her. It was fresh, and had a wonderful, slightly nutty scent to it.

"Oh no, really I get more than enough fish at home!" The cheese was soft and creamy, and just strong enough to offset the bite of the little green onions. "This is lovely!"

He watched her eat with evident enjoyment, and made good work of the food himself. She savored each bite; the common food of Nippon was based on rice, not bread, and though it was good, she had missed the baked stuffs she usually enjoyed in the Drylands. Cheese, well they did get cheese beneath the sea, but it was all firm stuff, and of course every bite was flavored with the salt water. This was—delightful.

She tried not to be greedy. But it came to her, as it did so often when she was on the Drylands, how tired she was of the taste of salt. *Everything* there tasted of salt. Fruit, even. Maybe if she never came to the Drylands again, she would get used to it, but she never seemed to.

It was possible to get cooked foods and even baked things in her father's Kingdom, but you had to leave the Palace grounds to do so. Elsewhere, people could use magic to cook food and even to make little pockets of air where you could have something baked and eat it, too, if you were the sort that could breathe air as Katya was—a gift that was rare outside of the Sirens, the mer-folk, and the seal-people. But Katya never seemed to have the time to go to one of these places anymore....

And anyway, everything *still* tasted of salt.

She realized he was watching her with a little half smile on his face.

She stopped eating. "What is it?" she asked. "What have I done?"

"Done? Nothing," he said pleasantly. "I'm just trying to figure out what sort of magical creature you are, Katya."

She froze, and he went on. "There are not a lot of human sea creatures in Led Belarus Tradition, except maybe a swan maiden—swan maidens do land on the ocean. But you haven't a suggestion of anything feathery about you, and anyway, swan maidens travel in flocks. So that means you must be outside the Led Belarus Tradition, and I'll admit you have me stumped." He scratched his head and grinned ruefully. "All I know about are the mer-folk and you haven't a tail. Well, and the Sirens, but you haven't tried to drown me, or sing at me to make me love you, so I think I'm safe there."

She opened and closed her mouth several times. It was taking her a moment to compose herself. Finally, "I'm the Sea King's daughter," she said.

He raised his eyebrows. "Really! And what brings you to Led Belarus, Princess?"

"Don't call me that," she said, blushing. "Call me Katya. And—you are what brings me."

Now it was his turn to open and close his mouth, as if about to say something, then thinking better of it. "Me!" he said finally. "But I'm not important. Well—"

"You're a Fortunate Fool, and a Songweaver," she replied, cutting him off. "And you're the Seventh Son of the King of Led Belarus. But it isn't so much you yourself that brought me here. It was what you're doing."

He blinked, and nodded. "But all I'm doing is making things peaceful—" he said feebly.

Katya laughed, and popped a grape in her mouth. "Too peaceful! Or so my father said. He was afraid that things here were about to turn very bad, the calm before the storm, you see. But then I met you and I heard you, and I realized you were a Songweaver, so then, of course, it was all right."

"I'm a—" He hesitated. "I'm a what?"

"A Songweaver. It's not moving big magics, like a Bard can. It's smaller things." She paused, not sure where to go with this explanation.

But he—oh he was a quick one. "Spinning songs for good harvests and fine weather. Catching evil things and singing them out by making them all too visible to both ordinary folks and their own enemies. Or just singing them out by making it too cheerful for them, because happiness is poison to them. That's what I do with ghosts, when they're vicious haunts…."

"Exactly!" She nodded with relief. "And you can make your songs do more than any other Songweaver I've ever seen or heard of, because you're a Fortunate Fool."

"Oho! That's the explanation!" He seemed pleased. "I had wondered. I thought the reason that the songs were working was only because I am a Fortunate Fool."

She wiped her hands off with a napkin and shook her head. "No, it's the two things working together. By themselves, each is good, but together you make your own luck."

"Within reason," he added for her.

She nodded. "Within reason. You can sing a ghost out of existence because you can make it unable to resist the pull of the other side. Ghosts are always in a kind of tug-of-war within themselves, and you just add a little push. But you couldn't sing a demon out of existence."

"But!" he said, raising a finger. "I can recognize one when I see him, and I can sing that a priest comes along at just the right time."

"And so you can," she agreed. "There's how the powers are working together."

"There's the powers working with my brain!" he corrected, tapping his finger on his temple. "So you came because your father sent you. But you've come back."

"My father has no need of me just now," she temporized.

"And neither has mine. I think we have been granted a rare moment of idleness!" he said cheerfully. "Perhaps it's the fortune of the fool!" Then he laughed. "You've no notion how good it is to keep company with someone who understands what I do besides my family."

She shook her head. "I have the same problem. No one is to know I am my father's eyes and ears, or they might be more reticent around me."

He sighed. "Welladay. There you have it. But for now, we are on holiday! So what would you care to do, Katya, Sea King's daughter?"

She settled her back against the boulder. "I should like to hear you sing."

It was about the middle of their third day together that Sasha realized that he was courting this young woman. Possibly she had known it earlier, but if so she had given no sign.

He said nothing, however. He didn't want to do or say anything that might make her take offense, and young women could take offense at the oddest things. *She* might only want to be friends. Or she might think that he was not courting her, but trying to seduce her—

Well I am, he thought, as he lay in his bed in the inn and stared up at the ceiling in the dark. *But my intentions are honorable!*

He would not think of what his brothers might say. He would not think of what his Father would do. All of them should know better anyway. The Fortunate Fool always went away from home and returned with an exotic bride, more often than not, it was a magical one to boot! They should all be expecting it by now.

Could he win her?

He certainly hoped so, because he could not imagine feeling this way about any other young lady, ever again. It was not just that she was beautiful, kind, clever, and intoxicating. It was not that he was madly in love. If anything, he was sanely in love. If ever two creatures were suited for each other—

They were out riding at the moment that he came to this conclusion; she was up behind him on a pillion. Now, his regular saddle didn't have a pillion pad, but true to the nature of his luck, there had been one left behind at the inn so long ago that no one quite recalled who had left it or why. Not that it mattered. It was his luck. So he was able to suggest to her that they go riding inland, and she readily agreed.

This was not a part of Led Belarus where they were likely to run into either trouble or people. It was, in fact, hunting lands belonging to one of the boyars, a man who hated to hunt. The people of the fishing village poached it with impunity. There might be a gamekeeper somewhere about, but if there was, Sasha had never seen him.

Sasha really wasn't at all sure who or what lived in this forest, besides the possible gamekeeper. He only had one hope—that the unicorns weren't around.

He felt his heart sink when he caught a flash of white through the trees.

"What's that?" Katya asked, crushing his hope that she hadn't seen it.

"I don't know," he temporized, because he actually didn't *know,* he only guessed it was a unicorn.

"There it is again!" she exclaimed, as the path curved, and there was the briefest possible glimpse of a white flank.

Oh, this was bad. This was very bad. How was he to explain the unicorns to her? Oh he could probably sing them away but—

They rounded another turn in the path, and ahead, the path led straight into a beautiful glade. Sun poured down into the pocket meadow, golden and sweet as honey. The sound of gurgling water was just audible, along with the song of a lark. Lush, deep green grass carpeted the ground, and in the middle of this tiny paradise, haloed by the sun, stood—

A white doe.

Relief made him flush. *Thank heavens.*

"Oh!" Katya said, as the deer turned her mild eyes on them and nodded. "Oh! She's lovely!"

She was more than lovely. Sasha quickly ran through all the lore in his head. A white *stag* could sometimes be a guide, but a white doe—

He dismounted, and slowly walked toward the beautiful creature. She let him approach. He got within a few feet of her, then stopped. "Are you under a curse or a spell?" he asked.

Slowly, the doe nodded.

"Can it be broken?" Sasha asked, as he heard Katya behind him respond to that answer with a swift intake of breath. Again, the doe nodded.

"Does it have to be a Prince of the Royal House?" he asked,

hoping that the answer would be *no*. Because all of the White Doe stories had a period of sorrow and trial to them, and he was hoping his brothers would be spared that. And oh no—he had chosen his bride, if it could be done, if Katya would have him, and in no way was he going to be this girl's rescuer. To his intense relief, the doe shook her head. "Any boyar will do, then?" he asked, and was rewarded with a nod.

Thanks be to the blessed saints. He thought about the man whose hunting lands these were. What he knew of Boyar Arkadij was all good. He was a kind man, good to his peasants—as witness the fact that poachers here went unpunished—faithful in his loyalty to the King, solitary by nature. Perhaps that was why the doe appeared here.

"I will send a message to the boyar whose forest this is," he told the doe. "I think you will like him. I suggest you start showing yourself near the hunting lodge in this forest as soon as possible."

The doe bowed her head and delicately pawed the ground. Sasha smiled as the doe reared a little, then whirled on her hind feet and vaulted off into the shadows under the trees so lightly he did not even hear a rustle of branches.

"Well," he said, looking around at the perfect little glade. "This looks like as good a place as any for our lunch, no?"

Katya had known from the moment her father had asked her if she fancied Sasha that she was falling in love with him. Since he'd begun making moves she could only interpret as courtship almost immediately, she could see no reason why she *shouldn't*. Traditionally, they were a very good match. The Fortunate Fool never, in any of the tales that she had ever heard, was paired up with an ordinary girl, not even a Princess unless she had some sort of magic about her or was the captive of a magical villain. He *always* found a wife who was a swan maiden, or a captive of some evil creature, or enchanted into the form of a bird, or a deer or—

That was why she realized, after Sasha himself had clearly figured it out, that the pure white doe must be exactly the latter. And her heart sank as she came to that conclusion.

But then Sasha had questioned it, and when he'd asked about how the curse could be lifted, then promised to tell the boyar who owned these lands about the poor thing, her heart had risen again.

She helped him to unpack the pannier they had brought with them, and set out a meal. There was far more food in there than two people could ever eat in a day, but Sasha explained to her that he *always* tried to pack a great deal of food, in case he should meet a little old lady begging, because such little old ladies popping up in the path of princes were almost always witches. That was even more the case when the Prince was a Fortunate Fool. Mostly they just gave him their blessing and let him ride on if he fed them, but once he had been sent to a treasure, and once he had been sent to the aid of an old hermit.

"That was a very kind thing you did just now, Sasha," she said, going to the stream and returning with both their cups filled with water. She could hardly get enough of pure water when she was on Drylands. It was almost intoxicating in its sweetness, after the heavy salt of sea water. Sasha found that very amusing, she imagined, though he never said anything.

"Kind? I suppose so." He helped himself to a boiled egg and began to peel it. "I was just hoping she hadn't come for me, or for one of my brothers. She won't have an easy time of it. The boyar will break the curse, I am sure, but whatever cursed her will know that the curse has been broken and come here to plague her. Something bad will happen to her, and she and her boyar will have to work through it before they can be happy." He shook his head. "Usually the firstborn child is stolen, and the witch makes it look as if the mother has murdered it. Often the girl is actually at the stake to be burned before the truth is discovered. There is a lot of grief, pain, and fear before the proper people are found and punished. I don't want that kind of trouble in my family."

She nodded soberly. He sighed. "That's the thing, you see. There is a lot I can do…but there is a lot more that I can't. I'm not powerful enough to make it so that poor girl won't have to endure that suffering. I can make a choice of paths for The Tradition, but I can't send it out of its chosen path once it's in. There are too many things I can't do. I can sing a ghost into the afterlife, or a demon to sleep, but I can't cure someone's illness, nor do anything at all about boyars that are mean-spirited and cruel to their peasants. It's—" he looked down at the half-peeled egg in his hands, as if surprised to see it there "—it's frustrating."

She felt a surge of pity for him, as well as a burst of affection. How could you *not* love a man like this one? His heart was so big….

And with all that he did for people, he himself was treated as the fool, the nuisance, the fellow best gotten out of the way when something important was going on. *Even though his family knew what he was.* They still discounted him,

"Why do you keep doing these things?" she asked finally. "You get scant thanks from it, even from your own people, who know what you are. You get kicked around by everyone else. And there is probably at least one of your brothers who thinks you are a fool anyway for making yourself miserable with trying to help everyone else and not going off and finding treasures and coming home a rich man."

He pondered that a moment. "I do this because…I have to, Katya. I have to, or I won't be true to myself. I'm not a legend or a hero, I don't slay dragons, I don't do any of the things that a real hero can. But I can make things better, one day at a time, for most of the Kingdom. We're given a choice in our lives, to make things better, or worse, or merely endure like sheep. I choose to make things better, as much as I can."

She nodded. "I'm lucky," she said ruefully. "Even if only a handful of people know what I do, at least I'm not abused the way you are."

But he laughed at that. "Oh, my family makes sure that I never have to worry about truly being abused. And it's not so bad, really. I get to pull some pretty outrageous pranks and I get away with it, too. So there're some advantages to it."

As they ate, he told her about some of his funnier stunts. How he'd left a sheep in the bed of a visiting boyar who seemed to think that his rank gave him the right to use whatever servant girl he wanted. How he'd arranged for another who was drunk nearly all the time to get only water while he stayed. How he'd blundered into a group of mutually antagonistic boyars and tangled them all up together in their own cloaks so that they *had* to talk to one another.

She had to smile at the image that called up in her mind.

By that time, they were both full, she had packed what they hadn't eaten back into the hamper, and the sun was making them both drowsy. Finally he stretched and yawned. "Would it be terribly ungallant of me to take a nap?" he asked. "I didn't sleep much last night."

"No, not at all," she hastily said. "Bad dreams?"

"No, the opposite." For some reason, he was blushing.

She smiled. "You go right ahead. I'll keep watch."

He stretched himself out on the blanket they had used for their picnic. "Thank you, Katya," he murmured drowsily.

And then he was asleep.

She watched him for a while, as he slumbered so deeply that he scarcely seemed to breathe. She wondered what had happened to keep him awake. And then, the warm sun overhead felt so good…her eyelids started to droop. She woke with a start twice, but the third time she could not fight sleep off anymore.

She woke up curled against Sasha's chest. She could tell he was asleep, or mostly asleep, but his hands were caressing her hair and shoulders, slowly.

Now what did she want to do about this?

The sensation of his hands on her body made her tingle, made her skin feel alive, made her feel entirely wanton. Which was perfectly fine for someone like her, all of her brothers and half of her sisters had taken lovers already and no one had second thoughts about it. Things only got complicated when the lover was someone who would then try to use the relationship to gain influence from the King. So far, that hadn't worked, and the lesson had been learned by the sibling in question so it never happened again.

Magic creatures were like that. Humans thought they were fickle, when in fact, it was a matter of knowing that for a creature of magic, there were lovers and there was Love, and an emotion as powerful as Love tended to get all tangled up in the magic and make for complications.

But for ordinary folk, the humans of the Drylands, there were a hundred thousand social codes and religious considerations and things they thought of as "moral behavior," never thinking or knowing that one group's "moral behavior" meant nothing to a different group. The question was…where was Sasha in all of this? How would he look at her if she—

Then, mentally, she shook her head. She was what she was. He would love her as she was, or there was no point in continuing this. She moved a little and put her hands on either side of his face and kissed him.

"Hmm?" he murmured, his arms tightening around her. Then he opened his eyes and looked at her blankly. "Uh—"

"Good. You're awake. Are you completely awake?" she asked, her mouth quirking in a little smile.

"Uh—" he flushed bright red, and she felt something hard and insistent stirring against her leg.

"Very good." She kissed him again, this time letting her lips part, teasing his with the tip of her tongue. She could feel his indecision; whether to respond or not, and ended the kiss.

"Um…Katya…your father is going to kill me—" He was bright crimson. "I want—I mean—you're wonderful and—but—"

She chuckled. "My father has never interfered in the lives of his children that way," she said. "We're not like you, we sea-people. My father concerns himself only where matters of the Kingdom are concerned. We don't make alliance marriages. He would not care if I had a dozen lovers so long as I was discreet…and it did not interfere with my doing my duty."

We don't barter virginity for a higher seat at the table. And he'll only care if you hurt me, she thought, but did not say.

"Um…" He hesitated a moment longer, then bent his head down to return her kiss.

It was inexpert, but so was hers. She had only the benefit of her mother's advice, and surreptitious watching of her sisters and some of the other women, young and not so young, of the Court. But he wasn't impatient. He moved very slowly and carefully, despite the hardness she could feel pulsing against her thigh. She nibbled and licked at his lips, he slipped his tongue into her mouth, and she met it with hers, as his hands moved down along her shoulders, then hesitantly, one hand cupped her breast. His thumb brushed her nipple through the thin fabric of her blouse, and she gasped as it sent arrows of sensation to ignite a fire at her groin. Her legs parted without thought, and her hands moved to his buttocks and pulled him against her.

She threw one leg over his, and insistently tugged at the buttons fastening the collar of his shirt. He had it easier, one pull at the drawstring of her blouse and it slipped down over her shoulders to her waist, and he began kissing his way down her neck, both hands now on her breasts, thumbs circling the hardened nipples as her breath came faster and the fires raced through her entire body. Then he moved his mouth farther down and began to trace the same circles around her nipples with his tongue, while one hand pulled her skirt up and the other unfastened the front of his trews.

She knew what was there, and she wanted it, her insides cried out for it, and she helped him, eagerly.

There was some fumbling on both their parts. He raised his head from her breast and looked at her, ruefully, absolutely scarlet with embarrassment.

"I've—never done this before—" he whispered hoarsely.

"Neither have I," she replied, and pulled his head back to her breast.

Finally, his hardness found her secret place, and with a desperate thrust, he entered her. She bit back her exclamation of pain, as with a few sharp lunges, he climaxed.

He cried out, shuddered, and was still. But she very well remembered her mother's instructions about men and lovemaking, given when her breasts had first begun to bud. And after his breathing steadied, she began to kiss and fondle him again. Slowly, he responded, kissing her, making the fires rise in her again, making more free of her body this time than he had the first. He found new places to make her gasp, new ways to raise shivers. She made him gasp, too, nibbling at his earlobe, holding and slowly stroking his member, running her nails lightly along his sides. By the time the pain between her legs faded, he was hard and ready again.

And so this time, they came together slowly, with care, and

fell into a rhythm of thrust and response and what she had thought was a fire before became a conflagration, a ravenous hunger that built and built until she thought she could not bear it, and then it exploded within her, making her world go white for a moment as it swept over her and carried her away. A moment later, he cried out as well, and the two of them shuddered, stiffened, and then collapsed, still entwined.

Their breathing slowed. A breeze cooled the sweat on her body. His arms tightened around her.

"Marry me," he said into her ear.

"Of course," she replied.

He chuckled. "Good."

Chapter 9

By common consent, they elected not to talk about all the complications, the hows and the whens and the wheres. "We'll talk about this—" she began.

"Tomorrow," he agreed, as if he had read her mind. "Or the next day. But not now."

They made love again, in the warm afternoon sunshine, then bathed in the stream, then ate, feeding each other little tidbits. They told each other stories of their childhoods, and laughed a great deal, and kissed a great deal more. He played and they both sang, and then suddenly in the middle of a song, he stopped and began laughing hysterically.

She looked at him askance, as he bent over, shaking his head. Finally he got control of himself, and wiped his eyes on a napkin.

"The next verse is about the unicorn that follows Kalinka about," he said, still wiping tears of merriment from his eyes. "That's all very pretty in a song, but the reality is a plague—"

Her eyes widened and she began to chuckle. "Oh, *that* is why you were so stiff when you saw the White Doe!"

He nodded. "I thought it was another unicorn. I can't get rid of them. They follow me everywh—"

"Not anymore," said a voice full of disgust from the place where the path entered the glade. They both looked up.

A unicorn stood there, her lip curling, but her eyes wet. "Oh, Prince. How *could* you?" she cried. "And not even with a proper Princess after a proper wedding!"

"I wouldn't want a proper Princess," Sasha replied. "I'm not sure what you would call a 'proper' wedding. And I've been your mascot for far too long. It is time I had my own life. Now go and find some good little farmer's boy and bring some magic into his world, for he surely needs it."

With a snort, the unicorn turned and trotted back into the forest, every muscle expressing silent outrage.

"Why am I not a proper Princess?" Katya wondered aloud, more amused than anything.

"Because you are not pink, and white, and demure," said Sasha, with a flip of his hand that said wordlessly how little he cared for pink, and white, and demure. "A proper Princess would not survive me. I should drive her mad in the first day." He leaned over and kissed her, and she answered the kiss with rising passion. "Now, now!" he cautioned, laughing, as he pulled away. "More of that and we will never get back to the inn."

She sighed. She really didn't want to get back to the inn. She didn't want to go back under the sea and be parted from him. But he was continuing. "I will bespeak the bigger room. There is no reason why we cannot share it, is there?" Now he looked anxiously at her. "You don't need to be immersed in water every day do you? Or have to put on a fish skin?"

He wanted her with him! More, he wanted her with him in public! Her heart bubbled over with happiness. "No, and I only need go down to the shore to make sure my father hasn't sent any messages," she assured him. "There is no reason why—" she blushed, and stammered out the last "—why we cannot be together."

But that was skirting perilously close to the subject that they had both agreed to avoid for a little, so she said nothing more, and he did not ask or comment.

They packed up the pannier, saddled the horse, and he lifted her up onto the pillion. After a rueful look at the now-stained blanket, he folded it up so that the blood didn't show, and tucked it in the top of the basket.

"I can fix that," she said quietly. For of course, she could. She need but leave it in the ocean for a little, and at her direction, almost invisible sea creatures would pick it clean.

"Oh, I was just thinking that when my brother weds, they will display his sheets like a banner in the morning," he replied, making a face. "A barbaric custom—"

"And rather difficult to manage in the sea," she pointed out wryly. "Which may be why we set little store on that."

He had to laugh as he mounted the horse. "Then that is wise," he replied. "Very wise. You will have to excuse our barbaric ways."

"Oh, we have barbaric ways enough of our own," she replied, making a face. But she didn't elaborate. Time enough later to warn him that he would have to fight a token battle to prove he was worthy of her hand. He was clever; he would find a way to do so even though he was no warrior. That came under the heading of all the things they would talk about on some other day.

During the ride back to the inn, she kept her arms clasped about his waist and her cheek pillowed on his shoulder, reveling in the warmth and the scent of him. He was a very cleanly man. She had been around any number of unwashed Drylanders, and she was glad she had not fallen in love with one who scorned bathing.

They reached the Inn of the Jolly Sturgeon at dusk, and he lifted her down from the saddle while the hostler came to take the horse. She had never actually been here before, although in the course of her duties, she had seen the insides of many taverns, inns, and the like. The outside was in fine repair, if a bit weather-beaten, made of wood that she suspected had to have been scavenged from shipwrecks. But that was to be expected in a place so near the sea. The Jolly Sturgeon herself was painted on either side of the door, and she did look very jolly indeed, which was odd considering how many of her kin must have been brought here, split open for their eggs, and then made into soups and stews.

Sasha led Katya by the hand straight up to a woman who was tidying the tables in an otherwise empty common room. She was a sturdy, though not at all stout, woman of middle age. A bit of dark blond hair peeked out from under her kerchief, and her cheeks were pink from the heat of the kitchen. "If it is not inconvenient, good hostess," he said without any preamble, "I should like to bespeak a larger room."

The innkeeper's wife eyed both of them with a frown. "I do not run a bawdy house, sir—" she began.

"And I would not frequent one," he replied. "This is my betrothed."

Her frown deepened, and Katya felt suddenly uneasy. "Prince," the woman said, "for Prince we know you are—do you know what it is you hold by the hand and call your betrothed? It would not be wise to betray her."

At that moment, a chill seemed to fill the air, and Katya shivered. She could *feel* the magic of The Tradition suddenly looming over them like a wave about to break. And she felt her mouth go dry and her heart start to race. And she begged, silently, *Oh don't go making promises, Sasha! The Tradition is waiting for a promise! It is waiting for you to say "I will never betray her," so it can make you do just that!* This was precisely the sort of moment that tragedies were made of....

But Sasha just smiled. "I know, good hostess," he said softly. "And I will make no vows of undying love. *Never* and *Forever* are not words for mortals to use. But I will love her as truly as I can and as long as it is given to me to do so, and I hope I shall never hurt her, either by accident nor deliberately,"

The sense of portent faded. The feeling of great power looming turned into the feeling of great power shuffling off, disappointed. The innkeeper's wife laughed. "Well said, Prince. We need no tragic spirits here. We were long in laying to rest the last one." She smiled, and her eyebrows rose until they disappeared beneath the rim of her kerchief. "Now go take your sea-bride to the chamber next to yours and I will have Boyra bring your things to the new room." She winked. "If you choose to anticipate the wedding, well, so has half this village. I think you will find the bed to your liking."

Katya found herself blushing, and in her confusion almost overlooked something. Then as Sasha started to turn, she blinked. "How do you know what I am?" she demanded.

The innkeeper's wife smiled. "And who do you think is the witch of this village? I know a seabride when I smell her. You have the scent of the ocean clinging to you, and always will." She made a shooing motion. "Off with you, and I shall see to it that dinner is taken to you. I think you will not want to trouble yourselves with the stares of the company, who will suddenly see the lone minstrel with a lovely maiden that none of *us* know."

Laughing, Sasha tugged on Katya's hand, and nothing loathe, she followed him.

He lit a spill at the lantern in the hall, and opened a door as a boy clattered up the stairs behind them. Holding the flame over his head, Sasha located the candle and went to light it as Katya stood just inside the door and to one side, waiting for her eyes to adjust.

It was, by the standards of any inn she had ever been in, a good room. There was a large window, just now shuttered closed, two blanket chests, and a perfectly enormous curtained bed. A moment later the boy came clattering in—he was an extraordinarily noisy child—burdened with what must be Sasha's things. There were two bulging saddlebags, the balalaika case, and what looked to be a flute box, plus a fine cloak and a rain hat made of oiled leather with a broad brim. He put all these things down atop one of the blanket chests and clattered out again. Before Katya could so much as breathe a word, one of the serving girls from below came up with a laden tray, her footsteps lighter than a sylph's compared to the boy's. This she set down on top of the other blanket chest, curtsied to Sasha, and slipped out again.

Sasha closed the door and pulled the latch-string out.

"Well," he said. "This is certainly a step up from my old room. Our hostess must favor you, *belochka*."

She blushed at the word *beloved* and shook her head. "I think it's you she favors," she said instead, and unable to resist, sidled over to the bed.

In all her life she had never slept in a bed like *this* one.

With heavy curtains on three sides for privacy and warmth in winter, it would easily sleep four. It had a fine bearskin coverlet, four fat pillows, and the plumpness suggested a wonderful soft featherbed beneath the coverlet.

"Hmm," said Sasha, from behind her. "Our hostess has sent us things that are all good cold." He came up behind her and put his arms around her. "So shall we test out the bed?" he breathed in her ear.

"Perhaps." She slipped out of his embrace. Then slowly, deliberately, she unfastened her wide leather belt and dropped it behind her. With a tantalizing smile, she plucked at the drawstring to her skirt and untied it, letting the skirt drop to pool around her ankles, until she kicked it aside. Pulling at the drawstring of the neck of her blouse and loosening it, a moment later it, too, followed the skirt to the floor, leaving her standing only in her shift.

He stood quietly, arms crossed over his chest, a grin on his face. "What's this then, seawench?" he asked.

"You didn't see much of what you were bargaining for," she

replied, with a sly smile. "I just want you to be sure you haven't been cheated." A quick pull of the drawstring of the neck of her shift, and it, too, fell to the floor, leaving her standing there wearing nothing but air. Pulling both the bows from her hair, she shook it loose from its braid, letting it fall about her, hanging to her knees. "Well," she said, turning on one toe as she lifted her hair in both hands. "What do you think?"

"I think you should have a look at your half of the bargain," he replied, stripping off shirt, trews, and singlet, and tossing them all aside in a heap. He spread his arms wide. "Going to send me back to the market?"

She ran her gaze over him, slowly. He was not a tall man, but now that he was naked, she could see that there was nothing at all to be asked for in the way of strength. He was also not a particularly hairy man, which pleased her. Sculpted chest muscles and strong arms, a flat stomach—

But her eyes would go no farther as she saw how ready he was for her.

"I hardly think so," she replied breathlessly.

"Good!" He scooped her up and tossed her into the middle of the bed. "Because I have no intention of letting you."

He followed her into the bed, knelt between her legs, and looked down at her, greedily. "You are a tasty little morsel. Where shall I begin? Ah, I know—" He bent swiftly and took a nipple in his mouth, his hand cupping the other. The sensations of his tongue and gently nibbling teeth made her shiver and gasp, and the slightly roughened skin of his thumb on the other made her wild with desire. She threw her arms and her legs around him and drew him to her, arching her hips against his.

His free hand cupped her buttocks and pulled her against him, and she stifled a cry of pure pleasure as he entered her.

Then, maddeningly, he paused. "Slowly," he murmured against her breast, then sucked gently on the nipple, moving against her in time with his mouth. She found herself nibbling his neck and his earlobes, caressing his back and squeezing his buttocks with her hands as the movement of hips and mouth quickened gradually, grew more urgent. He switched his attentions to the other breast, both hands now holding her to him, then, as pleasure began to overcome her and she drove her own hips against his, his hands tightened on her and the amble became a gallop, the pleasure became a screaming need, the need became all, and fire exploded inside them both.

Somehow they didn't get to that supper after all that night.

It was three days later that the summons came.

Katya went down to the sea as she always did, first thing in the morning and the last thing at night. But this time, there was someone waiting for her.

It was one of the mer-folk, an earnest-looking young triton with a shock of jet-black hair and a worried expression. His eyes went from Katya to Sasha and back again. "Princess," he said. "I have a message for you. Your father needs you with all speed."

She bit her lip, and glanced at Sasha herself. He was nodding, though he did not look happy. "We are the servants of our people and our fathers, *belochka*," he said, firmly. "Duty comes first."

"With all speed," repeated the triton, and dove into the sea. Sasha seized her by the shoulders and turned her toward himself. "Duty comes first," he said. "But love follows. If you do not return in a reasonable time, I shall come looking for you, and I will find you." He bent his head to give her a hard, passionate kiss. "Now go! And remember that I am a Fortunate Fool, and I get what I want!"

Not daring to answer with anything except a whispered "I love you!" she turned and dove into the waves, allowing the magic to melt her Drylander clothing away and give her back her armor.

Ahead of her she could see the tail of the triton flashing as he flexed it in powerful pulses, dolphin-like, driving him at high speed into the depths. The fact that he had not waited for her made her feel cold. Whatever this was, it must surely be bad for her father to have put that much urgency into the triton's head. She thought she knew this one; a youngster that her father was grooming for a high position of trust. Had he told the youngling what she was? What she did for him? If so, then that could very well account for the triton's reticence.

Especially if the matter really was grave.

She turned her swim into the dolphin-kick herself. Although she had not got the advantage of flukes, the undulating swimming motion was much faster than any other form. As she swam, she "felt" for the magic of the sea, and asked it for help, and a moment later, a dolphin came shooting out of the distant waters. Though he wasn't wearing a towing harness, she could, and did, still seize hold of his dorsal fin, and lay herself along his back. As soon as she had positioned herself, he put on his full speed, catching up with, then passing the triton.

She released the dolphin with silent thanks at the edge of the Palace grounds and cast around for her father.

She spied him swimming toward her and knew then that this must be the most serious trouble he had ever yet needed her for.

"There is a threat," he said without preamble. "Do you know where the castle of the Katschei is?"

She nodded. "Just over the border of Led Belarus, in the wilderness. But the Katschei is dead, father. He went to another land, thinking that since their Tradition did not know him, he could conquer it. But he did not reckon on the ways of a God-mother, and he was killed in the trying. The castle is empty even of his followers."

"Not anymore," came the grim reply that sent shivers up her spine. "He may be gone, but something else has taken his place. And whatever that something may be, it is not of the local Tradition, it is very powerful, and altogether evil. Something, perhaps, has learned from the Katschei's mistake and is moving to take advantage of his absence."

She bit her lip, but he was not yet finished. "Whatever is there has taken one, or perhaps two, magical maidens. A swan maiden was taken right from under the noses of her sisters, and they came to me to ask for my help. There is a Snyegurochka, a Snow Maiden, missing, and she has not melted. I should not think twice about this except that she was walking in the cool of evening in the same area where the swan maiden was taken, and she did not return. The place where both vanished is very near the Katschei's castle."

"Have you sent anything to spy there?" she asked, knowing she would probably not like the answer.

He nodded. "Yes. And there is the trouble. My spies were seabirds and they have not come back. Your sister's magic cannot pierce the dark veil about the place. You are the only one I have that can go to the Drylands with impunity."

She nodded gravely. "Then that is what I must do," she replied. She thought fleetingly of going back to Sasha and asking for his help—but the Katschei was not in his Kingdom, and he could not in good conscience leave home to help her. Right now, this was a concern only for the Sea King. The swan maidens had asked him for help, not the King of Led Belarus.

"Though your fighters cannot come that far onto land, I can get help should I need it with my paper bird," she continued. "And if need be, you can trade future aid for me against aid from your allies. Besides," she added, smiling slightly, "I have allies of my own."

The Sea King nodded. "Then go with all speed, daughter. I feel great foreboding when I turn my mind in that direction. Whatever it is must have plans beyond the kidnapping of a maiden or two. The swan's sisters are awaiting you on the shore at the point nearest to the castle."

Somberly, she saluted him, and left. As she went to the stables to find another dolphin-helper, she tried to imagine what could have gotten wind of the Katschei's absence and also known enough to subvert all her father's formidable powers to keep him from discovering what was afoot.

For that matter, even vacant, the Katschei's castle had some nasty protections on it. The Katschei had never been one to leave a door unlocked behind him. So whatever it was that had taken it—

Must be as powerful, or more powerful, than the Katschei itself.

* * *

The swan maidens were inconsolable.

There were five of them left, all told, and they huddled in their feather cloaks on the shingle and wept, and in between bouts of tears, told her their history. They were all sisters, and there had been seven at one point, but the youngest had been claimed by a mortal husband, who had won her freedom. She they saw from time to time—but this!

Patiently, Katya tried to unravel their tale; she appealed to the eldest as being, perhaps, the most sensible, sitting beside her and trying to make sense of what she was saying through her sobs.

"I can't help you if I can't understand what happened," she said, trying not to sound impatient. "You have to tell me exactly, from the beginning, precisely what happened to your sister. Every detail. Details are important and tell me much."

That elicited a wail from all of them. Finally the eldest managed to choke down her tears long enough to blurt out, "It was just like every morning! We went to the lake where the hot spring is to bathe and play in the water! Even when the Katschei was in his castle, no one bothered us there!"

"We thought it was safe!" cried another—Katya had stopped trying to tell them apart; really, between their floods of tears and identical swan cloaks, it was like trying to distinguish among a flock of real swans. And, sadly, they seemed nearly as bird-witted as real swans.

That called forth another spate of sobbing.

"All right, you went to enjoy yourselves. Why did your sister leave the rest of you?" she asked.

"We wanted to sun ourselves, but Yulya wanted to sleep in

the shade," wept a third. "So we—we—we—left her! Alone! And we heard a scream and a loud wind, and she was gone!"

"Show me the place," Katya demanded. They looked at her doubtfully.

"It is dangerous," said one, and "It is a long way away," said another. "We can fly. You can't," said a third.

"This lake drains by the river here, yes?" she asked, suppressing her annoyance. "I can swim up the river as fast as you can fly. Show me the place."

As they continued to hesitate, timorously, she lost all patience. "I can see you do not want my father's help," she snapped. "I will return to him and—"

They mobbed her, clung to her, wept all over her, begging her not to go. Finally, after far too much dithering, the eldest agreed to show her where they had left Yulya. With a sense of relief, Katya pulled loose from the others and dove into the river.

Though swimming upstream was generally an effort, the current was slow and the river placid—exactly the sort of stream that swans preferred—and Katya was at the lake only a little behind the eldest swan maiden. The girl was waiting on the bank, every feather in her cloak trembling as she shivered with fear.

Good heavens, Katya thought, with no little disgust. *As timid as these girls are, I am amazed they ever leave their father's palace.* Perhaps it was nothing more than the force of The Tradition, for every swan maiden tale that Katya had ever heard involved one or more of the maidens being taken, or seduced, or hunted beside a lake far, far from their home. Perhaps they had no choice. Perhaps it was The Tradition itself that forced them into leaving home.

If that was the case…

Well, she could sympathize even while it made her impatient with their timidity.

She leaped out of the water like an otter, startling the girl, who jumped and squeaked.

"So, where was your sister when you left her?" Katya asked, looking around at the lush forest that surrounded the lake. She was not surprised that the swans came here. Not more than a few feet away, a hot spring bubbled up out of the ground and cascaded down a gravel bed, steaming, to end in the lake waters. The grass at the verge of the forest presented an attractive place to doze in the shade. And, she presumed, there were good places for sun-basking not far from here. Traditionally speaking, swan maidens, like her father's mermaids, must spend a great deal of time sunbathing and combing their hair.

Don't they ever get bored? She'd have gone mad.

Well, evidently not. Perhaps The Tradition ensured that all swan maidens were born as brainless as the birds themselves….

That's unkind….

"Here," said the girl, shaking in every limb, pointing to a spot where the feather cloak still lay.

But true. "You didn't take her cloak with you?" she asked, a little stunned.

"No. Should we have?" The girl blinked at her.

"What happens if someone who isn't one of your sisters puts on the cloak?" Katya demanded.

The girl blinked again. "They become a swan like us, I suppose...."

Katya did her best not to smack herself in the head in frustration. "And it didn't occur to you that someone could put on the cloak, become a swan, and follow you back to your father where he—or she—could then enchant you and put you *all* in his power?"

The girl's eyes widened, and she dropped to the ground, crying. "Oh no—oh no!" she sobbed "Oh this is terrible, dreadful—"

"Oh for—" Katya strode over to her and took her by the shoulders and shook her hard. "It didn't happen! The cloak is still here! Get control of yourself, for pity's sake!"

Startled, the girl stopped sobbing.

"Now, take your sister's cloak and go," she ordered. "Leave this to me."

She didn't have to give the order twice. In the blink of an eye, a swan stood where the girl had been. It picked up the cloak in its beak and flew off, white feathers streaming behind it.

Katya went back to examining the area where the swan maiden had been taken. And she was not too terribly shocked when she found a patch of moss in the deepest shade where the temperature was considerably colder than anywhere else. And beside that patch of moss, a cluster of snow-drops was blooming.

So, now she knew that both girls had been taken from the same place. What else did they have in common?

Magic, she decided. The likelihood that it was any other common denominator was vanishingly small. The snow maiden was a peasant, the swan maiden was a princess. One was born of magical blood, the other made by magic. One lived in a simple hut in the forest, the other in a palace East of the Sun and West of the Moon. One was hardworking, the other pampered.

Well, there was one good way to test this theory. And Katya didn't think she was going to be able to get into the Katschei's palace any other way.

But first, she needed a disguise.

Bereginia. She would disguise herself as the riverbank maiden. Magic enough, but not too much magic, and surely exactly what this kidnapper was looking for.

She waited for The Tradition to notice her, waited to feel it focusing on her. *I must be a bereginia,* she told it. *This thing that hunts maidens does not belong here. I will make it go back to its place. But I must be a bereginia to do so—*

She felt the magic of The Tradition gather around her, she pulled it to her, and felt it settle on her like a heavy cloak—

The sunlight gathered around her and dazzled her eyes. Then it was gone.

And there she was, dressed from head to foot in brown and green, green as the reeds and the rushes, green as the grass and the river water. Brown as the mud of the bank and the stones. She felt something on her head, touched it, and realized she was wearing a crown of water iris and plaited rushes. Her shift was of filmy brown linen, light as gossamer, with huge sleeves that swept the ground, embroidered in green. The sarafan, the over-gown, was green, and embroidered in a hundred different colors of green and brown. A green half cloak, slung over the right shoulder and under the left, was also embroidered in green and brown.

She was enchanted. She had never actually seen a bereginia;

she'd no idea what they looked like or what they wore; she had only been hoping that it wasn't entirely hideous, some strange primitive thing of rawhide and rattling bones.

She didn't get much time to appreciate it though—

She heard a strange sound above her head, and looked up.

There was a whirlwind in the sky above her, descending rapidly down onto her. Her first instinct was to run—but of course, that was not what she needed to do. She stood her ground as the sand-colored, top-shaped vortex homed in on her, whining a high-pitched note that set her teeth on edge. Of course, this thing had waited until she was alone.

She ducked as it hit her, and used those long sleeves to screen her face; a good thing she did, or she would have been blinded by the debris in the wind. She was in the center of a whirl of hot, dry air full of sand and dust that engulfed her and almost stole her breath away. And then she felt her feet lose contact with the ground.

Despite her best intentions, she screamed. It did no good of course. She felt it take her, and with a sickening lurch, felt it hurtle up and sideways with her suspended in the middle of it.

All she could think of at that moment was Sasha....

It seemed to take forever, but the time between when the whirlwind picked her up and when it deposited her on the battlements of the Katschei's castle could not have been very long at all. It had been mid-afternoon by the sun when she had called on The Tradition to disguise her. It was still mid-afternoon, though perhaps just a bit later, now.

But when the whirlwind dissipated and she could see again, she got a tremendous shock. The Katschei's castle had once stood in the heart of a bleak, oppressively dark and overgrown forest, one where all the trees were droop-branched pines, more black than green, where the ends of the branches dripped endlessly, where fog wreathed the landscape and the space between the trees was host to unwholesome-looking mushrooms and briars with thorns as long as a finger.

Not anymore.

Now the castle stood in the heart of a desert.

In every direction, all she could see were sand dunes and little patches of scrub. The sun beat down on her like a hammer on an anvil, and the sky was like an upturned enamel bowl, glaring and pitiless.

"Hmpf."

She turned, hearing the sound behind her, and stared.

He was twice as tall as she, and barely half-clothed. His skin was the color of beaten bronze, his eyes black and slanted, and his head mostly bald except for a topknot of black hair as coarse as a horse's tail, bound at the base with a gold ring. He wore baggy silk trews of an eye-watering scarlet color, and shoes that matched with pointed, upward-curling toes, a pair of gold bracelets around his biceps, and nothing more. He looked down at her, arms folded over his hairless chest.

"And what are you?" he asked in a strangely accented voice.

She didn't have to act to get her voice to tremble. As it happened, she *knew* what this was, because she had heard about them from her father, in his tales of his family's war with Drylanders of the Southern Kingdoms. It was a Jinn. And most Jinn were evil. "A bereginia, sir. A simple dweller on the riverbank—"

"Enough." He cut her off with a gesture. "Go down and join the others. You serve me now, whatever you are." His voice rang in her ears, with overtones like a brass gong.

She looked where he pointed, down into the central courtyard of the castle, which was, at least, still a garden. She saw three other young women down there, one listlessly reading a book, one picking at embroidery, and one sitting and staring at nothing.

She glanced back at the cruel, scowling face of the Jinn and scuttled down the cut-stone stairs from the battlements to the courtyard, feeling entirely too much like a mouse in the gaze of a cat that is not quite hungry…

…yet.

She entered the garden not sure of what her reception was going to be. The first thing she noticed was that all the young women were wearing a very different set of garments than the ones she would have thought they'd have been captured in. Instead of blouses, skirts and vests, or shifts and sarafans, or even the brocaded silver-white gowns the swan maidens had worn, they all had on a variation in color and embroidery of the same outfit; filmy, baggy trews of the sort that the Jinn wore with a short skirt over that, an equally filmy blouse with very short sleeves, and a vest. Most of them had their hair braided and wrapped around their heads, for coolness, she thought. Katya entered the garden near one dressed all in white and silver, who had been the one staring listlessly at nothing. The girl gave her an indifferent glance; Katya recognized in her features the stamp of her sisters. This then must be Yulya, the missing swan maiden.

"You had better get a servant to show you the way to our quarters, and change out of that, if you don't want to roast," the swan maiden said indifferently, then went back to staring at nothing.

"Never mind the servant, I'll show you," said another in blue, the one who had been embroidering, making a dismissive gesture at Yulya. "And never mind her, either. She's terrified, so terrified it's made her go all numb." The girl managed a shaky smile. "So am I, but it hasn't made me go all numb. I almost wish it would. That bronze fellow says his magic will protect us but—" she glanced up at the sky with a shuttered look of terror "—I keep expecting to melt at any moment."

So this would be the snow maiden.

The third girl, all in red, looked up and nodded solemnly. "It's a Jinn, you know," she whispered. "It's trying to do what the Katschei did, only much more cleverly. It's trying to come here, where The Tradition doesn't know how to cope with it. It took over the Katschei's castle, though, so The Tradition is making it do what the Katschei did—collect girls."

"He doesn't like it, either," said the snow maiden. "Every time The Tradition makes him send out one of his whirlwinds, he gets very irritated."

"It doesn't like being forced into anything," the other said, closing her book. "It was like that all along, of course, but being confined to a bottle for two hundred years has made it very…" she seemed to be searching for the right word "…angry."

"How do you know all of this?" Katya asked, eyeing the other doubtfully.

The girl sighed. "Because I was the first one it took captive, before it even came here. I was an apprentice to a hedge- wizard, and he was the one that let the Jinn loose. He bought the bottle from a sailor—he thought it was just some odd magic potion. He broke the seal and opened the stopper on it to analyze it— now, of course, I know that the stopper and the seal were part of the spell that kept the Jinn confined—and the Jinn came boiling out and destroyed him. Then it began wrecking his tower. I was down in the cellar decanting things and heard the noise and hid. By the time the Jinn got down there, its anger had cooled somewhat, and it decided to take me captive to serve it." Katya noticed at that point that the girl looked very, very tired. "Not like a servant. It leaches power from anyone that has it to save his own. I'm sure it would *much* rather take more powerful people to leach from, but it decided to take over the Katschei's castle, so young women are all that The Tradition will let it capture. Still, it must keep us alive so we can recover more power he can steal again. It means we are generally safe."

"Unless, of course, he can use us as bait to lure in other things. Princes. Sorcerers." Katya shrugged. "Why do you keep calling him *it*?"

"I—don't know," the young woman confessed. "I suppose because it didn't show any interest in…" She blushed.

"I had as soon couple with a donkey." The brass-toned voice made them all start, and the Jinn faded into view, looking down at them with scorn. "You are mere animals, for all that you talk.

Your conversation is like the chattering of apes. You irritate me. Go to your quarters."

Yulya, the swan maiden, shrank back the moment the Jinn appeared; she went absolutely white and, like her sister, she trembled in every limb. The snow maiden and the apprentice, however, though pale and frightened, stood their ground, at least insofar as not falling to pieces in front of him. The snow-maiden took Katya by the hand and led her off toward a doorway in the wall of the courtyard, while the apprentice took Yulya's hand and tugged her insistently away, breaking her out of her paralysis.

The thick stone walls of the castle, built to withstand the assault of any foe the Katschei could imagine, give immediate relief from the desert heat. The snow maiden sighed involuntarily as they penetrated deeper into the corridors, with Yulya's quiet sobs making a melancholy counterpart to their footsteps.

"I'm Ekaterina—Katya," Katya said, into the uncomfortable silence. "Marina," and "Klava," the other two volunteered. Yulya just whimpered.

The room that Marina brought them to must once have been one of the Katschei's audience chambers—although it was possible that this chamber might have once held the Katschei's own collection of captive girls. Although there were no windows, it was illuminated brightly enough, with glowing lanterns spaced at intervals along the walls. The light that came from them was a cool blue, which made all of them look just a touch cadaverous. It was furnished very simply, with heaps of pillows and low cots. There were books here, neatly arranged in a bookcase that looked out of place. Yulya went straight to one of the cots and lay down on it. Marina went to a chest and rummaged around, coming up with an outfit just like her own, in green. Taking the hint, Katya changed into it, and realized that no matter what it looked like, it was very cool and practical. Wardrobe taken care of, the three of them arranged themselves on pillows as far from Yulya as possible.

"I don't suppose you've tried to escape?" Katya asked.

Klava rolled her eyes. "Marina is a snow maiden," she pointed out. "Even if we could escape, she wouldn't last very long out there in the desert."

Katya nodded. "Still," she persisted. "Did it ever even look like there was a way to escape?"

"Nothing that I ever saw," Klava said, after a moment of thought. "Some of the Katschei's servants were still here when the Jinn took this place, and they simply accept him as the new master. Some of them came back. And the Jinn has servants of his own, and a lot of them are human. You didn't see them, but he has lots of soldiers."

Katya pondered. "Does he stop you from exploring this place?"

Marina shook her head. "That's how we got all the books. He doesn't bother with us as long as we don't try to kill ourselves or try to escape in any obvious way. And don't worry," she added, "I can tell when he's about, invisible. Right at the moment we can talk about anything."

"Right," Katya said, and set her chin. "Then let's talk about how we are going to get out of here."

Chapter 10

When three days went by without so much as a word, Sasha began to worry. When a week had passed, he became certain that Katya was in trouble. And when a fortnight had come and gone—

—that was when he decided that he was going after her.

He sent only a short message to his brothers and father. *I will be traveling and am not certain where.* Unlike Katya's duty, the tasks of the Fortunate Fool had never yet involved an emergency. With luck, nothing would fall apart in his absence.

So hear me, my Luck. Let nothing fall apart in my absence.

He took the message with him out to the innkeeper, who had sent messages on for him before. The man looked at the folded, sealed piece of paper, then at him, and nodded. "Tinker just came in this morning. Heading to Vasilygrad."

"Perfect," he replied, and handed over a half-dozen silver coins. The innkeeper would keep one, give one to the tinker, and promise the rest when the tinker returned with proof of delivery. The man would do as he promised of course. The innkeeper was a good judge of men.

Then again, you didn't cross someone married to a witch. It was pretty obvious now why no one ever stole things from this inn.

Sasha had no real idea of where he needed to go, but that had never stopped him in the past. Now, if ever, was the time to rely on the Luck of the Fortunate Fool, the Luck that would put him in the right place, at the right time, without fail.

He went straight to the innkeeper's wife after sending on his message. As she was the local witch, she would be the best place to start.

"Your betrothed is long away," she said shrewdly, the moment he walked into her fragrant kitchen. The door stood open to let out the heat, and the air was full of the scent of perfectly baked bread. "I sense this was not planned."

"My betrothed answered the summons of her father, and it has taken longer than either of us thought," he replied. "But I do not think it is her father that is detaining her."

The witch nodded, and bent to remove loaves of rich, dark bread from the oven. "I do not, either, though I have no real word to give you. Whatever has gone amiss, it has a land-feel to it, not a sea-feel."

He did not even have to think what his answer would be now. If Katya's father was not the problem, then she was in trouble; and if she was in trouble he would find his way to her. "I was already going to go to her. Is there any help you can give me at all?"

"These." She nodded at the bread. "I dreamed you would go, though I did not know why—I only saw you taking to the road and the road stretching on before you farther than I could see. I began my baking for it last night, when I woke from the dream. Other than that—" She shrugged, and then looked up at him, a rueful expression on her face. "I am not very powerful. My abilities lie mostly in seeing what is to be seen here in the village, some healing, a little advice, once in a while, a dream. And bread."

"Then I will have that, and your blessing, little mother," he replied, and bent to kiss her hand, a little rough with honest work, and so very different from the hands he usually had to kiss.

"Oh get on with you!" she said, blushing, as she snatched her hand away. "Take my bread and my blessing, and bring your love back."

So when the Fortunate Fool rode out a short time later, it was with the blessing of the Witch of the Jolly Sturgeon, a pannier full of rich bread wrapped for travel, and only the vague direction that the troubles had a "land-feel" to them.

But Sasha was not stupid. He knew The Tradition like few in this kingdom. He knew his land and its people. And he was accustomed to looking at the vaguest of hints and turning them into answers.

Sasha had only just ridden the boundaries of the kingdom. He knew where the trouble spots were and he had dealt with them. So whatever had happened, whatever it was that Katya was to look into, there were two things he knew for certain. The place had to border the sea, or the Sea King would not be concerned about it. And it was not *inside* Led Belarus.

So. The logical place to start would be to follow the coastline northward, to cross the border into wilderness claimed by no Kingdom. There were plenty of nasty things there, lurking in ancient, be-spidered and be-haunted forest. There were no few things he had sung out of Led Belarus that could have gotten stronger since he removed them. There were also rumors of very, very powerful Old Things. If one of *them* had decided that decades, centuries of quietude were about to end, then things could be very interesting indeed.

So northward he went. As it happened, there were a few creatures he could ask for advice on the way, and it would be in the true Tradition of the Fortunate Fool to do so.

He pressed his horse as much as he could to reach his first destination by nightfall.

The woods to the right were still haunted-looking, but nothing like as sinister as the last time he passed this way. Instead of oppressive, endless shadow beneath the trees, there were will-o'-the-wisps, not dancing off into the distance, mockingly, but hanging quietly in one place or at worst, drifting about a little. The scent of the place was of fallen leaves, cool, old—not of death and decay. Still unnerving, but not terrifying.

The trees, though they stirred without a breeze to move them, and made ominous creaking noises, did not reach out to grab him or his horse as they made their way down the path. The path did not grow holes, or roots, or stones to trip the horse. It did not suddenly seem to squirm in a different direction. In short, it remained an ordinary, common path.

So far the Rusalka was keeping her promise.

He arrived at the lake as the moon was rising, and looked

around. The atmosphere was little changed, but, nevertheless, it was changed. Again, the scent was subtly different; not rank with a hint of corruption, but cool, a bit damp, and ever so faintly scented with waterlily. There were still wafts of fog on the surface and wreathing around the verge, but they didn't go above waist-high, and the moonlight illuminated the area quite brilliantly.

There were no evil little silver slivers of fish in the clear water. Just an ordinary carp nosing about the bottom, a few tiny sticklebacks darting past, and a perch dozing just under a lily pad. And frogs were singing all around.

He dismounted from his horse, took the first loaf of bread from his pannier, laid it on a stone near the edge, and waited.

He didn't have to wait for very long.

A head shot up out of the water, shaking long, silvery-blond hair out of her eyes. "Bread!" the Rusalka exclaimed. "Do I smell fresh bread?"

"From today's baking," Sasha replied. Rusalkas, although technically ghosts, still ate. It was a contradiction that Sasha had never been able to reason out, and so he had never bothered to try. "A bargain for a little information. Sorry I don't have butter."

The Rusalka jumped out of the water and seized the loaf of bread, sitting right down on the stone to tear a chunk off and start eating. She paused with the bite halfway to her mouth. "What sort of information?" she asked.

"Is there anything you know of that might be stirring to the north that would attract the attention of the King of the Sea?" he asked.

Frogs punctuated the silence. "Hmm." She ate her first piece while she thought.

"Just guesses would be fine," he said encouragingly.

"Well...I *would* have mentioned Katschei the Deathless, except that he didn't manage to live up to his name," she said, smirking. "His castle is vacant, but I doubt that anything would have moved into it. He was a vile thing, and would have left it completely filled with traps of all sorts." She shook her head. "It is not a place *I* would venture into, no matter what treasures are there."

He made a mental note of that anyway. If something was strong enough, clever enough, to get past the traps, it would certainly be strong and clever enough to capture Katya. "Anything else?" he asked.

"Baba Yaga roams up there."

He bit his lip over that one. Baba Yaga never was, and Traditionally never would be, the sort to stir up the kind of trouble that *would* get the Sea King's attention. Not that she didn't stir up trouble! And not that she wasn't absolutely deadly! But she didn't ever involve herself in the matters of Kingdoms. He suspected that she just didn't enjoy the sort of impersonal misery that conquest and subjugation created. She performed her evil one person at a time.

So, probably not Baba Yaga, though it was entirely possibly that Baba Yaga could have ambushed Katya on the way *to* her goal. "Anything else?"

The loaf was half gone. The Rusalka must have been starved for the taste of bread. He made a mental note to see that she got it more often. "They say Chernobog is seen there." She looked up then, and shivered, eyes going opaque.

He didn't blame her. Chernobog was said to be a god, though who knew? It was impossible to say. Whatever, the Dark One *was* very, very powerful, and *was* interested in the lives of mortals, and was entirely arbitrary so far as Sasha could make out. You could not tell what he would and would not do. Like many ancient spirits, he acted only as he pleased, and in tune with some balance and some logic that only he and The Tradition understood or could predict.

Though if it was Chernobog, the Dark One would not be acting directly, but rather through someone else. He had no interest in being a king himself—for a spirit as powerful as he was, that was a distinct demotion—but oh, how he loved to meddle in the lives of mortals! Meddle, then stand back and watch and laugh. No use appealing to him either; he let you get yourself out of whatever situation his meddling had put you in.

The Rusalka finished the last of the bread, and licked her fingers bare of crumbs. Nearby, a nightingale began to sing, adding his voice to the frogs.

"I cannot think of anything else," she said. "Although there are plenty of evil things there. Plenty. More than enough to give your Katya a nasty surprise."

He nodded. "But that is a start. Well—" He looked up at the moon. "I should go while there is light to ride by."

She shook her head. "No. Stay." At his askance look, she smiled. "I have no designs on you! I scent the Sea King's daughter about you and I have no desire to challenge her! No, you can safely sleep here. I will guard your rest." Then she added, softly, "You are a good man, Sasha."

He flushed. He did try to be. Even if he didn't know The Tradition as well as he did, he'd have been the sort to share his bread with an old beggar woman....

"Thank you," he said, just as softly.

Then she laughed. And shook back her hair, and winked at him "And you are a Fortunate Fool! Such are always finding help in unexpected places!"

And so, somewhat to his own bemusement, Sasha unsaddled his horse and left it tethered to graze on the verge, while he rolled himself up in his cloak and slept through the night to the sound of frogs and a lovestruck nightingale, beneath the protection of a Rusalka.

Katya scanned the battlements carefully from her place in the Jinn's garden. The other girls—and there were more of them now, for the Jinn had added a fifth maiden to his collection—were all in their rock-walled room. The new one might be very useful. She was a Wolf-girl, the opposite of a werewolf, a young Wolf-bitch who could take the form of a human at will—legends said it was by taking off her skin, but Katya had watched her, and she merely shape-shifted. She was very like the bear-people in that way, or a real werewolf, as opposed to the swan maiden who was human to begin with and took the form of a swan by putting on the feather cloak. As a Wolf, the girl was able to sniff out things that the others could not see nor sense. Like drafts or fresh air where neither should be. Katya had her exploring the cellars and dungeon as much as she could without getting caught.

The garden had never been all that lovely when Katschei the

Deathless had lived here; he had been much inclined to dark and poisonous plants. In his absence though, most of those, needing nurturing, had died. So the weeds, and what good plants that once had flourished here and had somehow survived, had taken over. And then, just as the garden was at its most tangled, someone had taken a clumsy hand to it.

The Jinn, she supposed, was the one who had ordered some of that cleaned up. The fountain flowed clear, bushes and even trees had been cut back, and paths were newly graveled. But the Jinn clearly could not tell weeds from flowers, and the weeds were slowly choking out the flowers, in all but a few places. Granted, some of the weeds did look very lush and green, but stinging nettles were not what anyone would want in a garden, even if they did look like mint.

She sat next to one of those places where the flowers were winning, a bed of primroses that had completely taken over whatever else had been in there with them. The delicate pink blossoms, only faintly scented, spilled out over the cobbles containing them, looking cool and lively in what to her was dreadful heat.

The heat was enough to flatten anyone used to the climate of the north as she and the other girls were. The devastation this Jinn could wreak here if he spread his desert was appalling. The heat alone would kill many animals—and people, too.

She was here, not because she wanted to be, but because she was both testing something and waiting for her moment to finally act to get some help.

What she was testing was her own ability to tell when the Jinn was moving about invisibly. After a good deal of observation she had realized that like the snow maiden, she, too, could tell when the creature was spying on his captives and his own men invisibly. There was a kind of hum in the back of her mind, like the buzz of a fly that would not land, whenever he was about. That hum did not go away when he was invisible. And the more she thought about it, the more certain she became that this buzz was because the Jinn did not belong here. Perhaps what she sensed was his dissonance with The Tradition here, like an improperly fitting wheel, or the grating of a movable joint that had not been smoothed.

So, that was something. He could not watch her without her knowing that he was about. So long as she did not hear that hum, she could operate knowing that he could not find out about it.

She waited until the hum went away—and actually, she watched him go. He gathered one of those whirlwinds about himself and lofted into the sky, the bizarre thing forming a kind of brown blot against the blue. When he was out of sight, and the hum was gone for a bit, she took her waterproof wallet of oiled eelskin and unsealed the paraffin holding the edge shut. From it she took her paper crane. The Jinn had taken every-thing from her that looked like a weapon, but not this. He probably thought it was a lover's token.

It might not be a bad thought to moon over it as if it were when he was about.

Carefully, she wiped her hands and forehead with a soft cloth, to avoid dampening the paper or dropping sweat on it. She unfolded the bird, and with a bit of lead stolen from a window, wrote swiftly on its interior. She used a tiny bit of magic of her own, the magic that allowed her to speak and read in any language in any land. Whoever got this would see it as the script of his or her own native tongue.

Captives being held by Jinn at Castle of Katschei. Jinn plans conquest. Champions needed. Follow bird.

That was all she had room for.

She had thought, and thought hard, about sending for Sasha—and she would, when the bird came back. But although he was a Fortunate Fool, he was no warrior, and it was warriors who were needed here now. The Jinn had to be stopped. Not just for the sake of the Sea King, but for everything else hereabouts. If the Jinn could transform one piece of forest to desert with only the power at his personal disposal, what could he do with the nearly unlimited power he would have if he took many folk captive? He could lay waste to entire Kingdoms without ever leaving the castle grounds. The more she thought about it, the more alarmed she became.

And she could not send the bird to her father, not directly. It was, after all, paper. Nor were any of his forces useful for this— not in the Drylands. It would take time for him to gather help from his allies, and time might be in short supply. A Champion or two could stop the Jinn now, before he became too powerful, but the longer they waited, the harder it would be to stop him. So she would send him word only after she sent word to Sasha.

She folded the bird back up, held it in her hands, and concentrated. *I need a Champion, or more than one. I need the nearest. I need the strongest of the nearest, something that can take on a Jinn, someone clever, someone skilled. I need you also to find the nearest Champion who qualifies that can also read, so that he or she can read your message.*

The nearest, strongest literate Champion; yes, that was exactly what she needed. There. That should do it. She folded the crane again and held it on her palm, balanced as if to fly. "Do my bidding, bear my word, then come you back, my paper bird," she breathed to it.

With a rustle, the bird sprang to life.

It hovered over her hand for just a moment, tiny paper wings a blur, then shot off into the sky, just as she felt the hum return. She bit her lip. The Jinn could probably sense magic being worked. Had he felt her at work? Had he sensed the bird? Swiftly she turned to the rosebush beside her.

A moment later, the Jinn appeared in the middle of the garden, with a sound like a thunderclap and a puff of smoke, his bronze face creased with a ferocious frown. She froze in place, as if terrified, as his eyes lit on her, then moved to the branch of the rosebush in her hand.

The barren branch was now showing life, in fact, the entire bush had come back to life. Green leaves were slowly unfurling and there was a hint of buds where there had been only dry thorns before.

The Jinn stalked over to her.

"What are you doing?" he demanded.

She shrank back. "T-tending the garden," she stammered. "They were drying dying, these roses. Green things…it is what I do…."

"A waste of magic!" he growled. "Putter about in the dirt if you wish, but waste no more magic on it! Your magic is mine to draw on!"

She nodded, and let go of the branch. He stalked away.

And only then did she heave a sigh of relief. The illusion of greenery about the bush faded away. It took very little magic to create an illusion, especially when it was one that someone would reasonably believe.

But while she was at it—the bush *was* still alive, it only needed coaxing. And today in the bottom of a chest she had found a very practical set of the baggy trews and a sleeveless shirt of some light beige stuff that was not linen and was not silk, being softer than the former and tougher than the latter. She went to change into those, to nurture the garden the hard way while she continued to think and plan as hard as she ever had in her life.

There was no fence or border or even a border guard on the road where the Kingdom of Led Belarus ended and the wilderness began. The only sign of the transition was the road itself, which went from being in relatively good repair to degenerating to a rutted dirt track within a matter of a few hundred yards. This was forested land, the beautiful hardwood forest of the north, mostly untouched even by woodcutters. The trees reached high into the sky, and the track lay deep in shade. Where fallen trunks lay, they were covered in soft moss. Here the leafy trees were mixed with cedar, and the scent of them was sharp on the air. There should be mushrooms. He wished he had the time to look.

It was there that he encountered the old beggar woman.

He had been expecting one all along. In fact, he was rather surprised that The Tradition hadn't supplied him with old beggar women between every village. If ever there was a situation that The Tradition must surely be agitated about—if something like the Tradition could be agitated—it was this one. The Sea King's daughter missing, some dire problem in the north, and not a Godmother in sight. By now it must be spinning around like a dancing mouse, trying to find a solution to a problem. It was, he thought, dreadfully ironic that usually it was a Godmother working to find a way to steer The Tradition into an alternate path in order to solve a problem. Here it was The Tradition itself frantically casting around to heal itself.

It was too bad that he didn't yet know what the problem was.

Needless to say he was not at all surprised to see the old beggar woman there just over the border, as if she had been placed there to intercept him.

She was a small, bent bundle of black and rusty-brown fabric beside the road. He couldn't see her face, only the fold of her shawl over her head and a curling lock of white hair. She looked up at him from under her shawl as he rode near, and held out her hand to him, entreatingly. "Please, young man, can you spare an old woman a crust?" Her voice was soft and quavering.

"Little mother, I can spare far more than a crust," he said, dismounting. "You look fair famished and you are terribly far away from anything like a village. Come—" leading his horse with one hand, he took her by the elbow with the other, and escorted her to a fallen log. "Here, now sit down, rest your honored bones, and let me tend you, as surely your own son would want you to be tended."

"Alas I have no son," she replied, looking startled as he spread out a napkin and broke open a small loaf for her, stuffing it with the cheese he had bought at the last village. He put the bread down on the clean napkin, then handed her his own waterskin to drink from.

"Eat and drink, little mother," he said, "and when you are done, I will take you up behind me and take you to your home. You should not be alone out here, and you should not have to walk when I can carry you."

The "old woman" made a sound between a snort and a giggle and pulled the shawl off her head, revealing a not-so-old woman. "That won't be needed, Prince Sasha," said the witch, in a perfectly normal and pleasant alto voice. "I don't know why anyone ever bothers to test you anymore. You clearly expect every test we could give you."

"No more do I know why you test me," he said cheerfully. "But I like finding living folks on desolate roads, I like giving beggars something to eat, and I like witches. So as it's about midday, do have some bread and cheese and share a meal with me. It's very good bread. Another witch baked it for me."

"Did she, then? Well good, thank you, I will." She took the half of the loaf he had already stuffed with cheese and began making a hearty meal of it, while he tore open the other half and served it in the same fashion. "Well the warning I was to give you, if you passed the test, was that in order to get where you're going, you'll have to deal with Baba Yaga."

"Hmm. That's not good news," he replied, starting on his own half. "In fact, I have to say that is very bad news indeed. Of all the creatures in the world that I would rather not meet, she is high on the list."

"But she will have something you need if you are going to succeed." The witch shrugged. "The saints only know what that thing is, I certainly don't. It could be anything from a single pin to an elephant."

The mental image of Baba Yaga riding an elephant made him blink, and he shook his head to clear it. There was such a thing as having too vivid an imagination.

"A single pin is more like, but you never know," continued the witch.

"Anything else you can tell me?" he asked.

"Only that The Tradition is not happy about something that is north of here. Whatever it is, it's an irritant now, and if it stays there it will become deadly as well as dangerous and we will all find ourselves in rather a pickle. Now you know everything that I know."

He nodded. The witch was a very pleasant-faced, tall, thin woman of about late middle age. Unlike the illusion she had worn, she was not stoop-shouldered, nor were there more than a few streaks of white in her light brown hair. "In that case, may I give you a ride anywhere?"

She shook her head, and helped herself to his waterskin. "I live just off the road. I live in a rather nice, dry cave, actually. It's been used by the witches hereabouts for generations. It's warmer in winter and cooler in summer than any house I've ever had, and I never have to fix the roof. I share it with a bear."

"A bear!" His eyebrows rose. He saw no reason not to take her literally. "That's likely to keep you even safer than having a wolfhound!"

"And he is very pleasant company, when he hibernates, he is warmer in winter to curl up against than a dog, and in summer, he feeds himself. He is not a bear-man, but he is a Wise

Bear. We get along." She smiled. "Now, I wouldn't turn down another loaf if you happen to have one to spare."

"Even if I didn't, I'd give you my last one," he laughed. "But as it happens, I do." He dug out another of the loaves, tight-wrapped in dried, tallow-soaked kelp, and handed it to her. "I came prepared. I had no idea how many of you kind ladies I would meet—or even how many genuine beggars."

As he finished his meal, he was planning. Baba Yaga... She was the thing you frightened small children with, but she was one of the most deadly witches there was. The only thing that kept her from being a real menace to be hunted down by a Champion was that encounters with her were so infrequent, and took place only in the wilderness. And that she did as many good turns as she did vile things.

The trouble was she usually did the good turns to good little girls; he had never heard of her doing one for a young man.

Armed with the knowledge that he was about to encounter the dreaded witch Baba Yaga, he needed to change his plans.

If he was going to encounter Baba Yaga, the best thing he could do would be to look as if he wasn't worth a ransom.

Not that he had ever heard of Baba Yaga holding anyone for ransom. It wasn't as if she couldn't have anything she wanted. She wasn't bound by the conventions of "good" witches to use her powers unselfishly. She could be just as selfish as she liked. He'd heard tales that inside that weird hut of hers it was like a hundred palaces rolled into one.

But at bottom she was an evil old peasant woman with more grudges than a cur had fleas, and when an evil old peasant woman of that sort got her hands on a prosperous- looking young man…the results were generally less than pleasant for the young man.

"I don't suppose," he asked as he finished the last of his meal, "you'd be able to keep my horse?"

The cave-witch considered that for a moment. "I don't know why not. There's a side cave I could use for a stable. There's plenty of grazing. And if you aren't back by autumn—"

"If I am not back by autumn," he said a bit grimly, "then I am dead, and you had best think about using my horse to get yourself as far from whatever is brewing in the north as possible."

So he left his horse with his new friend, bundled his things on his back, and set off down the road. It wouldn't be the first time he'd traveled afoot. Even a Fortunate Fool can have accidents, though even accidents generally tended to be the sort that got him where he needed to be at the time he needed to be there. He didn't expect to be afoot for too long, anyway.

And he hadn't gotten more than a league down the road when it happened.

The road passed through an area of rocks, where the trees thinned out a bit. There was now open sky above him, rather than branches. The first thing he heard the moment he set foot on that stretch of road was a strange roaring sound. It was something like the wind in the trees—except that there was no wind. Then he heard a wild, high-pitched cackling that made the hair stand up on the back of his neck. It wasn't sane, that laugh. In fact, it was the laughter of someone who never had more than a nodding acquaintance with sanity.

But he kept going, pretending he hadn't heard, either, because he had decided that he was going to pretend to be a deaf-mute. He marched down the road, head high, foolish grin on his face as if he hadn't a care in the world.

He pretended not to know that the roaring, and the cackling, were approaching him from behind. He forced himself not to react as it drew nearer and nearer.

And then—

He found himself knocked flat on his face by a sudden burst of "wind" as the most improbable vehicle in the world shot down the road and skimmed just over the top of where his head had been the moment before.

The thing, and its driver, spun around in a tight circle and landed right in front of him as he picked himself up out of the dirt.

It was a giant grey mortar, the sort that apothecaries and herbalists—and witches—used to grind up ingredients in.

It looked as if it was made of stone, and the pestle somehow hung off the back of it, as if the witch was using it as a rudder. The mortar was fully large enough that it came up to the witch's waist, and she was not small.

As remarkable as the vehicle was, the rider was even more striking. She had wild, bright red hair, red eyes and skin of a pale green. Tusks protruded from beneath her withered lips, and her face had more wrinkles than an oak tree's bark. She wore at least three blouses, each a different clashing color, all layered on top of one another, all in various states of tattered, so that the colors of one showed through the holes of another. She had a kerchief tied loosely on her head, but not as a good, modest housewife would, so that none of her hair showed; no, the witch's bright red hair stuck out in every direction as if squirrels had been nesting in it. There was a black shawl about her shoulders, three more in different colors tied about her waist. It looked as if she had on as many skirts as she did blouses and for the same reason, because all three of them were torn and tattered. Her neck was hung with necklaces of bones, teeth, tiny skulls, and charms, and her arms were loaded with gold bracelets. She looked down at him out of those red eyes, and there was no more sanity there than you'd see in a goshawk. He scrambled to his feet, bowed, then stood before her, grinning foolishly.

"Don't you know better than to get in my way, fool!" she screeched. Her voice was as harsh as a screaming cat's.

He allowed puzzlement to creep over his face, though he never stopped smiling, and tilted his head to the side. Then he pointed to his ears and shook his head.

She spat into the dust. "Bah! Not only a simpleton, but a mute, too!" With a sour look, she flapped her hands, miming speech. He shook his head again. Then, thinking quickly, mimed wood-chopping, then rubbed his belly and looked at her entreatingly.

She growled and mimed shoveling, then eating, and pointed to him, then to herself.

He nodded eagerly.

"Hmph," she said, though she didn't seem as irritated as she had been a moment before. She made a gesture; he felt his eyes widen as the mortar began to grow, until it was more than wide enough for both of them. She pointed at the mortar, then at him, then pointed down beside herself.

So clearly she had just hired him to do her heavy labor, just as he had hoped she would.

Because if she had something that he needed, this was no bad way to find out what it was, and maybe even get hold of it. And if she thought him to be a simpleton, she would not set him any impossible tasks, such as sorting out three kinds of grain from a heap of several bushels worth.

Grinning foolishly again, he clambered inside the mortar.

She hardly waited until he was over the rim. With a shout from the witch, the mortar shot into the sky, tumbling him into the bottom of it. With difficulty, for the mortar was moving as swiftly and as violently as a tiny sailboat on a windy day and heavy seas, he got to his knees, clung to the stone sides of the thing, and peered over the edge.

They were so far above the trees that the birds were no more than specks, and the ground was shooting past at a rate that made him dizzy.

He closed his eyes and hung on for all he was worth, wondering if this time he had let himself in for far more than he could handle.

Away over the hills, a tiny paper bird shot across the sky, as swift as an arrow, swifter than a falcon. The spell that animated it had found a target and it was closing in fast.

Chapter 11

There were six girls in the Jinn's keeping now, and one of them was trying to kill the other five.

It wasn't the Wolf-girl, either. Katya got along perfectly well with *her*. She was clean, polite, a little shy, but just as determined to find a way out of this captivity as Katya was. More than that, she better understood the ramifications of this terrible desert than any of the rest of them.

No, the one that was trying to kill the rest of the girls was a Rusalka.

How and where the Jinn had gotten hold of her, Katya could not imagine. *Why* he had stolen her, she also had difficulty in understanding. This one was not a ghost; she was a true water spirit, which did make her something of a rarity, and indeed, did make her very, very magical.

But—

She was vicious. She had taken over the fountain as soon as

she was put down, and the first attempt at a friendly overture by the young sorceress was met with slashing talons. She drowned one of the Jinn's men the very first night; after that he made the garden off-limits to them, which was a mixed blessing, because even though it meant there were no more guards posted in the garden itself, it also meant that the Rusalka could do whatever she wanted there.

And what she wanted was to kill everything that wasn't her.

Now, she *was* a water spirit, and as such, Katya could probably control her. The trouble with that idea was that she did not want the Jinn to know she was that strong in magic. She wanted him to think her powers were very minor. If he tried to drain her, she wanted him to underestimate her ability to fight back. Part of her ability to disguise herself was an ability to mask part of her magic.

Katya had made several attempts at making friends without using magic, and they had all ended badly. The truth was, the creature was a stupid, vicious, violent *thing* in a beautiful young woman's body. There was nothing there to make friends with. There was nothing anyone sane would *want* to make friends with.

Katya was beginning to get worried though. The paper crane should come back at any moment, and she wasn't sure if it could find her in their room—

Worse, surely a brightly colored paper bird flitting down the hallway was bound to be noticed.

But the Rusalka had made the garden impossible for any of them to stay in.

As Katya was thinking just that, the Wolf-girl, Lyuba, dashed in wearing her Wolf form. She skidded to a stop and her shape writhed in a way that made Katya's eyes water, and instead of the Wolf, there was something halfway between Wolf and human on all fours in the middle of the room.

"Quick!" the thing snarled frantically. "Help! Yulya!"

Then she transformed back to the Wolf and dashed out, with Katya and Marina right on her heels.

Katya was expecting the worst, so when she spotted the Rusalka with both hands around Yulya's neck, trying to shove her under the water in the fountain, she was hardly surprised. Lyuba snarled and charged the evil creature; she slammed into the thing with her shoulder, but couldn't dislodge it. Marina flung herself at the Rusalka and tore at her hands, to no effect.

Katya weighed the alternatives all in a moment, closed her eyes, and then exerted her power over water creatures, closing her hand into a fist and concentrating on the Rusalka's throat.

The Rusalka choked and gasped, and let go of Yulya.

As the creature's hands went to its own throat, Marina and Klava ran in and pulled Yulya out of reach, and Lyuba slammed her shoulder into the thing a second time. *This* time she managed to knock it off balance and into the fountain. Katya released her hold on the thing, and the five of them retreated to their room.

Yulya's throat was bruised and she was gasping for breath, but there was fire in her eyes at last, and she looked ready to go back and take on the Rusalka.

"Don't even think about it," Katya warned, before she could gasp out anything. "Think back to all the fights you must have had with your sisters. Who got in trouble? The one who started it? Or the one who got caught hitting back?"

Yulya frowned, rubbing her neck. "She almost killed me," the swan maiden whispered hoarsely. "Surely the Jinn—"

"I think," Lyuba put in, speaking slowly, as she always did, "that the Jinn cares only for how many of us he has."

Katya nodded. "That was my thought." She held up a hand. "I have an idea. I have a trick in my pocket—and I just made that insane creature very angry with me. If the Jinn catches her in the act of attacking me, I do not think he will be lenient with her."

Klava blinked. "You mean to let her try to kill you?" Even Yulya stopped massaging her bruises to stare at Katya then.

"Only when the Jinn is there," Katya reminded them, and grimaced. "I'd rather not have a bruised neck myself, but she can hold me under the water all she likes and I won't drown."

They all gaped at her then. She listened as hard as she ever could for the telltale hum of the Jinn, and heard nothing. One corner of her mouth quirked up. "Oh yes. Water is the same as air to me. I'm not a bereginia. I'm the Sea King's youngest daughter."

After a moment of shock, they began to babble at her. She held up her hand for silence, and got it.

"I will tell you more, later. Right now, before that devil gets her wits about her, we need to arrange for the Jinn to get rid of her himself."

Sasha's eyes felt as if they were going to pop out of his head when he saw their destination.

He had *heard* about Baba Yaga's hut, of course. Who hadn't? But hearing about it and seeing it were two very different things. In tales it had sounded utterly absurd, laughable almost.

Take a small peasant hut, no larger than a single room.

Now attach two giant legs to the bottom of it, so that the hut was easily two stories tall when the legs stood up. And not just any legs. Giant chicken legs. Complete with feathered thighs.

Now take away the keyhole to the front door and replace it with a mouth full of teeth even a shark would be proud of.

Now, while the hut squats on the ground like a broody hen, surround it with a fence made of bones.

Describe it, and it sounds comical. But view it, and it is utterly terrifying. You shouldn't graft something that is living to something that is not. You shouldn't have a fence made of bones, with skulls as the decorations on the fence posts. Above all, you shouldn't have a house that exudes so much malevolence that you expect it to stand up, chase you down, and devour you. How much magic would it take to create a hut, a living thing, with giant chicken legs? What sort of demented soul would imagine it in the first place?

And then…the fence of bones. Plenty of them were human. Baba Yaga's victims were so common she *made a fence out of their bones*. The eye holes of the skulls glowed red, and they all turned to look at him as the mortar circled the house.

The hut had its back to the front gate. Baba Yaga waved her hand at it. "*Turn your back to the forest, your front to me,*" she called out.

The hut rose up on its legs and began to spin, emitting blood-curdling shrieks as it did so. It spun around thirty-three times before settling back down, with the door facing them.

He shivered. Baba Yaga noticed. And with a casual air that was as macabre as her hut, she patted him on the head like a dog. "You just be a good lad," she said absently, as she steered her mortar down for a landing in front of the hut. "You just be a good lad, do as you're told, and you won't end up in my fence."

He shuddered again. He had to remember that he wasn't supposed to be able to hear. He looked up at her, letting the fear in his eyes show in an exaggerated manner, and cringing. Again she patted his head, pointed to the fence and shook her head.

With a flexibility and spryness at odds with her apparent age, Baba Yaga sprang out of the mortar, leaving Sasha to follow. He clambered out, and followed her when she crooked her finger at him. "I'm calling you Ivan," she told him, as they went around the bone fence to a stable and yard behind the hut. "All my menservants are called Ivan. It saves time, I don't have to try remember their names."

Sasha could only grin foolishly; as a deaf-mute, it wouldn't matter to him what she called him. She waved him over as she flung open the stable doors, then pointed at him and into the stable. "Here're your charges, and they haven't had their stalls clean in a long time." Before Sasha could look into the shadows there and make out what "they" were, she continued with mime, making shoveling motions, pointing at him, then into the stable, then making eating motions. "Muck out the stalls first, eat second."

He nodded his understanding vigorously, until his hair flopped into his eyes and he had to push it back with both hands.

She trotted away toward her chicken-legged hut, chortling. The hut stood up and a ladder dropped down from underneath.

The witch scrambled up it as nimbly as a ferret; the ladder was pulled up and the hut remained standing. But it turned so that the door was facing him.

It didn't have eyes…but it felt as if it was staring at him.

With a shudder, he turned and went quickly into the stable.

Out of "sight" of the malevolent hut, he waited for his eyes to adjust to the darkness of the stable. His nose, however, told him that the witch had not been exaggerating. It had been a long time since these stalls were last cleaned out. The smell of dung and urine was thick enough to gag a fly. Quickly, he walked across the stable to the opposite door and flung it open, and a stiff breeze blew through as if conjured, carrying the worst of the stench away.

And not everything in here was a horse. The sharp smell of predator droppings added a pungency to the overriding stink that was quite unmistakable.

He pitied the poor animals closed up in here without ever coming into the light—since clearly Baba Yaga did not put them out in the yard by day.

Well, he might as well make a start.

Behind him, leaning against the wall, he found a shovel and a manure fork, and before he began, he paused for a moment. To his right, he heard shuffling, growling, and grunting; to his left, sighing. Face the dangerous side first?

Well, a deaf-mute wouldn't hear any of that.

All right, then, he thought, steeled himself, and went to the right.

The first two stalls were empty. The second contained the largest Wolf he had ever seen in his life. A great, grey, grizzled thing, it was so large that it could easily look him straight in the eyes without trying. It was obviously a Wise Beast, able to reason and communicate.

It did just that, looking over its shoulder, yellow eyes narrowing in speculation. "So," the Wolf said, red tongue lolling out, "the old crone sends my dinner in alive now, does she?" It flattened its ears back along its skull and grinned at him rapaciously.

"I think, sir," said Sasha carefully, giving up his pretense and hoping they wouldn't tell the Baba, "that eating me would be a mistake. You might upset the witch who hired me to clean her stables, you would certainly upset my betrothed, who is the Sea King's daughter, and you would still be standing in filth when you were done eating me."

The Wolf tilted his head to the side, ears going up. "Good arguments, all of them," he admitted. "Very well, I will not eat you."

"If you don't mind, I should like to move you while I clean your home," Sasha replied, making a little gesture toward the chain holding the wolf to the watering trough, which had a scum of green algae in one corner.

The Wolf yawned hugely, showing white teeth as long as Sasha's fingers. "It is all one to me," said the Wolf. "Until the old witch needs me to track down an enemy and turns me loose, one place in this stable is much like another. I am bound to her with the enchantment on the collar."

Sasha moved into the stall, bowed once to the Wolf as if to a boyar, then unchained the beast. Its shoulders were on a level with his, and it was easily big enough to ride, if it would allow such a thing.

"If you are hungry, I have some bread," Sasha said, as he led the Wolf to the next stall.

"Bread! It is long since I tasted bread! Yes, I will have some," the Wolf replied, its ears up, and its tail wagging ever so slightly. Sasha went to get one of his remaining loaves of bread from his belongings, and also fetched a pail of clean, cold water from the well.

"Here you are, my lord Wolf," Sasha said, unwrapping the bread for him and putting down the water. "I shall have your home cleaned in as little time as may be."

Big as he was, fierce as he was, the Wolf began nibbling daintily at the loaf. "A kindly woman baked this bread, and she thought well of you," he said, yellow eyes softening and losing some of their fierceness.

Sasha said nothing, only went to work with shovel and fork and barrow to clean out the stall, then returned with armfuls of sweet straw mixed with rushes to make a thick bed. There were some bones that he thought were not human, stacked ready to repair the fence perhaps. He took some of them and left them in one corner for the Wolf to chew on to ease its boredom, then filled the clean stone watering trough with sweet water. He returned to the Wolf, mane comb and brushes he had found in hand.

"If you don't mind, sir, I think it is long since you had a brushing," he said diffidently.

The Wolf looked at him down its long nose. "I think that you are right," it replied, "and I would not say you nay."

So before he returned the Wolf to its stall and chained it up again, he worked hard with brush and comb until the Wolf's pelt was as soft and shining as a lady's lapdog, and free of clumps of winter's underfur. He then took a broom and swept all the fur out the door for the birds to take to line their nests.

That was all that there was on the right-hand side of the stables, but Sasha cleaned up the stalls anyway, and moved in fresh bedding. Then he went to the left-hand side.

Once again, the first stall was empty, but the second contained the biggest black he-goat that Sasha had ever seen in his life; it was easily the size of a warhorse. Sasha bowed to it, as to a boyar, while it looked at him down its long nose.

"If you don't mind, sir, I would like to move you while I clean your home," Sasha said to it. The he-goat shook his massive head till his ears rattled against his huge, curved, and cruelly pointed horns, and looked at Sasha sideways out of his big golden eyes with their bean-shaped pupils.

"Well, it's all one to me," the wise Goat said. "I'm doing nothing here until the witch decides to hunt something and saddles me for riding." And Sasha looked at the side of the stall and saw a proper-sized saddle of bronze and a bridle of gold.

He untied the Goat and led him to the next stall, then asked, "Would you like some bread to eat while I clean your home?"

"Bread!" the Goat exclaimed, and his eyes grew greedy. "It is a long time since I had any bread!"

"Then I am happy to share mine," said Sasha, who got another loaf from his belongings. He brought it and a bucket of cold, sweet water for the Goat, then set about cleaning the stall thoroughly. As with the Wolf, he then brushed and combed the Goat until the beast's long hair was soft and silky again, as lovely as a maiden's hair, and free of all the knots that had been in it.

"You've done me good turns, young man," the Goat said as Sasha returned him to his stall, now deep with clean straw and rushes, the manger full of hay, the bucket full of grain, the trough full of pure water. "I won't forget them."

Sasha moved on to the final stall, at the end of the stable, in a melancholy corner where very little light penetrated. He could see something small moving about in the darkest part of the stall, but couldn't make out what it was.

"Hello?" he said, tentatively. "I'm here to clean your home."

There was a huge sigh from the darkness, the same one he had heard when he'd come in through the door. "It's not my home," said a sad voice. "And I don't know that it makes any difference. When you're done here, she'll eat you and add your bones to the fence and my stall will just get dirty all over again."

"That's no way to think!" Sasha said sharply, and came into the stall. And to his amazement, as his eyes got used to the deeper shadow, he *knew* the creature that was in there. It was as small as a child's pony, as small as a donkey, with ears a yard long and two humps on its back. Its coal-black eyes were dull with depression, its coat unkempt and dusty, so that nothing of the original color could be seen.

"Sergei!" he exclaimed, gazing with astonishment at the Little Humpback Horse. "But—how did *you* end up here?"

He had never seen the Horse himself, but he had heard the tale often enough of how his grandfather jad won Sergei and his two handsome brothers from their mother, the Mare of the North Wind. The Horse raised his head sorrowfully and looked at him. "Do I know you?" it said wearily.

"My grandfather made a bargain with the Mare of the North

Wind for your services," said Sasha. "But I thought that a Godmother—"

"Oh it is my own stupid fault," Sergei replied, dropping his head down to his knees again. "That wretched witch lured me with apples from the Garden of Solomon and acorns from the oak where the Katschei used to keep his heart. If I hadn't been so greedy, I wouldn't be here now. She has me well and truly trapped and even Godmother Elena couldn't find me and free me."

Sasha bent down and lifted up one of Sergei's long ears to whisper into it. "I am the Seventh Son, a Songweaver, and a Fortunate Fool, and I will get you out of here. As my grandfather took your service, I will release you from your bondage."

Slowly Sergei's head came up. Light came back into his eyes, and he gazed at Sasha with renewed hope. "You would do this for me?" he asked.

"As ever I can," Sasha replied. "For now, let us get your stall clean and made fit for you, and I will give you bread to eat while you wait."

Sasha went and fetched the last loaf of bread. He redoubled his efforts on Sergei's filthy stall, cleaning until it sparkled, then returned Sergei to a much more comfortable place. Sergei looked at the now clean stall, the thick bed of straw, the filled manger and bucket and water trough, and two tears rolled out of his eyes and down his cheeks. "It has been so long since anyone cared for me," he said softly.

"Well now someone does," Sasha replied, and proceeded to brush and comb the Little Humpback Horse until the dark grey coat shone like the tsar's favorite steed on parade.

"She has me bound with a spell," said Sergei. "She plays it

on that flute thing." And he nodded at a peculiar instrument hanging on the wall beside the stall.

And at that, Sasha smiled. *A musical spell, hmm?*

Fortune was favoring her Fool.

If this goes wrong, Sasha is going to kill me, Katya thought, as she lurked in a still-overgrown corner of the garden, just out of sight of the fountain where the Rusalka was sulking. Then again, if this went wrong, Sasha wouldn't have to kill her....

She was waiting for the moment when she felt the Jinn appear, and hopefully she would even see him when he did. Then she would go down to the fountain and let the Rusalka attack her. Even if the Jinn didn't see the attack, he should sense the small magic she would use to help to cover her ability to breathe water. Since he had already reacted poorly to her use of magic once, that should bring him, and then he *would* see the attack.

She fingered the high, uncomfortable gold collar she was wearing. She and the others had found it rummaging through the jewelry the Katschei had accumulated. Hopefully it would be enough to protect her neck and make the Rusalka switch from trying to choke her to trying to drown her.

There were a lot of things depending on hope, here. But then again, this Jinn was like a grain of sand in an oyster shell. The Tradition didn't want him there, and was secreting layer after layer of magic to try to be rid of him. If she could only tap into that, her schemes would go much smoother.

Her head went up as she sensed the Jinn.

The hum was faint and far off, but growing nearer. She only wished she could tell what direction he was coming from.

The hum grew louder. Nearer now…

She looked about from under cover of the trees she was hiding among. No sight of him on the battlements. He might be somewhere inside the building.

Or not. The hum was still approaching.

Then it stopped moving. She looked around again, but still couldn't see him. She was just going to have to take her chances.

Taking a deep breath, she walked out into the garden, the sun hitting her like a hammer, taking the path that was going to put her walking right past the fountain, as if she had forgotten that the Rusalka was there. And it took everything she had to pretend that she was focusing on something else, something off to the other side of the garden and not on the fountain.

There was no sign of the Rusalka, but then, there wouldn't be. The evil bitch was hiding under the water, waiting. She'd spring out at the last moment….

Katya drew even with the raised basin of the fountain. Went a little past—reached about the middle.

With a shriek of pure rage, the Rusalka erupted from the fountain and seized her neck.

Katya didn't have to feign a scream; even though she was expecting the attack, the Rusalka surprised her. She felt the strong hands closing around her neck, heard the Rusalka's grunt of surprise as her hands encountered the collar. Meanwhile Katya was fighting back, kicking and scratching, pulling hair. The goal, after all, was certainly not to appear passive! As she scored the Rusalka's face with her nails, the creature shrieked again, and with a sideways twist of her body, flung them both into the fountain with a tremendous splash. The water cushioned their fall, but the stone coping around the basin hit Katya in the leg so hard she knew it was going to leave a black-and-blue mark the size of her own head, and her head bounced off the bottom of the fountain hard enough to leave a lump. For a moment, they floated together in the water; it was a very deep fountain, quite deep enough even for a water creature like the Rusalka to swim in comfortably. Katya had both hands full of hair now and was pulling as hard as she could, all the while kicking viciously at the Rusalka's legs. But the Rusalka was in her element now, and got her flipped over, and the next thing she knew, Katya was face down in the fountain with the Rusalka kneeling on her back, and the Rusalka's hands pushing her head down.

Now, of course, her native ability to breathe water came into play. But now was the time when she worked that little bit of magic....

She went limp. And though she was breathing just fine, it would appear to anyone else that she had lost consciousness at best, and had drowned at worst.

Now as long as the Rusalka didn't think to unlock that collar and start choking her just to make sure—

The weight was suddenly taken from her back, and she floated to the surface.

There were hands all over her, and as her head broke water, she heard her fellow captives shrieking in a quite convincing manner as they pulled her from the fountain and down onto the gravel path. While the others interposed themselves to keep the Jinn from seeing exactly what was happening, practical Marina turned her over and began pounding her back.

That was her signal to cough, wheeze, and gag, as if she were expelling water from her lungs.

"Katya!" Marina cried, "you're alive!"

The others kept screaming, though—which was not what she had told them to do. And there was a roaring sound, and more heat than was coming from the sun. And a very odd, burning smell.

She rolled over onto her side, wanting to see what the Jinn was doing.

He was incoherent with rage. A circle of fire flared around him, and at least one set of shrieks was screams of pain, because they belonged to the Rusalka. The Jinn's hands were burning her arms where he held her, feet dangling, well off the ground.

Not a word did he speak. He only held her, looked into her eyes, and laughed cruelly.

"I told you there would be peace!" the brazen voice boomed. *"I told you that you would not touch the other captives! Now you pay the price of disobedience!"*

Then he burst into flame, exactly as if someone had soaked him in oil and lit him.

She hung in his hands, on fire as he was, but alas for the Rusalka, she was not immune to his flames. Katya and the others watched in horror as she screamed and screamed, as the scent—not of burning flesh, but of burning water weed—filled the air. They watched as she stopped screaming, but still writhed in his hands, watched as she finally stopped moving, and then watched as, with a burst of white-hot fire, the last of her corpse was consumed and the pitiful caricature of a husk crumbled into ash in the Jinn's hands, and the ashes rained down as a pile at his feet.

The fires abruptly vanished, as if they had been sucked into him.

He turned, slowly, and stared at them all, as they sat there, struck dumb. His eyes blazed still, burning like twin suns in his head.

"You will obey me when I give an order," he said.

They all nodded, numbly.

"Go to your room."

They fled, Katya being half carried between Marina and Lyuba, her legs rubbery with a weakness she did not have to feign.

The little paper crane had found what it had been sent to find. There was only one small problem. How to get the two Champions' attention? They were very large....

Chapter

12

Sasha waited patiently beside the door to the stable, arms crossed, leaning his back against the wall. The newly cleaned shovel, fork, and barrow stood beside him. The stable was now lit by two cleaned and filled oil lamps. There was not the slightest trace of stink about the place. The only aromas in the air were the smell of fresh straw, the scent of fresh-cut rushes, and the sharpness of the bunches of fleabane he had hung in each stall.

Wonderful smells were coming from the witch's hut; baking bread, roasting meat, the sweet smell of little tea cakes, all wafted from the chimney. Sasha reminded himself over and over, even as his stomach growled, that he should not get his hopes up, however good the food smelled. Now, it was possible that Baba Yaga might feed him well, give him the hospitality her bargain entitled him to....

Or she might treat him as she had treated the creatures in the stable. And truth be told, if she did the latter, it would be better for him. The Tradition would treat that as her breaking her bargain with him, which would leave him free to do what he was going to do anyway. There would be no repercussions if she was the first to be the one to break the deal. And that would be good.

Because he was going to free Sergei, and he would need every bit of his Luck and The Tradition on his side to do that.

And maybe, just maybe, the bread he had given the Goat and the Wolf would free them as well. By accepting his bread and the tiny bit of salt he had sprinkled on it, Traditionally speaking, they had accepted him as, not master, but liege. If they chose to. That was the key. If they had accepted him in their own minds, deliberately, then once the witch released them from their physical bonds…

But that was something he would not know, and could not know, until the moment they chose to act. If, in fact, they would.

The Goat, at least, had implied as much. But the Wolf?

The Wolf was the unknown.

And the Wolf was the most dangerous to his plans.

For the first time since he had started this quest, he had leisure and was able to think about the reason for his search. His heart filled with longing and just a touch of fear. Katya… Where was she? Was she safe? Or if not safe, at least in no immediate danger?

Or if not that…

She is brave, competent, clever. She will likely only need a little help from me, or none at all. I only hope when we finally meet, she isn't angry at me for coming after her. He tried very hard to convince himself of that. Tried to believe that the reason she had not returned, had not sent word, was that she was safe and secure, but in hiding and dared not break her secret cover. He tried to think about her as he had last seen her, plunging into the sea, ready to race to discover what it was her father needed her to do, full of high courage, and wit, and intelligence. But all he could really think about was Katya in his bed, sweet and fierce and...

And he needed to stop thinking about that right now. Because the rising in his groin was not going to be easily explained if the witch came out right now....

Suddenly the hut spun around to face him, and all amorous thoughts vanished in the baleful glare of those windows.

The hut squatted down, and Baba Yaga emerged, this time from the front door. If anything, she was even stranger to look at than he had thought. He hadn't noticed her hunched back in the mortar. And somehow, the fact that her nose was so long it almost touched her chin hadn't made much of an impression on him, either.

Or maybe it was possible she could change how she looked, and this even more grotesque face was her true one.

She scuttled up to him, and looked him up and down. He'd cleaned himself up, so he was fairly presentable. He gave the old witch a respectful bow, and she replied with a sneer, and stalked into the stable.

She emerged only a few moments later, with an interesting look on her face. Surprise, mingled with smugness and self-congratulation.

Oh ho. She thinks she has gotten herself a bargain. Which means, I think, that she is about to cheat me.

He presented her with a look of pure grinning idiocy. She mimed him following her to the hut.

He lost the grin. He shook his head vigorously, and looked at the door of the hut with exaggerated fear.

Or maybe not so exaggerated. He really did not want to go in that hut. Once he was in there, he was truly in the lion's den.

She looked at him with impatience.

Then, unexpectedly, her hand shot out as fast as thought, and she seized him by the ear like any babushka with a naughty grandchild!

It was all he could do to avoid yelling something coherent. Her grip on his ear was as tight as a vise and painful. As she hauled him, stumbling, towards the hut, he gave voice to his feelings in a series of animal moans. Deaf-mutes could do that, he'd heard them. And he didn't strike at her, much though he wanted to. But he did flail his arms wildly for balance, something that the old hag seemed to find very amusing, for she began chuckling.

She pulled him in through the front door—which, recognizing its mistress, did not devour them.

Once through, she let loose of his ear. Jumping away from her, he stood just out of reach, rubbing his sore ear and looking around with unfeigned wonder and no small amount of apprehension.

Outside, it was a tiny peasant hut. Inside, it was the biggest room he had ever seen in his life.

It seemed to stretch on in every direction forever. The ceiling was certainly a good five stories above them. But it was hard to tell where the walls were, because there were trees growing up through the floor, making this a forested room, if there was such a thing.

It was very brightly lit, with what must have been hundreds of lanterns hanging from the tree branches. And beneath those lanterns were enormous piles of…well…everything.

Within arm's reach of where he stood, he could have picked up a chunk of raw amber from a pile of the same about as high as his shoulders, a sable skin from a huge pile of furs the size of the bed he and Katya had shared, an iron cooking pot of virtually any size from stacks of pots, or a ball of yarn of just about any color out of one of a pyramid of baskets brimming with yarn. There were similar stacks and piles and heaps of anything he could think of in every direction, with little paths between them. There had once been a crazy old noblewoman living in the palace who had never, ever, in all her life, thrown anything out. When she'd died and the servants had gone into her room, this was what it looked like. Or rather, this is what it would have looked like if she had been able to magpie everything she wanted for a thousand years.

And he didn't touch *any* of it. In fact, he tucked both his hands behind him like a little boy who had been instructed *not* to touch.

He looked at her, anxiously. She chuckled, and crooked a finger at him.

He followed her as she scuttled down one of the paths beneath the trees, weaving in and out through piles of things that were, some of them, taller than his head. There were unset gems next to piles of wheat, barley, or rye. There were sacks of flour next to bars of silver. There were gold coins beside piles of turnips. She led him to a spot where there was a little wooden table, exactly the sort of thing you would expect in a peasant hut, with a stool beside it, and a wooden bowl, cup, and spoon on top of it. In the bowl, despite all of the appetizing aromas that had come from the kitchen, was borscht. He sat down at the table at her direction, looked up at her and at her nod, picked up his spoon and dipped into it.

Borscht indeed. And not even very good borscht, either. If this soup had more than a nodding acquaintance from all the way across the kitchen with any sort of meat, he would be very surprised. It was mostly beets and cabbage, the cabbage cooked until it was transparent, with a few lonely bits of carrot and turnip floating like sad little trading ships caught forever in the ominous red of the Cabbage Sargasso Sea.

In the cup, thin, sour kvass, poorly made, poorly brewed, the drink of choice when your only other choice was swamp water.

There was not even any bread, that staple of diet, the very essence of hospitality and goodwill, that thing that no meal was complete without, from the tables of the kings to the hovels of the peasants. There was always bread; when there was nothing else, there was bread. It was the wealth of the land, the life of the people.

She had given him no bread. And there was no salt in the borscht. She had accepted his bargain and withheld her hospitality and her protection.

He had worked honestly and hard for her. He had done more, far more, than she'd asked. The stable was clean enough that a tsar would approve. Entire families would have been willing to move in there. And she had seen how hard he had worked—and this was how she had repaid him.

He felt the pressure of The Tradition looming over him. And he did something he had never, ever done in all of his life.

Wordlessly, as he spooned up the tasteless soup, he asked it, *Is my bargain broken? Can I free her beasts? Can I rescue Sergei?*

He did not get an answer in words, but the pressure lifted off, and he sensed currents moving and a kind of vague *yesness* settle over him.

She waited impatiently for him to finish. He looked up at her face, just beginning to scowl, and quickly drank up the last of the soup, using it to wash down the bitter kvass. She crooked a finger at him, and he jumped up and obediently followed her out through the piles to the door, then out into the open yard.

It was very late evening; already the stars were out, and the moon was just rising. She pointed at the stable and mimed sleeping. Well that was pretty much as he had expected. And really, the last thing he wanted was to be sleeping under the same roof as that hag. The saints only knew what she would do to him in the night.

Obediently he trotted out to the stable and bedded down in the stall next to Sergei's, using a pile of hay for a pillow and an old horse blanket for a coverlet.

But then—he heard her shuffling footsteps as she entered the stable herself.

He curled up in a tight ball like a hedgehog, and feigned sleep. He heard her go off to the right first.

"Wolf, Wolf," he heard her say, "am I your master?"

He heard the Wolf growl then, and reply, "As long as I only eat flesh slain in anger, you are my master."

She gave a grunt of satisfaction, and this seemed to be the answer she was looking for, but his heart leaped, because the Wolf himself had told him earlier that he had, inadvertently, freed it! It had eaten bread, his bread, the bread baked in kindness by a woman who thought well of him—

He heard her shuffling over to the left, and heard her pause at the stall of the Goat. "Goat, Goat," she grated, "am I your master?"

The Goat gave a derisive baa. "As long as I only eat that which was harvested in despair, you are my master," the He-Goat replied sarcastically. And Sasha had to wince at that, because of what that implied about the grain, the hay, and the straw that Baba Yaga had provided for her slaves. The saints knew that the life of a peasant farmer was hard...but there were lords who made those lives harder still. When a peasant was not merely a peasant, but a serf or a slave...every grain, every blade of grass, every stalk was grown in despair...it would be easy enough for the witch to supply a hundred stables with such provender.

But Led Belarus was not such a kingdom...and the bread had been made with hope and happiness, not despair.

She shuffled over another few feet. He not only heard her stop at the door of the stall he was "sleeping" in, he practically felt her eyes boring into him.

He wriggled a little and tucked his head down farther, putting his arm over the top of it.

Satisfied, she moved on.

"No bargain would hold you, now, would it, my slippery little devil?" she chuckled. "And few spells. A pity I am the master of most spells, eh?"

He heard her take the odd flute down from the wall, and then she started to play.

He concentrated as hard as he could. It was a strange little tune, no more than five notes, and oddly minor. It had, he guessed, nine bars to it, and she repeated it nine times. By the third time he knew he had it memorized, but he still concentrated on it as hard as he could. He wanted, he *needed* to have every note exactly right.

The witch shuffled out again, pausing to hang the flute back up on the wall.

Sasha waited a long time, waited for the sounds outside to settle, waited to make sure the witch wasn't coming back out.

Only then did he whisper to Sergei, "Has she gone to bed?"

"Oh yes," the Little Humpback Horse said. "She won't awaken until dawn. And since she has you to do the work of tending us, not then. What did she feed you?"

"Sour kvass, and a bowl of bad borscht with no salt. No bread."

Sergei sighed. "That's good on two counts. She's not fattening you up to eat yet, and she hasn't bound you to her will."

"Three counts. She broke our bargain. She may have hired me, but she's gone back on it by not giving me bread and salt and not feeding me properly." He chuckled. "Now I can do what I want because she's the one who broke the bargain."

"Oh! I hadn't thought of that!" Sergei exclaimed. "But—"

"You just let me take care of a little something. Tomorrow you and I and Wolf and Goat will be free." He knew he wouldn't need to raise his voice for the others to hear him, and he was right.

"We're still bound by the rope and chain," the Wolf pointed out. "Those are still enchanted. We can't leave the stable unless she takes them off with her own hands."

"Oh she will," Sasha chuckled. "She will. Now, I'm going out into the woods to see what can be done about Sergei's spell."

He had never seen a flute that looked like this one, and he had certainly never heard a flute that played the notes this one did. The scale sounded all wrong to his ears—a series of pensive, breathy notes in a minor key. He didn't want to play it around the stable or around Sergei for a couple of very good reasons. He didn't want to be so close to the hut that there might be a chance that the witch would hear him playing. And he didn't want to be near Sergei on the chance that something he played might have bad consequences when crossed with the spell that was already on the Little Humpback Horse.

That would be bad. Very bad.

So he picked his way across the yard until he came to a path into the woods. He had the feeling that there would be at least one good path, if only to a pond or a stream, or a place where the witch could cut her firewood.

And so it proved. There was indeed a pond, and from the looks of it, a good deep one. As he neared the verge, he heard ducks quacking quietly in their sleep, and smiled. Good. They would give him the alert if anything crept up on him.

He sat down on a tree trunk, put the flute to his lips, and blew, very carefully. There were stories of instruments like this that screamed or shrieked if anyone but the owner tried to play them.

But not this time.

The first note sounded out, breathy, but true, low and tremulous.

He ran the scales, slowly, getting used to the progression of notes, of where his fingers had to go for what. It was a deceptively simple instrument. He found he could get half and even quarter tones out of it if he was clever. But the witch had not been a musician, and she had stuck with the simple tune of the song.

So now he practiced it, although he took care to break it before he got to the ninth repetition, inserting some other little ditty. And when he was certain he could play it in his sleep and backwards—

Then that was what he did. He played it backwards.

He had had an odd feeling about that music when he had heard it. It had seemed to him that this spell was powerful—but simple. Baba Yaga had never been known to be any kind of a musician. He suspected that any spell that she cast by means of music would *have* to be simple.

So it followed—

It followed that the power was in the magic that Baba Yaga controlled. But the spell itself should be easy to undo. She was familiar with the use of her own power. She was unfamiliar with music. If he played the same music backward…he should be able to unravel the spell.

It was rather like knitting. It took a great deal of time and skill to knit up a garment. But it only took one snip of a scissors and it was easy to unravel, and took little time and effort at all.

And certainly no skill.

When he thought he was ready, it was very nearly dawn. The sky was beginning to go grey in the east, and he didn't want to take the chance that the witch might decide to wake up early and kick the deaf-mute awake before going back to her bed.

He returned to the stables.

"Now this is what we are going to do," he told them all. "I am going to try to break the spell on Sergei. If I succeed, he and I will escape—"

"What about us?" the Goat asked suspiciously. But the Wolf was already laughing.

"Brilliant!" the Wolf chuckled. "How long before I raise the alarm?"

"As long as you think you can get away with and not be punished," Sasha told him honestly. "At least give us as much of a head start as you can."

"Oho!" the Goat exclaimed, his ears coming up. "With us raising the alarm, she won't suspect *us!* And the hunt will be on! She will loose the Wolf to track and loose me to ride!"

"And you can be rid of her however you choose once you are set on the track." Sasha nodded. "If I were you, Goat, I would wait until you were a good long distance from here. I don't think she can summon that mortar to her, so the longer her walk, the more time *you* will have to make your own escapes."

The Goat nodded. "Best get on with it, Prince. Your luck may not hold forever."

That was very good advice indeed, and he set about implementing it. "If you know any ways of helping this work, I suggest you start doing them now," he said, and began to play.

He narrowed down his concentration to get each note exactly right, to keep track of exactly how many times he had played through the reverse tune. This had to be perfect. He might not get another chance.

He finished the last note.

And the flute shattered in his hands.

There was a muffled sound. He looked up to see Sergei's long ears clamped over his mouth to keep his laughter from escaping as he danced around for joy. The rope holding him had disintegrated into fibers and he was free.

The Goat was dancing in place, too, and the Wolf was laughing silently, tongue lolling.

"Go!" said the Goat, shaking his horns. "We'll give you as much of a head start as we dare."

It might have seemed like a waste of time to gather up his belongings before he flung himself on Sergei's bare back. But he didn't dare leave anything for Baba Yaga to use to bring him back, or even worse, somehow get to Katya.

But with his pack on his back, his legs tucked up, because otherwise they would drag on the ground, and bent over Sergei's neck, they tiptoed past the hut. Despite that both of them were afire to flee, this of all times was the moment to take care.

The hut did not appear to notice as they passed, and remained standing on one of its legs like a slumbering chicken. Then they were out of sight, and they ran like the wind itself, careening down forest paths only Sergei seemed able to see.

"Can't you fly?" Sasha shouted, for now that they were well away from the hut, Sergei was going for speed and his little hooves were hitting the ground so fast it sounded like continuous rolling thunder.

"She has a host of spirits that serve her, and serve her well," Sergei shouted back. "I dare not fly, they will be on us in an instant."

Well, then they would just have to run.

The only trouble was…they suddenly ran out of forest.

Sergei burst through the trees and skidded to a halt, as he realized that they were on the side of a mountain, and were now above the tree line. They had been running so fast, and so hard, that neither Sasha nor Sergei had realized they were gradually climbing the shallow slope of a very large mountain indeed. And before they could turn and run back under the cover of the trees—

It was too late.

The horde of spirits bound to Baba Yaga, who must have been following them above the trees, descended on them.

Sergei gave a little buck and Sasha tumbled to the ground. "Go!" Sergei shouted. "Run! Hide! It's me they're after!"

And before the spirits—the ugly tattered ghosts of the evil dead—actually reached them, Sergei shot off into the sky. "Try and catch me, boneless, bloodless rags! Servants of a feeble old witless hag! You couldn't catch a sneeze, much less me!"

The horde sped off into the sky after Sergei. Only a few hesitated. And while they were hesitating, Sasha bolted.

He had no clear idea where to run to—and a moment later he tripped, fell over, and began a headlong tumble down the steep slope of a ravine he hadn't even seen before he fell into it.

All he could do was curl up as tight as he could get, and hope he didn't hit anything lethal—

At least the three tattered ghosts kept missing him as they darted at him, claw-like talons extended to shred him into rags.

It was one bruising impact after another. He gritted his teeth and endured the punishment, trying to keep his head tucked in and out of danger. And it was nausea-inducing dizziness too; even if he did come to a stop rather than hurtling down a hole, would he be able to stand up and stagger off before the spirits got him?

And then, with a bone-jarring *thud*, his back hit something solid enough to stop the tumble and knock the wind out of him for good measure. For several moments after he uncurled he was too busy thinking about trying to get a breath back into his lungs and to make the world stop spinning around him to worry about ghosts or much of anything else.

When he finally did gasp a lungful of air, it was cool and damp. And he realized that he had rolled into a cave.

And the spirits hadn't followed him.

Which might have been because there were about half a dozen copper-armored, green-faced fighters around him. Half of them had their weapons—their *glowing* weapons—pointed at the cave mouth.

The other half had identical weapons—a sword, a spear, and a crossbow—pointed at him.

The little paper bird had fluttered about in frustration for far too long. It didn't exactly have a mind to think with, but it did have a purpose, and that purpose was to be read.

It had tried every means it had to be noticed, and it was always dismissed as a leaf, or a bit of debris. It seemed there was no way to make these Champions pay attention!

Except—

Now one of them had pulled out an enormous book, and was opening it! The Champion was going to read something!

But not before it read the paper bird!

Swift as a thought, the bird dove for the book, plastered itself against the page, and unfolded before the Champion's astonished eyes.

Chapter 13

Sasha was just about dead on his feet; a night of no sleep, coupled with the frantic race for freedom and ending with the tumble down the ravine had pretty much put paid to the last of his energy. He kept stumbling over unseen lumps in the tunnel floor, and more and more often, ended up falling to his knees. His legs felt as if they were made of lead, and soft lead at that, and he thought that at this point he must have been walking down these tunnels for leagues and leagues. It certainly seemed like leagues and leagues.

And oh, how he hurt. He thought that surely if he took off his shirt, he would find that his entire body was nothing more than one enormous bruise that extended from neck to ankles. The number of lumps on his head did not bear thinking about.

And he was starving. And thirsty. One little cup of kvass and a single bowl of watery borscht was not much to sustain someone for a day and a night.

It seemed that his Luck finally had run out.

But if Sergei wasn't caught—he knew a Godmother. Surely Sergei would go to her and try to get help!

Except that Sergei didn't know he was in trouble. And even if he knew, he wouldn't know where to look for the one who had freed him.

This was just…grand.

Just grand.

He stumbled and fell to his knees again, and this time he just fell over and then lay there on his back, on the cold stone, eyes closed. He couldn't find it in himself to care. "I don't know who or what you are," he said into the silence, "but I am too tired to go any further. So as far as I am concerned, you can just—"

There was the *twang* of a crossbow followed immediately by a strange tickling between his legs.

He opened his eyes. A crossbow bolt, head embedded completely in the stone, was sticking up between his legs. It had passed so close to his apparatus that the tickling sensation he had felt was the still-vibrating shaft brushing the cloth of the crotch of his trews.

Miraculously, he found himself on his feet again.

But finally, the tunnel opened up into a vast cave, which seemed to be the end of their journey, for his six guards stopped, and he simply dropped where he stood, kneeling exhausted on the floor. This time no one prodded him to get to his feet.

In the center point of the roof of the cave was a huge chandelier. It glittered and sparkled with thousands upon thousands of quartz crystals, strung like beads, and looped about it like so many frozen flower garlands. They gathered the light and reflected it out into the room, filling it with a dancing inter-play of light and shadow.

It didn't take him long to realize that this was an audience chamber. It was fairly empty of furnishings, and entirely empty of people except for himself and his guards, but it certainly was nothing like a room where you would take prisoners. You didn't take a prisoner to a room with a chandelier, as a rule.

At the far end was a single throne, a simple and graceful piece of flowing lines that echoed the stone of which it was made: malachite. He had never seen a single piece of malachite that large before, never seen carving of that level of expertise before. Behind the throne was a tapestry in which every stitch held a bead, so that the tapestry too glittered in the light. And the subject was the portrait of a mountain, presumably the same one he was now inside. The lower slopes were a kaleidoscope of verdant greens, the upper third, a misty blue. There was no snow on this mountain; it was held in this tapestry in an eternal spring and summer.

The throne, the tapestry, the huge and empty room. Now, it occurred to him that maybe his Luck hadn't run out after all. Whoever was in charge here could have had him thrown straightaway into a cell in a dungeon. Instead, he'd been hauled into the audience chamber.

Someone wanted to see him. Someone wanted to be seen by him. Either. Both, perhaps.

This was a room that dwarfed the inhabitants, but he got the sense this was accidental, that an existing cave had been used rather than a new room had been cut from the rock for the purposes of cowing visitors—or prisoners. On the far side of the room there was another tunnel entrance. He wondered where that one went. How many people lived here? For that matter, who were these people? This did not match any Traditional tale he knew.

There was a stirring where the tunnel picked up again on the other side of the room; he had the feeling that he was about to find out just who it was that wanted to see him.

The cause of the commotion entered the room, followed by her entourage of ladies, secretaries, guards, and assorted flunkies. And if the world did not acknowledge her as one of the most beautiful in the Five Hundred Kingdoms, it was because the world hadn't come down here to see her yet.

Her skin was pale as cream, and as smooth and—he guessed—as soft. Her hair was the red of copper newly forged. Her neck was long and graceful, the overused word *swan-like* sprang immediately to mind; her legs and her back seemed just as long and graceful. It came to him at that moment, that if someone had taken little Katya and made her taller but proportionally the same, she would have looked like this.

He didn't know a lot about women's clothing, but he'd never seen any girl in Led Belarus dress like this. The gown looked to have been poured over her, the sleeves clung to her upper arms, the bodice to her body, and the whole flowed down to the floor and pooled there at her feet.

The body in the close-fitting green gown was lush, sensuous.

He started to get up, but a meaty hand on one shoulder disabused him of that notion. So he stayed where he was, as she approached him.

She gazed down on him dispassionately. Her eyes were as

green as her gown, which, on closer inspection, clung closer to her than he had thought, and made guessing about what was beneath it unnecessary.

"I am the Queen of the Copper Mountain," she said. "And what are you, that Baba Yaga's servants pursue you so relentlessly?"

Sasha swallowed. She wore some sort of perfume he didn't recognize except that it was rich and sweet. "I am Sasha Pieterovich, Prince of Led Belarus," he replied. "And I made the old witch annoyed."

The Queen laughed. "I like you, Prince Sasha," she said. "Come and sit with me."

Sasha wondered how he would "sit with her" on that enormous throne, but she clapped her hands, and two flunkies brought chairs.

Meanwhile his mind was frantically racing through everything he knew about supernatural creatures outside of Led Belarus. Had he ever heard of this Queen of the Copper Mountain? He couldn't recall anything. What was she? Some sort of creature of the earth, but she was hardly a troll, and her minions, though green-faced, were not unhandsome. For that matter, in any other place, her ladies would have had men panting at their feet. But she outshone them as an emerald outshines a mere beryl.

She was handed into her chair by two of them, and motioned to him to take the second. It was, needless to say, lower than hers, and smaller. She might not be sitting in an actual throne, but there was no doubt that a Queen outranked a mere prince.

"So." She looked at him with an unreadable expression. "Tell me, then, what is it that you did to annoy the witch? She is no friend of mine."

"I freed some creatures that she held captive," he admitted, "but not before she had broken her bargain with me."

The queen sat back on her throne, a faint smile on her face. "You dared? Now I am impressed!"

He shrugged. "My family has some association with one, the Little Humpback Horse. I could not leave him in those unkindly hands."

"So, so." She leaned forward, elbow on knee, chin on hand. "Loyalty is a good thing. So tell me, have you a woman you are loyal to as well?" She lowered her eyelids suggestively, and he flushed.

"Yes," he said shortly, then added, "Gracious Queen."

She smiled a little secret smile, then looked up at her servants. "Take the prince and let him bathe, tend his wounds, eat and sleep. For now—" the smile broadened "—for now he will be my very special guest."

Should he have felt alarm at that smile? As he got up and felt as if every bone in his body was made of lead, as if every muscle was made of boiled noodles, and—

Well enough. He had no more energy to feel alarm. He let himself be led away.

"Blessed saints." Marina applied cold cloths to the enormous bump on Katya's head, while Lyuba bathed Yulya's bruised neck with wine in which wormwood had been steeped. It smelled vile, but it was easing the pain of the bruises, and there was no doubt that it was healing them. Already they were more yellow and green than black and blue.

The state of Katya's head and Yulya's throat, however, was not what was on anyone's mind. For all that the Rusalka had been a crazed thing, it was—or had been—a living creature. And that had been the most horrible way to die that any of them had ever seen.

"It was a mad thing," Lyuba said at last. "It almost killed Yulya and it would have killed you. You put down mad things, or they hurt the pack."

Katya winced.

"Well, it's done, and hopefully the Jinn will be sated for a while," Marina said finally, and shivered.

Katya listened for the hum, and did not hear it, even distantly. "We absolutely *must* find a way to defeat this Jinn!" she said, fiercely. "Even if *we* don't have the resources, we must devise some way that someone can!"

Lyuba nodded fiercely, and showed her teeth. "Given the chance, he would not stop at consuming a few, he would consume all, until the world ended."

Katya was not at all sure of that, but she let it pass. Consume the world or not, the Jinn was quite bad enough all on its own.

"We—" Yulya said, and coughed, and struggled to swallow. "We know his power comes from fire. Might he be some kind of fire spirit?"

It seemed fairly clear to Katya that the wretched Jinn was anything but mortal, but perhaps that wasn't as obvious to the others.

"As the Baba Yagas are spirits of the earth?" Klava asked, brows narrowed.

Katya gaped at her. "There is more than one Baba Yaga?" she asked, somewhat aghast.

Klava shrugged. "So it is said. I could believe it. It is difficult to imagine how one Baba Yaga could wreak so much havoc. The tales I have heard say that there are three. But the point is that they are not really ancient human women but spirits created when the forests were young."

Marina nodded sagely. "So my parents who made me said. And so Father Frost says, when he comes to visit me and ask how I am, and remind me not to jump over any fires—"

She stopped there, and a look of horror came over her. Small wonder. A snow maiden would last no longer than a breath if the Jinn set his fires on her.

Lyuba leaped to her side. "I will protect you! He will have to face my teeth if he tries to—"

"The point is to find a way to deal with him so that none of us have to face him without the power being on our side," Katya reminded them, and Klava nodded.

"I have been going through every book I could find in the castle," the wizard's apprentice said. "I wish I had more information. There is not much there about the Jinni. They once lived in a place called the City of Brass, but why they no longer dwell there, the book does not say. Another said that some were good spirits that were imprisoned by evil magi to force them to serve them, and that some were evil spirits locked away by good magi to keep them from harming mankind, and the only way to know which that a Jinn-bottle held was to know the seal of the magi that sealed it in." She sighed. "Of course, we already know what sort this fellow is."

Yulya cleared her throat a little. "Are there any laws of magic that could work in our favor?" she asked diffidently.

Klava looked at her, startled. Yulya shrugged. "I am not

entirely bird-witted," she said. "I used to listen to father's friends. One is a wizard. The Laws—"

"Well," Klava began. "The Law of Names, really. If we could discover his True Name—"

They all fell silent at that. Everyone knew the power of a True Name. The difficulty was to get hold of it. Magical creatures, spirits like the Jinn, kept their True Names to themselves, and in the normal course of things, probably only one other person or creature would know it, that being the one that had given it to them in the first place.

There were ways to learn the Name; it could be tricked or coerced out of someone, and a powerful enough magician could find a Name with scrying and spells. The trouble with all of those was that they weren't powerful magicians, and the Jinn wasn't likely to be tricked.

"Other than that?" Katya asked dryly, and then stopped. "Good heavens. In order to seal him in his bottle in the first place, the magician would have to have known his True Name, right?"

Klava's eyes widened. "Almost certainly."

"And it must have been written on the bottle as part of the bindings."

Klava nodded. "Definitely."

"And I very much doubt he would have left such a thing lying about to be found and meddled with!" Katya continued, triumphantly. "So his bottle must be here in the castle somewhere."

Klava's eyes lit up. "Of course! He must have brought it when he brought me! When we find it—" But there Klava faltered. "I couldn't read the language myself the last time, and neither could my master. How can we expect to translate enough to tell what his name is?"

Katya's eyes sparkled. "How do you think I can speak to all of you?" she asked. "It is one of the things that *I* can do" She looked around at all of them. "Marina, Yulya, you are best suited to talking to the Jinn's servants. You are both gentle and sweet—no one would suspect you of anything other than curiosity if you asked questions. See if there is some place odd that the Jinn is known to go to, or he has forbidden his servants to enter."

The snow maiden and the swan maid nodded, and Yulya brightened. She liked talking to people, she was gregarious by nature.

"Lyuba, you can use that clever nose of yours, not only to see if there is an escape from this place, but if you find a place that the Jinn visits often in the castle."

The Wolf-girl grinned. This just meant she could spend more time in her preferred shape. And Katya could not blame her. The Wolf was ever so much more powerful than the pretty human girl.

"Klava, there may be a way you can find the bottle. Did you not once hold it in your hands?"

Klava brightened. "Oh! I did! The Law of Contagion! That which once touched always touches! My magical abilities are not strong, but perhaps they will be enough!"

Katya nodded, decisively. "There, we all have important jobs. Since I can sense him, I will keep watch for the Jinn and warn you when he returns to the castle. And then—find the bottle and I can read it and tell you the Jinn's name if it is there."

* * *

Sasha drifted off to sleep feeling monumentally better. A good bath, a good meal, and the ministrations to his multiple bruises by—

No, not a comely wench, which he was just as happy about. A competent young fellow who seemed more than happy to rub some sort of pine-smelling green goo all over him in a very impersonal manner. Whatever it was, it worked wonders. He stopped aching and fell asleep immediately without really paying attention to his surroundings.

But when he woke up again, clearheaded, he wondered with a shock if he had been drugged, precisely because he had been so incurious. He couldn't even remember what the *bed* looked like, much less the room....

Well the former was easily remedied; from the feel, it was a good featherbed, and there was a feather comforter over him, which was just as well as he was stark naked. He remembered getting undressed, but he didn't remember getting into bed....

And there was a moment of panic as he made sure that he was *alone* in that bed.

The repercussions of bedding a supernatural creature were ones he really didn't want to contemplate, and just about everything down here was probably magical or supernatural in one way or another.

The repercussions were especially critical since he had already pledged himself to another magical creature. Traditionally speaking...that was a recipe for disaster.

But he was alone and there was no sign that he had ever been anything but alone in this bed. One worry dealt with.

The bed was curtained; another good thing. He rolled over to the side, noting as he did so that although he still ached it was distantly, as if the bruises were a week, rather than a day, old. He parted the curtains slightly.

The room beyond was lit, dimly, by a single glowing globe in a sconce fastened to the rock wall. He couldn't tell just what was in that globe that made it glow. A candle? An oil lamp? Something magical? A fire-bird feather? There was no way to tell. It didn't flicker as a candle flame would, though. That in itself was interesting.

It wasn't a large room, but it was luxurious by his standards. Just about everything seemed to be beautifully carved of stone. He had never seen such artistry in his life; it wasn't that the carving was elaborate, because it wasn't. It was that it was so very perfect. Every flowing line, the polish—perfect.

What wasn't stone was metal, copper in fact, just as most of the stone was malachite, and the metal was as exquisitely wrought as the stone.

There was a stone bench and two copper chairs, a stone chest, a small stone table beside the bed, which itself was made, he now saw, of stone.

There were, of course, no windows. But there was a huge, highly polished, copper mirror. And on either side of the mirror, two narrow beaded hangings like the one in the throne room, but smaller. Each one showed half of the mountain.

The air felt slightly chilly, but there was no fire…but of course there was no fire. How could anyone get a chimney to reach down here? And you really didn't need a fire, the temperature in a cave was always the same. But it would make those feather-beds and comforters and blankets a necessity.

He parted the curtains a bit more, noting that they were heavy velvet. Very luxurious. Either he was a most honored guest or the Queen was wealthy enough to supply even her flunkies with this sort of luxury.

Then again…this was a woman with a malachite throne….

There seemed to be a neatly folded pile of clothing on the bench. He slipped cautiously and quietly out of bed, and eased silently to the bench. For some reason—and he was not sure why—he didn't want the "assistance" of any more of the Queen's attendants. At least, not until he had clothing on.

This was not the clothing he had brought with him.

More luxury; a high-collared honey-colored shirt of heavy, dull silk that felt like cream against his skin, and a pair of amber-brown lamb's wool trews, dark brown boots so beauti-fully made that the cobbler back home would have wept to see them. They fitted onto his feet like stockings, and the leather was butter-soft. There was even a heavy silk sash for his waist, fringed at the ends, cunningly woven in a pattern that combined the colors of his shirt, trews, and boots.

All of this only made his mind race as he tried to think out all the possible Traditional ways this could go. With a sinking heart, he reckoned that the most likely was—

"Ah, my lord Prince, I see that you are awake."

He jumped at the voice behind him. The young man of last night had just come around from the other side of the bed, bearing a copper tray with covered dishes on it. The dishes were also copper. He sensed a theme here….

"I hope you are hungry." The young man set the tray down on the bench, and frowned a little. "There was no need to dress yourself—"

"I'm used to tending to myself, actually," Sasha replied, with a little laugh. "I've gotten into the habit of it."

"Please sit, my lord," the young man replied firmly. Sasha bowed to the inevitable. He knew this sort of very superior servant. There were Proprieties. They must be met. And if you didn't meet the Proprieties…a servant like this one had a way of making you feel like a barbaric cad.

Breaking one's fast here was evidently considered of grave importance, judging by the number of dishes on that tray….

The moment he sat down, the servant produced a tiny table and set it in front of him, whisked a napkin into his lap and laid out knife and fork. Then the parade of food began.

The manservant presented him first with a cup of hot tea and a small plate of blinis with sour cream and caviar. These were followed by cheese blintzes, boiled eggs wrapped in ham slices, thick slices of bread that the manservant buttered for him, then layered with a thick slathering of jam, sliced fruit, sausages, egg pie, berries in cream…all washed down with more tea. If this had been Baba Yaga's hut, he would have been seriously alarmed at this point, but he was fairly certain no one here was planning on making dinner out of him.

It was a far cry even from breakfast at his own father's table, which, while certainly generous, was nothing like this.

"There," the manservant said, whisking away the last course and deftly removing the table—which, being solid copper, must have weighed more than Sasha cared to think about. "Now you are ready for Her Majesty."

Well that had an ominous ring to it. Nevertheless, he stood up and straightened his shirt. He needed to find a way to persuade the Queen to help him—or at least, let him go. Katya was out there, somewhere, and she needed his help and she wasn't getting it with him in here.

The manservant paused a moment. Sasha glanced at him. There was something about his expression—

He had something to say. The question was—was this one of those cases where, Traditionally, it would be disaster and an insult to ask a question? Or was it the case where it would be "help from an unexpected source"?

"You've been very kind to me," Sasha said, diffidently. "I hope you know that I appreciate it. I know you haven't just been doing your duty, you *care* about doing your duty and doing it well. That is a difficult thing, and very admirable."

The manservant's green face darkened with a blush. "Most would never notice, and those that do never give it a second thought, my lord," he replied.

"Well the only reason I didn't say something last night was because I was so tired I was drunk with exhaustion," Sasha said, and laughed ruefully. "I may be a Prince by title, but I have to tell you, I am a peasant compared to your Queen. And all this—" he gestured broadly "—is not the sort of thing I am used to. I hope I haven't offended you with my barbarous ways. You've probably got nobler blood than I do!"

Now the manservant chuckled dryly. "Blood is as blood will be, my lord, and it was and is a pleasure to serve you. But..."

He paused. "It may not be my place to tell you this, and I am hoping you won't take it amiss, my lord, but the Queen my mistress…is….an easy woman to serve, but a difficult one for someone who aspires…higher…." He paused significantly. It was easy for Sasha to read between the lines. The manservant was warning him about the consequences of courting the Queen's attention.

"I aspire to my Katya and no one else," he said firmly. "Your lady may well be the most beautiful in all of the Kingdoms of the world, but it takes more than beauty to win a man's heart." He chuckled. "And love isn't logical anyway."

And his own heart warmed just thinking of Katya at that moment.

The manservant relaxed just a trifle. "Well then, my lord…the Queen my mistress is a most powerful creature as I am sure you are already aware. She rarely means anyone harm…but she is a creature of appetite and senses. She is fond of taking mortal lovers but…she is by her nature rather hard on them." He sighed. "As I say, she rarely means anyone harm, but she can never really *love* a mortal. You are so short-lived, you see. The poor fellows generally end up breaking their hearts over her and coming to bad ends."

Sasha shook his head in commiseration. "Ah, that's just a tragedy all the way around. Sad for them, sad for you who has to watch it, and sad for the Queen who means them no harm."

"Ah, sir," the manservant said with relief. "You see how it is then. Well, follow me, and I will take you to the Audience Chamber. If you can amuse her or interest her, then there is much she could do for you in return."

Definitely help from an unexpected source.

Sasha followed his guide down tunnel after tunnel, cut right out of the living rock and lit by more of the globes in copper sconces. Finally the servant paused and waved him through a doorway, beyond which Sasha could see a much smaller room than the chamber he had first encountered the Queen in.

She was on another malachite throne, this one draped and softened with a throw made of sable fur. Her attention was occupied by two men with the manner and demeanor of advisers, but she glanced at him and smiled before turning back to them. He waited patiently. Waiting patiently was a job that princes, as a whole, got very good at.

Eventually, whatever business was being transacted was quickly dealt with. The advisers bowed themselves out. Sasha was beckoned to, and he came forward and made the most elegant bow that he could. The Queen smiled.

"I imagine that this is all a bit overwhelming for you, Prince," she said indulgently. "There are few mortals in the world that can match the wealth of my realm."

"I would not imagine that there are any at all," Sasha said, and grinned. "But it isn't so much the wealth that I admire, it's the art. Majesty, the littlest and most ordinary of furnishings here is a work of art! Your carvers must be not only gifted but inspired!"

He went on for a bit—quite genuinely—about his admiration for her craftsmen. But it was clear, at least to him, that she was trying to tempt him with her wealth. And truth to tell, yes, it was tempting. It would be a fine thing to live like this, surrounded by luxury and beauty, and every need or desire answered. A fine thing for a while.

But it would get boring very rapidly.

And in the meantime, what would he be *doing?* Nothing to make the world any better.

No, this was not the life for him, even if he hadn't met Katya. As it was, he would rather roam the Kingdom for his father with her than live in luxury without her.

She stared at him clearly intrigued, reclining gracefully over one arm of her throne with her chin on her hand. "You astonish me, Prince. Most mortal men see only the value, not the beauty. But my people have had centuries to perfect not only their love of beauty, but their ability to create it. It is refreshing to meet with one who appreciates that."

He bowed his head to her. "It is a sad thing that mortal or any other creature cannot see a thing of beauty without wanting to know what it can buy, or lusting to possess it so no one else can have it."

"Or to possess it for the power it gives." She leaned back, and gestured at the chamber. "This is merely the outward aspect of power, Prince. It is not just that this realm has great wealth— it has equally great power. If we chose to exercise it in the world above us—"

"Ah." His eyes darkened. "But that would bring unpleasant attention down on you. As you yourself have said, there are so many who see something and lust to take it to prevent anyone else from having it. No, my Queen, in the world above, there are far too many greedy creatures that would see your power, your wealth, and yourself and desire to command all three. One, two, or even three—yes, you and yours could hold against them. But they would never stop coming, my Queen. And eventually one of them would win. No, your power is best kept here, where it is. It is nonetheless strong for being hidden."

Her eyes lit up, and she beckoned to him to come nearer.

Now, when a Queen and a powerful magician wants you to come closer, it is generally a good idea to obey. But Sasha knew very well what she was going to do. And it would be all without intending any harm at all, and second nature to her. All of that magic was about to be channeled into an attempt at seduction aimed at him.

He had, in his way, fought many battles. This was going to be the hardest.

It was just a good thing he'd had some practice at this sort of thing. How many Rusalkas had he encountered since he'd begun making the rounds for the King? The one thing they had in common was that they almost always tried seduction first.

"Wealth and power do not move you, Prince," she breathed, her green eyes fixed on his, full of promise, her scent filling his nostrils, the heat of her body calling to him. "But beauty, now…is that your passion? Is that what can lure you when nothing else can? Come closer—"

She bent down and curled one arm around his shoulders, like a velvet snake. The scent of her was a mingling of vanilla, musk, and amber. "Is beauty your heart's desire?" she murmured, bending to kiss his lips. Hers opened as soon as they touched his, and her tongue darted into his mouth. He felt his body yearning for hers, felt the heat of her kiss shooting straight through him—

But the one thing that saved him was this: her seeming passion was dispassionate. It was the form of passion but not the substance. There was heat, but no feeling; what she wanted was only sensation and nothing more. Compared with Katya, this was like the picture of bread compared to a fresh-baked loaf. And eventually, even through the kiss, his body realized that, too.

She felt it, felt the resistance. She sat back up and stared at him, astonished.

"There is a girl I love, Majesty," he said, simply. "You are more beautiful than she, more radiant, more of everything. But the heart does not listen to anything but its own logic, and it is she whom I love."

The Queen of the Copper Mountain blinked at him, as at a marvel the like of which she had never seen before.

"So I see," she said finally, and without rancor. "So I see."

Chapter 14

The Queen of the Copper Mountain had listened patiently and with growing interest as Sasha recounted the course of his adventures so far. By the time his narrative reached the point at which he had come into her hands, she was leaning forward on her throne again, an intrigued and amused smile on her face.

The only time she had shown any sign of impatience was when he had waxed a little too lyrical on Katya's virtues. As soon as he'd realized that, he had quickly moved on at that point, and privately chided himself for praising one woman to the face of the one she could not compete with. Not clever. Not clever at all. He then set about making his story as funny as possible to make her forget his little faux pas. It was actually a lot easier to do, if he ignored the growing anxiety he had for Katya, the growing uncertainty as to whether or not she was still all right. The business with the Goat and the Wolf was actually quite funny—although he had not seen the two rid themselves of the old hag, he could certainly imagine it, and he happily made up a description that was both vivid and funny enough to have her laughing aloud.

When he finished, she nodded and steepled her fingers together as she leaned back into her fur. "You are loyal, Prince Sasha, a trait which I have seldom seen in the mortals who come into my world. You are loyal and steadfast." She smiled a bit. "And you are most amusing. I have not laughed so much in a very long time. I am tempted to keep you here—but I think that you would not be so amusing if I made you my prisoner, however comfortable the prison. So I have instructed my people to provision you and take you to the surface—well away from that evil hag, Baba Yaga."

He wondered for a moment how she could have already "instructed her people"—but then, she and they were magic, and there was no telling what she could and could not do. So he merely bowed. "Thank you, gracious Queen." He hesitated. "At this point, I have no idea what direction I should look in—"

"Then if I were you, as your betrothed is the Sea King's daughter, I would begin at the sea. My people will put you within reach of it." She looked up; hearing a footstep behind him, he saw that the advisers had returned and were waiting in the doorway. "Now I must to my duties. Fare you well, Prince Sasha."

Well versed in the way of royalty, it did not take having the manservant appear at the other door to tell Sasha he had been dismissed. He left the Queen of the Copper Mountain sitting on her malachite throne and followed in the wake of the manservant.

"You did remarkably well, my lord," the manservant said, leading him through tunnels that slanted upward. "You amused her without offending her."

"Call it my Luck," he said with a shrug. "I try, but an honest man in my place would admit that what happens is as much because of Luck as skill." The tunnels, low-ceilinged and only lit at intervals, were beginning to make him nervous. He found himself longing to be out and seeing the sun again.

"I think it is more than merely luck. And here we are."

The room they entered was what Sasha would have called a guardroom or a muster-room. There were weapons and weapon racks hanging on the walls, and crates and barrels of supplies. Presiding over it all was a wizened old man, who, oddly enough, looked completely human.

"Greetings to you, Pavel Romanovitch," the manservant said to the old fellow. "The Queen wishes you to provision her friend so that I may let him out into the world above again."

The old man eyed him with astonishment. "By gad! She's letting him go?"

The manservant nodded gravely. "She was much amused, but he has a love to whom he is faithful, and she has released him to seek her."

The old man cackled with glee. "See! I win my bet! I *told* you that one day there would come a man down here who would resist her wiles! By gad! This is good seeing!"

The manservant smiled. "And now you are to provision him, and provision him well, we can send him on his way, and you and I will share that bottle I promised you."

"With a good heart!" The old man began getting things down

off walls and out of barrels and boxes. Sasha watched with
interest and growing glee as the man put together a rucksack
stuff full of everything a traveler might want.

"Weapons?" the old man asked, his hands hovering over a
heavy crossbow.

"Dagger and hunting bow," Sasha replied, looking with regret
at the armament arrayed along the wall. "Frankly, I'm not all
that good with anything else, and no point in loading myself
down with things I can't use."

"Smart fellow," the old man said with a nod, getting down a
good hunting bow, a quiver of arrows, and a belt with a long
dagger. "Now lad, as pretty as that outfit may be—"

"It's not fit to travel in," Sasha interrupted, "I take it you have
something better?"

The old man laughed, and brought out much more practical gear. The only thing that Sasha retained was the boots.

"Can't better those," Romanovitch said, with a nod of
approval. "You might not believe it, but they'll wear like iron.
Now, the Queen said to provision you well, lad, so put this
inside your tunic—" And he handed Sasha a coin pouch so fat
it barely jingled.

Sasha took it with astonishment. "But I didn't—"

"'Course you didn't ask for it. That's why you got it. Now go
on with you! Take that tunnel there. It'll open out facing east.
Just keep going east and you'll strike the sea."

Sasha nodded, and took himself out, leaving the manservant
and the old man deep in a discussion of just what drink the
manservant was going to supply for losing the bet.

This last tunnel was mercifully short, and ended in a massive door. For a moment Sasha wondered how he was going to get it open alone, then he shrugged and tugged at it.

It swung inside silently, with scarcely any effort at all on his part.

He stepped out into the sunlight; the door swung shut again behind him, and when he turned around, he could not tell where, in the rock of the mountainside, it was.

Face east, and keep going.

He stood on a small ledge; a gravel-covered slope lay before him. He had emerged well above the tree line and, as he had expected, the sea was nowhere in sight. The Queen's idea of what was within reach and a mortal's were apt to be different. It looked as if his little sojourn with Baba Yaga had taken him far, far out of his path. But there was no hope for it, and the journey was not getting any shorter for standing there.

The slope was quite slippery; he had to descend it by moving obliquely across the face of it, which was pretty much adding three times as much to the distance between him and the tree line. And what he was going to do when he got there—

Make camp, I suppose, he thought dubiously, looking at the sun. *If I don't do so before I lose the light, it'd be awkward to try to find a place to hole up in the dark. The saints only know what's in those woods, or out of them for that mat—*

And then, he froze, as the howl of a Wolf echoed across the face of the mountain.

He looked frantically in all directions, but there was only one place where there was any cover at all—the forest down below. If there was a hunting Wolf out here, he needed to get somewhere that he could get out of reach. In a tree would certainly be his first choice—

Throwing caution to the wind and with his heart pounding wildly, he began a precipitous run down the mountainside, boots slipping and sliding in the gravel. The Wolf's howl followed him; it was definitely at his back and closing.

Closing fast, by the sound of it.

He wouldn't look back. His heart raced, and his vision narrowed. He concentrated on the tree line. The Wolf might be getting nearer, but so were the trees. If he could just make it—

A heavy, hairy body slammed into his from behind, and involuntarily, he screamed as he went face-down into the gravel. An enormous paw flipped him over onto his back—

And a tongue the size of a cow's slapped into his face and licked him from chin to hairline.

The Wolf stood with both forepaws on his shoulders and grinned down at him, tongue lolling. "I knew if we stuck around this mountain long enough, you'd come out," it said, its hot breath washing over him. "Was the Queen nice?"

"The Queen—*oof*—was very kind indeed. And if you'd get off my shoulders so I can get up, I would be a lot more comfortable." The Wolf leaped lightly back, and Sasha sat up. Fortunately, he had not actually hit the gravel with his face, but his healing bruises were telling him a sad story indeed. "I'm very happy to see you, Wolf. I take it the lady of the unusual hut was unable to persuade you to enjoy her hospitality any further?"

"Fortune was all against her," the Wolf said mockingly. "On her way home, before she even managed to fetch her mortar, she got into a quarrel with a leshii, and she now has quite enough to worry about. True, she is Baba Yaga, but he is the master of the forest, and it's two bulls locking horns, is what it is. She'll win in the end, but it will cost her. That's what she gets for breaking her bargains."

Sasha sighed with relief. That meant Sergei was also probably fine. The moment the witch had got herself into difficulty, she'd surely called back her ghosts to help her.

"And speaking of locking horns—" The Wolf turned up his nose and howled again. "We still do owe you our thanks, and I think you'll be glad—"

There was a sound like thunder in the distance, and over the slope of the mountain came the Goat at an all-out run, head down, negotiating the steep slope as easily as if it were a flat meadow. He skidded to a stop beside the Wolf in a shower of small stones, and shook his horns.

"Slow, slow, slow," mocked the Wolf. "It is a good thing I am not inclined to eat you, because I would have no trouble catching you."

"On the flat, maybe, but I should like to see you chase me on the cliffs!" the Goat replied, with a baa-ing laugh. "And then I should knock you over the side of one, and then where would you be? So Prince! I have a request to make of you and an offer to pay you back for your kindness."

"I've paid back already, I tracked him down for you," the Wolf said, with another grin. "Travel well, Prince! Perhaps one day we'll meet again!"

And with that, the Wolf bounded off into the forest, and vanished from sight among the trees. The Goat snorted.

"As you can plainly see," said the Goat, turning toward Sasha, "I still have on this pesky saddle and bridle. I am not inclined to ask just anyone to take it off, since I would likely end up a captive again. However this is a good thing for both of us; since I still have it on, I can carry you to wherever you want to go, and when we get there, you can take it off for me. I am happy to take you anywhere you like, in return for your kindness in freeing me."

"That would be wonderful," Sasha replied with heartfelt relief. "It would be more than wonderful. I need to get to the sea—a port, if possible—"

"Then climb on my back, Fortunate Fool, and hold on tight!" said the Goat merrily. "You will be eating fish for dinner!"

He really should have expected that a Goat the size of a horse was not the ordinary sort of mount.

The Goat did not fly, as Sergei did, but it might just as well have. It leaped. It made enormous leaps that took it right over the tops of the trees, and in fact, so dense was the forest canopy that once it *was* above the treetops, it used them instead of the ground as its landing and leaping platforms. It was dizzying, and at once terrifying and exhilarating. Each leap seemed to cover about seven leagues, making Sasha wonder if this was how the owners of those famed seven-league boots got about.

He held onto the Goat's horns instead of the bridle; a bridle, after all, was for someone who knew where he and his mount should be going, which he particularly did *not*. They bounded along so fast that Sasha really didn't get to see much of the land-scape; when the Goat finally landed just as the sun was setting, and then didn't move again, it took him a moment to realize they had reached their destination.

When he did so, he immediately swung his leg over and dropped down onto the ground, then took off the saddle and bridle. The Goat sighed and shook his whole body.

Sasha looked down at the town. It was a proper town indeed, with streets and shops, a fine church, and the port and docks. There were several ships tied up at the docks, and surely one of them would be going north.

"Oh now, that is good to be rid of that tack," the Goat said. "What are you going to do with those?" He pointed his long nose at the saddle and bridle. "They look valuable."

"They probably are," Sasha said, absently. He noticed that they had landed not that far from a peasant hut that looked rather in need of repair. A sad-eyed little girl played listlessly in front; his heart ached to see her, for she looked too malnourished even to play properly. He picked up the tack and carried it over to her. She leaped up and stared at him as he approached.

"Tell your father," said Sasha, "that I make him a present of this, having no more need of it, and that he is to sell it and buy you a she-goat. But you must take very, very good care of the goat, because she will give you milk to drink, and to make into yogurt and cheese. Do you understand?"

Wordlessly, the child nodded, and he went back to the Goat, leaving her squatting down beside the saddle, touching it with one hesitant finger.

"That was well done," observed the Goat. "Prince, you have a good care for the people."

He shrugged. "It saved me having to sell it myself, or find some other way of disposing of it. I expect my Luck has seen to it that it goes where it will do the most good."

"Well, with all the good turns done, I am off," said the Goat. "Fare you well, Prince Sasha, and I hope you find your way to where you need to go."

And with that, the Goat leaped into the sky and out of sight. Sasha turned toward town, pausing only to wink and wave goodbye to the little girl, who shyly waved back.

It did not escape Sasha's sense of irony that he probably could have avoided the whole entanglement with Baba Yaga and the Queen if he had just stayed where he was and tried to contact the Sea King from the village where the Jolly Sturgeon lay, or, alternatively, taken a ship there for the North with people he knew, or at least, who knew people he knew. Here he was, in a strange town, with no real idea of where to go except for an insistent tugging at his heart whenever he thought of Katya that now pulled him Northwards again. And if it was pulling him north, then not even the sea knew where she was.

But this was a place without roads, and in any event, he was without a horse. If he went North, it would have to be a ship that took him.

He spent the rest of the evening making the rounds of the taverns, looking for a vessel that would be heading North in the morning. He was glad of that pouch of coins; he barely made a dent in it with all of the drinks he was buying, and he could not have done this without that much money. One thing he did not have, and that was a hard head for liquor; he bought far more than he drank, until he finally encountered a dour old man who soon, under the influence of a great deal of vodka, agreed to take him as long as he came aboard at that very moment. Since everything Sasha had was with him, Sasha agreed, and the two of them reeled out together into the moonlit street.

Sasha, who was far more sober than he appeared, quickly realized when he saw the vessel just why it was that the captain wanted him aboard that instant. The ship was not in good condition. She listed slightly to port, and her sails were in desperate need of mending.

Still, it was summer. The season of storm was not yet upon them. And all this beast of a ship had to do was to get him Northward.

So he staggered up the gangplank behind the captain, and obediently tucked himself up in a cabin barely large enough for the hammock strung there. But it had been a long day, a very long day, and exhaustion was hammering him on the anvil of bone-weariness. Riding the Goat had been more than an experience, he had used an entirely different set of muscles from the ones he used to ride a horse. He just could not find it in himself to think too deeply about this.. He would trust to his Luck.

With the vodka fumes still making his brain whirl, he flipped himself into the hammock, used his rucksack as a pillow, and was asleep in a moment.

He woke with the hammock swaying with a fair amount of vigor, and when he caught the edge of the porthole and looked out, he realized that the ship had left port even before the sun rose. Small wonder the captain had insisted he get aboard last night. The man was probably skipping out on port fees.

Oh well. His stomach growled then, reminding him he'd done a great deal yesterday on two meals. It occurred to Sasha that the best thing he could do right now would be to stay right where he was. There might be repercussions from the crew on the captain's pulling out of port so fast. It would be better for the stranger to appear after those had been sorted out.

And as for breakfast? Trust the food provided by a cook on a ship like this one?

Oh not even his Luck could save him there.

He still had food in his rucksack and water in the bottle that he hadn't even touched. He'd bought his dinner in the first decent tavern he'd walked into. It might be better for everyone if he didn't put his nose out of the cabin until, say, noon, or thereabouts.

Besides, he was still plenty tired. More sleep would be very welcome.

So he rummaged in his "pillow," and pulled out a packet of what looked like a cross between good dark bread and a cracker, wrapped in oiled paper. It wasn't quite bread, whatever it was; it had a very chewy crust and dense interior, and had a nutty flavor to it, and left him feeling quite satisfied. A little more wriggling and rummaging got him his water bottle, and a few sips of that and he was ready to sleep again. If he'd been in a bunk, the ship's obvious sideways list would have probably made it difficult to sleep, but in a hammock it didn't matter. He closed his eyes and never minded the slap of the waves against the hull.

But it was a peal of thunder that shook the ship that woke him with a start.

His heart hammering, he tumbled out of his hammock and peered out the porthole. What he saw raised the hair on the back of his neck and sent cold, cold chills down his spine.

They were still sailing through relatively calm water and sunshine—but looming directly in their path, covering half the sky and all of the horizon, was a Baba Yaga of storms.

The clouds were blue-black, and laced with lightning. More spears of lightning were lancing into the ocean beneath the clouds. And those clouds were racing toward them at the speed of a falcon—he heard shouting overhead as the crew tried to react, and the fear in their voices told him that this thing must have sprung up, literally, out of nowhere.

Hearing their fear made his chest tighten. Then the porthole went black and he was tossed to the floor as the storm hit them.

A gout of cold seawater surged through the porthole as he struggled to his feet again, drenching him and everything in the cabin. He fought his way to his feet, coughing and spluttering, and managed to get to it and slam the cover shut, locking it in place, before being thrown to the floor again.

He lurched upward, grabbed the door frame, and wrenched the door to his little cabin open. There had to be something he could do to help the crew—he didn't know what, but there had to be something! But as he clawed his way up to the hatch, pushed it open enough against the wind to squeeze out onto the deck, he wished that he had stayed below.

Overhead, the black clouds boiled and seethed, lightning was striking all around them—waves towered high threatening to break over the bow. The little ship somehow managed to crawl to the top of a wave as he held onto a stanchion, hands frozen in place, then plunged down the back side of it with a sickening lurch. Icy spray whipped around them, and foaming water sloshed over the deck as the ship wallowed drunkenly from side to side. There was no rain—not that it mattered. Or maybe it did, because rain would have hidden the most terrifying thing of all.

Just off the starboard bow was something he had only heard and read of, never seen. A whirling, white column of air and water that began in the clouds and ended at the sea. He stared at it in horrified fascination. A waterspout; it had to be. It didn't seem to be headed for them yet, but—

A clamor behind him made him look up; the captain stood there on the bridge, wrestling with the wheel, as the ship heaved and shook and dove in the huge swells. Three or four of his men were causing all the ruckus, shouting at him over the roar of the wind in the rigging and the rolling thunder, telling him that the Sea King must be angry with them, saying that someone had to be sacrificed or they were all doomed— they shook their fists and screamed at the captain while clinging to whatever they could that was not the wheel, and the deck bucked and rolled under their feet.

That was when the captain glanced down and saw *him* standing there, holding onto a stanchion with both hands. And where his eyes went, so did those of the sailors.

And Sasha didn't even have time to blink, didn't have time to react to the crazy way their eyes lit up when they saw him.

One moment, he was standing there staring up at the captain. In the next, he was swarmed by three of the sailors who had been arguing with the captain who let go their holds to leap over the rail to grab him, plus another three or four more who had come up from behind.

They seized him. He fought desperately against them, but they had their sea legs and he didn't, and there were two of them to each of his limbs and a couple extra besides. Even though the tangled knot of him and his attackers was tossed around on the deck every time the ship heaved over, they still had him.

He looked up once and saw the captain, still at the wheel—totally ignoring what was going on below, his eyes fixed on the sea in front of him.

There would be no help coming from there.

The mob surged toward the rail, reeling drunkenly as he continued to try to fight. For a frozen moment, he was held up above their heads, illuminated by a dozen lightning bolts.

Then he was over the side, hitting the cold water with a jolt. It hit him with a shock, or maybe it was a real shock—the jolt of a lightning bolt snapping into the sea too near him. It paralyzed him, he gasped and went under and got a lung full of seawater. He tried to struggle to the surface and cough it out, but he couldn't find the surface, and his coughing only brought in more seawater. He had felt fear before in his life, but never like this. This was terror. His lungs were on fire, black and red flashes took up all of his vision, and he felt everything slipping away even as he clawed and fought and clung to life with a frantic urgency, and all he could think of was surviving and Katya—

Then something stuffed a ball of seaweed in his mouth. He felt hands on his arms and legs, and without knowing why, he chewed and swallowed the weed.

The water in his lungs somehow seemed to turn to air. He heaved in great shuddering breaths as he stopped struggling and sank, slowly, into the cold, cold water, into the peace of the deep, away from the terror of the surface. The red and black cleared away from his sight.

That was when he wondered if he wouldn't have been better off drowning, for he was surrounded by seamen, both with fish tails and with two normal legs, and they were all armed to the teeth. They all had spears with barbed points as long as his arm, and all of those spears were pointed right at him.

He swallowed. Smiled feebly.

There were no answering smiles.

He sat…well, half sat and half floated…in a room in the Palace of the Sea King. There had been no doubt in his mind, even though his captors had spoken not a word to him, that the enormous, fantastical pastel confection he was taken to was a palace, and who would have a palace like that except the Sea King?

The room to which he had been brought, after much swimming through what he could only call "gardens" and in and out of corridors, was as plain as the exterior was embellished. Four white walls, one door. Two armed guards inside, two outside that door. No windows, but there were huge seashells mounted on the walls that glowed. By now, he was getting used to arcane lighting, he supposed; he scarcely spared them a glance. He'd been brought here long enough ago that he was beginning to get bored.

From terror to boredom…well, perhaps he shouldn't be complacent. It might just be that the Sea King really had been angry with the owner of that ship or its captain, and he had just been the convenient sacrifice. After all, how could the Sea King have known that he was on that particular vessel, much less have found out about him and Katya?

Unless, of course, Katya had told him....

But still, the course of his journey from the Jolly Sturgeon to here was far from predictable. It made no sense for the King to have known....

Then again, there were all manner of spells for scrying and finding....

But then, why leave him here for so long?

Because the King wanted him nervous...or wanted him off guard.

He thought about that. And he reminded himself of several important truths. That this was Katya's father. That he needed to make an ally of this man. No matter what happened in life, you came with either the burden or the support of your parents, and that never changed, no matter what else did.

He knew what his own father's reaction would be; the King of Led Belarus would welcome an alliance with the Sea King with open arms. Sasha's father would think Katya was adorable, and probably consistently underestimate her, which was not a bad thing at all.

But what of the Sea King?

The room looked as if it was used more for storage than as a prison. It was lined with chests made of shell and metal—or at least, he thought it was shell. He wondered if there was anything in them that would be of any use to him....

He sidled over to the first one and opened it. The guards paid him no attention at all, so there probably wasn't anything here that *they* would consider a weapon. Yes, well…if ever he got out of this, he would have to have a word with their trainer.

The first two were empty. The third contained odd bundles, soft cloth drawstring cases that contained—strangely lumpy objects. Well, he thought the cases were cloth. It was hard to tell, really—would cloth disintegrate down here? This was a more surreal world than that of the Queen of the Copper Mountain. He pulled one out, and pulled open the drawstring and looked inside.

He gaped with astonishment to see a balalaika.

Quickly, he slid the instrument out of the bag. It was a bala-laika, all right. But *such* an instrument! It was carved of pearly yellow shell, and he couldn't imagine the clam or oyster that was large enough to have supplied the top and bottom of the instrument. All the frets and the tuning keys and pegs were ivory. The sounding hole was a delicate lacework cut into the shell. It was a stunning piece of work. And he discovered by trying it that it was perfectly in tune.

At this point he didn't even trouble to wonder how the sound could carry underwater. It just did. That was all that mattered.

He held very still for a long moment, letting everything settle into his mind; what he knew, what he did not know. This moment was important. He sensed that he was at a crossroads of sorts and that what he did now was going to set the tone of his life for a very long time indeed.

Now he *could* use this instrument for any number of purposes. He was a Songweaver, and the fact that it had fallen straight into his hands could only mean that The Tradition was working powerfully in his favor. He was, with no doubt, intended to use it.

The question was for what?

He could *probably* put his guards to sleep and escape, trusting to whatever spell made it possible for him to breathe underwater to keep him from drowning. He could definitely make for the surface. He might be able to escape pursuit. He might even survive on the surface long enough to find land or be rescued by a passing ship.

He could most definitely subvert one of more of the guards to his aid, as he had done with the Goat and the Wolf. In that case, with allies, his escape would certainly be a success. He could get to land. His new allies might even know where Katya was.

Or—

Or—

He could do the honorable thing.

Katya was out there somewhere and probably in need of help. Her father knew where she was because he had sent her himself.

If Sasha made a clean breast of it, told her father what had gone on between them, and told the truth, that he was trying to find Katya to help he—-

Well, the Sea King *probably* would not kill him until Katya was safe again.

It would be hard to do. It might be dangerous. There might be costs and repercussions he had not dreamed of. But that, and not escape, was the honorable thing to do....

With a sigh, Sasha searched for words and music in his mind, and began to sing. This song was going to take all of his craft as a Songweaver.

He sang of how he and Katya had met, how they had felt their spirits akin from the moment they had first set eyes on one another. Then he changed to a minor key and sang of the loneliness each had endured because of what they were and had to be for their people. He sang of Katya's loneliness as well as his own, for by now he knew the shape of it, too. Part of him had served to fill that loneliness, and his spirit retained the impression of it.

By this time, his guards were listening, and one or two of them had tears in their eyes—

At least, he presumed he had moved them to tears. He hoped it wasn't laughter. But the two in question had turned away for a moment and were rubbing their eyes. If he had moved them, that was important because he needed them to fetch the King; he needed the Sea King to hear this for himself.

He changed back to a major key, and though he did not go into the kind of detail that would have turned this from a ballad of love into a bawdy one, he made sure that there was no doubt of what he and Katya were to each other. Now all four of the guards were hiding smiles; he tried not to make this part sentimental, for coming after the previous section, that would be cloying. He kept it respectable, but earthy.

And if that didn't get the Sea King's attention, nothing would. Hopefully the King would not demand his head…

Now he changed to a minor key again, and sang of how duty had called her and he had waited, waited, realized that something had gone wrong and she had been taken from him. He sang despair, then resolution, reprised the theme of loneliness and—

"Oh for the sake of all that is sane, do stop."

His hands, which had been forming a complicated chord, fumbled it into a dissonant twang as he looked up.

There was a tall, blond man standing in the doorway, hands on his hips. He wore a golden-scaled, fish-skin tunic, and tight-fitting trews of sharkskin. If the coronet hadn't given it away, the demeanor, and the resemblance to Katya, certainly would have.

"Apparently you are unaware of just how well sound carries underwater. You have half my courtiers and family swimming about looking for me to plead with me to forgive you," the handsome, strong-featured fellow said, arms crossed over his chest, wearing—to Sasha's intense relief—an expression of amusement. "And the other half are swimming about looking for a way to help you escape." One eyebrow rose as he examined Sasha. "You'll be a very useful sort of Drylander to have about, I think. Between the two of you, you and my daughter *might* just equal a Godmother." He raised the other eyebrow. "Of course, you'll have to marry her. You *did* intend to do that, I assume? I'm giving you the benefit of the doubt here, on your intelligence. I am supposing you were going to ask me for her hand, otherwise you wouldn't have been wailing about your undying love in the heart of her father's palace—"

Relief suffused Sasha, and he was very, very glad that he could answer, honestly, "I already asked her, gracious Majesty. She consented, and if you would grant me the honor I—"

"Ah good, that's settled then. Now, let's get down to tactics. Here—" the King took the balalaika from his nerveless fingers and thrust it at one of the guards who had been wiping his eyes. "You put that away. You, Drylander, come with me." And as he grabbed Sasha by the elbow and bustled him away, the King turned and shouted back over his shoulder, "And stop *snif-fling*."

Chapter 15

"I know exactly where my daughter is," said the Sea King, leading Sasha through a bewildering array of corridors and out into the "gardens" again. It was very peculiar to follow someone swimming rather than walking. It was even more peculiar to be walking through "gardens" and see fish rather than butterflies and bees darting past. "The problem is that neither I nor any of my people can help her. She's the only one of us that can freely walk on dry land." He made a face. "Well I can, but one old warrior isn't going to do her much good right now. She got herself some Champions, but *they* can't come underwater. You, my good fellow, are exactly what I need. A foot in both worlds. So time to go talk to the Champions and see what they've found out." He made an abrupt turn into a netted enclosure. "We'll need some mounts. We need speed we can't supply on our own."

Sasha looked at the half-dozen smiling faces that pointed

their snouts in the King's direction and bobbed their heads with excitement. "Ah, sir, these are dolphins—"

This was the first time he had ever seen dolphins up close. They were bigger than he had thought, and very agile. Their eternal smiles were quite charming. From time to time one of them would leave the enclosure to go to the surface to breathe, and it was breathtaking to watch them shoot away so gracefully, and return just as quickly. The graceful grey bodies, wonderful to watch from above the surface of the water, were astonishing from below.

Thanks to the dragon's blood, he could understand what they were saying, too. "Me! Me!" "Pick me, Majesty!" "No, me! I'm fastest!" "I'm strongest!" "I'm both!"

"Exactly," said the King, and looked over the choices. "Bowwave and Spinner, if you please."

"*Awwwwww.*" There was a disappointed chorus as two of the dolphins separated from the pod and presented themselves for harnessing. Both bowed to the King, then nudged each other like a pair of teenage boys before settling. The King waved away any help from a young Triton who came swimming up belatedly to serve him; as one of the two dolphins went to pluck a second harness off the net wall, the King harnessed the first. Then he fed both dolphins the same seaweed balls that Sasha had eaten.

"Just hold onto these handholds on the harness here and here. Then you lay yourself along Spinner's back like this—" The King demonstrated, and awkwardly, Sasha tried to copy him. "Now take us to the Champions, lads."

There was no warning; with a powerful surge of his entire body, the dolphin shot forward.

Sasha hung on for dear life. It was a good thing he had strong arms; he was not so much riding as being pulled along. The sea floor shot past, and then, abruptly, dropped away, and they were in a place he could not even have imagined—beneath the surface of the deep sea.

First a mortar, then a Goat, now a dolphin, he thought, with a combination of bewilderment and irony. *So what do I ride next? A dragon?*

As the water rushed past him and he did his utmost to keep from interfering too much with the dolphin's powerful undulations, he had to laugh a bit at that thought. *No, that would be a bit much. Even for me.*

He had never been aware of just how serene—and just how *empty*—the wide sea really was. He and the King and the two dolphins appeared to be suspended in a zone of endless milky-blue water. From where they swam, you could not see anything of the bottom, the water went on into the distance with no horizon. He cast a glance upward. The surface was visible only as rippling reflections. With no landmarks to go by, he couldn't tell how fast they were actually going. It might have been faster than a galloping horse, they might have been crawling. The pressure of the water moving past told him "fast," but his eyes told him nothing. Neither he and the King, nor the dolphins, had to surface for air because the dolphins at least were under the same spell that he was, allowing them to breathe water instead of air. As for the King—probably the Sea King could already breathe water, just as his daughter could.

Then something dark loomed in the distance, and it was coming up fast—

And they were in the middle of life again.

The dark thing was a rock wall rising up from the deeper sea floor, and life clung to every crack and ledge of it. Kelp and other seaweeds, sea fans, some coral, lots of barnacles and shellfish. He spotted crabs and lobster scuttling about, and plenty of fish flitting in and out of the kelp patches. This, it seemed, was their goal, for the dolphins shot to the surface, taking their "riders" with them.

Sasha spasmed in a cough, spat a little water, and was breathing air again. The two dolphins spouted a blast that was more water than air, and did the same. All four of them bobbed in the sunlight, in a relatively placid cove. At a nudge from his escort, Sasha swam toward the very narrow beach of what appeared to be an island. It was quite a precipitous one; a shallow cliff rose abruptly from that beach, a dark basaltic cliff, jagged and showing only a few patches of green where moss and bushes found a foothold. And it wasn't until part of the cliff face moved that he realized that it wasn't cliff face at all.

It was a dragon.

"What ho!" the dragon said genially, as Sasha froze. "Visitors? Oh good! Oh the Sea King, even better!"

As if one dragon hadn't been enough, a second dragon's head popped up over the back of the first. "The Sea King! Wonderful! Then we are finally going to be able to get on with the rescue!"

The word *rescue* resonated with another he had heard on the other side of this journey. *Champions.*

He stared. "You're the Champions," he said, making it a statement and not a question.

The first dragon, who was a sort of dark translucent grey,

nodded. "Adamant and Gina, Champions of the Order of the Glass Mountain," he said proudly. "We don't really have a Chapter House." He chuckled. "Really, how would we fit into one?" The second dragon, this one a dark seagreen also nodded.

"I didn't know there were any dragon Champions." Sasha felt rather dumbfounded. His mind was running in tiny circles of reasoning trying to fit "Dragon Champion" into what he knew of The Tradition and failing utterly. "Isn't it usually Champions *slaying* dragons?"

"Oh now *that* was tactful," the Sea King said sarcastically, emerging from the water onto the beach. Sasha noted absently that it was sadly obvious how much more practical the Sea King's garb was for this than Sasha's was. The Sea King's sleeveless tunic and trews shed the water and were already dry. Sasha was still dripping.

Sasha flushed, as the second dragon sighed. "All the ugly old prejudices. As if we didn't have enough problems with nasty sorcerers trying to force us into the Traditional Path of maideneating. Really sir, I could just as well have said, 'Oh, a Seventh Son, so how dimwitted are you? Must I limit my conversation to monosyllables?'"

Sasha flushed. "I deserved that," he acknowledged. "Let's try again, shall we? My name is Sasha, Prince Alexsandr of Led Belarus to be precise, and yes, I am a Seventh Son. I didn't know that it showed."

"It does when you are by your nature magical," the second dragon said. "And when you know what to look for. I'm Gina, and this is my mate Adamant." She turned her head, and gazed fondly at the charcoal-colored dragon. "We were ambushed by a paper bird that gave us a message about captives in the castle of the Katschei. Not knowing what that *was,* we went looking for an explanation, found a Triton, and—" She shrugged. "The Sea King has good agents, and this Triton was one of them. The Triton suggested we come here and gave us a good grounding— when we got a full explanation, we decided to wait for His Majesty to see if he had anything more he could help us with. We are *not* from this part of the world, and we really need an expert on The Tradition hereabouts."

Sasha made a self-deprecating face. "I don't know about expert, but I know a bit. Katschei the Deathless used to live in a castle north of my land of Led Belarus, but I'm afraid he couldn't live up to his name. It was rumored that he thought he would be clever and invade some land that didn't have him as a Traditional evil, where no one would know what he was or be able to defeat him. Since most of the enchantments around his castle suddenly evaporated, we assume he came to a bad end. The castle has been vacant since."

"Well it isn't now." The first dragon—Adamant—shook his massive head. "Can I assume that it was *not* originally in the center of a hot, sandy desert?"

Sasha blinked at both of them, dumbfounded. "Ah," he managed to say. "No. Rather impenetrable forest, then a hedge maze, according to The Tradition."

"Hmm. Then the desert must be the work of this 'Jinn' that the note refers to." The green dragon gave the impression of a frown. "So far we have a 'Jinn' moving into the castle, creating a desert around it, and evidently kidnapping maidens who have some link or other to magic, which is how you, Majesty, got involved in the first place. I assume from what the Triton told us that you sent your daughter to investigate and she is the owner of the paper bird. Would you say that your daughter is clever?"

"Second to none," the Sea King said with pride.

"Then a clever girl would arrange to have herself carried off just like the others. I think we can assume that is what she did." The green dragon Gina looked at her mate, and Sasha could have sworn that she smiled at him. Could dragons smile? "It is what I would have done."

"You are clever and rather too inclined to charge in before reconnoitering," said Adamant, but there was amusement in his voice.

"A dragon can afford to do that," she pointed out, and laughed.

"You did it when you were a knight, too." Adamant shook his head at her. "Don't forget, I was there. I remember it very well, you charging up to the cliff, and shaking your fist at me." He pitched his voice higher. "*Come back here, fell beast! Coward! Scum! Wretched thing of evil! Come back here and taste my steel!*"

Sasha looked from one dragon to the other, and couldn't help but feel any vestige of control over this situation slipping away. And—the dragon was once a knight? This was seeming evermore impossible. "Ah, excuse me please, but my betrothed is in danger—"

"Ah—I beg your pardon." Adamant immediately became all business, and Gina sobered. "I don't think this girl—"

"Ekaterina—" said the King, and "Katya," Sasha said at the same time. They looked at each other.

"Katya," said the King.

"Katya is not in *immediate* danger, but that could change. Do either of you know what a 'Jinn' is?"

Sasha shook his head. "A Fire Spirit," the King said. "It lives in deserts. Some are good, some are bad, and I think we can assume this one is bad." He shrugged. "That is all that I know, I am afraid. We're not much given to deserts around here."

"Any reason why it would kidnap maidens?" asked Gina.

The King shook his head. "From the little I know of them, this is not the sort of thing that Jinni do. They can't be bothered with humans, much. They despise mortals."

But several disparate pieces of information clicked into a whole in Sasha's mind at that moment, and he spoke up with the answer. "Because it is living in the Katschei's castle," replied Sasha. "The Tradition is trying to make it fit."

"Aha. That makes perfect sense." Gina looked at Adamant again. "Are you thinking what I am thinking?"

"That the Jinn is making the best of what it is being forced to do by taking maidens inherently magical so that it can use their magic?" Adamant hazarded. "That means they will probably be safe for now if they don't go making trouble." He pondered again. "Time to reconnoiter. And look for allies. They should be easy to come by. Even the nastiest of creatures native here is going to object to having this Jinn drop a desert in their garden." He pondered again. "Do you think we need the bird anymore?"

Gina shook her head. "We know where the castle is. I think we can let it go." And before Sasha could say anything, she lifted a rock, and a brightly colored paper bird shot up into the sky and was gone.

He looked after it wistfully. If they hadn't been so hasty, he could have written something on it. Even just *We're coming* and his own name. He rather doubted the dragons had been able to write on something that small.

Well, it was done. At least now she would know she wasn't alone. He took comfort in that, and turned his attention back to the planning.

Katya worked at the ground around the roots of the roses. Whoever it was who had built this place first, it was not the Katschei. The original plants here had all been lovely, not the nightshade, the belladonna, the spider-lilies that the Katschei had favored. This bed of roses in particular was responding to her ministrations, and those of Klava, with a vegetable gratitude. New shoots were forming, the bushes were covered with healthy leaves, and two of the bushes in particular, a red and a white, were in full bloom. The white roses especially were ones that Katya loved; the blossoms had a unique honey scent she would gladly have worn as a perfume.

It was in this mood that the paper bird found her, darting down from the sky like an attacking wasp to hover in front of her nose.

She forgot all about the roses in a surge of shock and elation. "You found help!" she breathed. "Show me what they say!"

The bird unfolded. The inside of the page was blank.

She faltered. "But—you *did* find help!"

The bird folded itself back up and bobbed madly.

Suddenly it dawned on her. "They can't write!"

The bird bobbed again.

She had specified that her Champion be able to read—but not write. Perhaps there just hadn't been anything to write with…not everyone would think of writing with a bit of soft lead, or a piece of charcoal from the fire—or maybe they didn't have a fire, or lead around.

But the bird was unfolding and refolding itself, and when it was done, it was no longer a bird, but a tiny paper dragon. Her eyes widened.

"A *dragon* is the Champion?" Affirmative bobbing. Now moving so fast it was a blur, the bird unfolded, refolded, and became a man—then a balalaika—then a dragon again. She frowned over that. "A dragon—wait—*two* dragons? And a man—not Sasha?" It had become a bird again, and the bird was bobbing affirmatives like a mad thing. "Oh, little bird, you did well!" she crowed, and the bird dropped into her hand, just paper once more. She tucked it into her waterproof envelope just as she "heard" the Jinn swiftly approaching. The wretched thing was infernally sensitive to magic—or at least, to the magic happening around *her.* Or maybe it was only to spells in use. Or maybe it was spells he didn't recognize.

She felt him looming over her, but did not turn around. "Were you wasting magic again?" he growled from directly behind her.

"There was a wasp," she said shortly. "It stung me, and I purged myself of the poison. Would you rather I sickened?"

He grunted; she sensed him turning on his heel, and felt him leave.

But he did not leave the castle; she still could not tell exactly where he was, but she knew he was near enough to be within its walls. She decided to wait things out in the garden. There was no point in rushing to the others with her news, especially not if he had suspicions of her.

The others—there were ten of them now. Klava was not the only human; there was a young gypsy hedge-witch, and a girl who talked to animals without ever having tasted dragon's blood. There was a bear-girl who was just as irritated at being taken as Lyuba was, if not more so. And there were two creatures from a Tradition that Katya did not even recognize; a fragile girl wearing what looked like a wedding dress, and a silent dark-eyed, dark-haired girl who had yet to say a word to any of them—not that she seemed hostile, just very wary. Katya had her suspicions about the one in the wedding dress; she had the notion that the poor thing was a ghost, and not a girl at all. If that was true, then there was an escape for her, and as soon as the Jinn was gone and she was able to relay her news, she was going to try talking to the poor thing.

As for the dark one…she had no clue at all. The Jinn must be straying far afield to have gathered that one in. Katya didn't blame her for being wary; in her shoes, Katya would have been the same.

The humming faded and finally vanished. She left off her gardening, dusted off her hands, and headed for the shared room. By now it was rather full, but no one really wanted to move out. Probably they all felt safer together. Katya certainly liked having the others about. True, the Jinn's guards and servants had never offered any offense, but they had also never been given the opportunity to.

There must have been something about her that alerted all of them as she stepped in through the doorway because they all fell silent and looked at her expectantly.

She nodded and smiled. "We have Champions," she said simply.

They were all too cautions, too careful about attracting attention, to cheer. Cheering would bring down some form of notice, if not from the Jinn himself, then certainly from one or more of his guards. But each reacted according to her nature. Lyuba jumped up, transformed to Wolf form, and capered for a moment. Klava clapped her hands, as did the girl who spoke to animals. Yulya bent her head and heaved a sigh of relief, as did the new girl in white. Marina threw her arms around Yulya, who hesitated, then hugged her back. The gypsy bit back an exclamation of triumph, and the dark girl and the bear-girl merely looked fiercely pleased.

"Tell us!" Klava demanded. The rest gathered closely around to hear what she had to say.

"One of them is Prince Alexsandr of Led Belarus, my betrothed Sasha," she said, and blushed. "But he is not one of the Champions."

"What is he then?" asked Klava. "A great warrior?"

She had to laugh at that. "Better. A Songweaver."

No matter what Tradition they came from, it seemed that all of the girls knew what a Songweaver was. "We call that a Skald," said the dark one, looking impressed. "Is he a Greater or a Lesser Skald? Does he tell The Tradition a new path and make it listen and heed him, or does he cajole it into believing that his way is the Path it wishes to take?"

"Oh, it is persuasion he does." Katya smiled. The dark girl nodded.

"That may well be of more use to us," was all she said, but Katya felt her warm approval.

"The other two—" she paused for effect "—are dragons."

Well that certainly put the fox in the henhouse! It was a

good thing that the Jinn was gone because the babble that arose was enough to wake the dead. Katya just let it run out, since she knew she wouldn't get a word in anyway. Fortunately it wasn't so much noisy as it was confusing with everyone trying to talk at once. When they all finally ran out of things to say—mostly about frying pans and fires—she spread her hands.

"I haven't got a lot of answers for you. The amount of information I can get from my bird is quite small." They nodded at that, and accepted it. That was a relief. "All I know is this. They *are* Champions, or my bird wouldn't have gone to them. I was very specific on that point. If they are Champions, that means that they will fight to free us. And Sasha wouldn't be with them if they weren't going to help us. He is not easily deceived."

There were glances all around. Finally it was Klava who said, a little reluctantly, "Well, if they really are Champions…"

Lyuba began to chuckle. "Oh think! Dragons! No matter how powerful the Jinn is—these are dragons! They'll make him think twice, at least!"

"And we really need to find that bottle," Katya said firmly. "It does us no good to fight and defeat the Jinn if we can't confine him again, because I don't think we can actually kill something like him. It's time for all of us to put every moment we can into the hunt."

"You know," the bear-girl said slowly, "we might be going about this all wrong. Instead of finding where it is, it will be easier to find where it isn't. We need to make a map of the castle and start eliminating places."

"There is one. It's in the guardroom. The old one, that the

Jinn's people don't use." That was the gypsy. "I'll bring it here. Then we can search every room completely."

Katya nodded. "And it might sound like a waste of time, but I think each one of us ought to go over every room. We each have abilities that the others don't." There was a sly look from the gypsy, and Katya thought wryly, *And I know what yours are,* because she knew for a fact that the "old" guardroom had been locked the last time she'd checked it. Well, having someone who could pick locks around was going to be heaven-sent.

As the gypsy slipped out, and the others gathered to discuss how to perform the searches, the girl in white sidled up to Katya. "You want to talk to me," she whispered.

Katya nodded, and put her hand comfortingly on top of the girl's. It was ice cold, as she had suspected. "You aren't alive, are you?"

Two slow tears formed in the girl's colorless eyes and trickled down her cheeks. "No," she said, simply. "I am a Wili. We are the spirits of women who died because of the treachery of men. The man I loved deceived me, and I—died."

Suicide, she suspected. Not unlike the Rusalkas, then, these Wili. "Oh, you poor thing—" Katya left her hand atop the girl's despite the chill. "Can you tell me your name?"

"Guiliette." She sighed. "I should not be here—I can only walk by night. I do not know how this Jinn managed to capture me—nor how he keeps me walking by day—" A faint blue flush suffused her cheeks. "Nor how he keeps me from what I am cursed to do."

Katya sighed. "Murder young men, is it?" she asked.

The Wili started. "How do you know?" she gasped.

"Because the Rusalkas of my Tradition are much the same." She gave Guiliette a long and measuring look. "And I think that there is an escape for you, not only from here, but also from your curse, so you can go on."

Now the Wili went so pale she was almost transparent. "Why do you tell me this?"

"Because if any of us can escape from here, we should. Because I don't think you are happy with what you are. Because—" She shrugged. "Because, Guiliette, you should stop being a Wili, and—and go on. I know that this works for Rusalkas, so it should work for you. This won't be an easy thing," she warned. "But it's deceptively simple. You have to forgive, really forgive, the man who betrayed you."

The blue flush suffused the Wili's cheeks. "Ne—!" she began, enraged—

—then stopped herself.

"That is the point, isn't it?" she replied slowly. Katya nodded. "Forgiving the one that betrayed me…forgiving all that pain, the despair…it is almost impossible."

"That is why so few Rusalkas manage," Katya said gently.

"I…will think on this," Guiliette said, and sighed. "But I can do one thing that none of you can. I can still pass myself through things. So—"

She lifted her hand, and it passed right through Katya's with a feeling of terrible chill and a vague nausea. Katya repressed her shivers.

"I can look for hidden passages, hiding places, in the walls," the Wili continued. "And I do not sleep. So I will do this. Yes?

And whatever betides I will not leave you all until you have found that bottle."

"Yes, please," Katya said, and smiled warmly at her. "You are a treasure to us, Guiliette. Thank you."

"It is little enough I can do, and none of you deserve to be here," Guiliette replied. Then out of nowhere came a tiny little smile, the first that Katya had seen on her face. "It is good to feel useful again."

"Yes it is," Katya said softly, watching the ghost-girl drift out of the room in search of the castle's secrets. "It always is."

There were Tritons and Mer-folk in the waters closest to the Jinn's desert, waiting to hear if there was anything that the rescuers needed that the Sea King could provide. Sasha had gotten his ride on a dragon, much to his terror and delight. Take the ride in Baba Yaga's mortar and add to it the ride on the Goat, and the result might be half of the experience of riding on a dragon. When he slid shakily down off Adamant's back once they were on the mainland, it was with two conflicting feelings inside. He wanted to do it again immediately. He never wanted to do it again, not under any circumstances.

But right now they had some other priorities. Sasha needed clothing that wasn't crusted with salt, and food and drink. Gina scouted him a village, although he would have been willing to swear there couldn't be any such thing here, and Adamant put him down near it while the two flew off to scout conditions around the Castle of the Katschei. If there was any way to reach it without being seen...

He went into the village, after beating the worst of the

damage out of his clothing. It was too bad about the boots; they'd need oiling and oiling and re-oiling to get them fit to wear. There were, fortunately, people here who, if not actual merchants, were still willing to sell him things. He still had the Queen of Copper Mountain's coins, and silver spoke a universal language—though he could make himself understood, as the tongue spoken in that remote place was not unlike that of Led Belarus. He found a woman doing laundry quite happy to part with a shirt and trews right off the line, a cobbler who had a pair of boots in his stock that fit when Sasha had on two pairs of socks, and several folks who would cheerfully sell him all manner of odds and ends. Once again, for the third time on this journey, he found himself with a new set of clothing, pack, and traveler's essentials.

And when the dragons returned to him with the dismal news that there was no way in which they were going to be able to get anywhere near that castle without being easily seen, even by night, he already had a plan in mind.

"What we need," he said, "is someone who can get into *and* out of the castle. Something insignificant, that wouldn't be noticed or missed. I think I know just the person, but I have to track him down."

With that, he explained everything he knew about Sergei, the Little Humpback Horse.

"That is a good notion," Adamant observed. "The information we can get or give with the bird is very limited, but if you can find your friend—he would be ideal."

"The other idea I had was this," he continued, and grimaced, just a little. "We don't know just how apt these girls will be at helping us to fight, and I think we have to assume that they won't be of much use. So before we take on the Jinn, we need to get them somewhere safe. If we can't go through the air or on the ground to get them out—we could go under it."

Both dragons regarded him with a jaundiced eye. "We don't burrow like moles, you know," Adamant said, a little testily.

"Not you. I was thinking the Queen of the Copper Mountain. Look there—" From enough time staring at those beaded tapestries, he would know the shape of the Copper Mountain anywhere, and he pointed to it. "There it is. The Jinn's desert is—there."

Adamant and Gina both blinked. "They are…surprisingly close."

"I wouldn't be the least bit surprised to learn the Queen already has tunnels under the Katschei's land," he admitted. "She's a neutral creature, neither good nor evil. I have no doubt she traded with him. I have no doubt she trades with virtually everyone and everything in this part of the world. Think of it— she is secure in her mountain fortress, and can cut off access merely by collapsing tunnels. She has no wish to conquer anything above the surface. She was and is in the perfect position to trade with everyone and favor no one. The trick will be to get her to agree to extend those tunnels into the Katschei's dungeons. If she'll do that, we can get the hostages out."

Adamant's eyes glinted dangerously. "Then it would not matter what we did to the castle and its inhabitants in the course of fighting him. We would not need to restrain ourselves in the least." He flexed his talons, tearing up the ground, and Gina did likewise.

"Exactly." He wondered, could he be persuasive enough? "If we can find the cave I tumbled into, I'm sure I can get inside. Then it will be a matter of talk."

"What about the door you left by?" Adamant wondered. "That would be easier to find." They both gazed out at the mountain, blue in the distance, pondering all the possible ways to get inside.

But Gina just snorted. "Men. Why should you go hunting? They will come to us."

Sasha blinked. "Ah…how?"

She laughed, a deep rumble in her chest. "Trust me. If two dragons show up on her mountain, the Queen will certainly send someone to find out why. Being that she seems to be relatively peaceful by nature, I suspect that would be an envoy rather than an army."

Sasha and Adamant looked at each other and Sasha grinned wryly. "Gina *is* another female, and probably knows better than we do how the Queen would think," Sasha pointed out.

"Aye. And that being so, why don't we just go?"

So it was another flight by dragon back, another terror-filled takeoff and landing, and then Sasha found himself with two dragons at his side, admiring the view on the eastern side of the mountain. He thought he was probably quite near the door he had left by. The stretch of gravel-laden slope seemed about right, as did the nearness to the tree line.

"I could get very fond of this view," Adamant said meditatively. "Very fond."

A heavy sigh greeted his words. As one, the three of them turned to see a green-skinned man in elaborate silk robes regarding them with a dubious expression. "I certainly hope you don't plan—"

And then he stopped, and peered at Sasha.

"Prince?" he said, in an entirely different tone of voice. "I hope there is no—dissatisfaction involved in having you and your—friends—here?"

"Not at all," he replied, stepping forward from between the two dragons. "I just needed to get your attention quickly, so I asked them to come along. You must admit, they are rather— "

"Prominent?" the adviser suggested. "I would not say 'threatening,' of course—"

Sasha widened his eyes. "I absolutely pledge you on my honor and soul, there is and was no threat intended. But I did need to speak with the Queen and not have to wait about hoping someone would let me in. If I may, I really, truly, do need to speak to Her Majesty on a matter of terrible importance."

The adviser eyed him, and evidently decided that Sasha was serious. And that it was a matter of urgency. "In that case, please come inside." He eyed the dragons. "Do you wish your—friends—"

"Oh no, Prince Sasha can speak for all of us," Gina said cheerfully. "We'll just continue to enjoy the view."

Chapter

16

The Queen of the Copper Mountain was just as stunning as he remembered her. She wore a different sort of gown today, one that seemed to be made of a pale green silk, cut like a chemise with long flowing sleeves, and it provided the backdrop for a kind of gold-and-malachite collar that covered her shoulders and chest, with a matching belt that encircled her hips and depended to the floor. "You didn't find your wandering lady?" the Queen asked, with just a touch of a smirk.

"Actually I sort of did, and that is why I need to speak with you, Majesty," Sasha replied earnestly.

They were not in an Audience Chamber, nor a Throne Room. This was a very different sort of room altogether, but it was one that displayed the wealth and skill of the people of her Kingdom as nothing Sasha had seen before.

Sasha had gotten the impression that one never saw the sun in the Queen's little Kingdom.

He had been wrong.

They were in a fascinating chamber hollowed out in the very peak of Copper Mountain. The floor was paved with malachite tiles; the furnishings were all malachite as well—two low, padded chairs, a tiny table between them, and a very long table behind them. Most of one wall was a single glass window, the likes of which Sasha had never seen. It was clear, flawless and all a single piece. He could hardly imagine how it could have been made without magic. All of the glass windows he had ever seen were made of thick, wavy glass, full of bubbles and imperfections. This was as clear as air.

And the view was amazing.

They sat, not facing one another, but side by side facing the window, with that tiny malachite table between them. Behind them was a servant at a samovar at the larger table. On the smaller table, within easy reach of either of them, were delicate teacups and plates of tea cakes.

"So did the lady reject you?" the Queen asked, nibbling a cake, as an eagle flew past at eye-level.

He shook his head. "Nothing of the sort, Majesty. No, the lady is held captive, with several others, in the Castle of the Katschei."

She paused, tea cake halfway to her lips. She set it down. "The Katschei is dead," she said flatly.

"But something else is in his Castle." Sasha contemplated the view, then leaned forward a little. Yes, if he leaned forward, he could just see the edge of a zone of pale yellow. "I think you know that, Majesty."

She nibbled the cake, but it had clearly lost her interest. "Hmm, yes. I believe I was informed. Overtures to trade were met with silence, so I shall not trouble myself with what is there now."

"Perhaps you should look more closely, Majesty," Sasha said, getting to his feet and walking over to the window. Yes, there it was, a smear along the edge of the view, a haze of dust above it, marring the cerulean-blue of the sky, a blot of arid, alien color bespeaking death and desolation amid the greens and blue-greens of the wilderness. "What is there has changed the landscape."

She waved a hand dismissively. "It does not belong there. The Tradition will arrange for it to be taken away."

"Perhaps. Or perhaps The Tradition will be changed." He continued to stare at the Jinn's desert. "The Tradition has been changed before, and it can be again. Do you know what is there?"

Silence for a moment. "Personally? No...."

"It is called, I believe, a Jinn."

She murmured something to the attendant. Sasha continued to stand, staring out of the window, as the attendant left, then returned. He turned back to see that there was now a fourth person in the room, a fellow with the bent-shouldered look of a scholar about him. The Queen looked to Sasha. "What did you call the creature again?" she asked.

"A Jinn," Sasha repeated.

At a look from the Queen, the newcomer cleared his throat. "A Jinn, Majesty, is a being said to be born of fire. Although physical, it is not, and never has been, human. My sources are mixed as to whether it is or is not mortal. It cannot abide water or many green things, finding its home in the desert. In some ways, it acts very mortal, having dwellings, marrying, begetting children. There are said to be two sorts, the lawless and the law-abiding. The latter dwell in the City of Brass, in the Kingdom of the Empty Quarter, so called because it is all desert. The former may be anywhere in the lands surrounding that Kingdom." With a significant glance at Sasha, he continued. "It is, I believe, those with which we are concerned. The Lawless Jinni acknowledge neither master nor ruler, nor abide by any laws, and seldom make alliances even with their own kind. Each seeks to create a Kingdom of his own, accumulate power, and eventually, to overwhelm and enslave all Jinni it encounters, turning the land to desert and slaying or capturing all that are not Jinni. Being powerful magicians, and able to accrete power by extracting it from others, they have little or no use for the items most other beings consider valuable. Wealth they count only in terms of power. Art gives them no joy. They are immune to most feelings."

"That," Sasha said into the silence, "is probably why the Jinn rejected trade with your Kingdom, Majesty."

The scholar nodded cautiously.

The Queen looked just the faintest bit irritated. "Then let him sit there in splendid isolation. If he has no need of what I can offer, then I have no need of him."

Sasha scratched his head. "There's a bit of a problem with that, Majesty. You see, he isn't satisfied with just having what he has. By his very nature he wants everything. In fact, unless I'm very much mistaken, you'll find his patch of desert has been growing since he arrived."

Again the Queen sent a sharp glance toward her scholarly adviser, who nodded reluctantly. "It has doubled in size, Majesty."

"The Tradition makes him do what the Katschei did—hold

lovely young women captive. But he's using that, using The Tradition against itself. He needs more magic than he has just in
himself, and The Tradition makes it easy for him to abduct
young women—so he abducts only those that have power,
either inherent or because they are naturally creatures of
magic." He grimaced. "Like my betrothed, except that she
allowed herself to be taken on her father's orders to find out
what had happened to a missing swan maiden. The message she
got out to us said there were several more captives in the Castle
and if I were to venture a guess, I would say that every time he
takes a girl, his desert gets a little bigger."

The Queen bit her lip and narrowed her eyes. "I do not see
what this has to do with me," she replied.

Sasha paused while he sorted through possible answers.
"Well…for one thing, you are going to lose your trading
partners. Nothing can live in that desert but him. Sooner or
later, everyone you've traded with will be gone as his desert eats
what used to be their lands."

The glance that the Queen sent toward the scholar was
like a spear now. He coughed. "We, ah, already have, Majesty.
The Leshii of Mosswood, the Shaman of the Cave of the
Bones, and the Firebird of Aen Jar. The Firebird fled," he
added. "We do not know what the fates of the Leshii and the
Shaman are."

The Queen's darkening expression did not bode well for
those who had failed to call her attention to this. "I have no intention of going to war against this Jinn," she said ominously.

Sasha put on an earnest expression. "That shouldn't be
needed, Majesty. There are Champions—my two dragon

friends—who are going to attempt to take him. But this is where we *do* need your help. We need him weakened, we need to get the Sea King's daughter out to help us, and the only way we can do that is if we get his hostages out of his hands." He looked at her expectantly. "Without those young women to draw on, his power may well be halved."

She drummed her fingers on the arm of her chair. "You have a plan."

"We have one that requires your help, yes, Majesty." He licked his lips, and hoped he didn't look as nervous as he felt. "I told my friends that I would be very surprised if you had not had tunnels driven well into the Katschei's grounds. For trading purposes. As is your right."

"What of it?" she asked. "This Jinn knows nothing of them. We approached his gates rather than reveal our secrets."

"All the better, Majesty." He smiled weakly. "You see, I am fairly certain that the Jinn does not know of these tunnels, and he will be looking to the surface of the land or to the sky for any attempts at escape. If you were to drive those tunnels further, into his dungeon, we could free the hostages and weaken him by removing them from this source of power."

She sat in silence a while. "I will think on this. I must speak with my advisers. Stay here."

He bowed. She rose to her feet and swept out, pale green gown and long sleeves trailing after her, jewels chiming softly.

"Tea, sir?" asked the attendant. "And perhaps something more substantial than cake."

Sasha sat down, feeling very weak in the knees. He could scarcely believe he had managed to get this far. Matching wits with the Queen made him feel like a man with a knife facing a man with a sword. "That would be welcome, yes."

The attendant took away the cakes and placed buttered bread, cold beef, and pickles beside him. With a sigh of appreciation, Sasha helped himself. The view from that window was tremendous, and he had no doubt, had helped his case. She could see with her own eyes how the Jinn was encroaching on Copper Mountain. And being underground probably would not save her and her people if he decided he wanted what she had.

It wasn't as if the Jinn would know how the girls escaped, either, not if she was clever and he and the dragons were fast enough. If her people collapsed the tunnels behind the girls, the Jinn would never know who had driven them. And if Sasha and the dragons could start an attack or a distraction so that the Jinn had his hands full at the time of the escape, he wouldn't notice until his power began to ebb that they were missing, and by that point they would be long gone.

He repressed the urge to pace. Pacing would make no difference in how this came out. If she elected not to help, they would just have to make some other plan.

"Perhaps something a little stronger than tea, sir?" the attendant asked.

He thought about that a moment. "That might be a good idea."

Without another word, a glass of vodka replaced the teacup, and Sasha downed it, feeling it burn all the way to his stomach, and light a fire there.

Fire—

If nothing else, now he had far more information on what a

Jinn was than he'd had before. But fire and water…Katya was the Jinn's "natural" enemy, and Sasha had the uneasy feeling that if it came to a need to consume one of the Jinn's captives, she would be the first to go.

He had to get her out of there.

Had to.

Even if he had to fight his way in there alone.

Katya was reasonably pleased with their progress. Half the rooms had been explored, and thoroughly. The Wili had uncovered a veritable second castle of secret passages.

That much pleased her. The trouble was, still there was no sign of the bottle.

Guiliette had, however, found one hidden way out. There was a tunnel leading out under the walls from one of the cellars full of old and broken furniture that came out in what had probably once been the other side of the lethal hedge-maze that had surrounded the Castle. But, the maze was gone, vanished, leaving behind only desert. There wasn't a hint of cover out there; the Wili had cautiously investigated and come back to report that anyone using that exit would be quickly spotted by the Castle guards. No hope for it; unless something provided a powerful distraction, there would be no escaping that way.

She wondered if there was any way the girls could hide in the walls. Would that make the Jinn go looking for them, and leave an opening for them to escape?

But that would really accomplish nothing. As long as the girls were around the Jinn, he could leach their magic. That was probably why he allowed them to roam at will. As long as they were within the walls, he was going to be satisfied. It wouldn't matter that he couldn't see them, as long as he knew he had them.

On the other hand, if he decided he needed to consume one—those secret passages might come in very handy. Even if he could find the passageways—which, eventually, he probably could—he wouldn't know them the way the girls did.

Of course, that supposed that he wouldn't just blast a hole in the wall to get to the one he wanted....

In the tales, solutions were always so much simpler.

All right. She knew that Sasha was out there with the dragons. It was time to tell him what was going on. This time she found a real pen so that she could write as much detail as would fit on the inside of the bird. She told him how many girls there were, about the secret exit, that they were trying to find the Jinn's bottle and why. She included everything they knew about the Jinn, which was, sadly, not much. When she was done, she had room for exactly one letter, and after much trepidation, she made a neat little heart.

Then she let the bird fold itself up, and went in search of some of the other girls. She found Klava deep in conversation with the gypsy over a handful of herbs, in a small square tower room with a window overlooking what was now desert. The other half of the tower floor was dark, and she couldn't see what lay in the room. This one was furnished with four chairs, a table, and chests lining the walls.

They both looked up at her entrance.

"We were discussing whether or not it is possible to poison

a being of fire," said the gypsy, without preamble. "Am thinking not, but is good to discuss anyway."

"I'm about to send the bird off again, and the Jinn will surely come looking for the source of the spell he senses when I do," she replied. "Twice now he's sensed it around me, and I think a third time—"

Both the others nodded, and the gypsy grinned. "I give him something to think about, I think. You send bird, then hide—" She cast around, and pointed at a chest. "Is empty, yes?"

Katya raised the lid. It was empty and big enough for two of her.

"Klava, you getting ready to close lid on her. I start spell." The gypsy took out a pack of cards and began to shuffle them. Katya stood in the chest, and whispered the words of the spell to the bird, thinking hard about Sasha. The bird shot out the window, she dropped down into the chest, Klava shut the lid on her, and she felt the Jinn approaching quickly from a distance. Within moments he was practically on top of her, as if he had flown in through the window. She knelt, all bent over, inside the chest, and hoped he would not think to look there. She would have a hard time explaining why she was hiding.

Flickering light played through the cracks in the chest as the Jinn's presence filled the room in a way she could feel even inside the chest. *"I told you—"* he roared.

Then stopped. The light dimmed immediately. "What are you doing?" he demanded, sounding a little surprised.

Katya breathed in dust and old wood, keeping her breaths

shallow, as she listened to the others. "Telling future," the gypsy said, an insolent tone in her voice. "Hoping to see you *not* in it."

"You are wasting magic," he replied, surprise giving way to his usual irritation.

"Is mine to waste," she said indifferently. "If you wanted tame, timid girl, you should have taken tame, timid girl. You carried away Django girl. You get what you took."

"Insolent mortal!" the Jinn growled. "Very well, if you are going to waste it, I must take more from you from now on, so you cannot!"

Klava gasped, there was a strange, discordant sound—

Katya stifled a gasp of her own, as she was overwhelmed by a feeling that something was pulling all the blood from her body. She thought for a moment that she was going to faint.

Then the moment passed, though Katya still felt weak, and the Jinn sounded as if he was speaking from a great distance. "Heed my orders in the future," he said.

"If I choose," said the gypsy, and laughed, though weakly.

The Jinn growled, and Katya felt the hum that signaled his presence receding.

She continued to breathe shallowly, all her limbs as heavy as lead. After a moment, the lid to the chest came up, and she sat up. "I think I'll just stay here for a while," she said weakly. Klava nodded.

"That was rather nasty," the apprentice said, looking as unexpectedly exhausted as if she had run for seven leagues, then spent a sleepless night.

"Was expecting same," the gypsy replied. Katya looked to her, and saw that, though she looked a bit drained, she did not look as wretched as either Klava or herself. At Katya's look of puzzlement, the gypsy smirked.

"Source of your magic is *you*," she said, pointing to Katya. "And same being for you, Klava. Source of *my* magic is all gypsies. He takes only what I have at moment, and no more. I call upon magic of my people, it is all returned to me again." And indeed, she was looking better and better as time passed. "I think we do this again, when bird returns. Yes?"

"He'll mark you as the troublemaker," Katya warned weakly.

"This is not new thing for me." The gypsy lost her smirk, and shrugged. "Everywhere gypsy goes, are marked as trouble-maker. Me, he will not kill, I am knowing how far to push, and no farther." She looked about furtively. "I am Anya," she whispered, giving them her name for the first time.

Katya gave her a little bow; she had noticed that the gypsy girl never offered to take anyone's hand. "Thank you for your name," she said, taking care not to repeat it. *Names are power.* The gypsies must take the opposite tack as her father, keeping their names hidden as much as possible to keep people from taking that power. "But I shall call you Magda."

The gypsy's face lit up with a smile. "Is good name. Was name of babushka. Am liking name."

Looking completely recovered now, she offered Katya a hand out of the chest, which Katya sorely needed.

"Did you notice?" Klava said suddenly. "He didn't seem to know he was taking power from three, rather than two."

Katya blinked at that. It was true. And there were other things, now that she thought about it. "And he never appears when Lyuba and Shura transform, nor when Guiliette passes through walls."

"I think," Klava said, slowly, "perhaps those things that we do that are a part of us do not count as spells. I have never seen nor heard Lyuba say anything when she transforms."

Katya pondered that. "I can't think how that could be useful, but it might. We should remember that."

"Magda" laughed. "Is useful because he cannot tell when we are searching!" she said triumphantly. "But we must tell others. In search, some might think to use spell, and that would be bad."

Katya nodded. "I will, when we gather for dinner," she said. "But now—I really think I will go and lie down."

"Be lying down here," Magda said firmly. "Is place in other room I use when want to be alone. I keep watch."

Katya and Klava both staggered into the tiny room that Magda pointed to, and found a pallet had been made up there on the floor, with a plethora of pillows and so many shawls, curtains and draperies that Katya blinked. Why on earth would Magda have decorated this room like a draper's showroom?

"Oh…it looks like a tent," Klava said instantly. "Oh poor Magda—she's homesick…."

"Then we'll have to get her home," Katya said firmly, which ended up being the last thing she said for a while. The inviting pile of pillows pulled her into itself and she fell asleep listening to Magda humming a strange, wild melody.

Sunset painted the landscape outside the window in hues of pink and rose, with the shadow of the mountain etched across the face of the forest. Sasha didn't know whether to feel encouraged or discouraged that it was taking the Queen so long to make a decision. The attendant kept faithfully filling his teacup and feeding him the entire time. From time to time, trays of new food were brought in, and the samovar was kept topped up; Sasha had so far gone through an entire banquet of courses in small portions, from blinis and sour cream, to mushrooms, to tiny portions of baked fish and a whole quail treated like a larger bird. It would have been a glorious afternoon if he had not been so anxious.

Finally, as he was considering asking for another round of vodka to take the edge off his tension, the door opened, and one of the advisers walked in. Sasha leaped to his feet and bowed; the adviser gravely returned his salutation.

"The Queen is with her tunnel planners even now," the green-faced man said, without any preamble. "She has, in her graciousness, elected to help you."

Relief made Sasha as giddy as three glasses of vodka. "And we are grateful beyond telling," he replied, with as much enthusiasm and sincerity as he could bring to bear.

The adviser smiled thinly. "Actually, we of the Council wish to thank *you*. We have long felt the presence of this interloper to be a threat to the Kingdom of Copper Mountain, but we could not persuade her most gracious Majesty of this. You have, and we are in our turn grateful."

He blinked. "Why ever wouldn't she believe you?" he asked, bewildered.

The adviser examined his nails closely. "Her Majesty is…much older than she appears. *Much*. In all that time, there has never been a threat to our Kingdom from the surface dwellers. Since there never has been, she believed there never would be. She was of the firm belief that remaining neutral, and trading with all parties, made us too valuable to threaten—and too well allied. We who live shorter lives cannot afford to be so sanguine."

Sasha nodded in sympathy. "That's something I can understand, and it isn't just those who live long who fall into that trap," he replied. "I have to allow a certain amount of danger into Led Belarus, even though I'd rather not. People who never face danger never believe that danger can come to them, and never recognize threats until it is too late."

The adviser looked up, and smiled. "You are a wise Fool indeed. Now, I am sent to tell you that we think there are tunnels leading out from the Castle already. If such exist, we will find them and strike for them. As I am sure you assumed, we tunnel very quickly indeed, especially when we need only carve a small and temporary passage. I think that is the only information you may need?"

"It is. Thank you for your help, and thank you for your hospitality." Sasha stood up, and included both the adviser and the attendant in his bow. "You have been gracious beyond measure."

"It is not often we have so pleasant a visitor from the surface world." It was the attendant who replied, rather than the adviser. "Usually they are here only for lust or greed, and concentrate on the Queen and perhaps on her obvious advisers, and treat the rest of us as mere bagatelles."

As Sasha's eyebrows shot up, the attendant laughed. "We are all equals here, Prince. Today I served you tea and dinner. Tomorrow, if my expertise is needed, I may don the robe of an adviser. Very few of us are set in one position during our lives. We find it makes for more balanced judgment."

"Well, some positions are better than others," the adviser murmured diffidently.

"But taking on the onerous ones for a time makes us all aware of our fellows' feelings," the attendant concluded wryly. "We believe that all those who are served should also spend time serving. Shall I see you to the door?"

"Yes, please," Sasha said weakly, glad beyond measure that his usual habits of treating everyone well had reaped such a bountiful harvest.

He left the door he had come in through, after a friendly nod to the old man in the guardroom as he passed by. He found the two dragons enjoying the last of a bountiful meal in the fading blue of twilight, which eased a bit of his guilt at having left them for so long.

"Well, there you are at last!" Adamant said, gulping down a raw goose whole by tossing it up in the air and catching it like a trained dog with a treat. "They treated us like honored guests, so I assume they did the same for you?"

"Very much so," he replied, and grinned. "She's going to help us. She's with the tunnel planners now."

"Ha!" Adamant said with delight. "Then it was worth the wait!"

"You said that about the geese," Gina said dryly.

The grey dragon laughed. "You'll say that, too, eventually. Just wait a few years and you find out how hard it is to catch a goose when you're our size."

"Now wait a moment—" Sasha said, because by now his curiosity had gotten to the point where it was an unbearable itch that had to be scratched. "The things you keep saying make me think that Gina wasn't always a dragon—"

"Oh I wasn't," the emerald dragon said cheerfully. "I was a human Champion for Glass Mountain. It's a long story, but I exchanged places with Periapt, Adamant's brother, so that he could be with his human mate and I could join this fine and handsome fellow as his."

"Keep flattering me, wench, and I shall never get my head out of the clouds," Adamant chuckled.

But Sasha was still blinking at the idea of a human becoming a dragon. "That's—powerful magic."

"Yes it is, and it couldn't have been done without The Tradition practically breaking over us like a wave, and without human and dragon being willing to exchange places," Adamant said, soberly. "And not without Godmother Elena. I don't think there will ever be a piece of work that powerful again in our lifetimes. Certainly not in this part of the world."

"Well I insisted on staying a Champion, and Adamant decided he wanted to be one as well," Gina continued, nuzzling behind the charcoal dragon's frill affectionately. "I was very glad of that. Time enough to settle down and have hatchlings when we are tired of flying to the rescue!"

"It does give us a certain amount of immunity from roving adventurers who want to make a name for themselves by slaying whatever dragon they happen to meet," Adamant said dryly. "Besides, it means we become part of some amazing stories. Godmother Elena's Champions do tend to get involved in unique situations."

"That is like saying that the ocean is a bit damp," Gina

laughed, then sobered. "Well, we have accomplished one goal. Now we need to find that little horse you were speaking of. Have you the least idea where you might find him?"

Sasha sighed. Frying pan….fire. "I last saw him around here, but he could be almost anywhere, I suppose."

"Well, in that case," said a low, growling voice with a tinge of laughter in it, wafting in from out of the darkness. "I suppose you are going to need a tracker again. You humans! So careless with losing your friends!"

Chapter

17

"Wolf!" Sasha shouted with joy, and flung his arms around the huge beast's neck. "I am beyond glad to see you!"

"Piff," snorted the Wolf. "A simple calculation made me realize I still hadn't really repaid my debt to you. Nasty things, debts. Have a way of creeping up on you and jumping down your throat when you least expect them to. Thought I would hunt you down to deal with it, and lo! Here you are in my hunting grounds! Who are your large friends?"

Hastily, Sasha made the introductions. "First a Fox, now a Wolf," Gina murmured to Adamant. "I expect before the year is out we'll have collected an entire menagerie."

"Ahem," the Wolf said. "I heard that. Pot, kettle. You aren't exactly running around on two legs yourselves."

"Don't mind me," Gina replied. "My mate will tell you I talk before I think sometimes."

"But if I do, she'll hit me," the grey dragon said, his red eyes sparkling with humor in the light of the rising moon.

"We really need to find Sergei," Sasha said urgently, ignoring them both. "It's about that Jinn that's in the Katschei's Castle."

"The one making the forest into a desert?" The Wolf growled. "Even if it wasn't paying off my debt, I'd help you with that. What call has he bringing his wretched desert into my forest, I ask you!"

His tone was light, but underneath it was a deadly seriousness.

"He thinks to conquer us easily, because The Tradition here does not know him," Gina replied.

"Bah. What need have we for The Tradition to guide us, when we know what to do with interlopers?" He snapped his jaws. "I wish I were something more than large and fierce and a good tracker. But never mind. I will find the Horse. He is still on this mountain somewhere, I scent him now and again when hunting. It could be, Prince Fool, that he is hunting for you."

"I hope so." Sasha smiled a little in the dark. "If you can find him, he could be a key to being able to defeat this Jinn."

"Then I go!" the Wolf said, shaking his huge head. "You *are* staying here, yes?"

"It's too dark to fly," said Adamant. "Crashing into things in the dark is bound to get you mocked when other dragons hear about it."

The Wolf laughed deep in his chest. "Makes me glad I am not able to fly then," he said. "And that I can see in the dark. If the Horse is on this mountain tonight, I will find him!"

He was a bounding silhouette against the night sky for a moment, and then he was gone.

Sasha sighed. "The Tradition seems to be working for us, Champions," he said to the dragons.

"It does not like this Jinn," Gina replied. "I think—"

She was suddenly interrupted by a howl of triumph in the distance. All three of their heads swiveled in that direction.

"You don't think—"

The howl came again, nearer.

"Surely not—"

The howl came practically on top of them, and the Wolf bounded in like an oversized, overexuberant dog, tail and head high, tongue lolling. "What did I say! What did I say! I am the best tracker on the mountain!"

"And it is not as if I was trying to hide!" said a voice in midair above them, crossly. "In fact, I have been rather obvious! You could have found me at any time today, but *no!* You wait until I am just falling asleep! I ask you!"

"Oh, land and be done, old woman!" the Wolf laughed. "The Fool will think you are more foolish than he is! He will set you up as a jester!"

Sergei trotted down toward them; the moonlight, from a moon in its first quarter, was just bright enough to show that he was trotting in a descending spiral, as if the air were hard and he was using a ramp to come down. He heaved an enormous sigh as his four hooves touched the ground, then his long ears pricked up and he shook his head so that they flapped. "Hello Prince! I am pleased to see that the Queen has not made you forget everything but her!"

Sasha rapped him lightly on the top of the head with his knuckles. "She is the loveliest creature in the world, but my heart goes elsewhere," he replied. "And right now, she who has my heart is behind the walls of the Katschei's Castle in the heart of that growing patch of desert!"

Quickly, he and the dragons explained the situation, as Sergei listened quietly.

"I have a feeling," he said. "I think that it would be very dangerous for her to use that paper bird again." The Horse pawed the ground. "I will be your go-between, as you hoped. I think I can get into the herd and the stables tonight and tell her what you plan. And if need be, I may well be able to get out again to carry messages. It is the least I can do."

Sasha impulsively flung his arms around the Horse's neck. "Sergei, you—"

"Are wise and noble, yes I know." The Horse whinnied a chuckle. "Just you capture that bird and don't let it fly back to—"

Something small smacked Sasha in the face. He batted at it with a yell, and found himself with a handful of paper bird.

"—speak of the devil and it shall appear," said Sergei in a voice heavy with irony.

"Bah, I need a light now!" Hoping he wouldn't somehow hurt or insult the bird, Sasha held it carefully in his teeth while he fumbled through his pack in the dark, looking for his fire-striker and the tiny lantern he had bought.

Suddenly it became much easier to see, and he dug through his things for a good long moment before a polite cough made him look up.

The Horse held some sort of glowing ball between his long ears.

Sheepishly, Sasha stopped going through his pack, took the

bird out of his mouth, and let it unfold. He peered at the tiny writing, shaking his head, until Sergei somehow made the ball glow brighter.

"Saints! How can she write so small?" Carefully, he puzzled through the words. Some of it repeated what he already had learned from the Queen's scholar. But one thing was completely new.

"This Jinn was imprisoned in a bottle, she says," he told the others. "One of the maidens was there when it was released by her master. She thinks the bottle has the spell to imprison him again on it, and perhaps—" he felt a sudden excitement "—perhaps even the Jinn's True Name!"

"None of us are mages, to force the thing back into its bottle," said Gina doubtfully.

"You won't need to be a magician if you have the thing's True Name," said Sergei decisively. "Even a child could command it by its True Name."

"They're hunting for the bottle now," Sasha continued. "She thinks that they are all safe for now, and says not to make any attempts to rescue them until they find the bottle."

"That makes good sense," Sergei said, as Sasha stared at the tiny heart at the end of the message, and felt his cheeks growing hot. And not just his cheeks. It was a good thing it was dark....

Even in the middle of terrible danger, she was thinking about him.

He felt amply rewarded for the way he had handled the Queen.

Then, as he watched, the ink slowly faded from the page, and the now-blank paper seemed to wait, expectantly, for him to fill it.

"Should I send it back?" he asked the others, looking up.

"No," Sergei said immediately. "It's too dangerous. If that Jinn can sense spells, every time the bird goes out or comes back, he will know."

Sasha looked down at the blank paper in his hand. "Wait for my answer," he told it firmly.

The paper shivered as if a breeze was about to pick it up. Then, slowly, it refolded itself and a paper bird lay quietly in his hand.

Sasha searched for a place that was safe to put it, and finally settled on folding it inside a piece of paper, which he put inside the coin pouch that he emptied of coins, and put that inside a stocking, which he carefully folded up, folded the second one around it, and wrapped the bundle inside his spare shirt, which went into his rucksack. If the bird could get out of that, it would be because The Tradition had decided it should.

Sergei clapped his ears together and the globe of light vanished. "I'll be going," he said, with a nod of determination. "So don't worry, Sasha, I'll find a way to get to her and tell her the bird isn't coming back yet. You keep track of those Copper Mountain miners. We'll need to make sure that when they break through, the girls have that bottle, know the spell or at least the Jinn's True Name."

With that, the Little Humpback Horse turned and galloped off, except that instead of galloping *down* the slope, each step took him higher and higher into the air, until at last, he vanished from sight.

They all stared after him in silence for a long time.

Then the Wolf said, genially, "Well, Prince Fool, I don't suppose you thought about how you're going to spend the night on the mountain, did you?"

"Uh," Sasha admitted, sheepishly. "No—"

Maybe the bottle isn't actually in the Castle at all. That had been Katya's first thought on waking, and she had hurried into her clothing, made an excuse of breaking her fast on a bit of bread that she took with her, and headed for the Castle outbuildings. It had been like a revelation in the night, that thought. It would have been infernally clever, to put the bottle where the Jinn never went. It could be hidden among all the broken and useless objects in one of the sheds, of course. Or wedged in among the wood in the woodshed—as hot as it was, the only fires were being laid to cook things. Or even in the stable—the place was full of horses, donkeys, and mules, all brought by the troops that the Jinn had hired, but no one ever rode anywhere except to exercise a favorite mount.

Katya decided to start with the stalls first. It would be just like that wretched Jinn to wedge the bottle in under a manger or a watering trough.

The stables were a substantial stone building with exposed wooden beams and a huge hayloft overhead. She supposed that in the normal climate here the stone was a necessity to keep the horses warm in the winter; now it served to keep them from baking in the heat. When she entered the double doors and paused in the doorway she was met by a breath of cool air redolent with the scent of clean straw, the dryer scent of hay, and just a faint whiff of horse droppings. She was also met by at least two dozen sets of eyes as every beast in the stable turned to look at her.

She had not been around horses much, but the legacy of the Sea King's children and the dragon's blood she had swallowed so long ago meant she could talk to and soothe most animals. The horses eyed her with suspicion, but a few words into the darkness convinced them that she was not an enemy.

This was just as well, considering that these were war-horses. She went slowly from stall to stall, stopping to speak, and to listen, quieting fears, dispelling suspicion, and convincing them before she ever entered a stall that she was a herd member. These were not Wise animals, merely animals, but they did listen to reason when it was given to them in their own tongue. Even the worst tempered eventually allowed her into their stalls.

She had finished with the last of the horses and had started on the few mules, when she heard it. She was hunting at the back of a mule's stall, just under the manger, feeling through the straw when the voice whispered to her.

"Psst. Sea princess—"

Startled, her head came up suddenly, and she banged it into the bottom of the manger. Red and black flashes passed in front of her eyes, she saw stars, and sat down abruptly in the straw, her head alive with pain.

"Ow!" was the first thing out of her mouth, followed by a stream of articulate and literate curses that were neither blasphemous nor prurient.

She'd had years to develop a vocabulary of invective that wouldn't offend anyone. It was the sort of thing a princess had to do if she was going to be able to adequately release her feelings.

She put up her hand and felt the brand new lump on the back of her head, wincing as her fingers probed it. "Ow."

"Good saints, princess, I am impressed!" said the voice. "I do not believe I have ever heard anyone call me a noodle-spined bar sinister son of a blind camel and a cactus before."

"I'm not," she replied crossly, slowly getting to her feet and peering over the top of the stall. "I'm not impressed, that is. I can do without being introduced quite so intimately to the underside of a manger, thank you. Who *are* you?"

She wasn't sure quite what to expect, but the ugly little creature, like a tiny horse with the long ears of a donkey and two humps on its back, was not it. "And while I am at it, *what* are you?"

"Sergei. Son of the Mare of the North Wind. Called 'the Humpback Horse' by some." The beast looked around furtively. "I don't think there is anyone here to overhear us, is there? I don't sense anything. Sasha sent me. We all think it's not safe to send back the bird."

She blinked, felt the lump on her head again, and stared at him. How—where had this all come from? Had she hit her head too hard? Was she seeing things, hearing things? How could this little fellow have come from Sasha?

Then it occurred to her: Fortunate Fool. Help from unexpected places. This was Sasha's Luck at work, the first she had ever seen of it really.

Of course she knew of the Mare of the North Wind and her sons. The Humpback Horse was the most famous of them, and also the cleverest. How Sasha had managed to get the Horse's help would probably be a story in itself.

It was, after all, the way that the Tradition of the Fortunate Fool worked. He went about doing good deeds without thinking about it, just doing them. And The Tradition saw that he got paid back for them.

But he was probably right about not sending the bird back. "I'll need to send him information. You got in here, can you get in and out more than once?" she whispered back.

The Horse smirked. "Easily. Most of what I do depends on looking worthless. If I slip out of the Castle and go wandering off into the desert, who's going to go out there to retrieve something that looks like me? And even if they tie me up, there has never been rope or halter that could hold me if it wasn't magical." He stared for a moment at the lead rope fastening him to the manger. His eyes crossed, and the rope unknotted itself and fell to the ground, followed shortly by the halter that had come unbuckled.

"In fact," he continued, "even if a bond is magical, most of the time I can get out of it."

Alarmed, she hissed, "The Jinn! He senses spells!"

"Ah, but it's not a spell," the Horse corrected. "It's just me. Now where was I? Ah, yes. Sasha sent me. There is an ally that is carving a tunnel towards the Castle, evidently as easily as a mouse eats its way through a loaf of bread. Are there any tunnels leading out of the Castle? Escape tunnels, perhaps?"

"One," she whispered back, fascinated. "How did you guess?"

"I could sound all superior, and point out that it *was* the

Castle of a creature who was suspicious of everything and everyone, but the truth is, our ally thought of it first," the Horse replied. He cocked an eye up at her. "Well, I presume they have some means of sensing these things, and I was told that if such a thing exists, they are going to drive for that tunnel, which should make things easier. Sasha wants you to have the girls ready to get down there at all times. Since at that point it won't matter, he can send back the bird as the signal that our ally is going to break down the last bit between the two tunnels. Then you and they and anyone else you feel moved to rescue can run far away as fast as you can."

"We need to get our hands on the Jinn's bottle first!" she whispered urgently.

"Well, yes, obviously." The Horse sounded impatient. "I might be able to help with that. I knew the Katschei and I knew all the hiding places he had for his heart. Well, it wasn't really a heart per se, it was—never mind, I'm rambling. There are some hiding places. It's possible your Jinn used one."

She nodded. "But what about places like—well, the stables? Unlikely places? Places where people wouldn't think to look because no one would ever put anything valuable there?"

Sergei considered that for a moment. "Would you say that the Jinn is subtle?" he asked, with one ear raised.

"Not—really." She thought about the little she had actually seen of the Jinn. He had come in with a whirlwind to abduct her; presumably he had done the same with the rest of the girls. That was hardly subtle. He seldom appeared except to briefly watch them—or perhaps it might best be said, to glower at them. That wasn't even remotely subtle. When he felt a magic spell, he rushed in from wherever he had been, and immediately threatened whoever he thought had cast the spell, without waiting to see what had actually happened. Definitely lacking in finesse. He had said that he considered them all animals....

"Not subtle at all," she said.

The Horse nodded. "Fire spirits seldom are. Firebirds being the exception, but then, they are female, and gender might have something to do with that." She got the impression of a smirk, the sort that invited you to join in the joke. "That being so, I think we can eliminate subtlety in the choice of a hiding place. I think we can eliminate creativity as well." He laid his ears folded over the top of his head. It looked very peculiar, as if he was trying to hold his head down with his ears. "Now, when the Katschei died, I suspect his minions proceeded to flee rather than looting the place. I would in their shoes. He wasn't called 'the Deathless' for nothing, and you never know when a creature like that is going to bounce back from apparent death. So the good saints only know what got left behind. I suppose you've found that out to an extent, but I am talking about dangerous things. You might find other items in these hiding places besides the bottle. If I were you, I wouldn't touch them, no matter how attractive or harmless they appear."

She shivered, thinking of all of the deadly potions, possessed daggers, gems and pieces of jewelry that had either curses or inimical spirits attached to them that she had encountered just in *her* travels. "No worries there," she assured him. "I'd rather not spend my life as a toad."

"Or worse, find yourself dead and your body hosting the Katschei's spirit. Or anyone else's spirit for that matter," the

Horse said darkly. "There are more nasty things in pretty packages in the world than most people would believe. All right. The first hiding place was the most elaborate. There was a fountain in the garden. Is there still a goose in it?"

"No, not when I got here," she said.

He heaved a sigh of relief. "Good. That one was a nightmare. You'd have to be an expert archer to deal with it. Have you looked for a secret compartment under the throne?"

"Not yet. We were leaving the throne room until last. The Jinn is sometimes in it, and it's generally guarded." She couldn't imagine why the Jinn would be in the throne room, but she had caught a glimpse of him there once or twice.

"There's a second hiding place in the throne room. If you sit on the throne and stare directly at the wall opposite, you'll see the reflection of light from the facets of a jewel no larger than a grain of sand. Press that jewel and the hiding place will be revealed. Another hiding place is in the well in the root cellar under the kitchen. Lower someone down on the rope. Halfway down is a niche." The Horse sighed. "The Katschei used all of those before he hit on what he thought was the perfect solution, and that was an elaborate version of the goose. There was an oak tree in the forecourt—it's gone now. There was a dragon curled around the foot of the tree. In the tree was a chest. In the chest was a fox, in the fox was a rabbit, in the rabbit was another duck, in the duck was an egg and in the egg was his heart. You had to get past the dragon, climb the tree, open the chest, kill the fox before it got away, then kill the rabbit, then kill the duck and break the egg."

Katya's brows rose. "Good heavens. That just shrieks 'I am

an important hiding place, look into me!' Why didn't he just put a big sign on the tree that said My Heart Is Up Here?"

"He should have." The Horse sounded amused. "Thank the saints that The Tradition favors villains making mistakes. But we can't count on that this time. The Jinn isn't in our Tradition. Any mistakes he makes will be due only to himself, not to The Tradition. We will have to be careful as well as clever. I think that bottle is our only hope of really ending this."

"Once I find the bottle, Sergei, I still have to read what is on it," she reminded him. "That brings me to another question, when I find the bottle. Should I move it, or leave it where it is?"

His eyes widened. "You *are* careful as well as clever! Leave it, by all means, if you can manage to read it without touching it. We won't actually need the bottle until the time comes to confront him."

She smiled. "Thank you for the flattery." Now the question she really and truly wanted answered. "Sergei—how is Sasha?"

"Worried sick about you. Missing you. Blushing when he thinks about you. Blushing and other things that is, making me wonder how blood can rush to two places at once." She blushed, but laughed. "And great friends with your father, despite the fact that your father sent a storm to fetch him." The Horse sounded amused again. "Did your father intuit his existence, scry on you, or did you tell him?"

"I told him. I'm his agent, it's my duty to keep him informed." She sniffed. "Father could use some lessons in subtlety himself. All right. I will try those hiding places right now—if the bottle isn't there, we're no worse off than we were before. I will be back before nightfall and let you know of my progress."

Or lack of it, she thought, as she left the stable. And she felt her head again. This task was turning out to bid fair to break her skull. *Ow.*

The view from the minstrel's gallery above the throne room was superb. You could see everything with nothing in the way. There was only one guard on the throne room. The three captives eyed him dubiously. He was one they all recognized and he was a good enough fellow, but they probably could not get away with strolling into the throne room and rummaging around in secret hiding places.

"Should we distract him with our feminine wiles?" asked Yulya in a whisper. She didn't look happy about the prospect, but in the past few days she had gone from timid and incapable to determined and capable of accomplishing quite a bit. That Rusalka would not have gotten the better of her a second time. She still wasn't the equal of, say, Klava, but her attitude toward everything had improved enormously.

"I don't think so," Katya whispered back. "Not that you don't have plenty of feminine wiles, Yulya, but it's one thing to chat up one of the guards when they aren't on duty. It's quite another to come marching up to him when he's on an important post and start batting your eyelashes at him."

"You think he'd suspect something?" Yulya sounded more relieved than disappointed.

"I would, if I were him. These fellows aren't stupid, more's the pity." Katya surveyed the room, looking for any more guards. Their hiding place in the minstrel's gallery gave them a good vantage point for any purpose; the carved screen across the whole of it allowed them to see without being seen. Evidently the Katschei or his predecessor believed that minstrels should be heard and not seen. "Remember what Sergei told me. Since The Tradition doesn't hold the Jinn here, we can't count on him making Traditional Path mistakes, like hiring stupid guards. And he hasn't."

"It's true that they do seem very smart," Yulya said thoughtfully. "Smarter than I would have expected."

"All right. He can't see the throne from where he's standing," Katya observed. "Guiliette, it looks as if the first hiding place is yours to look into. Literally."

The Wili nodded, and slipped into her semitransparent state. If she was moving, you would certainly see her, but if she was still, she could be mistaken for a trick of shadows. "I'll come through the corridor wall and then freeze in place."

The problem was this throne room was built in a kind of extension to the Castle itself, so that there were three outside walls. It had probably been planned in order to have as many windows as possible, taking advantage of natural light. However, that made getting into it a challenge. The four of them were in the minstrel's gallery on the one inside wall, facing the rear of the room and the throne, and directly above the corridor that gave access to the room.

The throne was not only on a dais, it was inside a kind of enclosure that was twice the height of the throne itself, gilded on the inside. The effect would be to make both the throne and its occupant seem larger and more important. Katya wondered what the Katschei had looked like. Had this been his idea? Had he been a wizened little thing, or the opposite?

She had the feeling he had been small and wizened, and very self-important.

There were two niches for guards behind the throne, in the two rear corners of the room. Because of the enclosure, the one guard on duty could not actually see the throne itself. But Guiliette would have to be very careful when crossing the floor between the wall and the throne. There was no real way to approach it without being in the guard's line of sight at some point.

Alas, that the Wili could not fly! It would have been so much easier if she had been able to drift in the rafters among the battle banners, and float down into the enclosure. There would have been a point where she was exposed, but not nearly for as long.

She slipped out of the minstrel's gallery and down the stairs to get to the corridor, for although she could pass through the floor, to do so would mean she would fall from the ceiling. It wouldn't hurt her, but it might make a noise. The guard would be watching the door, of course, but he might not be watching the wall, so that was why she was going to pass through the stones.

Guiliette had already checked the niche in the wall; that was easy for her, and accomplished just in the same way that she found the secret passageways and three other hiding places. It had, alas, been empty, but at least they hadn't had to go through all the rigmarole of sitting on the throne and finding and pressing nearly invisible jewels in order to check it.

So once Guiliette was out of the minstrel gallery, they waited. And waited. There was no sign of the Wili. Katya began to get impatient, then alarmed. What could be going on?

Then Lyuba chuckled throatily. Katya glanced at her sharply.

"Look at the floor," the Wolf maiden whispered. "Halfway between the wall and the throne."

It took Katya a moment to see it, because the stone of the floor was full of irregularities, and because she wasn't sure what she should be looking for. But then, finally, she made out something, as transparent as a jellyfish, moving along the stone. It was the Wili, who had plastered herself flat to the floor and was crawling toward the throne, taking advantage of the stone to hide her, and the fact that the guard was keeping watch for someone standing or walking, not crawling. This would be why she was taking so long, of course.

"Oh clever!" Katya breathed. "Good for you, Guiliette!"

"Does it seem to you that we are becoming more clever all the time?" Yulya asked. "I mean, I feel cleverer. Not that I'm getting overconfident! But I do feel much cleverer than I was before, and I know I'm thinking of more solutions to things by myself." Then she frowned. "Or do you think it's all The Tradition? Is there a Path for this sort of thing? Will I stop being clever when I am back with the flock?"

She really *had* changed. Katya nodded. "I suppose that being clever is like anything else. If you do a lot of thinking, especially thinking for yourself, you get better at it. I honestly don't think The Tradition is helping us much here, if at all. It can't—there's no Path for this. I think this is all us. I think that we are all getting better and better at finding solutions for problems."

"Really?" Yulya sounded rather happy about that. "Oh good. I've been thinking that I'm tired of having people think of answers for me."

Katya smiled. "You're a different girl from the one that was abducted. Yes, a cleverer one. I think you should be proud of that, Yulya."

You won't have to depend on anyone else to tell you what to do after this, she thought. "It wouldn't hurt to show your sisters how to reason things through, when you get back." She chuckled. "You're going to be the flock leader now, you realize this, don't you?"

Yulya giggled a little, embarrassed. "I probably will. There wasn't one after Oksana was married. She always was the truly clever one—"

Remembering that story, Katya said wryly, with her eyes still on the crawling Wili, "Not all that clever. Not when that husband of hers caught her by stealing her swan-cloak."

Yulya flushed a little. "Well…some of us suspect that was no accident. She had been saying for a while that she was tired of the flock and wished she could go somewhere alone. We couldn't understand it—why wouldn't she want to be with the flock? And of course, when she did get a chance to escape, she came straight back to us, but—"

"But she knew very well that husband of hers would follow. And she knew he'd find a way to get her back. Right? If he hadn't guessed she was his wife by her hands, she'd have found some other way to show him."

Guiliette was almost to the throne. The guard still hadn't spotted her—

Wait—

He peered in the direction of the Wili and stepped a little out of his niche, frowning.

Lyuba writhed into Wolf form and was off like a shot before

Katya could say anything. Katya clutched the sill of the screen and held her breath. What on earth was the Wolf maiden up to? She wasn't stupid—she might not always think quite like a human, but she wasn't stupid.

Lyuba loped into the room, tail wagging, head high, and dragging her feet just a tiny bit to make the same sort of sound that the Wili might, when crawling. The guard relaxed.

"So it was you I heard out there! Doing a run?" he asked. And he grinned, which made Katya relax. Evidently Lyuba had been making herself popular among the guards.

Lyuba transformed back into human shape. "By the Leshii, this place is like a cage! Worse, a cage in a cage, with all that desert out there! I don't know how you humans stand it! Yes, I was doing a run, is there anything you'd like fetched up from the kitchen?"

"A flask of water—I think the days are getting hotter, this throne room was like an oven earlier," he replied, taking out a handkerchief and wiping his brow. "Eh, it's a good job, but this is a damned odd place."

"You need to look into some other sort of uniform if you are going to keep serving this fellow," Lyuba observed, eyeing him critically. "I never have understood all the cloth you humans burden yourselves with, but in this place, friend, that is insane. Look at you! All wool! Even sheep know not to grow much wool in the desert!"

The man tugged at the collar of his tunic and grimaced. "I'll take it up with the Captain, Loobie, you have a point. Of course—" he looked around carefully "—I know I can count on you not to spill this…we might not be serving him much longer. Captain doesn't like some of what he's been hearing out of the Jinn's mouth. Little things like 'when you're all my slaves, there will be no complaining.' Our term is up in a fortnight, and I think he's looking at another job."

Lyuba grimaced; by now, Katya saw, the Wili had reached the throne and was well under cover of the enclosure.

"Well, you know," the Wolf maiden said, "you might look into Copper Mountain. I understand the Queen sometimes takes mortal mercenaries to guard the doors. And with this Jinn on her doorstep, she's likely to be thinking hard about just that. You could do a lot worse. The pay is good and she's not the sort to fly off the handle and start something you have to finish."

The guard shook his head. "No, not for us. I've seen what the Jinn can do when he's angry, and we have no defense against that. No, he's looking south, into the human Kingdoms. Ordinary soldier work, that's the thing for us. No more mucking around with magical types. There's some things that no amount of pay can compensate for, and seeing the Jinn burn up that Rusalka, you can't help but wonder what he'd do if you crossed him."

The Wili was crawling back along the floor, faster now, since Lyuba had the guard's attention.

"Well, fewmets. I don't like being in a cage, but some keepers are better than others, and you lot weren't bad." Lyuba looked melancholy. "I like you fellows and that's a fact. Don't at all mind running errands for you, you're not all growls and hatefulness just because you're guards. I hate to think what's going to replace you."

"Probably more like *him*," the guard replied, with sympathy.

"We're getting the idea that the bigger he gets, the more of his own kind he'll have working for him instead of us plain old mortals. Sorry, Loobie. You're a good girl, and I wish we could take you with us. You'd make a great Company mascot. We could put your picture on the banner and everything."

Lyuba chuckled. "I would, wouldn't I? I could run dispatches, scout, get in behind enemy lines, cut through their horse lines and turn their mounts loose, then chase them off, and when I wasn't doing all that, scare the crap out of new recruits when they get too full of themselves."

"All that and more." The guard laughed, and Lyuba laughed with him. Katya marveled. It was very clear that Lyuba had been making a lot of friends among the guards. Clever of her, for certain.

"Well let me run you that water, before you pass out." With another bizarre writhing of her form, Lyuba became a Wolf again, and dashed out the door. About that time, the Wili glided quickly into the minstrel's gallery. "Nothing," she said. "The hole was empty."

"Well that just means we won't have to deal with the throne room. That is not a bad thing," Katya pointed out as Lyuba dashed into the throne room again, tossed the waterskin she was carrying in her mouth into the air with a flip of her head, and waited for the guard to catch it. It was quite a performance, and clearly one she wasn't doing for the first time. With a bark and a tail wag, she dashed out again.

A moment later she was back with the rest of them. She jerked her head sideways toward the door; Katya nodded, and they all headed for safer areas. They were courting discovery in the minstrel's gallery.

As they entered a more public corridor, Yulya stopped. "I can't bear it anymore. My curiosity is eating me alive, and has been since you joined us. Lyuba, how do you transform and still have clothing?"

The Wolf turned around, and writhed into the girl again. She was laughing. "I'm not," she said. "It's an illusion. I'm really absolutely bare. People see what they expect to see, and they don't expect to see a naked woman running about. Oh, I do wear clothing when I'm going to stay human for a while, but if I'm transforming a great deal, I don't bother. Go ahead, try to see through the illusion now that you know."

Katya's eyes widened, as she did just that, and realized that Lyuba was telling the truth, because there she was…wearing… nothing but air.

Now, this was hardly shocking to *her,* since most of her father's subjects tended to be very cavalier about clothing. But Yulya—

Sure enough, Yulya gave a little squeak and hid her eyes. Lyuba transformed back again. But she was still laughing, Wolf-fashion, jaws wide and tongue lolling, as she ran off.

While the others pooled their information and tried to figure out where to look next, Katya was in the stable, consulting with Sergei. "It's not in any of the hiding places you mentioned," Katya told the Horse. "So if you were a Jinn, where would you hide a bottle? You don't want to destroy it, I presume."

"A smart magician would make sure that destroying the bottle would do something bad to the Jinn," Sergei replied. "I think we can assume that any magician wise enough to confine a Jinn is going to be sure to take that sort of precaution with the bottle."

Katya sat down in the straw of the Horse's stall, just under the manger, with her back to the wall. "Just out of curiosity— why would anyone put a Jinn in a bottle if they are so danger- ous? And if you have to imprison it, why put it in a bottle? Why choose something that can be opened again? That doesn't make a great deal of sense to me. I'd imprison him in a crystal or a sealed box and drop it into the deep part of the ocean."

Sergei tilted his head to the side and one ear flopped over. "Good questions, both. Hmm, well…I assume that you can't simply destroy a Jinn. The Katschei was supposedly Deathless only because he took steps magically to make himself invul- nerable. He wasn't really a spirit. And most of the creatures we think of as being 'spirits' are really quite mortal, they just live a very long time. The Queen of Copper Mountain is one of those, and so are the Baba Yagas. Then on the other hand, you have the Rusalkas that *are* ghosts, your Guiliette who is the same…and I presume, the Jinn. Pure spirits can take on a physical form, but they don't need it. And you can't really destroy them. In the case of a ghost, you can send them on to— whatever fate awaits them, or like the Jinn, you can confine them, or drive them away. But you can't destroy them. So if you want to be rid of them, you need to imprison them."

"Hmm." She thought about that. "All right, then why put them in something that can be opened? What possible reason could you have for not dropping the thing into a volcano or the deepest part of the ocean?"

Sergei blinked at her.

"Mercy," he said softly.

Her eyebrows rose. "Mercy? What, in the name of the good saints, do you mean by that?"

Sergei's eyes softened, and for once, there was nothing sarcastic, ironic, or comical about his tone. "These are creatures that cannot be destroyed. You can't allow them to run about loose, because of all the damage they can inflict. They are, simply put, a menace, and they do need to be confined where they can't hurt anyone. But they are also thinking beings, things that can reason and are aware of their own existence. Yes, they have chosen paths of evil and harm. But don't they deserve a chance to repent and reform?"

Katya opened her mouth, then shut it again. This was a question to which she really had no answer. "Can they?" she finally asked. "Repent and reform, I mean. Just listening to this one, it doesn't seem likely."

"I don't know. I don't know much more than you about Jinn. But the one who put him in a bottle obviously thought so." The Horse sighed. "I'd rather err on the side of mercy, myself. I might be in need of some myself one day, and it isn't only Fortunate Fools who get back what they give to others."

She considered this. "Could you find the City of Brass?" she asked. "I know you've found a lot of other places, probably more unlikely than that, like the Well of the Water of Life and Death."

"Probably. It wouldn't take me long to get there if I knew the way. But since I don't know the way, I don't think I can get there and back with help from the lawful Jinni in time to help us." His ears drooped with obvious regret. "It was a good idea though. I wish you'd thought of it sooner."

"That wasn't what I was thinking—or actually I was. If we lose, I think you should go there and get these lawful Jinni to help you, help Father, because we simply can't allow this one to keep destroying the forest with his desert." She bit her lip. She didn't want to think about losing, because if they lost…Sasha would probably die. Not only that, but she might die if the Jinn thought she was too much trouble to keep alive. In fact, she would rather be dead, because she didn't want to think of having to go on without Sasha. The very thought felt like a spear in her heart. "But if we win, the Jinn will be back in the bottle and no matter what we did with it, there would be a chance that someone would find it and open it again. So I want you to take the bottle to the City of Brass and the Jinn's own people. If anyone will know what to do with him, you would think it would be them."

"Good idea," Sergei said, brightening. I will do just that." His ears came up. "I promise."

"Now, help me think, here. If you were a Jinn, where would *you* put such a bottle?" she asked.

"I would want it some place where ordinary mortals couldn't touch it. Someplace where, however, *I* could. That would be— in a fire?"

She frowned. "Hot as it is, there are no fires anywhere around the Castle—" No—that wasn't quite true! "—except the kitchen!" she all but shouted. "The bread ovens!"

Sergei picked up his ears even farther. "Is it late enough for them to have been banked?"

"Should be…can you tell if I am going to alert him by moving his bottle?" she asked. "I'll have to take it out of the oven to read what is on it."

He nodded enthusiastically. "Go get the rest. I will meet you at the kitchen door."

"The rest" were not hard to find; all of them were sitting disconsolately around their shared room. They all must have been pinning their hopes to the throne room. When she explained her idea, life came back to all of them.

"We'll stand guard!" Lyuba said, as the bear-girl nodded.

"I'll watch for trouble coming from outside," Guiliette said bravely. "If the Jinn comes, I might be able to delay him."

"Huh…" Klava said, and then grinned. "Oh, I have such an idea!"

"What?" The sparkle in her eyes made Katya think that it was probably a very mad idea—and in this case, the madder, the better.

"Come on! No skulking, no hiding! Everyone laugh and talk! We're making cakes!" She seized Magda by the hand and hauled her out the door, laughing and chattering more than enough to cover up Magda's astonished silence.

"Oh *yes!*" said, of all people, Guiliette. She clapped her hands and began to giggle, in a little silvery laugh, and glided out the door after her. Whatever Klava had thought of then dawned on Marina, who also laughed, grabbed Lyuba, and ran after. The rest followed, though it was clear that most of them had no idea why they were making so much noise. Still, Klava seemed certain of her idea, and both Guiliette and Marina had also figured out her plan and liked it, and that was enough for Katya.

The mob of young women streamed down the corridors, occasionally meeting with some of the Jinn's hired guards. To each of them, Klava cried merrily, "We're making cakes!" and somehow this pronouncement turned puzzled and suspicious looks and even frowns to indulgent smiles.

"You go right ahead, dearies," said one grizzled old veteran, and "Make some for me!" cried a younger man.

Then they ran right into the mercenary Captain, and Katya's heart went cold. If there was anyone in the Castle who could and would stop them—

He eyed them as they approached. "And what—" he began in a rumble.

"We're making cakes!" Klava cried, dropping Magda's hand and dancing up to him. "We'll make some for all the men, too!"

And to Katya's astonishment, that hardened veteran paused, and slowly smiled. "Well now, and that's more like it, acting like real girls and not all this moping about," he said with a nod. "Time you brightened up. You go on, have your fun, and don't worry if them cakes don't come out. I'll make the mess right with the cook in the morning."

"Thank you!" Klava cried, and jumped up to peck the man on the cheek like a child. The Captain actually blushed, and waved them all past. Katya and the others managed to gather their wits enough to chorus "Thank you!" as they passed him, and a few corridors later, they swarmed into the kitchen where Klava shut the door and put her back against it.

"By the saints! I thought that would work!" she said, looking very well pleased with herself. "What's more, if the bottle is in one of those ovens, now we have an excuse to take it out."

"What, exactly, did we just do?" Katya asked.

It was Marina who replied. "Village girls, girls in big schools, sometimes in convents if they are not yet novices—this is something that we just do. Usually at night, when kitchens are clear; it often happens that everyone has been gossiping or telling fortunes, and everyone has gotten a little hungry, and someone says, 'Let's make cakes!' and everyone goes and does it."

"Exactly," Klava nodded. "I went to a big school for girls for a while before my wizard asked my parents for me as an apprentice. Now, we really *will* have to make cakes, but don't worry, it's easy, I know how, and I'll show you while Katya looks for the bottle."

The soft sound of a hoof on the outer door made them all start except Katya, who ran to it and opened it. Sergei stood there with his ears up and his eyes wild with curiosity. "We are covering our subterfuge with noise," she explained. "I need to start checking ovens—"

"I can explain," said Guiliette, "since I will be of very little help in the cooking."

So Guiliette explained what was going on to Sergei, while Klava apportioned the tasks in cake-making, and Katya began cautiously peering into the banked ovens.

And there it was, tucked into one side of the third oven—well out of the way of any actual baking that would go on, but safe enough from someone who didn't know where to look for it.

"I've found it," she called softly to Klava, who was instructing a bemused Yulya how to sift flour. "How do I get it out?"

The apprentice left her pupil and came to peer into the oven, then looked around the kitchen for something. "Ah!" she said with satisfaction, and went to a rack of cast-iron implements next to the fireplace. "These will do the trick, I fancy!" At Katya's bemused expression, she laughed. "These are called *tongs*. Not many fires under the sea, then?"

"Only volcanoes," Katya replied, and watched with fascination as Klava used the scissors-like object to deftly seize the long neck of the bottle and pull it out. She set it right in the mouth of the oven, though, where it was still very hot—

"Let it sit there, and I'll move it again in a little," Klava ordered. "Taking it out right now and putting it on the floor might make it shatter, and I assume we don't want that. I'll come back in a bit and move it when it cools some." She went back to the cake-making while Katya stared at the bottle, willing it to cool.

It was not like any bottle she had ever seen before. It started with a very long, thin neck, which then widened out into a wide, squat bottom. Instead of a wooden stopper, which would in any event have probably become charcoal in the oven, there was a glass or porcelain one, still attached to the neck by a chain.

"Klava," she called softly, "when you saw the bottle, was it only stoppered, or was it stoppered and sealed?"

"Stoppered and sealed," Klava called back, interrupting her own explanation of how to beat nuts into the batter. "But the seal was plain wax, there was nothing written on it."

"The wax was probably bespelled," the Horse observed, "but it shouldn't have been a vital part of the magic to draw the Jinn into the bottle."

She hoped so. It would be disastrous to discover they were missing part of the magic because the wax had burned away.

Klava came over to the oven with the first tray of cakes. She held her bare hand near the bottle and nodded. She slid the tray into the oven, then took the tongs and moved the bottle to the floor.

"Let it cool a bit more, then you can handle it," she said, going back for another tray.

But regardless of the heat radiating off the bottle, Katya was already leaning forward to try and read the writing—because what she had at first thought was only a spiraling stripe was actually a spiraling line of writing, inscribed into the dark green glass of the bottle, then filled with white enamel.

"Fire smite thee, Zephyr blight thee, Water blind thee, Earth then bind thee," she read, and looked up. "What does all that mean?"

"It sounds to me as if there are supposed to be all four elemental powers involved in stuffing him into the bottle," Klava said with a frown. "The fire power to actually fight him, the air to weaken him, the water to confuse him and the earth power to bind his power and send him into the vessel. Is there any more?"

She bent closer. "It's written there three times, then this: 'Iblis Afrit En Kalael, I command thee in the Names of the Law, be bound into this vessel until released by the hand of a virgin of five and fifty years.'"

Klava began to laugh. She had to put the tray of unbaked cakes she was carrying down, she was laughing so hard. Tears began to come from her eyes, and she wiped them with the back of her hand.

"What?" asked Magda, curiously. "What is being so very amusing?"

"Oh, blasted Tradition," Klava replied, picking up the tray and inserting it into the oven, and fishing out the first one with the set of tongs. "Honestly. I suppose you have to put a condition on these things, but I would have looked longer and harder for one, personally. Like 'Until twelfth of never' or some such thing. Still." She began laughing again. "Poor master! No wonder he always had a steady supply of unicorn hair!"

"But now we know the creature's true name," pointed out the Horse. "Iblis Afrit En Kalael. All we have to do now is assemble the company to fight and bind him. I will return to Sasha and the dragons. But first—" He yearned toward the tray of crisp brown cakes "—could I have one of those, please?"

Chapter 18

The forest they stood in was cool, verdant, flourishing. Five paces away, however, the land was all but dead. There was no sign of the trees that had once stood there; there was nothing but hard-baked earth, sand, and a little scrub. The landscape had not merely been altered, it had been erased and a new one put in its place. Not even the softening hand of night could disguise that. It made Sasha feel edgy, nervous. If the Jinn could do this, so quickly, what would he do if he had real power? "That is how matters stand," Sergei finished, and looked from the dragons to Sasha to the Queen of Copper Mountain. "It seems that it will require some sort of magic tied to all four elements in order to bind the Jinn back into the bottle. But we do have his True Name at last. We can command him."

"We are clearly Fire," said the dragon Adamant. "Ekaterina is Water."

"Zephyr blight thee," mused Sasha. "How can Air blight?"

"Weaken him?" the Horse suggested. "I haven't anything in my scant arsenal that could do that."

Sasha closed his eyes for a moment in thought; so much of what he did depended on knowing The Tradition and trusting to Luck, but this was not the time to trust to Luck. Was there anything he could do as a Songweaver? "I am not a fighter," he said, slowly, "but I could sing the strength out of him."

"Music is Air," Sergei agreed. "So that is three of the four. But the key one, the one that imprisons him, Earth, must be the strongest of all."

The Queen frowned, but said nothing.

Why is she so reluctant to join us? Sasha repressed anger at her recalcitrance. It would do no good to get angry with her.

After the silence had gone on long enough to be awkward, the Horse coughed. "How goes the tunneling?"

"One blow of a pick and my men are through," the Queen said shortly. "You need only say the word."

The four friends exchanged a look. "With or without Earth," Sasha said finally, "we must go now, and hope that something turns up."

"I concur," said the Horse. The dragons nodded.

"All right, Sergei," Sasha said, swallowing. "Go and tell Katya to get the girls into the head of the tunnel. I will send the bird as the sign we're going to break through. I'll come through in the tunnel itself and join her."

"We'll come down out of the sky," Adamant said. "The bird should bring the Jinn, and we'll trap him between us."

"It's as good a plan as we're going to get," Sasha sighed. It felt incomplete. Well, of course it felt incomplete. It was.

"I will tell my miners," the Queen said abruptly, and stalked off. Rather than one of her elaborate gowns, she wore a slim, calf-length green skirt, a tunic cut away at the neckline and shoulders in a fanciful pattern, and green boots.

Sasha would have preferred to see her in armor. But then, he had hoped that coming out to see the devastation first-hand would turn her more fully to their side.

Alas, it appeared that such was not to be.

"Have I left any argument out?" he asked the others, feeling obscurely like a failure. He *should* have been able to persuade her, shouldn't he?

The dragons shook their heads. "You pointed out that the Jinn is not likely to permit a rival power on his doorstep. You noted that although he might be a power of Fire, he is not going to find going underground any sort of hardship, and that he could very well call forth the Earth-fire in the form of volcanics and lava and never have to personally leave the surface to attack her. Her own advisers told her how she has lost or is losing half of her allies. I can't think of anything more that you could have said."

He sighed. "Nor can I." *Encourage them, Sasha. They need to think that you think we can all win.* He smiled weakly. "Well, my friends, dawn approaches. Let's get into place. Sunrise will tell us if Fortune favors us or no."

The ten captives were assembled in the kitchen, with the door to the root cellar open. Katya looked to the nine young women who had spent a fundamentally sleepless night until the arrival of Sergei. Her stomach was a knot, her nerves wound up tight. This was going to be, literally, the fight of her life. And she was not a fighter. She couldn't let these girls know how frightened she was, though, or the good saints only knew what they would do. "You all heard Sergei," she said quietly. "Get down into the tunnel, and wait. And I will, I hope, see you again when this is over."

They looked as if they wanted to protest, but bit their objections back. Klava stepped forward, looking more determined than Katya had ever seen her. "I'll take care of them, Katya," she promised. "I'll make sure everyone gets out. You fight the Jinn. You can beat him, I know you can."

Katya smiled, and it wasn't an insincere or weak smile. "Believe me Klava, that, all by itself, will make a big difference. If you all can get away, you take the power he is counting on with you. The weaker he is, the better chance we have to bind him."

Klava turned and went down into the root cellar.

"I wish that I was an earth-spirit," Marina said, bitterly. "I cannot even hope to help you. One touch from him, and I am gone."

Poor Marina! Given how fragile she was, it was amazing how much she had done in these past days. Her courage was amazing. Katya embraced her. "You have been more help than you think, and I am counting on you as our second line of defense if he defeats us. To do that, you have to flee. Get home. Be safe. If we don't win, warn others, tell Father Frost. He may be able to do something where we can't."

"I will," Marina promised.

Magda merely traced an odd pattern in the air, nodded soberly, and turned away, taking Marina by the hand. Blessing?

Protection? Both? And when the gypsy had started to tell the future with those cards of hers, what had she seen?

The Wolf and bear maidens stood uncertainly together, and Katya turned toward them. "You two can do something no one else can," she said firmly. "You are both neutral creatures and you both lived in the forest that was destroyed. The Queen may listen to you when she listens to no one else. Muster your pleas and present them if you see her. If you can bring her in, we *will* win!"

"We will," they chorused, and took themselves down into the cellar after the gypsy.

Yulya embraced her, and Katya heard a stifled sob, but when the swan maiden let her go, there was no sign of tears. "You will bind him," the young woman said fiercely. "You will win, and they will tell wonderful stories about this. And I will tell my sisters that they must be more like you."

She turned and fled down into the darkness. Katya looked after her, touched and just a bit bemused.

The small dark girl, and the one who spoke to animals, merely nodded and left. Katya sighed; she still didn't know their names. Now she might never learn them. But they had been steadfast companions, and she was glad to see they were escaping.

"I'm not leaving," said Guiliette from behind her.

She turned, and frowned with unease. "This isn't wise, Guiliette. You should go with the rest."

But Guiliette smiled. Smiled! And there was something about that smile that made Katya take notice. This wasn't a whim…and it was going to be important. "Let us merely say that I am going to provide a far more formidable distraction than the arrival of your paper bird. And that…it is not altogether true that I am not leaving. I am just not leaving by the tunnel. You did know that the fountain is not just a fountain, didn't you?"

Katya blinked at the sudden change of subject. "Ah, no?"

"It is fed by a spring. In fact, if it were not for the fountain being there, the spring would be gushing forth with a great deal more enthusiasm than it is." The Wili smiled again. "I think you can use that."

And then, suddenly, there was no more time.

With a sound like a bee shooting past, the paper bird arrived. Katya snatched it out of the air, stuffed it into its envelope, and stuffed the envelope into the bodice of her shirt. She heard the hum of the Jinn approaching at high speed, snatched up the bottle, and ran for the door; fear making her heart hammer, determination forcing her to move faster than she thought she could.

But Guiliette was faster still.

She sped out the kitchen door and through the gardens with Katya on her heels. They both reached the fountain at the same time as the Jinn.

He was already wreathed in flame, and his hands were clenched in anger. The fiery eyes were looking only at Katya, and she felt her mouth go dry with terror. *"You!"* roared the Jinn, his voice sounding like a thunderclap.

"No!" shouted Guiliette, interposing herself before the Jinn could act.

"Me!"

"Guiliette—!" Katya cried. This was not how it was supposed to be going.

But Guiliette was paying no attention to anything but the

Jinn; she spread her arms wide, staring him down with such intensity that he actually stepped back a pace, and then she began to glow.

Katya stopped dead, transfixed. The hair on the back of her neck rose, though not with fear. This was not like anything the Wili had done before. This was something altogether new. The glow did not come from within her, but somehow, from somewhere outside of her, and it was a pure white light that should have been blinding, but wasn't. Guiliette looked up, and her face was transformed in a smile.

Katya was filled with awe and wonder. She shivered, feeling that she was in the presence of something so far outside her understanding that there were no words for it.

Guiliette's lips parted, and she spoke; it was only in a whisper, but it echoed louder than the Jinn's shout.

"Rheinhardt! I forgive you!" she cried, in a voice full of incongruous happiness. "I forgive me! I forgive us both!"

In that moment, the sky opened, and glory came.

If the sun had turned into a column and stretched itself down to earth, that was, in the most minor way, the only thing Katya could compare to the column of white light that enveloped Guiliette then.

It made her want to sing for pure joy.

The Jinn cried out in pain, and flung up his arm to hide his face as he turned away.

Katya did not. Although the light was so intense it felt as if it were burning its way into the back of her brain, she could see perfectly clearly. She saw Guiliette looking with love and gratitude straight at her. Watched as the Wili—now no longer truly any such thing—put both hands to her lips and blew her a kiss.

Felt tears of joy sting her eyes as Guiliette dissolved into the light, still smiling, infused with the purest happiness Katya had ever seen in her life.

And then, she was gone.

And the column of light faded, leaving nothing of itself behind.

That was when the dragons struck.

Roaring down out of the sky, they came in from opposite directions, giving the still-dazzled Jinn two targets, rather than one. He didn't make up his mind in time.

Katya awoke from her own daze, filled with a fierce determination. It did not matter that they did not have the final Element. They would fight this creature, and they would win!

In perfect unison, at the bottom of their dive, the dragons opened their mouths.

Enormous gouts of flame fanned out to cover the Jinn in fire, and as they passed, each lashed out with talons at his head.

The Jinn roared with fury; in an instant, there was a sword of fire in his hand and he struck at the bigger grey dragon.

But he missed, and both of the dragons pulled up, shooting up into the sky, mocking laughter trailing behind them.

The Jinn began a gesture.

He never finished it.

With the power that was all instinct, Katya reached for the source of the fountain, found it, and called it with all the urgency that was in her. With an explosive force that shook the ground, the water answered her, blasting the remains of the fountain and its basin out of its path, surging for the sky. She grabbed the half-formed whirlwind that the Jinn had tried to call, infused it with her wild, untamed waters, and turned it loose on him. The whirlwind strengthened, tightened, became a white, churning column that engulfed the Jinn before he could move.

Fight that, wretch! she thought with exultation.

Her father's powers ran true in her. She had created her first waterspout. And the Jinn was caught, trapped, in the middle of it.

He shrieked, and shot up the center of it, trying to escape and clearly blinded by the whirling waterspout that had him in its grasp.

And behind her, Sasha started singing.

It was a mocking, painfully scathing song.

"What a failure you are!" Sasha sang. *"Look at you! A couple of half-magic creatures, a mortal and a girl are beating you! You couldn't manage to live with your own kind, and you can't manage to live on your own. You couldn't conquer anything in your own land and you can't conquer anything in this one, where you are a stranger. Can you feel it? Even the tiny power you had is trickling away! Failure, fool, you have the respect of no one, and no one fears you."*

Blindly, Katya reached for Sasha's hand and found it. The sense of his hand in hers made her feel stronger; she didn't have to look at him to know he felt the same. He had no instrument, no balalaika to carry the magic; *he* was the instrument, and even as she controlled her own magic, she marveled at his.

Each word was a barbed dart. It was a poisonous song. It was aimed straight at the heart of the Jinn, a probe to find the things that the Jinn himself feared.

And it was working! He escaped briefly from the water-spout. The dragons came in for a second pass, and scored him with fire and talon again and the waterspout recaptured him. Katya dared to hope they could take him without needing the power of Earth....

But then, searching for a foe he could reach, the Jinn turned in midair. She felt his hot, desperate gaze on her.

And that was when he saw the bottle in her hand, realized what she had, and his anger exploded.

"Never again!" he screamed in a voice filled with such rage that she shrank back, her determination withering. *"Vile, mortal worms! Never again will you hold me! Now DIE!"*

Sheer terror engulfed her, as the sky exploded with flame.

Dimly, she heard the dragons bellow a challenge; she clung to Sasha's hand as his song faltered, then began again. She reached for her power, sent the waterspout into his face—

Gouts of fire lashed the earth around her; she screamed as tongues of flame licked at her before she could call more water to deflect them. She felt Sasha's arms go around her, as he shielded her with his own body, still singing, defiant, mocking, throwing all that they had in the Jinn's face. *"You will always be alone,"* the song mocked. *"We have friendship, love, the strength of companions. You cannot conquer that. You can never conquer that. Your sterility will blanket the earth and you will still never conquer that, nor ever have it for yourself."*

She lashed at the Jinn with her waters, throwing them at him as spray, sleet, even sheets of fog, anything to confuse his sight. The Jinn screamed his anger and returned with gouts of fire that struck all around them. The dragons roared from somewhere up above and the occasional shrieks of pain from the Jinn marked the times when they scored a hit on him.

It was stalemate, she realized. He couldn't take them, but neither could they take him. With a tingling of despair, she wondered if the best they could hope for would be to be locked in a never-ending fight with the Jinn, until they all dropped dead of exhaustion—

"Die mortal worms!" the Jinn bellowed, as a gout of flame scored a direct hit on Adamant, and sent the dragon into a tumbling fall from which he only just recovered before striking the ground. Gina dove down to protect her mate as he struggled to fly, to gain the comparative safety of height. Icy fear clenched Katya's heart as the Jinn turned his attention to her— and to Sasha—

"And now I see the weakest link in your chain," the Jinn sneered.

With horror, she realized he was looking, not at her, but at Sasha.

"The song dies with the singer—" the Jinn snarled in triumph, and flames began to build around him.

"No!" Katya screamed, calling her waters to her— knowing that this time they would not be enough.

"Indeed, no. Enough."

The Jinn froze; Katya didn't blame him.

Literally rising from the earth, came the Queen of the Copper Mountain.

She was sheathed from head to toe in a—sculpture, was all that Katya could call it—of malachite. It began with an elaborately carved crown, which somehow flowed over her head and down her neck, into something like a gown, the sleeves of which covered her arms to the first knuckle of her hands and dripped down to the ground like the flowstone of a cave, the body of which did the same, to pool around her and become the column of stone upon which she was rising. It was as if an artist of exquisite genius had fused woman and statue into a living whole.

The eyes of the Jinn met the eyes of the Queen—and the Jinn's were the ones that showed fear.

Two voices roared out of the sky. "Iblis Afrit En Kalael, we smite thee!"

Sasha's arms tightened around Katya, as he sang, "Iblis Afrit En Kalael, I blight thee!"

Katya called up her waterspout again and shouted with all of her strength, "Iblis Afrit En Kalael, I blind thee!"

And slowly, the right hand of the Queen of the Copper Mountain rose, until the index finger pointed at the Jinn, the rest curled against her palm. *"Iblis Afrit En Kalael, I bind thee!"*

With a scream, the Jinn started to struggle, as wisps of fog, tendrils of flame, a blast of wind carrying the dust of malachite that lifted from the earth at the Queen's command, all began to circle him. Wordlessly he howled as Fire, Water, Air, and Earth formed into dark green chains, chains that encircled him, wrapped him in their coils, and bound him tightly.

Katya snatched up the half-forgotten bottle and pulled out the stopper, holding it with the open neck, pointing it at the now fruitlessly writhing Jinn. Everything she had talked about with Sergei surged through her mind, and she *knew* at that moment what she was going to say.

"Iblis Afrit En Kalael, we command thee in the name of the

Law, in the name of Justice, in the name of Compassion and in the name of Peace, to be bound into this vessel until you repent and reform, and join the ranks of the Lawful Jinn of the City of Brass!"

With a terrible cry, the Jinn, chains and all, dissolved into green vapor, vapor that was sucked into the bottle in the time it took for hearts to beat twice. As the last of it vanished, Katya grabbed the stopper and drove it into the top, and the Queen of Copper Mountain made another little gesture, and the last of the malachite dust still hanging in the air coalesced about the top of the bottle, forming into a malachite seal that covered the entire top. "There will be no more deserts here," the Queen said, coldly.

Only then did the Queen look into Katya's eyes, and smile.

"An interesting choice," she said. And the malachite column shrank back into the earth, taking the Queen with it.

With a thunder of wings, the dragons landed beside them.

"Looks like we won!" Adamant said with a gleeful grin.

Katya sighed, put the bottle down carefully at her feet, and with weary joy felt Sasha's arms go around her again.

"Yes," she said, and closed her eyes. "Yes we did."

EPILOGUE

The desert was gone. Once again, the Castle of the Katschei was surrounded by forest.

But it was forest that was very much changed.

Gone was the briar maze that had once surrounded the Castle. In its place was a lake—the water was far too wide to be called a *moat*—with the Castle as an island in the center of it. The miners and excavators of Copper Mountain, it seemed, were also superb engineers. A canal cut to the broad Viridian River kept the lake filled and provided access to and from the sea, at need.

Where the fountain had once been, there was now a much more elaborate construction that, paradoxically, looked utterly natural, a high mound that mimicked the shape of Copper Mountain, with the water from the spring flowing down the side in a waterfall, and channeled out of the garden to end in the lake.

The Castle, newly cleaned, revealed itself to be made, not of grim grey granite, but a rosier form of the same stone. The gardens were bidding fair to be second to none. This shouldn't have been a surprise, since they were in the charge of a small, dark woman with a mysterious smile and amazing ways with plants. She was aided in this by her partner, a quiet, contained girl who spoke mostly to animals and had made it clear to the creatures of the forest which items were off-limits and which had been planted for their particular enjoyment. Very few people noticed them, and fewer knew their real names. Most called them "Flora" and "Fauna," and they seemed perfectly content with that.

There was a new addition to the Castle, a single large building that almost rivaled in size the Castle itself; after all, dragons have a hard time fitting into ordinary rooms and through conventional doorways.

The lake played host to one of the most beautiful flocks of swans in all of the Five Hundred Kingdoms. And if now and again one, two, or three of them swam up to the castle, transformed into lovely girls, and left their feather cloaks in the formidable care of the bear that denned in a kind of gatekeeper's cottage by the lake, well, with all of the other wonders of the Castle, it was hardly noticeable.

What *was* noticeable, however, was the nightly frolics of the Rusalkas; their exuberant water ballet provided a form of entertainment—in good weather, that is—that furnished the Castle's inhabitants and visitors with a great deal of pleasure. None of these creatures seemed at all inclined to drown anyone, which often surprised newcomers.

Visitors there were many, especially now that this area had come under the aegis of the King of Led Belarus. In fact, in a peculiar way, the Kingdom of Copper Mountain was part of, yet separate from Led Belarus. The Queen and King had come to a very amicable alliance: she ruled everything beneath the surface, and he ruled everything above. This was a perfect arrangement, so far as the King was concerned. Let someone else have the reputation for wealth and opulence. Led Belarus was still known as bucolic, pastoral, comfortable, but wealthy only in the fruits of its fields and pastures. And Copper Mountain could drive its tunnels and mines wheresoever it wished.

And if anyone wished to trade with, or ally with, or acquire the services of the Queen and her people, they came here.

Because across the lake, new buildings were arising under the auspices of the Queen's people. The most prominent of them thus far was the Embassy of Copper Mountain itself, although the Sea King had a representative here, as did the Dragons of Light, the Fair Folk, and it was said that there were other non-human races considering establishing a presence.

Also under construction was what—according to rumor—was going to be a College for Wizards and Witches. Since it was going up with no visible workers in sight, that was entirely possible.

Across the lake from the Embassies and the College was a semipermanent Gypsy camp. Semipermanent, because although the camp itself was permanent, most of the inhabitants came and went as their fancies took them. The only truly permanent resident was a highly skilled fortune-teller known only as Magda, and her handsome husband.

Whatever needed policing or guarding around the lake was taken care of by the Company of the Wolf Brothers, a troupe of former mercenaries who still, on occasion, hired out some of their young recruits. These went out under the command of Piotr the Clever, and the Company mascot and Scout, his wife Lyuba. He was called *the Clever* in no small part because of his success in securing Lyuba as his wife. There were currently bets on about whether their offspring would be cubs or children.

All that would certainly have been enough to ensure that no one ever attacked this place. But there was, of course, more.

For the Castle had a new name and a new purpose.

This was the Belarus Chapter of the Champions Order of Glass Mountain. The Knight Commanders were the two resident dragons, Adamant and Gina, and there was even a Godmother-in-training here, a former wizard's apprentice named Klava.

And on almost any given day, the first hint of hostility would have been met with such a bristling of weaponry and magics that the air itself would probably withdraw a little, just in case.

The wagon approaching the Castle was not quite a gypsy caravan. It had much the same shape, but it was nothing like as brightly—one might say *gaudily*—painted. The two horses drawing it were also a bit odd for a gypsy caravan; they bore a suspicious resemblance to warhorses, though if that was what they were, they were also clearly past their prime.

The caravan however, despite its relatively sober colors of dusty-blue and midnight, was in excellent repair and condition. The woman driving it—

—was certainly no gypsy. Her coloring was wrong for one thing; she was tiny, and blond rather than dark of hair and eye. And very few gypsies could have afforded her clothing; blue, high-heeled boots of the finest leather, full, calf-length skirt of heavy silk twill, wide belt that matched the boots and laced up the front, and a pristine high-necked white silk blouse, heavy with embroidery down the arms and around the high collar.

"Are we there yet?" called a voice from inside the caravan, mockingly.

"You know, I could turn this caravan right around—" she said, laughing.

"Bah, you wouldn't do that, your father would have us ambushed at the first river crossing and hauled into his presence." Sasha stuck his head out through the curtains at the front of the caravan. "Ah, we are there yet!"

Katya ruffled his hair. "You know, you could have been the one driving. Then you wouldn't have had to keep asking."

"So you could lounge back there like an odalisque in splendid isolation? I think not!"

"Or you could have sat up here with me."

"But then I couldn't keep asking 'are we there yet?'" His eyes sparkled with laughter, then he turned to examine the lake and the Castle. "Well, hard to believe all this went up in a year."

She shrugged. "When you have that many magicians available to make things happen, that many magical workers, and that much magic that The Tradition is throwing at a place to erase the last little thought of something like a Jinn, things tend to happen quickly. Castle first, or Father?"

"Castle." He sighed. "While this arrangement of splitting our services between your father and mine is an excellent idea, I must admit I am not looking forward to a year of eating seaweed balls and raw fish."

"It isn't all seaweed balls and raw fish," she replied, then reached behind his head and pulled him to her to kiss him. The horses continued to plod along, not needing her hand on the reins, which was just as well anyway. "Besides," she murmured into his ear. "Remember how you liked the honeymoon underwater?"

"Hmm." He chuckled.

Katya had very fond memories of all of the ways that being buoyant improved lovemaking, and from the state of things, so did he.

"All right then."

"Horses," he murmured. "Drive now, canoodle later. Ditch bad, bed good."

"I hear and obey, master." She turned her attention back to the horses and the road, just in time to prevent them from going down the road to the gypsy camp and sending them across the causeway to the Castle.

They had sent word days ago via the paper bird that they were on the way, and Klava must have had people watching from a tower for their coming. The horses had barely stopped moving when there was a groom at their head to take them and the caravan off to the stables, and Klava herself came flying down the stairs to catch Katya up in an exuberant embrace. Only after she had hugged Katya and kissed Sasha, was Katya able to take a look at her outfit.

It was a confection in scarlet; panniered overskirt, brocaded underskirt, low-cut bodice, puffed half sleeves reaching to the elbow, with her hair put up and a wide scarlet ribbon with a bow at the back around her neck. Scarlet lace everywhere it was logical to put lace. "Well! I see we have chosen a theme, finally!" Katya remarked, eyes sparkling with laughter, since the last time she had heard from Klava, the latter had been unable to settle on a Fairy name.

"Cardinal Fairy. There is a lovely vine called Cardinal Climber, as it happens, and I love red," Klava replied, dimpling.

"And a good thing you do, too," Sasha chuckled. "Well, there will be no mistaking you for your mentor, for certain!"

"Godmother Elena the Lilac Fairy? They'd have to be blind." Klava laughed at that. "Not even at a distance! Come along, you two, you must be famished!"

"So tell me, what has been happening?" Katya asked, allowing herself to be pulled inside the Castle by her friend.

"Since you cheated us of a wedding here by having it underwater, Marina had hers right here," Klava replied, taking them to the old throne room, which was now, by the heavy tables and benches, the Chapter refectory. It clearly made a lovely place to eat, what with all the windows. The old battle banners of the Katschei's conquests had been taken down and replaced with new ones, presumably representing the victories of the new Chapter.

"So she married that bashful boy from her village? I hope he knows he's to do all the cooking," Katya replied. "One touch of a fire—"

"No!" Klava exclaimed. "That's the wonderful part! Do you remember that delegation of Flora's people, the ones that came in this winter on reindeer-drawn sledges?"

"I remember you writing me about them. Why?" Katya was momentarily distracted by the arrival of what looked like a child bearing bowls of meat-filled borscht and cups of wine. Except it obviously wasn't a child….

"She and the youngest fellow, Flora's cousin, I think, took one look at each other and simply fell head over heels! Here's the best part—he's from *so* far north, the snow never melts!" At Katya's astonished look, Klava clapped her hands and laughed. "It's true! Can you think of anything more perfect for a snow maiden?"

"Not unless she married Father Frost! That's lovely, but what about her poor old parents?" Katya nearly swooned when she tasted the borscht; she hadn't had any soup that good in—well—a very long time.

"They are very happy for her, but I think it was a relief for them to know that they were not going to have to guard against her melting anymore," Klava told them.

"It's a definite consideration," Sasha put in. "Good saints, Klava, who is your cook? This is amazing!"

Klava chuckled. "We have Brownies now. Wait until you taste the bread!"

So that's what the little person wa—ah, is! Katya thought, as the small fellow returned with a basket of bread so fresh-baked it was steaming, and a pot of butter.

"We'll have to spend more time here, that's clear!" Sasha said, cutting a slice and buttering it. "Oh—my—" he added around his first bite. "Definitely."

"The advantages of being an apprentice Godmother— though Elena keeps threatening to turn me loose on my own!" Klava didn't look the least bit unhappy about that idea however, which made Katya take a longer look at her.

Hmm, I should think so. It's time.

"Good. It's about time Led Belarus had a Godmother, what with all of this going on." Sasha waved his hand wide to indicate the entire lake complex. "A Fortunate Fool can only do so much, you know."

"I know, believe me, I know." Klava rolled her eyes. "The Baba Yagas alone could keep a Godmother busy. It's a good thing that they tend to do as much good as evil."

"And speaking of evil, we met with Sergei on the road," Sasha told her. "He's just back from the City of Brass. They have the bottle and have agreed to keep it, but he told us they were playing very aloof and not terribly communicative, so heaven only knows what they plan to do about the Jinn."

Klava pursed her lips. "Well…he's their problem now. Or their Godmother's, if they have any such thing."

"Definitely their problem," Katya said firmly, getting the last little bit of broth from the bottom of the bowl. "After we bottled him, I saw that the writing had changed. Now he's bound in there until he reforms. If he does, he gets out, and then they will *have* to deal with him."

Klava gave her a long look. "You know, I don't know that I would have taken that generous a hand with him. I still like 'Until the twelfth of Never.' Or 'Until all frogs become princes.' Something like that."

Sasha thoughtfully ate his last bite of bread. "We do have to deal with the repercussions of being a Fortunate Fool," he said, as Katya nodded.

"Then I'm glad I'm a Godmother. I can be vindictive on occasion." Klava laughed. "Now that you've had the edge taken off your hunger, care to come visit Adamant and Gina?"

"Of course!" Swinging their legs over the benches, they followed Klava out to the practice grounds.

There a number of would-be young Champions were hard at work under the direction of the two dragons. Gina was instructing one group in swordwork, while Adamant was patiently on the receiving end of blows from quarterstaves.

"More wrist!" they both happened to be saying, as the three of them came into view. Both looked up at the same time, and all work on the ground halted as the students craned their necks to see who was coming.

"Sasha! Katya!" Adamant reared up a little and arced his wings. "Oh good to see you! How do you like the changes?"

"Impressive," Sasha chuckled. "Anyone would think this was a place where important people came."

"Well of course it is!" Adamant said, grinning. "We're here, aren't we?"

Gina cuffed him with a wing.

"In all seriousness," the emerald dragon said, slowly. "This is something that has been needed for a while. Not just a Godmother for this part of the world, and not just a Chapter House, but a place where those who are not human can safely send representatives to those who are. There has been some very interesting talk going on over in those embassies. I think we've done a fine thing here."

"If so, it was entirely by accident," Sasha replied, and shrugged. "The way most things tend to happen with me."

"Trust to Luck," Katya added, and grinned.

After a few more pleasantries, they parted. Klava led them through the gardens, then paused, waiting for their reaction.

Before them was a statue carved from a single piece of quartz crystal, of a young woman in a dancing dress, arms and face raised toward the sky. The crystal had been carved, and the statue placed so that the sun filled it with light.

It was Guiliette.

Katya gasped. "How—"

"The Queen's carvers," Klava said with pride. "They asked me questions and made sketches until they got her face right. Then they carved the statue."

"It's perfect," Katya said quietly. And then she smiled. "If there is one single thing I am happiest about, it is that she freed herself."

Klava nodded, and they both gazed at the statue for a while in silence. The carvers had somehow managed to put on the statue's face the one expression that Katya had not seen on Guiliette's until the end.

Joy.

Finally Sasha cleared his throat. "If we don't see the others soon, they are going to have our hides," he reminded them.

Katya laughed. "I think I shall keep my hide thank you! Let's go!"

Magda was holding court, so to speak, in the gypsy camp. She insisted on brewing them tea and told them firmly that she would *not* read their fortunes, since she never read the cards for family. She introduced them to most of the camp, people who looked so much alike that Katya wondered how Magda kept them all sorted in her mind, and then she sent them on their way after extracting a promise to come back that evening for dancing and music.

Lyuba greeted them just as enthusiastically as Klava had.

Although they had both heard of the changes to the mercenary company that had once worked for the Jinn, this was the first time they had actually seen these changes with their own eyes.

The livery was now light and a dark grey and cotton mix had lightened the wool. All the men wore a snarling Wolf head on their tunics, and the company banner bore the likeness of a running female Wolf. Lyuba herself wore the same uniform as the men, and they all treated her with respect and as an officer—except for Piotr, who treated her with respect in public, and with relentless teasing in private. But she teased right back, just as relentlessly, and with the same good humor.

They paid their respects to the Queen's Ambassador. Sasha didn't recognize him, but he didn't expect to, though they both paid close attention to everyone else in the Embassy. After all, tomorrow the man who served them tea might be the Ambassador, and the Ambassador might be serving as a secretary. The Queen herself, it was said, would likely not be coming out of her mountain for a long while. Her appearance to put down the Jinn was a rarity, and it would take something even more powerful to induce her to repeat that incident.

And then—it was time to visit the Sea King.

The Embassy was half above, and half below the water, to accommodate those who couldn't bear the thought of venturing below the surface. For those who could—

There was a chamber where one could change into costumes more suitable for the half of the Embassy where, to be honest, the real work was done.

"Well," Katya said glancing at Sasha with resignation. "We might as well."

"If we do, we'll at least come back to dry clothes," Sasha pointed out.

She nodded. Katya put on her old fish-scale armor, and Sasha something very similar. Then, after Sasha swallowed one of the seaweed balls that allowed him to breathe underwater, they plunged into the pool that led down below the surface.

What the King was going to do when winter froze this lake over, Katya didn't know. It might be possible to have the same sort of magic put on the place that kept the waters of the Palace warm and comfortable. That wasn't her problem though, for which she was monumentally grateful.

She found her father tending to dispatches, and the moment he saw the two of them, he left all of it to greet them.

"I want to know everything you've been doing," he told them, drawing them off to another room, as his aides tactfully steered petitioners away. "I know you sent me reports, but there are so many things I need to know! For instance—about that rogue witch who was changing the weather—"

They talked for hours, it seemed, while the water about them grew dark, and the light globes began to shine. Finally he settled back with a sigh.

"I know that you just got here, but there are so many things I need you to investigate—" he said reluctantly.

Sasha laughed, and Katya chuckled. "I told him that was what you would say. It was just what *his* father said," she replied. "You two are frighteningly alike."

Her father paused, and looked seriously into their faces. "I hope that you know that you are more, far more to me than just my investigators, my solvers of problems, and my Fortunate Fools," he said, his earnest tone of voice making it clear that he meant this, felt it. "I have always loved my daughter, Sasha, more than anything other than my wife and her siblings. And since she loves you, you are a part of that. I don't want you to forget that. Especially when it seems as if all I am doing is using you."

Katya's breath caught, and she looked at Sasha. He looked incredibly moved. "I know that, sir," he replied softly. "I do know that. But I also know that things have to get handled, and not always when we have the leisure for them. We both know that. It comes with the duty." Then he grinned. "That said, if you ever find a sealed bottle at the bottom of the ocean and open it—*you* can handle what comes out on your own! And I am perfectly serious about that one!"

The King looked at his son-in-law for a moment, and blinked. "I suppose it would be all right if I got a Champion to deal with it...."

Katya raised an eyebrow. "With Klava here? What do you think?"

After a long pause, the King cleared his throat. "All right then. New edict. All sealed bottles to be strictly left alone. There's almost never anything in them worth bothering with anyway. Now, about this overture from Acadia—they claim they are having trouble with some sea creature they call a Kraken—"

Sasha glanced over at Katya. "Never a dull moment, is there?" he whispered.

"Would you have it any other way?" she whispered back.

"Are you two paying attention?" the King asked abruptly.

"Of course. Acadia. Kraken. Question as to whether we should investigate, or just tell them to talk to the dragons."

"Ah. Good." He launched back into his litany.

No I wouldn't, Sasha mouthed at her, and smiled. She winked.

Neither would I, she thought with contentment. *Neither would I.*